AF507234

THE NORTHERN ROSEAARDE SERIES

BOOK 2

DESPICABLE BOON

R.E. HOLDING

CLIFF CAVE
BOOKS, LLC

DESPICABLE BOON
Book 2 of the Northern Roseaarde Series
Copyright © 2025 by R.E. Holding.

All rights reserved.

No portion of this book may be reproduced in any form without written permission from the publisher or author, except as permitted by U.S. copyright law.

This book is a work of fiction. Names, characters, businesses, organizations, places, events and incidents either are the product of the author's imagination or are used fictitiously. Any resemblance to actual persons, living or dead, events, or locales is entirely coincidental.

Certified Created not Generated © – all text was created by a real person with images crafted using licensed stock images and real art, without the use of artificial intelligence (AI).

For information contact:
https://www.cliffcavebooks.com

Edited by Sara Kelly
Cover art by Mighty Pejes Studio
Interior design and propaganda pages by R.E. Holding
Cover format by R.E. Holding
Map design using Inkarnate by R.E. Holding
Previous Title: Reaper's Bounty

ISBN (paperback): 978-1-963125-34-4
First Edition (under new title): January 2026
10 9 8 7 6 5 4 3 2 1

Contents

Part 3

Other books by R.E. Holding

Horror:
Metaxysm
Hillbilly Vamp
Subcutaneous (2026)

Fantasy:
Despicable Boon (book 2)
Existential Pest (book 3)

Collections:
The Artist's Soap Making Workbook
The Northern Roseaarde Omnibus (2026)
Untitled Short Story Compilation (2026)

Sign up for the newsletter for upcoming releases and freebies by visiting https://www.reholdingauthor.com, or by scanning the QRC below:

Stay up to date with extras at the Cliff Cave Books website by visiting https://www.cliffcavebooks.com or scan below:

INDEX

Read as a reference to the main text - reading ahead may contain spoilers.

Anglia: a race of people marked by their paper-white skin and hair. Eyes are typically light-colored and can even manifest as pink or red.

Arts: a non-Guild sub-faction career path that includes crafters of all kinds, entertainers, guides, storytellers, and musicians.

Ascendia: the Engineering capital of Roseaarde. It lies in a cluster with the other seven cities on the western bank of the North continent.

Audioxine: an illicit street drug, claimed to be crafted by the Yeunish and circulated to the youth.

Audun: the capitol city of Roseaarde. Officials control the activities of the northern continent and the southern morass.

Beast Tamer: an enhanced version of a Shepherd, only present in the Yeunish.

Black eneris (obsenis forturum): life essence that comes from a failed pull. It can be used as ink or if corrupted, can become toxic.

Blood fish: Carnivorous fish that generally live in deeper parts of the sea.

Blue eneris (lapis piscus): the life essence that is pulled from aquatic creatures.

Breach: the festering rot at a root of Great Tree sealed shut by Maron Valoa'brenga.

Cap 1 and Cap 2: periods of time marking the beginning and end of each year.

Celerity: the Reader capital of Roseaarde. It lies in a cluster with the other seven cities on the western bank of the North continent.

Chitter Birds: Small, quick and dark colored birds that can swarm. They are known for being early risers and waking citizens in the desert with their calls.

Chromatis hominum: a special kind of essence pulled from a Weggevens skin walker midway between human and animal.

Cirv'e: the beast of the breach and tormentor.

Corl: small fishing town south of Kanckette on the coast where the border blends with the southern continent. The town is widely ignored by Audun, and its residents live off the land rather than ration blocks.

Danashi: a race of people marked by their dark skin and hair. They can have any color eyes, including hazel and dark brown.

Desert Maelstrom: the annual energy storm that occurs in the middle of the span that begins around day 140 (middle of period X) and ends around day 180 (beginning of Split 2).

Deygo Lilac: Multicolored flowers that bloom just before the maelstrom. Pleasant scent.

Draught: also known as a "pot," these are solutions crafted by Formulators.

E-disk: a communication device popular with the citizens of Roseaarde. Its functions vary from making calls to sending QuickChats, watching holofilms, and performing daily tasks, such as depositing plats.

Elementalist: a new type of Weggevens that manifests as the controlling of elements. Ayala is a fire-based elementalist and Quint is an ice-based elementalist. The power is strong and capable of rapidly draining the host if used for a prolonged period.

Eletonk: a species of large land mammal typically residing in the desert.

Eneris: the essence of life pulled from recently deceased (or living) organisms.

Engineer: a Guild member who can sense the potential of materials to craft technology.

Flash ink: a type of tech text meant to disappear once the intended reader takes in the message.

Formulator: a Guild member who can sense the potential of eneris and other formulations to craft draughts.

Foscan: a race of people marked by their grayish-tan skin, black hair, and white eyes. Foscans were accused of rebelling against Audun hundreds of years ago and have been forced to serve as slaves for various households and businesses.

Giltberries: A special gold-colored berry that's been extinct for ages.

Gold eneris (auris hominum): a special essence that comes from a Reaper who pulls their own. Extremely rare and widely not practiced.

Great Tree: an ancient tree that used to grow at the northeast tip of the North continent. It has since burned to ash.

Green eneris (verdigris plantum): the life essence that is pulled from plant material.

G-scan: a tech device that uses a touch of blood along with a fingerprint to determine genetic markers, as well as any hidden Guild talent. Eloria was subject to a G-scan when receiving her diagnosis, and Lor was given a G-scan when confirming his Yeunish identity (not explicitly stated in the text).

Guild (see Engineer, Formulator, Reader, Reaper, Shepherd): a special title given to individuals who attend the Heart Island program and leave with a special ability.

Guild Central: the Eastern branch of the Seven Cities, commonly abbreviated GC. Working at GC means living in the apartment halls, with all expenses paid. Working hours are, however, long.

Haerow: a small coastal area known to draw individuals seeking private, and oftentiems salacious vacations.

Hanso Fruit: A type of island fruit with a sweet smell and bitter flavor. The residents of Heart Island are fond of the aroma, and it is ever present at the resort.

Holoconfetti: a special virtual confetti used in celebrations to reduce litter.

Holofilm: a type of entertainment loved by everyone, starring non-Guild members of the Art faction of storytelling.

Holopic: an image viewable in 270 degrees.

Howie Rod: a popular construction piece meant for sturdy buildings. Made of metal.

Igni: an extinct race of people who were former guardians of the Great Tree.

Ivory Saltpeter: a white eneris-based formulation invented by Jack that acts as a mild poison and potential explosive, depending on use. Dill shoots Hammer with Ivory Saltpeter to weaken his strongman ability.

Jaune Spirit: a yellow phial invented by Jack that gives the user an intense burst of energy. Dill used the phial in the cavern tussle.

Jumper: a type of on and off-roading vehicle with large spherical tires that can rotate in all directions. Popular choice as a taxi vehicle.

Kanckette (a.k.a "tent city"): the only city in the desert zone known as the Span.

Kanckette is the last train stop, as the Desert Maelstrom always destroyed any further travel east. A band of people live under the tracks in a series of tents, usually collecting any discarded items from the station above to use.

Lapis Evening: a Yeunish sleep aid draught invented by Jack. Used by the team to keep Hare sedated.

Last Grudge: an offensive phial invented by Jack and using Fowler's chromatis, tossing the formulation creates a multi-colored windstorm intense enough to cut like razors. Anything caught in its path is obliterated. Crow was a victim of the draught.

Law: a non-Guild sub-faction career path that includes roundsmen, judges, officials, and barristers.

Leaper: a small amphibious creature inhabiting the Southern Morass. Not edible.

Medicine: a non-Guild sub-faction career path that includes medics, observers, apothecarians, and advisers. Mesaman: a race of people marked by their tanned and ruddy complexions. The most diverse race, their hair can range from light to dark, with eyes typically light and no darker than hazel.

Milaris: the Formulator capital of Roseaarde. It lies in a cluster with the other seven cities on the western bank of the North continent.

Mount Gehenna: the towering mountain on the northeastern tip of the North continent. It is known for its black sands and constant guard.

Nazagora: Dark alien creatures that inhabit the morass. Predatory, but edible with body parts that grow back. Amphibious.

Newslite: an old-fashioned news delivery format requiring a subscription.

Non-Guild (see Arts, Law, Medicine): any profession that doesn't fall into the Seven Cities' definition of prestige.

Noxeine (a.k.a. "Klik"): a recreational substance mostly used by teens for a numbing high. Hare claimed his childhood crush, Tilly, traded sexual favors for the drug.

Oatcress: a ration block consisting of oats and protein.

Obsidia: the Reaper capital of Roseaarde. It lies in a cluster with the other seven cities on the western bank of the North continent.

Orange eneris (naranis corpum): the life essence that is pulled from a specific species of fruit.

Pandemonia: the Weggevens capital of Roseaarde. It lies in a cluster with the other seven cities on the western bank of the North continent.

Patch: crafted from ancient tech and a silver alternative, the patch is a device surgically attached to a Weggevens to prevent the drain. Invented by Verena and using Jack's alternative silver, the patch is proprietary and not shared with the Seven Cities.

Pau'tan virus: a type of infection that became a pandemic in Lor's early years, and took many lives. The cities now have a cure.

Peakwood: a mid-sized city just outside the peninsula of the Seven Cities. Lor's hometown.

Phial: a specialized glass vessel used to collect eneris for Reapers or to store draughts for Formulators.

Phillo bloom: a pink bloom in tropical areas with a light perfumy aroma that goes well with the scent of hanso. Flowers are not edible.

Plat: the system of cash, with the symbol of pL.

Pohay'an: a small tourist location north of the Seven Cities and nestled in the mountains. Location of the famous ivory forests and hot springs, and home to Val when not serving in the program.

Puck: a species of fish.

Purple eneris (purpuris porum): the life essence that is pulled from any purple-colored plant.

QuickChat: a message sent to another user via e-disk.

Reader: a Guild member who has the ability to read minds. Skilled members can even push ideas and thoughts. Gaining the ability naturally isn't as common as a Shepherd spending plat to earn special training.

Reaper: a Guild member with the ability to pull life force (eneris) from any recently deceased (or living) thing. Other abilities granted to a Reaper have been shrouded in mystery.

Reaper's gold: the gold eneris within a Reaper, extractable only by self, or by tough metal gloves employed by the cities made with enhanced tech.

Red eneris (roujis emporum): the life essence that is pulled from land creatures.

Red Mash: an offensive phial invented by Jack that absorbs through the skin and erodes in a series of large blisters. Used to attack Hammer in the cavern.

Roseaarde: the world.

Runner: a type of Weggevens ability that grants super speed to the user.

Sarga Fruit: a type of yellow fruit that is sometimes sent in rations. They're juicy, fitting in the palm of the hand, and are a favorite of Lor's.

Saxeroot: a root vegetable, blue in color, that's been thought to be extinct for centuries.

Second sun: a purple-colored sun that rises at the 24th hour and lasts a standard hour.

Seven Cities (see Ascendia, Audun, Celerity, Milaris, Obsidia, Pandemonia, and Wild Crag): the cluster of cities on the western bank of the Northern continent that serve as governmental rule for Roseaarde, consisting of representatives for each Guild house.

Shepherd: a Guild member with the ability to communicate with animals.

Silver eneris (argenis hominum): a special type of essence that comes from humans.

Skin walker, or skin changer: a type of Weggevens ability that grants the ability to transform into an animal to the user.

Southern Morass: a second continent loosely attached to the North by stretches of sand banks. The morass is a bog-like zone where the cities banish the Yeunish to die.

Span: the entire middle section of the Northern continent, covered in desert and mostly uninhabitable except for the city of Kanckette. Several encampments litter the sand underneath the trains, and the vast poverty of the zone has bred brigands.

Split 1 and Split 2: the periods of time in the middle sections of the year.

Storyteller: a non-Guild profession in Entertainment. Someone who acts in holofilms.

Strongman: a type of Weggevens ability that grants inhuman strength to the user.

Trega's Sky: a city on the West coast, just north of Peakwood, where most holofilms are made. A very affluent city.

Two-mind: a type of Weggevens ability that involves the attachment of another "mind" to the user. Known to possess secrets of the dead. Highly deadly affliction.

Valoan (see void brothers): a cult group of members who forsake bonding with the Maker in favor of worshipping the breach.

Vegemeal: a ration block consisting of a variety of vegetable and fruit matter compressed together.

Verdigris Biosore: a deadly phial that can degrade the flesh rapidly. Its intensity depends on the strength or weakness of its victim. Pigeon was killed with a needle of biosore, and Hare was threatened with it.

Verdigris Mend: a potent and almost instant healing draught invented by Jack, that uses a small drop of Reaper's gold to formulate. Used to mend Verena after her attack, Gale after his attack, Hare after getting punched, and Lor after being shot by Crow.

V-Note: a touch sensitive tablet that is widely used as a job-related recording system. Lor uses a V-Note to capture his visions when reaping, and medics use V-notes to record patient data.

Void brothers (see Valoan): a cult group of members who forsake bonding with the Maker in favor of worshipping the breach.

Volatile: a new type of Weggevens with random and serious outcomes. Each one has a unique second personality that can come out in violent ways, often resulting in the death of the host.

Waterbird: a species of bird that congregates around larger bodies of water.

Weggevens (see runner, strongman, skin walker/changer, two-mind, volatile, elementalist): a Guild member with an unpredictable outcome. Whatever the outcome, the ability is volatile and has consequences for the user.

White eneris (witis volatus): the life essence that is pulled from air creatures.

Witis Rejuvenate: an important drug invented by Jack to help treat a Weggevens suffering from life drain.

Wild Crag: the Shepherd capital of Roseaarde. It lies in a cluster with the other seven cities on the western bank of the North continent.

X: the period of time in the middle of the year, marking the beginning of the Desert Maelstrom.

Yeuni / Yeunish: a race of people born by the Anglia and Foscan. Their kind is hunted and banished to the southern morass for reasons lost to history.

Climate and standard annum

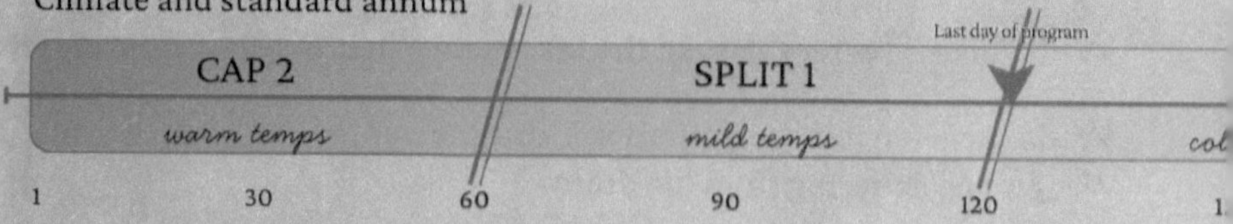

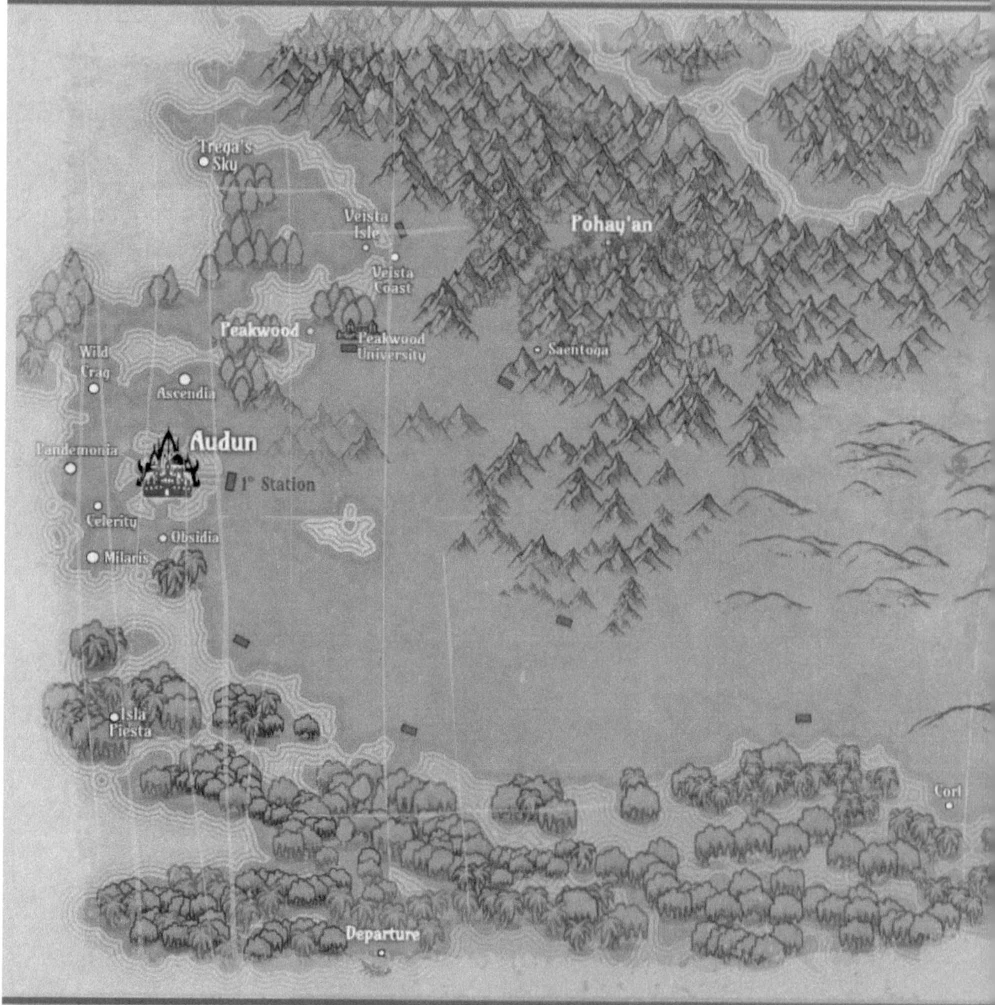

Daily sun rise & sun set

ONE DAY, 30 HOURS:
1st sun rise: 08:00
2nd sun rise: 24:00
Evening: 26:00-07:30

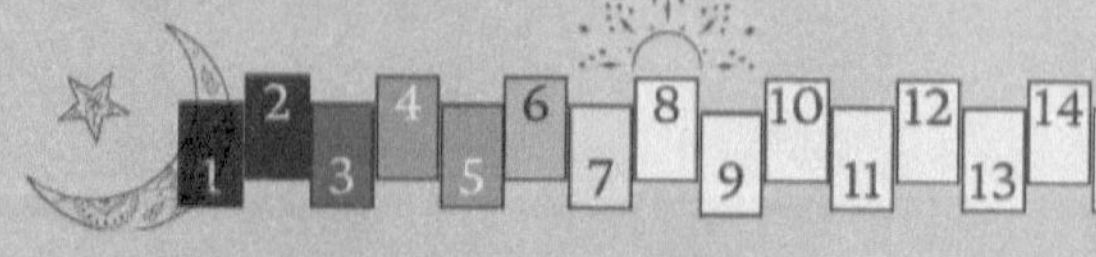

desert maelstrom
SPLIT 2
CAP 1
First day of program
temps
mild temps
warm temps
180
210
240
270
300
Moentaegar
Mt. Gehenna
Heart Island
Guild Central
Secas
Kanckette
Final Station
16
17
18
19
20
21
22
23
24
25
26
27
28
29
30
N
W
E
S

The Story So Far

Brief synopsis of Book 1, Nefarious Gift

Loren (Lor) Turtingas lives with his stepfather, Gale, in the mid-sized city of Peakwood which lies on the west coast of the Northern Continent near the Seven Cities. Living an isolated and lonely life, Lor has been studying the non-Guild *faction* of Law, specifically the role of the roundsman. Gale tries hard to convince Lor to enter the Guild program on the far east coast at Heart Island, but due to a bit of a misunderstanding and a dash of disrespect, Gale gave up being nice and forced Lor to go despite the cost.

On his first day in the program, Lor meets Paerli (Par) Harea, a beautiful Danashi stranger that takes an instant liking to him without any effort. However, once Lor meets Damaetra, his attention shifts to the demure Anglia, who teaches him about faith and how it might be connected to the colors he has always seen whenever he closes his eyes. Shortly thereafter, new friendships are forged between the handsome Mesaman, Nico Dicus, and the goofy fun-loving Danashi, Dill Storgut.

After a harrowing death in the first week of the program, the friend circle begins to question their safety and make the choice to remove the implant imposed on them on the second day.

As time carries on, each member discovers their ability: Damaetra and Nico as Formulators, Dill as an Engineer, and Paerli as the coveted Reaper—a class capable of pulling life essence, known as eneris, from the living and recently deceased. The odd man out is Lor, who doesn't discover his ability until the final week of the program when he has a violent seizure that turns him into a Reaper like Par.

Without much time to learn how to use his ability, and cryptic advice on avoiding "yaslecha" by the island Foscan, Val, he leans heavily on his prior connection to a strange Weggevens skin changer named Fowler that he met on the train on his way to the program. The group moves to Guild Central, where Fowler serves as their sponsor. While the job placement seems like a dream, they discover quickly that work is demanding, and they hardly have time to spend with each other, except for Lor and Par, who happen to be in the same apartment hall.

During a rough day at work, Par comes to meet Lor at his apartment that night, dropping a huge surprise on him by telling him that she has always been a Reaper and was specifically looking for him. She divulges a plan for them to become immortal together, but his fierce loyalty to Damaetra infuriates her to the point of assault.

The next morning, there is a box from Par on his floor that contains a phial of her gold eneris along with a note meant for him to drink it and bind himself to her. Stashing it away, he goes to work without her and meets up with his Foscan mentor, Krik'tha, for duties that day. While on the job, Lor asks Krik'tha how a Reaper can pull their own eneris, and it immediately sours Krik'tha. He refuses to talk with Lor for the rest of his shift.

When returning to the court, he runs into Nico, Dill, and Fowler, but no Damaetra. After putting the pieces together, Lor realizes Par kidnapped her and he has no choice but to find a way to gather his own gold and to drink Par's. That night, Lor reconnects with Krik'tha, who teaches him how to perform the "Ritual of Self" that withdraws his gold. After nearly bleeding out, he succeeds in pulling the gold and makes plans to meet with everyone to confront Par.

Once he drinks Par's gold, she finds him, instructing him to meet her team further at the edge of the desert. It is here Lor sees that Par's "team" has captured Damaetra, and that one of their members happens to be Nico's estranged twin brother. More secrets are revealed when Par drinks Lor's gold and discovers he's Yeunish—a disreputable race of people with a city-driven bounty on their heads.

Lor and his friends are ill-prepared for the encounter when Fowler transforms to get help but is immediately shot down by Par's team member, Crow. When Dill tries to go to him, Nico's twin, Hare, restrains him and ultimately blinds Dill while cutting off Nico's legs. As Lor tries to fight back, he's hit with another of Crow's projectiles and left to die in the desert until he is rescued by Gale, a revealed Weggevens runner.

Lor awakes in a modest farmer's home, where he discovers that Par's team mate, Jack (a.k.a. Cricket), has defected from her because he also hides his Yeunish heritage. Jack has powerful formulations that can heal Lor, but are unable to help Fowler, who exists in a fatally deformed transition state. Fowler begs Lor to put him out of his misery and pull his eneris, which ends up being an ultra-rare substance called chromatis.

The team returns to Guild Central, preparing for their next move to rescue Damaetra. Jack leaves Nico with some recipes to try, including a mysterious "last grudge," which contains Fowler's chromatis. Dill creates Engineering eyes for himself, and hyper fast modules for Nico's preserved natural legs.

During this time, Lor also discovers the danger of pulling eneris when angry.

Once prepared, they venture out to Mount Gehenna, or the burnt husk of what was once Great Tree, where Par holds Damaetra. They reconvene with Jack, and the guards allow them through the gates by the instructions of a woman on Par's team, Livia—a Reader with the ability of the push. Lor is led to the entrance of Gehenna by remembering a dream he had, and after they crawl inside, they see how much life has grown inside.

Par's team finds them, and Par leads Lor down the umbilicus while the rest standoff in the main cavern. Down in the deep corner of the umbilicus, the half-living ancient, Maron Valoa'brenga has been trapped for over a millennium, sealing the breach with his own body. They use a reverse reap to pull him from the breach, and afterwards, Lor attacks Par. He escapes the umbilicus with Damaetra and Livia.

Lor meets up with the crew in the main cavern just before they unleash last grudge on Crow. An enraged Par comes after them, and they escape when she is stopped by Maron, who tosses her necklace to Lor. He now carries it with him, not knowing what it's for. They capture Hare and impulsively bring him back with them to Guild Central, with no idea what to do with him next.

As the maelstrom dies down, children play in the desert, smelling a rotten odor. Just as the smell hits them, one of the children, Zane, seizes uncontrollably until bursting into flames.

PART 1

Prologue

THE SLASH OF BLOOD SMEARED across Lor's hand when he wiped his broken lip. In all the satisfaction of a downward spiral into emptiness, he grinned. It reminded him that no matter what these fools did to him, he would last. Longer than anyone in this place could fathom.

As he dodged the next fist to deliver his own, he thought of all those moments in his youth when he just knew he'd live forever. He was untouchable.

Not even fat Denny's torments could take him from the world when he pushed Lor from that hover lift outside the school's new wing construction. It landed Lor a torn hamstring, but he bounced back. He would always bounce back. Last he heard, Denny drank himself down an overhang while in a jumper. He didn't bounce back.

That renewal. It was something in his bones—he could feel them stitching over and over. Each old scar was a silvery pale ghost. Each new rip was just another tiny setback. The feeling... it washed over him like a thick, metaphysical influx of Verdigris Mend . He tasted it... every time it happened. It was the herbal green of early spring with a mineral coat of petrichor. He'd grown to love that taste. To expect it.

The taste came home, coating his throat with a welcome earthen zing, and his bloodied lip tacked shut.

What To Do, What To Do...
LOREN

"LET ME GO," HARE MURMURED.

It was uncanny. Lor peered at the new, volatile captive on his couch, who wore his best friend's face. *Hare*, like the gentle desert creature known for covering great distances in little time, was nothing like this man. This man was cruel, contemptuous.

Hare's face wrinkled inward when he realized Lor had been watching him, and he rotated his wrists, bound under hardened ivy cords. All the fine-tuned features Nico possessed were worn and patchy on his twin brother. Scars slashed his tanned arms, most likely from many years running for Paerli, doing Maker knows what. Dried scales outlined desert-whipped lips, and one of his teeth was missing.

The only reason Hare sat on his pristine couch, covered in dust and dried blood, was because of panic. Panic at the cavern confrontation, panic to save a human life from Par's ultimate attack, and panic for Nico to preserve some representation of a future with his estranged twin.

"Dad?" Lor said with a sigh.

Gale rifled through his pack, finding a solitary needle full of Lapis Evening. He sucked his teeth and stared at it. "I don't know if it's a good idea to give him, what... a third dose? At least not just yet," he said.

Lor clicked his tongue. "It's harmless," he said, snatching up the spare shooter from his table. The sensitive trigger pull almost had Lor miss his target, but the loaded needle nailed Hare in the shoulder. It threw him back, where his head bounced on the cushion and his dark, violent eyes slammed shut.

"Loren!" Gale plucked the barb from Hare's arm.

Lor shrugged and planted the shooter back on the table. "What? He deserved it! That guy nearly *killed* my friends."

"I hope you knew that shooter was loaded with Lapis Evening and not something more dangerous."

He didn't.

"Does it matter? I mean, look at Nico and Dill—whatever I could have hit him with would have been nothing compared to what he did to them."

"Don't wake Dill."

Gale always did that. He deflected when he knew Lor was right, but it was no use arguing, and he wasn't interested in waking his Danashi friend, already cozied up on his bed in the corner.

"Don't forget what he *did* to Dill," he muttered to himself.

Nico had been silently standing by, observing his brother with his thumbnail pressed against a front tooth. Not even the coolant liquid that kept his legs from rotting bubbled with movement. He sighed, then nudged Hare, who bobbed with stuttered snores.

An odd tapping sound thrummed on the kitchen counter. It was Jack, drumming slender fingers over the surface as if purposely attempting to stir a queer sort of dread through the room. Lor had forgotten the Yeunish Formulator was with them, and then he realized he had no idea about what to do with all their new *guests*.

Jack cleared his throat, propping the black buggy goggles atop his wind-blown, equally black hair. "We really ought to come up with a plan on how to either get him on our side or get rid of him," he said, yellow eyes scanning and judging the group.

"No," Nico said. He glanced up at the group, then zeroed in on Jack's glare. "I can't just get *rid* of him like a sack of garbage. Am I angry with him? Yes. Does he deserve my forgiveness? No—"

"You're not helping your case," Jack cut in.

"He's my brother. My *twin*. He was my whole world before he was sent away." Nico paced the room, setting the coolant tubes in his legs to burbling and squirting the liquid inside.

Jack hummed. "Well, your *whole world* will die either way unless he gets this shot."

Inside Jack's Formulator chest, a few silvery green syringes lay at the bottom, which Lor recognized as the same treatment Gale needed when he ran. Witis Rejuvenate. Crafted from abundant greens and whites with a splash of human spirit. It was a miracle Jack hadn't been arrested yet just for dreaming up this concoction.

Nico continued to pace, observing his brother. That look on his face was the one he always made when trying out all options in his head. It would take maybe a minute for him to weigh out all the positives and negatives of each scenario. His mind worked like an e-chip... always processing.

Nico spun toward the group. "What about a bribe?"

Jack tittered. "A bribe? You mean to bribe him with the treatment?"

A bribe assumed the other person was rational and willing to persuasion. There was nothing rational about this crazy dude. The group needed another idea. "Actually, since Nico knows how to make that drug now, maybe we can use that. In case things don't work out," Lor said.

Nico bit his lower lip and glanced at his brother draped over the couch, belly exposed and mouth wide open. "That's probably true," he said.

The sound of something hitting the floor in the bathroom roused Lor's interest. There was nothing they could do for Hare at the moment, and time was being wasted waffling about it—Damaetra was in that bathroom alone, with her own set of problems.

"Right. Well, I'm going to check on Damaetra. You know... because she's been through it," Lor said.

"Are you dressed?" Lor asked as he rapped a knuckle on the partition. Pressing his ear to the door, he heard a harried scraping and shuffling.

After a moment of silence, her muffled voice finally called out, "Yes, come in."

Lor slipped into the bathroom and slid the partition closed. A soft, clean aroma hung in the air—it was pleasant, but not her signature violet. It was the smell of standard issue washing soap, courtesy of Reaper's Hall. The scent reminded him of his own filth as he glanced down at his shirt covered in yellow sand stains, rotted cavern ash, and remnants of blood and blackened gold from Maron the Igni.

Damaetra stood at the counter, both palms resting on the surface as she gazed in the mirror. She turned to face him and apologized for dropping the tech caddy from the counter. It was probably broken, but Lor never used it anyway. Layers of hacked white-gold hair played around her ears and stuck out at odd angles. Her cleansed alabaster skin radiated under the artificial techlight, highlighting traces of still-bleeding cuts and bruises on her slender arms and legs. Seeing them made him seethe.

"Are you alright?" he asked.

She didn't answer him right away, continuing to gaze into the mirror with her eyebrows pointed inward. He went up to her and threaded his fingers through the hair around her neck. Little burs from hacked stubble hit him in patches, angering him even more. She closed her eyes as a glassy tear rolled down her cheek.

"Did you mean it? What you said back *there*?" she asked.

"Did I mean what?"

The day before was a mess to remember. From crafting, to traveling, to fighting, then escaping, he tried to imagine what he said in any single one of those agitated moments, specifically to her.

Then it hit him.

Lor had imagined the first time he would tell her he loved her, they would be somewhere magical, on a perfect day during the perfect time. He stood in front of the tree where she first asked him out in Secas, surrounded by hills of color and a gentle breeze sifting through feathered leaves of all shapes and colors. That image morphed into what they actually experienced: a pit of rot buried inside the root of Mount Gehenna, watched by the ancient Igni, Maron Valoa'brenga—a man only known in Dill's fairy tales and Foscan fables.

The Maker had weird ways.

"Of course I meant it. Did you?"

Her parched lips pouted under sunken eyes. It was the first time he noticed just how thin she had become. Nearly a week of captivity in a dank cavern, starved and neglected by her "friend." By *their* friend. The light struck her side, rippling down a jutting hip bone. If he held her, would she snap?

"Naturally," she said.

He almost forgot the question, as if she was affirming his fear that he would break her in half. He sighed in relief, yet something still bothered him. The confrontation in the desert had revealed so many secrets, especially the nature of someone he thought he knew. How many lies did Par tell Damaetra? More importantly, how much damage had been done?

Clearing his throat, he reached out to touch her hand. "I really hope you know that she lied to you before. About me."

She continued to look off toward the door and smirked. "That you're Yeunish? I won't tell."

"You know what I mean."

The tough smile she used to mask her grief faded.

"To be honest, I *didn't* know," she said.

Lor chewed on the inside of his cheek. Nico had tried to warn him about Paerli, and he ignored his advice. It left him vulnerable to her roving hands and put Damaetra in danger. The truth was, Par's big lie was only an exaggeration of reality.

I have to tell her.

"I need to tell you something about that night. The night *she* came to see me," he said.

"I'm listening."

Lor closed his eyes, not seeing his colors but a mental imprint of that night, cast in reds and golds with a vivid projection as if Par was standing there with him. The projection strode up to him, and just as it reached out to grab the same sensitive spot, he snapped his eyes open, seeing the heart-shaped face of Damaetra looking up at him, waiting.

What was even the point of Par crossing that line?

Suppose it was his fault. He knew nothing about women, what they wanted, needed, or conspired—nor did he try to understand. In the program, Par latched on to him, no questions asked, and Lor let it happen. In a way, he let life happen *to* him rather than take part. Had he learned nothing from his embarrassment in youth?

At only eight years old, a girl in first levels, Luci, had attached herself to him, much like Par did during the program. The cycle with Luci began there, where he *allowed* it to happen. Occasionally indulging Luci and talking about some random nonsense that was popular at the time encouraged her. It fueled her obsession with him.

Before long, she was holding his hand in the halls at school, drawing attention from friends and acquaintances. Handholding was just a gateway to more. The validation of attention was eclipsed by her desire for more from him. It eventually morphed into her tiresome and constant row of petitions to touch tongues with him.

As a boy who spent more time reading books on law and occasionally quarreling with Gale, Lor didn't know what it meant to touch tongues. Why would anyone ever want to do that? It sounded close. It sounded gross.

Luci was nothing remarkable, but she was cute enough, and Lor liked her somewhat. She was a Mesaman, similar to him, but with an olive cast over tanned skin. Eyes a shade of gray, like his own, her head was crowned in unruly red curls.

One day, his conviction broke. With a surrender to the strange ritual of the tongue-touch, he hoped to put a stop to the endless requests. She would see that it was gross too and quit asking.

Agreeing to meet behind the main building, she surprised him with an audience of classmates who urged them on. Everyone wanted to witness the peculiar exchange, hearing rumor that it was how babies were made. He didn't want to make babies with Luci and prayed they were wrong. But he couldn't turn back. He had to do it. Under giggles and whispers, he was all limbs and lank, eventually getting close enough to smell the cloying aroma of vanilla milk and berries in her hair.

The tip of his tongue slipped over hers. It was squishy and wet. She had just eaten a vegemeal ration, making her doughy tongue taste like stale grass. Everyone laughed at them when he recoiled sharply.

She turned red at the mocking and rewarded his displeasure with a swift palm across the cheek. The small cry he uttered at the impact made the others roar with more laughter, and his face turned hot.

As decent looking as Luci was, Lor no longer thought it was worth it to allow her to follow him around or hold hands with him anymore. He dodged her usual hangouts and wouldn't make eye contact with any of those who were there to witness their debacle.

If she knew back then that he was Yeunish, she probably wouldn't have offered. In fact, he imagined her puking at the thought, which gave him a sliver of joy.

Luci's tiny vegemeal-laced tongue-touch was innocent compared to Par's indulgent mouth thrust and grab. When he thought about it, Luci was his first kiss and Damaetra only his second. Par was... something else entirely.

Damaetra remained silent, waiting for him to tell her things about that night she would probably never forget.

"Paerli, she..." He paused. Damaetra had been through so much in the last couple of weeks, and her chest rose and fell with hurried breaths. "Par... she did something to me that night. The night she took you."

"Oh?" Her breaths quickened again.

"Yeah." He focused on the tip of her nose. If he couldn't see her eyes, she couldn't find his shame. At least, that was what he told himself. His tongue glued itself to the roof of his mouth, forgetting what it meant to speak in Northern Common. It reminded him of the day he tried to ask her out when his brain dumped out his ability to form complete sentences. "There's no real way for me to say this without hurting you," he blurted.

She sniffed and bobbed her head with a meek smile. "It will probably hurt, I know. But, truth is the rock we have to build on if we are going to make it work between us."

Truth. Why hide from it?

"Nico warned me so many times, and I was too stupid to listen."

Damaetra took his hands. "Stop. Just tell me, Loren."

The memory of Luci's stale vegemeal and Par's sour apples lingered in his mouth. "Par... she sort of..."

"Did she kiss you?"

Damaetra had grown tired of waiting. He had a feeling she would ask, and the fact that she asked so quickly told him it nagged her mind. He had to pull out the splinter. The big, fat splinter jammed between his ribs.

"Yes."

"Did she touch you?" Damaetra's eyes drifted down to his stones. In reflex, he pinched his legs together, feeling naked. Ashamed.

Lor closed his eyes, and he felt that foul tongue all over again. The colors buzzed under his lids in a frenzy, not knowing whether to arrange themselves into white gold or blood red. "Yes."

A drop of water swelled at her lower lid, reflecting the bird-shaped techlights. It clung to her thin white lashes before letting go and taking the bird with it.

He didn't want to cry. *Real men didn't cry.* It was a mantra heard from birth to death—at home, in school, at work... Lor's lip quivered. *This* man would cry.

The lingering taste of sour apple coated his mouth. As a linked immortal, it would stay there, just as Par would always be there. The sudden thought dried any tear that wanted to slip out.

Damaetra grabbed a small hand towel for her nose. Taking in a shuddering breath, she looked away. "Did she hurt you?"

Par didn't hurt him physically, no. It was his mind that suffered—any sense of ego he had. Nico was entirely right about her.

"Yes," he sighed.

Damaetra closed her eyes and nodded, holding the towel to her nose. She stood close to him. Close enough for the scent of her violets to come through the Reaper's Hall standard issue washing soap. It made him conscious of his unpleasant aroma.

"If I ever see her again," she said under the towel, "I'll tear out her damn eyes."

Lor raised his eyebrows. If that were a joke, he would have laughed. If Damaetra truly met Paerli again, she would probably tear out her eyes.

"Did any of those creeps touch *you*?"

She pursed her lips, observing him in silence for a moment. Her crystalline eyes had dried, and she was left with nothing but anger.

"*Damaetra.* Did any of those assholes put their hands on you?"

"Almost," she said.

Heat crept up his collar, filling his nose with the stench of the mineral desert.

The man had better be dead.

"What do you mean, *almost*?" He wasn't trying to be accusatory. The words came out that way, but she brushed them off.

She looked down at her nails, covering her eyes in a veil of thick white lashes. He hated when she hid herself from him. Angry red patches dotted the sides of her fingertips. She had picked up the habit of biting the skin around them.

Saying the words took effort. She pushed out the sound, and it came in skips and breaths. "Paerli was always busy. Sometimes it was with strategy, other times it was to get with that Hammer guy."

Paerli's aggressive sexuality surprised Lor that evening in his apartment. The day he almost died in the desert, he heard Par on the wind demanding

Hammer to take care of her. That wasn't the woman he met, befriended, and brought into his friendship fold. The woman had lost herself. She suffered yaslecha.

"There was this one time while she was away with the Hammer," Damaetra continued, her voice getting stronger, "that other big one... you know, the one she called Crow... the one who *shot* you." The word skipped as if saying it would make it happen again.

The heat scrolled back, and he felt the cooled breeze brush over his nape at the realization that vengeance was had. The man called Crow *was* dead.

"He went after you?" Lor asked.

She paused again. Always with the dreaded pause. The most subtle curve bent at her mouth as she glanced at the bathroom partition.

"He was stopped, don't worry." When she glanced up at him, her clear eyes were covered in slender red threads weaving through the whites.

"By what? Or who?"

Damaetra nodded at the partition.

"The one on your couch."

Impossible.

"*Hare?*" There was no way. There was nothing but a mean spirit in that guy. "I'm confused. He had no problem cutting off his *own* brother's legs, blinding Dill, then leaving us all for dead."

"Yes." She looked down at her nails again. That tiny smile melted into a frown. "Maybe despite that, he has a little good left in him."

Hare was a rat. No good could have existed in a man that could so easily discard his twin brother, never mind what he did to the rest of them. Damaetra was kind-hearted and naive about him.

She sighed, letting the last bit whistle from tightened lips. "I thought I was going to die in there," she mumbled.

Aedras came to mind when she said that. If he wanted any future with her, Lor had to get on Aedras's good side. Aedras would strangle him if he knew how close his youngest daughter had come to defilement... or death. It was enough to convince him to hate himself for it.

I'm such a weenie.

Rubbing one hand over his arm, he squeezed, nearly able to wrap his hand around a bicep. Damaetra needed a protector, not a lanky skin sack of bones and sinew.

"I thought... *you* were dead," she continued, taking his hand. A tear plunked onto the floor, then another. "I'm so sorry about Fowler."

Hearing his name brought back the last image he saw of Jacob Fowler in his prime. In the end, he was a twisted amalgam of man and bird, barely recognizable as a living being during his final moments. Damaetra didn't know what Lor had to do to him... she wasn't there. What a waste of a good man.

He didn't want to talk about it, only offering that Fowler was "with the Maker."

She smiled at that at least. "There was a night in the cave, after you were shot," she said, "I felt you there. That's how I knew you were alive."

Lor dreamt about her in that place. It was real after all. "It *was* me," he said.

Her mouth split into that tiny grin again. "I knew you were coming for me."

"Always."

She closed her eyes. "At least Livia was kind to me."

"Livia? The Reader?"

"Yes, the Reader. She snuck me food and water when Paerli wasn't looking... or when she was 'occupied.'"

"I'll thank her for that somehow."

"I think her freedom was gift enough." Damaetra wrapped her fingers around his palm, and he finally felt her warmth. "About that *other* thing...."

Other thing... other thing... what other thing?

Lor pressed his brows inward and his jaw flexed. Her expression had softened with mere curiosity.

Oh. *That* thing.

"About being a Yeuni?"

She tittered. "Yes, that thing."

The Yeunish were cursed. He was lucky to be standing there, and he intended not to find himself at the mercy of the Southern Morass. Harboring one was equally punishable, and the conversation shifted. He hooked his eyebrows up, setting lines in his forehead as he looked off to the side. He couldn't look at her, afraid of what she would say. What would an Anglia do with a Yeunish reject? Sucking in a breath, he closed his eyes and waited for the breakup words.

Silence throbbed his ears as the faint buzzing of techlights crescendoed to unbearable. If only the cursed light would pop, tossing bits of bird-shaped debris through the bathroom and sink a beak into his throat. It would spare him the worse death of losing her.

"I don't care what you are... I *still* love you. I just wanted you to know that."

Real men don't faint either, he told himself when he realized he had been holding his breath.

"You are my everything," he said. Those words were the last ones he sent to her after she had been taken. The message was still unread on his e-disk.

CHAPTER 2

Just a Small Bribe
LOREN

NO ONE NOTICED WHEN LOR came back into the room. They watched Hare snoring on the sofa, making a plan for what to do next.

"Help me bring him to the chair," Nico said while tugging at his brother's elbow. The wheelchair Nico used while missing his legs sat in a corner, brought there by Foscan staff after he abandoned it in the crafting courtyard.

The Lapis Evening had such an effect on Hare that Gale and Nico sagged under his dead weight while hoisting him onto the seat. Gale rubbed his face like he always did, until it was pink. "Well, he's clearly not happy about this," he said.

"No, but maybe we can make him just a little desperate. It might soften him up," Nico said.

"Or just make him desperate," Jack offered.

Nico had a thumbnail between his front teeth. "I know I can't take him home to Mom and Dad, so now what?"

Of all souvenirs to bring back from Gehenna, it had to be the cantankerous brother. A constant dose of Lapis Evening until the end of the maelstrom sounded good in theory, but that came with the chore of cleaning up shit and piss. The thought was enough to sour Lor's mood.

Hare snapped his eyes open as they considered their dilemma. He glanced down at his wrists and ankles, now connected to the wheelchair. "Let me go," he croaked.

Rotating his wrists around, he narrowed his eyes at the petrified ivy tying them together. Raw layers of skin peeled under the friction, bordered by pink irritation and flecks of old ash. The ivy cables creaked, and it was only a matter of time before they snapped.

Nico stood over him, arms crossed and knees locked. "Niki..."

"Don't call me that."

"That's your name."

"Last I knew, Niki *died* in that bedroom," Hare growled.

Nico jabbed his thumb into the crease of his chest. "I *agonized* over that."

"I don't even *know* who you are."

That had to hurt. Nico played it calm, titling his head with thumb still pointing at himself.

Jack took the opportunity to interject, moving to Hare's side. He fidgeted with an object in his pocket and a look that suggested he was going for the bribery route. "You need your treatment," he said.

Hare curled his lip, stretching his neck forward and snarled, "Put your damn goggles back on, you prickish *Yonch*."

Nico boxed Hare in the nose.

A red fan opened across his chest, turning orange on the yellowed dust staining his worn white short sleeve. The hit jolted his head back, then forward again as he shouted at Nico, who now hopped with pain heating his fist.

"Dammit, Nico! You broke my nose!" he groaned. The complaint was pinched under damaged cartilage.

Nico squeezed at his fist as the middle knuckle swelled to crimson. He didn't bother looking at his brother, only examining the new pearl of blood swelling at the abrasion from Hare's tooth edge. "And you cut off my *legs*."

Nico never expressed his feelings about his legs, relenting to the idea that this was "his life now." Any normal person, brother or not, wouldn't try to rationalize with the man who held the weapon. That guy would have died in that cave, with only the algae as witness and final resting place for his bones.

Hare tilted his head back, dismissing Nico's anger. "Yeah, and look at them… they're way cooler now."

Gale pushed a tissue in Hare's bound hands. "Tilt forward and pinch," he said. "Jack's right, you know. You need your shot."

On cue, Jack pulled out one of the syringe cylinders, holding it up enough for Hare to see but out of reach.

"Give it here," Hare said with nose pinched and leaning forward.

"You're not in any position to make demands, *Hare*," Nico spat.

Gale yanked the barrel back, farther from reach. "Not yet. I need you to do us a favor and behave."

"*Behave?* Who in Gehenna are you anyway?" Only Hare's vowels sounded proper under the fluids dripping in his throat.

"Right now, I'm the only person between you and this dose. So, will you behave?"

Hare rolled his eyes and glared at Gale before bobbing his head.

"Fine, whatever."

The drug tease had his hands in a subtle tremble, but he tried hiding it by folding his fingers inward. Gale noticed the shift, bringing the syringe back into view. Silver swirled in the barrel when he flicked it, and Hare licked his dry lower lip, nearly taking the end of the bloody tissue into his mouth. After popping off the cap, Gale expelled the air, loosing a thin arc of the liquid from the tip. As it splashed to the floor, Hare's eyes widened. They almost took on a blackness, shadowed by the sunken bluish hue of fatigue. Gale guided the needle into the patchwork of pock marks littering Hare's bicep.

The dose Gale gave was just a tease. "Give it! I need the whole thing!" Hare demanded.

Gale remained as unsympathetic as Lor remembered during his epic meltdowns as a child. He recapped the needle and gave the barrel another flick. "You'll get more when you calm down and apologize to Jack."

"Look, I'm sorry, alright? Just, give it... *please*." The tremor extended to Hare's knees as they vibrated in the chair. The ivy cords threaded around his ankles left their mark in his flesh.

It was a pathetic display of someone with such an attachment to Jack's substance. The desperation part came quicker than Lor imagined, and Jack must have felt the same, because the Formulator shook his head and frowned.

Noticing Jack's disappointment, Hare deepened his frown. "What? What do *you* know about being a Weg, half-breed? You can shut your hole," he said.

Jack smirked. "I didn't say anything."

They should just take the formulation and leave the runner to die. But, Damaetra thought there was good in him, and it was Hare's lucky day.

Hare glanced over at his twin. "Nico... please."

Lor glowered and stepped in front of Nico, pointing a stiff finger at Hare's broken nose. "Why should we help you after you tried to kill us?"

Hare tittered. "Look who's mouthin' off... another half-breed bastard."

Nico raised his fist at his brother again, making him flinch. "I should break your eye socket next. How about that?" he said.

"I'll pass."

The shooter sat on the table, making Lor's trigger finger itchy. He seized it again and took aim at Hare, who stared at him over the bloodied tissue with a smirk.

"*Do it*. Bastard," he said.

It would be easy. Right between the eyes. Lor nodded at Nico. "Want me to?"

"Just wait, Loren." Gale tried pushing his wrist down, but he wasn't going to be made foolish in front of a pathetic Weggevens with nothing to lose.

Lor remained firm, resisting Gale's pressure. "I was asking Nico, Dad."

When Gale actually let go, Lor finally felt that taste of autonomy, unyielding on the shooter, but finger far from the sensitive trigger.

Nico sighed, relaxing his fist. "No. I don't want to have to clean up his piss."

Hare chuckled. Desperate, but amused. It was disappointing, but Nico was right. They wouldn't get anywhere with him if they just put him out again. Damaetra also kind of owed the fool a debt.

Lor set the shooter down. "You're lucky your brother is better than I am," he said.

"What happened to you?" Nico asked.

"What do you care?"

"I shouldn't care, you're right. If you were anyone else, I wouldn't care. But for some stupid reason I do, and this isn't the Niki I knew."

"That's because Niki is dead. You're talking to *Hare*. Born again Weggevens runner, makin' Mom and Pop so proud."

"You know I didn't want that... you could at least talk to *me*."

The dull thud of plastic pulled Hare's interest as Gale flicked the syringe again. "Talk to your brother and I'll give you a little more," he said.

Without a word, Hare made a hard look at Gale. "Fine," he said, "I'll talk to Nico for a *whole* standard minute. Then you'd better give me that damn shot."

Lor sucked in a breath. Gale never liked being told what to do by someone he deemed his inferior. That was the feeling of growing up under his roof. Gale's palm rasped over chin stubble as he rubbed it pink—the not-so-subtle signal that he was irritated. When he raised his hands and turned away, Lor's skin went cold, never knowing him to let any affront go like that. Especially since Hare let a smug grin crawl across his face under the shadow of his reddening tissue.

"I was banished to '*tent city*' under the tracks," Hare said. Each word was a sharp tug.

"You were in Kanckette? This whole time?" Nico asked.

"Yeah. I was in Gehenna's *asshole* while you were living your best life in Secas, no doubt staying oh so colorful. Minute's up."

"Niki, I wouldn't have wished that on you in a million standard, you know that."

"Stop calling me that. I don't *know* you."

"How did you meet Paerli?"

Hare huffed. "Give me the shot and I'll tell you."

Nico nodded at Gale, who stuck another half dram into the pock-scarred arm.

With a fake goofy smile and a trickle of blood edging around his upper lip, Hare sarcastically smacked his mouth. "Well, I just feel so much *better*!

Like I could sing!"

"Please don't."

Gale rolled his eyes and capped the needle. "Jack, can you fix his nose, please?"

"I think he looks better like this," Jack said.

"Jack, please?"

"Yeah, it's gross," Lor said.

"Yes, Cricket, pwetty pwease? The bastard thinks I'm gross," Hare said, flicking red drops from his lower lip with a bitter chuckle.

Jack studied his former accomplice. Digging through his Formulator chest, he let out an exaggerated sigh.

"That's the spirit," Hare mocked.

Swiping a phial of Verdigris Mend, he dabbed two plugs of mesh with the solution, then marched up to Hare and slapped his hands away from his nose. The bloody tissue flew from his hand and made a wet smack on the clean tile.

Never comfortable with the sight of blood, it made Lor queasy, even if pouring from someone he hated.

Jack pushed the plugs up each of Hare's nostrils, then gave him a sharp shove to the forehead. "There. Better?"

"Much," he grumbled. The two plugs were comically large and stretched his nostrils to twice their size. They resembled two large half-picked boogers hanging from his face.

"What are *you* looking at?" Hare asked. His lip curled in a sneer, but stiff from the plug of mesh in his nostril. Lor didn't realize he'd been staring.

Lor smirked. "Not much," he said.

"Oh, taking a turn back at me, are we, *half-breed*? Why don't you kiss my sack?"

Nico chose the open palm slap, sending one of the green plugs flying from his nose. It collided with the tile and stubbed out like a smoking butt.

Lor couldn't help but chuckle at the insult. Call it immature, but he tried to choke back the laugh.

"Dammit, Nico, *stop!*" Hare stretched his jaw, raising a clawed fist to the red side of his face.

Dill's visor must have plugged his ears when he turned it off because there was no way Lor would be able to sleep through the noise. Curled in the corner on the bed, he hadn't moved.

"How about you stop insulting my friends and answer my question?" Nico spat.

"I'm so sowwy, bwofer, you must have knocked the widdle qwestion from my head. What did you want to ask me?"

Nico's expression turned leathery in frustration. Rather than ask, he repeated the question in a deadpan demand. "How did you meet Par."

They were all tired. They were tired from the fight in the cavern, they were tired from the arguing, and they were tired of Hare. He was beating them. The entire time, he kept a leg up on them, not even allowing the bribe to happen. He was desperate for the shot, but not enough to save his life.

"She visited us." Hare stretched his jaw again and wiggled his nose. The blood began to snake its way down his lip again. Jack prepared another plug and shoved it into Hare's empty nostril. "Ah, thanks, servant. You may go now."

The sinister glare Jack gave was made more so by the yellow cast in his eyes. Thin muscles rippled in his jaw.

Hare pointed at Jack with both wrists pressed together under the ivy rope. "Why are you asking *me,* anyway? That half-breed knows her better than I do."

Everyone in the room glanced at Jack, who shrugged.

"We'll talk to Jack later," Nico said, "Right now, this is about *you* wanting to follow her."

"Why did *he*?" Another accusation, another smirk.

Nico grumbled and approached the Formulator chest. Withdrawing a green phial, he sucked the fluid into a different syringe. "Since you're being difficult," he said, preparing the new barrel, "if I feel you're being a smart-ass, I'm going to jab you with this new stuff. If I think you're being genuine, you get another real dose. Understand?"

Hare tittered and complained. "But that's subjective! What if I'm telling the truth but being a jerk about it? I've been known to do that."

"You'll have to stop being a jerk."

"What's in the new syringe anyway? Widdle wussy tears? Yeunish brand squeezins?"

"Actually, I'm glad you asked. Jack, can you explain it to him?"

Jack opened his mouth like a bony puck fish. He studied the remnants of the phial Nico pulled from, then gave him a look. Nico nodded and smiled.

"Uh, y-yes, that would be Verdigris Biosore," Jack lied. Hare couldn't recognize the lie, but Lor did.

Pleased with Jack's choice, Nico curled his lip, then turned back to his brother. "And you should have seen what it did to your mute Shepherd friend in the cavern. I bet there's nothing but bones left."

"So you killed Pigeon, eh?" Hare said. "Her and her rapist son can rot in Gehenna."

"And now you're faced with the choice of whether or not to join them."

Hare studied the unknown substance... squinting and turning his head as if it would reveal its secrets if he looked at it sideways.

"Bastard Yonch and your twisted formulations. No wonder only someone like you could come up with a cure made from the *dead,*" he grumbled.

"If I hear you say that slur one more time, I'm going to squeeze this whole damn syringe of Biosore in your eyeball."

"You know just as well as I do that a Yeunish Formulator is an *abomination.* A draught like that is some kind of ancient sorcery."

That was new. Not much was written in the tomes about the Yeunish, so if what Hare said was accurate, did that mean the Yeunish had a different relationship with Guild abilities? What did it mean for one to be a Reaper?

"Jack isn't the only one that can make this drug," Nico said, wagging the new syringe between his first two fingers. "I can too."

"That's a load of crap."

"Honest to Maker. So it looks like you need me a little more than you thought you did."

Clever.

Hare peered at his twin, then tossed his head back. "Fine. What is your next silly question?"

"What is the breach?"

"What?"

"*What* is the *breach*?" Nico hissed through his teeth.

"Whatever, I don't know."

Nico rushed toward Hare and pointed the uncapped needle at his face. Hare jerked his head back, holding both hands over his eyes in a fleshy shield. "Dude, I really don't know, Nico. I only know bits and pieces."

"Such as?"

Hare rolled his eyes. "It's a source of power, from what I heard."

"From who?"

"Just whisperings in the meetings."

"Are you a Valoan?"

"That's four questions. Give me a dose." He peeked through fingers laced over his eyes.

"I'll give you a dose when I'm satisfied with your answers." Nico pointed the new needle at him again.

"I'm no damn Valoan, Nico. Now give me a dose. Please."

Grabbing the drug from Gale, he poked Hare himself with another half dram. "I don't want to hear your stupid, sarcastic remarks," he said.

Hare raised his hands in surrender with a lip curled and quivering to hold back some insult.

"So, what kind of power? And why did you want it?" Nico continued.

"I don't know. All I heard was power... and why *wouldn't* I want that?"

Nico sighed and looked over at Jack. "I'm done."

"Come *on*, Nico. Just give me the rest of the drug. Or ask me whatever you want, I don't care. I'll tell you what I think about while rubbing one out at this point."

"Now you're just being crude to be crude." Nico observed his brother sitting there with a half grin staring back at him. He activated the legs to burst toward Hare and jab the new green liquid into his leg.

"Oh Maker! Oh, shit! Nico, what did you do?" Hare writhed in the chair, bouncing the wheels and nearly tipping himself onto the floor. He undulated his torso like a dry, suffering worm, cursing and cursing while Nico chuckled.

"It's not funny, Nico! Oh Maker, have mercy!" Hare writhed some more until Nico unscrewed the needle and tossed the barrel into his lap.

"It's just green eneris. You're fine."

Hare said nothing, pursing his lips and looking at his leg. Slumping his shoulders, his head bobbed to the side. Gale stepped forward, pulling out a small pen beam and tilting Hare's head back to shine the light into his eyes. He drifted the gadget back and forth and hummed. "We'd better stop. His pupils are hazy."

Purple-scarlet circles hung from Hare's lids, and his posture had weakened. The tremor remained—constant and cutting into his wrists at the bindings.

"So what does that mean, they're *hazy*?" Nico asked.

Gale clicked the light off and watched as Hare swayed. "It means he's dying."

Nico closed his eyes and rubbed his temples. "Alright," he said.

With heels touching, Hare's feet formed a crooked "V" as he let his legs relax. The soles of his shoes were practically worn through. The white rubber, no longer white, had been splashed with yellow stains, black scuffs, and curled pieces of material peeling back from deep scratches. The canvas had endured much, with rings of yellow-brown stains spread over the material from rainy days. He looked like a child sitting there. The dirty child everyone knew in class. For a moment, Lor felt sorry for him.

That was their homecoming. It went about as well as Lor imagined, considering the situation. Hare's core was drained, and no amount of sarcasm or hatred could charge it that night. There was always the next night. And the next. Once the ivy they relied heavily on to hold their captive failed, Hare would be gone, and there would be a price on Lor's head.

"Just give it to him," Jack mumbled, continuing to stare at a weakened Hare.

There was no witty insult or hurtful retort. Hare's eyes were hardly open anymore, and he yawned several times. Nico gave him the rest.

Hare shuddered. "Thanks," he mumbled as he closed his eyes. The tremor in his hands slowed until he fell asleep, then they stopped.

Dill stirred on the bed, rolling over to sit up. "What'd I miss?" he asked as he pressed the center button on his visor. A purple line of light traced across his face in an arc.

"You timed that, didn't you?" Lor said.

"What? No way—you know how I like drama."

"Well, you didn't miss much… only Nico punching out his brother," Lor said.

Dill tittered and complained, "Aw, man! I miss all the good stuff!"

"You woke up just in time for bed."

It was past second sun. Hard to believe only a few hours ago, they were still in that cavern, fighting for their lives.

"Dang, I can't go back to Engineering Hall now or they'll fine me. Can I just stay here?" Dill asked.

"You're already here, may as well. All of you."

There were too many of them and only one paltry bed big enough for maybe two, a couch, and one chair passable to sleep in. Then there was the floor. The cold, marble floor with flecks of Hare's blood on it.

"Make that dude take the floor," Dill said, pointing at Hare, who had passed out in the wheelchair.

Nico shook his head and turned to Jack. "Is he going to be alright?"

Jack pried open one of Hare's eyelids. "I've seen him in worse shape. He'll be fine—just let him sleep."

"On the floor," Dill added.

The partition for the bathroom *shuffed* open, and Lor spun around to see Damaetra standing in the archway.

"Hey," she said. "Can I stay here tonight?"

Something told him that a fine of plats wasn't the big scary thing bothering her. It was being alone.

"Yes, of course," Lor said.

She stepped back and grinned. "I think you probably need a shower first."

Lor turned crimson and smelled his armpits. A funky expired sweat smell with an undertone of deep cavern musk hung there. It was a smell so thick it was almost visible.

"We should all wash up before sleeping," Gale suggested.

"Me first!" Dill jumped up and ran to the bathroom, closing the partition.

Water splashed into the basin before anyone could object. The armpits would have to wait. Lor went to the bed, seeing a silhouette of Dill's filth on the top cover.

Pulling it from the mattress, he held it toward the group like a plague cloth. "Anyone want to sleep with this?"

CHAPTER 3

Seven Was A Crowd
LOREN

FIRST SUN SCORCHED OVERHEAD, CUTTING *through layers of dank bog in the wasteland surrounding him. A single rotted log leaned against a dead gray tree with slender knobby branches reminding him of Fowler's bony fingers. Fowler wasn't there, but Karl was.*

A crudely stitched pack-sac sagged next to the log, with Karl's name scribbled along the side in black ink. It was most likely written with obsenis forturum, the common and widely discarded eneris he'd heard about. The stocky companion sat hunched on the log, scratching at a twig snapped from the dead tree with an engineering switch. He cared for that twig like nothing else existed around him. When Lor approached the man, he didn't know who it was, just that it was someone.

"There's an old Foscan saying..." Karl said, turning around. "Oh, it's you."

"What do they say?" Lor asked, hearing a strange tone come from his throat.

"Bah, it's nothing. I don't know much about those folk, but I do know they're quite superstitious." Karl continued to whittle his twig to a point, then proceeded to pick his stained teeth with it.

"The Foscans were responsible for Great Tree. You know that, right?" Lor's voice warbled. Why he would say such a thing was not like him.

"Were they now?" Karl raised his eyebrows, then eyeballed his toothpick. "Tell me then... what makes you say that?"

"You know."

Karl looked up at him with red-brown eyes and his lip curled. "I know the silly story you told me. But if I'm gunna say truth, I don't think you were being wholly honest with me."

"I told you the truth."

"If you say so," he said, nodding to something beyond Lor's shoulder. "It's time..." The last word echoed in his head as blackness rolled over the bog like a scroll.

Once the last bit of light blinked away, he remained there, floating in the abyss, willing himself to wake up.

Wriggling his legs in the open space, he dangled on invisible strings, looking around at nothing... total emptiness. That was until a pair of silvered eyes watched him deep in the dark depths.

They flickered once—twice. As he hovered in the void, it occurred to him he felt naked. The eyes searched him. A low grumble gurgled from within—it surrounded him.

Loren... it hissed. *His own name felt unclean.*

Loren Turtingas-s-s-s. The voice growled, and a shimmer passed over the silver specks as they slithered forward, meeting his face with haste. Icy tendrils forked through his blood as the entity faced him. I foun-n-nd you.

Lor shuddered awake, making Damaetra stir next to him. He stroked her hair, trying not to tangle shaking fingers in her strands. The blood slogged through his veins, still chilled from whatever met him in his dream. He opened his e-disk and swiped in several notes. That didn't feel like an ordinary dream.

The dual nature of the encounter with Karl, to the way the entity approached him, he documented every last detail of the dream. It took him a standard thirty to get it all down, and when he shut the e-disk off, he sat there, staring into the room's darkness. Those sinister eyes swimming toward him... he glanced around, half expecting to find them in an especially dark corner. But he didn't.

Who or what that was didn't sit right. One thought he had was that maybe it had something to do with his new immortality. There was no *Immortality: The Why's and How's for Idiots* manual he could turn to, and nothing to tell him what these dreams meant. Par had tricked him into something sinister, he was sure of that.

The black pendant Maron ripped from her neck sat on his nightstand, glittering red stars from its center. He wished she would die. He wished she *could* die. Again, there was no *Killing Immortals for Dummies* handbook either.

In the corner, he noticed Jack lounging in the chair he slept in, except his eyes were open and fixed on the ceiling. Lor crept out of bed to get to the bathroom. Once inside, the black silhouette of Gale lay bundled up in the bathtub. Surrounded by towels and resting on the bathmat, he couldn't have been comfortable, but he seemed to be sleeping anyway. Lor closed the shower curtain and quietly lifted the lid to pee.

As the stream hit the water, his mind wandered. When he drank Par's gold, he expected to feel some kind of energy, or something that flipped a switch in his body chemistry that told him he was different. Or more alive.

Par was good at lies, though, so maybe she lied to him about the whole thing.

"Loren?" Gale's groggy voice came from the tub.

"O-oh!" Lor's spray hit the back of the lid, and it echoed like hard rain on a window. "Yeah, it's me. Sorry, I had to go."

"When you're done, we should talk."

"Yeah, sure." Nothing makes the pee crawl back up like family listening. Lor labored to squeeze out the rest.

"So what did you want to talk about?" Lor flicked his hands in the basin and turned to face Gale, who had already pushed the curtain back. He didn't expect comedy that morning, but Gale's sleep-wrinkled face and yawns as he sat upright and cross-legged in a bathtub, of all things, delivered. Lor chuckled.

"Well, first the maelstrom. The train isn't running, so we have to figure out what to do with your extra friends." He peered up at him with his glasses perched on his nose. "Otherwise, we're riding out the storm at Kanckette station."

The thought of camping out with overflowing trash cans swarming with gee flies, and the occasional streaker zipping through the station with all their exposed bouncy parts didn't appeal to him. "I'd rather not."

"Didn't think so... but I don't think Guild Central is going to be very accommodating to them. Especially that runner."

"Speaking of running, do you need a treatment all the time, or only when running?"

"Only when I run."

"So now that Hare's had his treatment and can't go anywhere, we don't have a bribe."

"We just have to pray that he behaves," Gale said, sighing.

They needed a better strategy. First, there was the matter of a more effective restraint. Dill's improved Engineering abilities might prove helpful in that. There was no way those ivy cords would last through the end of the storm, and letting Hare go wasn't an option when he knew what Lor was.

"Jack plans to return to the desert after the storm," Gale said, grunting as he stood in the tub. "Before you ask, he mentioned it to me last night while you were in the shower."

"But what about his Yeunish—"

"He knows the risk. Plus, he's a grown man and can decide that for himself."

"So *during* the storm...?"

"He'll stay with Nico in Formulator Hall and try to blend in there. Like an uncle or something."

Lor huffed. "They look nothing like family."

Gale shrugged, and his familiar, routine gestures took Lor back home. It put him into a mild sort of melancholy, where all his old bad feelings of home had become a nostalgic desire to return and never leave again. Family was in Peakwood. His real mother was back West.

A cheerless veil hung around at Guild Central, and Lor wasn't sure he even wanted to stay. Par's nasty tricks, Fowler's death, and Damaetra's trauma were reason enough for him to bounce out of there. It didn't matter how colorful the paint, plants, or holoconfetti scattered all over town was, they all took on shades of dismal. If Damaetra didn't want to go, he'd stay with her. She was the only thing that could tether him to Guild Central.

A subtle knock rapped at the partition.

"Everyone's waking up," Jack said as he nosed through the crack in the door.

Gale projected the time on his e-disk. "It's still early," he said.

"Good. We can sneak everyone back to their halls," Lor said. He turned back to the door opening, where the slice of Jack's face peered in at them. "What about the running jerk?"

"He's awake."

Lor tittered. Leaving Damaetra in the living space with that creep was not an option. Savior or not, there was no telling what rude thing he'd say to her.

Back in the living area, Damaetra lay on the bed, facing the wall. She practically snuggled up next to it. Dill made himself into a ball at the foot of the bed, except one left foot jutting from the edge. Nico had nested on the one couch in the room.

"Ready to untie me yet?" Hare asked in a deep rumble.

"Nope," Lor said.

"Come on, man, I need a shower so bad."

"Yes, I know." Lor scrunched his nose. "Not so loud. Damaetra's sleeping."

"Not anymore," she said, rolling over to face them.

"See what you did?"

"It's alright, Loren," she said through a wide yawn.

Hare watched her open mouth with great interest, and it wasn't lost on Lor. "What are you looking at?" he asked.

Hare turned his attention to Lor, scanning him up and down. "Not much."

"Nice comeback. Did you think of that all by yourself?"

Jutting his lower lip out, Hare whined sarcastically.

More of his friends woke up, and the room got noisy. Dill rolled to sitting, turning on his visor with a great yawn.

"Nice *eye*," Hare said with a snigger.

A wise teacher once told Lor that to give in to your bully's taunts was to give him a gift. To ignore their challenge was a ball of black eneris in their stomach. Painful. Dill must have had the same teacher.

In the room's silence, plastic squealed and the familiar squeeze of liquid passing through coolant tubes burbled when Nico sat up.

"Gale and I talked earlier," Lor said, gesturing at all in the room but Hare, "and now *we* need to talk."

Everyone glanced at Hare, who had busied himself picking his nails, but they knew he was listening. The bubbles in Nico's legs shifted, and the purple glow of Dill's visor advanced toward the wheelchair.

As their shadows overtook him, Hare glanced up from his nail duties and gave them an ironic innocent look. "Oh, hey, guys, what's up?"

What he didn't notice was the shooter Dill stole from the night table when he rounded the front of Hare's seat. Preloaded with a final shot of Lapis Evening, the barrel traced Hare's torso.

Dill frowned. "Sorry, dude." The needle thwacked Hare in the chest, and he slumped over to snoring.

Reaper's Hall was an echoing cavern of stillness. Not a soul wandered in the earliest hours, choosing to sleep in for the weekend. They whispered through the atrium, passing the plump and testy attendant who chose not to engage with them after the night before. At the exit, the same two blocky Mesaman guards stood sentinel at the double glass. All it took was a somewhat understanding look from Lor at the attendant to get a nodding approval and release from the building, no questions asked.

Once outside, the sun had barely winked over the horizon, creating a near paranormal cast of orange over blue. There was something irritating about the dawn sun—Lor always felt that way, even as a kid. It was light, but not bright enough to bring everything into focus, and the two contrasting colors created a dim-bright muddled color that didn't know what it wanted to be. It was uncomfortable and sometimes painful. Amid the silence, only the fountain in the middle of the court sent its rushing din, reflecting the uncanny pre-dawn hue.

Dill skipped in front of the group. "So the plan is to ride out the storm after I make a new set of cuffs?" he said.

"That's what Gale thought was best," Lor said.

"Or how about this—you could have *this* crazy speedster drive you through it." Dill pointed toward Damaetra with a smirk.

She grinned in mild amusement and shook her head. Their escape jumper sat at the end of the circle, parked overnight without getting tagged. Another loose end they didn't know how to tie. Lor suggested leaving it there for a tow, which no one seemed to argue against except Dill, who wanted to scalp the thing for material.

"I'm pretty sure Guild Central would have questions about a random jumper sitting there, let alone a random jumper stripped to its pegs," Nico said with a laugh that was a mild rib but mostly serious. It was agreed that it was easier if Guild Central could just tow it.

The less attention they drew to themselves, the better. There was already one provocative question Lor was afraid they'd ask: "Do they even know Fowler's dead?"

He didn't mean for it to sound as callous as it came out. He was just being practical. As their mentor, Lor figured whoever wanted to know would ask each of them what they knew. Honestly, he had no idea what to say, as the truth was a thing out of fiction.

"It's been a crazy week... I feel guilty about it, but I didn't even *think* about that." Nico glanced down at Hare, still under the effects of Lapis Evening with the silver splint still poking out of his chest.

"I say we let Guild Central find out about that too. No sense in making it hard on us," Dill said. "Besides, we've got more problems to worry about with your brother..."

Dill's voice faded into a droning ambiance as Lor stopped paying attention. Maybe it was the way Fowler's death was treated as trivial. It could have been exhaustion and hunger. Whatever it was, Lor didn't want to listen to it, only catching snippets here and there. *Make new shackles...*Dill told Nico, and *it'll be easy because I'm awesome...* and such talk. Even Damaetra seemed to have forgotten their sponsor. They didn't know Fowler that well. It wasn't their fault—Lor didn't really know him that well either. Was it wrong to still think about him? Was he being overly sentimental?

"Hey, can you make more needles too?" Nico asked, pulling Lor out of his own head. "We shot a bunch of them in the cave, and I'm down to just a couple."

"That's easy. Make more of that knockout juice to fill 'em. I think your brother likes it."

Nico tittered. "I shot so many of them in that big guy. What was his name? Hammer. It took forever for him to go down. Dame, I can teach you how to make it."

Lor felt like an outsider. Just a slack-jawed extra in the backdrop of their own film. He flexed his fingers out as far as they would go, then squeezed them into a tight fist. Sharp nails dug into his palm, and he realized they needed to be cut. It was so weird, knowing that his ordinary, clammy hands could draw out a person's life force... maybe kill them. What good was his ability for needles, draughts, and shackles? "I might be able to get some extra eneris," Lor said, "but I don't know what it will be. They never tell us before we go."

Nico patted him on the shoulder as if to say, *aw, such an adorable offer.* "Any help is good help," was what he actually said. "We'd better split up before the sun comes up and we're found near this jumper."

"Actually," Damaetra interrupted, reaching a hand out to touch Nico. "May I ask you a favor?" Lor glanced at her fingers wrapped around Nico's tan, muscular wrist.

Don't be jealous, Loren. Envy is unattractive. It was something his fake mother, Surai, told him once when Lor was too young to know what attractiveness meant. He couldn't remember what he did to prompt her to tell him that, but the thing wasn't as important as the words she used to correct him. She was right, of course. In her wisdom, Lor tried not to show the green in his complexion.

"Would it bother you, or would it be alright if... I mean, *can* I stay with you? I don't think I'm ready to be alone."

Envy is unattractive.

Nico said nothing, only studying her with that concentrated look Lor always wanted for himself. It reminded him of the carved stone monument at Peakwood Park of Waegvar the Wise. Despite being the namesake of the Weggevens curse, the statue of Waegvar was a fetching cast of him in his early thirties. Perfectly striking. Impeccably wise.

Envy, Loren. It's unattractive.

"I-I mean, I'm alright with it as long as you don't mind these two." Nico pointed at Hare and Jack, who had been standing as still as the statue of Waegvar, but without the beauty or brains. "And, of course, if it's alright with you, Lor?"

Was he blushing?

Lor narrowed his eyes.

Why am I even jealous... Nico is my best friend. He got her out of the cave. He helped me find her. He's asking for my approval...

"I-I..." Nico paused, still focusing on Lor and his tightened mouth to form an answer for him.

Would she get close to him and want him? No. She can't stay with three men. That's absurd!

But she's scared; I have to let go of my own insecurities if it makes her feel better.

No, you can't, she'll get too close to him. Just think... she'll get so scared one night that they'll crawl in bed together. One thing would lead to another, and they would eventually laugh at how stupid you are—letting her stay with them.

She needs someone; she needs protection under the weird Guild Central Hall rules... he's your best friend and can watch her for you.

But he's just so much better than me!

"Loren?" Damaetra squeezed his hand.

Licking his bottom lip, he realized it had dried out from his mouth being parted open. How long had he stood there like that?

He smiled at her. "You don't need my permission to do what makes you feel comfortable. Nico?"

Nico nodded with his pensive Waegvar expression.

She wrapped her arms around his long, slender torso, briefly resting her head on his bony chest. His stomach rumbled a little. Hopefully she didn't hear it. "Message me every hour," she said with a cheeky grin.

"You're joking, but I'm going to," he said.

"I'm not joking. Every hour."

"I'll help you catch up with Formulating too," Nico offered finally in his pseudo-sage contribution.

Damaetra frowned. "I've missed so much," she said. "I hope I haven't been kicked out of the ha—"

"Master Loren!" the familiar Foscan voice called out from a small side building he'd never noticed. Krik'tha jogged to them with a stack of thin boxes. That long black tail he wore in his hair trailed aimlessly behind, bouncing off his back and nearly reaching his rump.

"Hey, Krik'tha, good to see you. Call me Lor, remember?"

"Yes, sorry, Lor. I come with good news."

After taking a handful of heavy breaths and stringing together several slanted sentenced in bad Northern Common, Krik'tha informed them that the lot of them had been stricken with parasites.

"You told them we had *worms*?" Dill raised his lip and glared at the Foscan with greater contempt than he usually had for them.

"That doesn't sound like good news." Damaetra dragged out her words as she looked at everyone for confirmation that she wasn't crazy.

"Not *worm*, parasite only. Halls are forgiving of very bad illness. Is on record, and your jobs stay safe."

The slender boxes teetered in his arm, and he about lost the top one. With a graceful catch, he shoved it toward Lor. Each of them had a box, even Hare, whom Krik'tha had only seen briefly the night before. "New clothes for you. Clean."

Lor collected a second parcel for Gale, thankful that someone was looking out for him.

"Wow, that's incredibly thoughtful, Krik'tha. And you've been so very helpful," Lor said with a wide grin at the servant, who beamed back.

"I am happy to help. Now I must explain the new... *guests*." He pointed at Jack and Hare.

"Right. We'll catch up later." Lor waved at Nico as he pushed Hare away with Jack and Damaetra trailing behind. She spun around and gave him a coy wave, then tapped her palm and mouthed: "*every hour.*"

After watching the exchange, Dill ruefully stubbed his toe into the stone walkway. "Man, I feel so *alone.*"

"Hey, you have all of us! And no one here is going to distract you from your greatness."

"Yeah, that's true."

The line between agreeing that they wouldn't distract him versus his greatness was a myopic blur.

"Is that going to go to your head?" Lor asked.

"Probably."

They watched the group walk away, waiting in the promise that Krik'tha would return to gather Dill and get him checked in properly. The farther Nico was from them, the more stilted his movements looked. Robotic. Either he still wasn't quite used to his reformed legs, or they needed an adjustment. Dill seemed to be thinking the same thing when he scratched his chin and said, "You know, I should put this greatness to work and make him a new set. Something less... fleshy."

"Will you have time with everything else you're going to make?" Lor rubbed his chin like Gale, feeling the prickly thick layer of blond stubble he itched to shave.

"I can make it work. Gotta get my hands on some new material. But I think I can make something he can swap."

"I think he'd like that." Lor smiled.

Good news, citizens of the North! Our non-Guild climate casters have predicted an early end to the annual Maelstrom that plagues our rich desert lands.

What does this mean for you? Princeps Renae has begun preparations for early reopening of train services, so you can be rest assured that any delayed travel plans can be restored to normal sooner than anticipated.

Thank you for being a valued citizen.
Details to come.

CHAPTER 4

Hall of Bad Memories
DAMAETRA

PROPER LADIES MUST MASK THEIR fear and show strength of resolve to the public. At least, Damaetra told herself as much.

Stepping through the front doors of Formulator Hall, she was reminded of the sharp shift in smell from indoors to the outdoors the last time she passed through the double glass. The stink of sweat and hot breath pouring from that beastly Engineer in the warmth of the building was traded for a cool slap in the face of crisp deygo lilac once outside. Both made her ill.

Decorative tiles tapped under the thin soles of her shoes as she marched with Nico to the attendant. The thin box from Krik'tha rumpled under her grip as she held it tight to her chest. To distract herself from the stress of retracing her steps from that night, she tried to imagine the flowy, frilly things he might have picked for her. After all, Loren liked her delicate dresses.

Was there underwear in here?

Oh yeah, your generous servant friend was thinking about my butt and picked me out a nice thong, Loren. What do you think of that?

She giggled to herself.

Watching the back of his head bobbing in determination as he led them to the central desk made her giggle a little harder. Underwear shopper or not, Krik'tha was an interesting man.

He reminded her of the servant she had at home, and not just because they were the same race. Feck the Simple, he was called... the poor guy suffered a blow to his head that knocked him silly. He could never read normally after that. Maybe Krik'tha was a reminder because they both had a disability. Maybe that was shallow of her, but she still adored Feck. He was there when her father died.

"May I help you?" The desk assistant grinned at the group. Her voice was overly cheerful, and Damaetra found it irritatingly fake. A sharp, angular item with *Loyal Advocate* inscribed in gold sat on the counter. It was similar to those trophies she'd seen in various offices she'd visited growing up in Audun. Heavy and sharp, sure, but just as fake.

"Yes, I am here to register family stay with Master Nico—brother and uncle."

As she alternated typing and swiping at her console, Krik'tha caught her up on Nico and Damaetra's "illness." Earlier when he told the group that they had parasites, it probably wasn't too far from the truth. Who knew what kind of bug she caught while wallowing in the ash and old death deep inside Mount Gehenna? Several notes hovered over her console, with images of her and Nico. Red letters were stamped across their smiling faces, reading "indisposed." The woman eyed them suspiciously.

"Vacationing in Haerow?" she asked with a wry grin, continuing to type into the console.

It was a joke but an unpleasant reference to an island on the southern coast of North Roseaarde known for its unclean waters and near invisible bugs that found their way into the body by... intimate means. "N-no!" Damaetra didn't mean to shout, turning scarlet. For one, she'd never been farther south than Kanckette, and if she had, it wouldn't have been to visit Haerow.

The woman snorted a laugh before finishing their entries. "Is he alright?" she said while dragging her finger to point at Hare.

Everyone glanced at him hunched over in the chair. A thin trail of drool hung like a pendulum, swaying in front of his dust-blotched shirt.

"A-ah, he is resting," Krik'tha said. He leaned in and whispered, "Too much fun last night."

It would be a miracle for her to believe that, considering the end of Dill's needle still protruded from his chest.

"I see..." She paused mid-thought, opening her mouth again before finding a new distraction in Jack's goggles. "Hey, you can't have those on inside."

Krik'tha cleared his throat. "Man is blind." His smile wavered, and Damaetra prayed his resolve wouldn't crack.

The attendant sighed harshly. "I suppose that's alright. May I see your card?"

Was his hand shaking? In the current climate of Yeunish hate, it made sense. The law had gotten harsher over the years, extending near-equal punishment for anyone caught supporting one. That would include Dame herself, if anyone else found out about Loren.

He handed her the trembling pass, which she took without notice.

Crap, I don't have my pass...

It was sitting on her night table next to her e-disk. Of course she wouldn't have had the permission to grab them as she was being snatched from her room by her former friend. The situation felt even worse by the fact she nearly didn't get into Guild Central to begin with. She was beginning to think that she wasn't meant for this place at all. Would Loren want to leave?

The assistant swiped Krik'tha's card, then stuck out a greedy hand to Damaetra.

"I, uh... I'm sorry, I accidentally left mine in the room."

The woman softened at her meek posture. "Don't worry, hon. Name?"

"Damaetra Praes." She hesitated. "It's Anglia. Should I spell it for you?"

"I got you." The woman smiled, tapping in her name. A digital holo copy of Damaetra's picture popped up on the receiver. Reaching under the desk, she pulled out a printed temporary pass with a wink. "These are normally 150 plat per extra copy. Just don't tell anyone I did that for you."

Damaetra sighed. "Thank you so much, I really appreciate that."

"Stay colorful," she said with a wave and a smile as they made their way to the lift.

Krik'tha left the group in a hurry to get back to Dill.

Living just down the hall from Nico, the patterns on the carpet were a dizzying reminder of her path out of there the week before. She should feel relieved to be back, but she wasn't. Each fleck of color against the navy-blue low pile carpet had a name. Each scuff mark in the wall was a trail marker. Seeing them now made her anxious for home and fueled her bitterness.

Nico's room was identical to hers. The crisp purified air nipped her cheeks and set her nose running. It was there, in that corner, where she was interrupted in her sleep. Where the bed leaned against the far wall, with a tall and heavy wardrobe that stood like an ancient guard at the foot. Standard issue room fragrance lingered in the air. It was different than hers, and a much welcome change. It was sweet and musky, a scent she could associate with change.

"You can take the bed tonight." Nico's voice was a distant echo in the background of her own thoughts.

"Thanks, you don't have to do that," she said.

He wouldn't take no for an answer, claiming she deserved to be comfortable, or something like that.

"Hare can stay in his chair," he continued as he pushed the wheelchair next to the couch. "I'll sleep on the couch and keep an eye on him, and Jack can have the tub or the floor. Whichever."

Really, she would rather sleep underneath the bed where no one but wandering dust clouds could find her. A mattress sounded comfortable, but it would leave her exposed.

The Maker would still listen if she kept her eyes open, right?

Hare's head bobbed to the side. Strips of purplish green branched out from the inner corners of his eyes toward his reddened cheeks. There was a slight bend in his nose, right at the bridge. There was no sense in getting sentimental... but she felt the smallest bit sorry for him.

"Do you need anything from your room?" Nico asked while stripping the mattress.

The only thing in that room other than a coiled wad of hair on the floor was her e-disk and ID, which she definitely needed. Nico held his hand out for the temporary card, volunteering to fetch them with reassurances he'd only be a minute.

And then she was alone. With two men from Paerli's "team." She knew nothing about Jack, even during the short time he was still with the group. He was weird as hell.

Hare may have helped her once, but she felt better knowing he was unconscious. If he could easily mangle his own twin, in what other twisted ways would he turn on a stranger, especially if money was attached to it?

She jumped when the door clicked open, but it was just Nico. He must have used super speed up and down the hall because there was no way he could have done that so quickly. It was a relief to have him back. He held out her e-disk and ID card.

As she took them, she remembered how Aedras had stressed the importance of independence. She should have gotten them herself.

Swiping the surface of her e-disk, she had several missed messages.

LOREN: You are my everything.

CAE Bee: How's li'l sis doing? He better be treating you right. Or else.

ELO-LO: Answer Cae. She thinks you're ignoring her.

CAE Bee: I didn't mean it really. I'm sure he's a nice guy.

CAE Bee: Seriously, how have you been? Are you mad at us? This is about the program, isn't it?

ADDY Daddy: Hey darling, please answer your sister. She's going mad.

MUMMY: Hey honey, I have a question for you when you have time. It has to do with your ability. How did it... manifest? Love you!

ELO-LO: Did mom text you about your ability? Just ignore it... she's being weird.

Addy Daddy: Dame... could you please call one of us?

Cae Bee: Dude, for real, I just miss you! I've been having these really weird dreams lately and I want to talk to you about them.

Elo-Lo: Did Cae text you about her dreams? Just ignore her.

Between the messages were several missed calls from each of them. While they increased in concern, they kept their distance, giving their youngest girl a bit of that independence Aedras was so keen for. As she held the e-disk, a new message from Loren hovered above the glass.

Loren: Miss you

The message hurt a little. She loved him, truly... but a bittersweet longing for how things were when they first met came rushing through her. It was the innocence they had, of learning new things about each other, and her attraction to his clumsy trips over ancient tech hidden in the sand. Sure, they knew more about each other now, and had been through a slice of hell together, but he still didn't know her stories. There was still time.

Damaetra: Miss you more

That wasn't a lie... and she hated this place.

Her e-disk buzzed again with a little winky face from Loren. It made her smile for the brief moment before remembering the several missed calls from her family. She put her e-disk down and spun it slowly on the table, watching it wobble. If they called again, she'd answer for sure. Otherwise, they could wait for her to call that evening.

"So, did you have a plan for him?" she asked. Nico was remaking the bed with clean sheets while Hare still slept.

He shrugged. "I wasn't thinking about a plan when I saw him that day." He bit his lower lip and flapped the blanket over the bed, letting it float down. The coolant tubes bubbled in protest with every bend at the knees.

"How could you forgive him?" she asked. Nico froze without looking at her, wiping his hands down his sides and shaking his head.

"I don't know if I can," he said.

The answer came as a surprise. Everyone dealt with their problems differently, and Nico was rather soft toward Hare.

"So, what's the story here?" she asked.

"What story?" Nico wandered toward the kitchen and lifted a can toward her. "Want a water?"

"Sure. With Hare. What happened?" All she knew was that he was twitchy and weird. Before meeting them in the desert, she had barely seen him, not realizing how much he resembled her own friend.

Nico shook his head. "To be honest? I'm not sure. One day we were normal, then the next he was having a seizure like Lor had the day he became a Reaper."

She didn't want to think about that day. It was the first time she thought Loren was going to die. "Your brother had a seizure?"

"Yeah." Nico took a gulp of water, ripping out a belch he tried to keep quiet. "Sorry about that. We were thirteen. Actually, we used to be very close and had our own nickname and everything." He chuckled to himself, disbelieving and sad. "Then he had that seizure, and my parents told me he was dead."

"That's terrible..."

"Well, maybe. I don't really know why they told me that. Maybe they thought it was shameful to have a Weggevens. Maybe Nik... Hare became a danger to us. I won't ever know. I just felt it—that he wasn't dead. Like a twin thing or something."

Damaetra nodded, turning the unopened water can around on the table, letting it get warm. There was always a sliver of jealousy when she thought about her own twin sisters. They had their own secrets and their own language with each other. Nico and Hare must have been the same, or similar. "My sisters are like that. I'll admit, I don't understand it."

Nico took another drink of the water, careful not to swallow air. "It's not something I can explain. But I know for sure that life wasn't as easy for me as he thinks it was when we were separated."

"Oh, do tell." The low voice rumbled from behind them. They spun around to the corner shadow where Hare sat, annoyed. The needle remained buried in his chest, winking at them under the techlight. He nodded at the pointed end. "Do you mind?"

Damaetra stood. "Here, let me..."

She pinched the silvery projectile. It was smooth and too slippery, evading her fingers and any attempt to pull it. Pushing a hand against his chest, she finally managed to slide it out as Hare grunted.

Hollow, with no tooled markings, she could almost see her reflection in it. Fascinating! "Did you say Dill made these?" she asked.

Nico nodded and was about to speak when Hare interrupted with an exasperated sigh. "Who *cares* about those? Just stop sticking me with them."

"We'll stop sticking you with them when you stop acting like a dick," Nico said.

"Watch your filthy-ass mouth around the lady." Hare turned up a lip and grinned under the shadow of his broken nose.

"Please," Damaetra said with a hard swallow. The last thing on her task list was to get in between estranged twin brothers. That was a fantasy for someone else.

Thankfully, Nico ended the last-word war, letting Hare grin stupidly in victory. Instead, Hare chuffed and looked around the room with the occasional sardonic murmur. The words and phrases he used hardly clocked above a whisper, but Damaetra wasn't deaf. *Spoiled bastard* was one such utterance. Maybe he was right. Or maybe they were all spoiled bastards. At least to him.

Hare was still child-like in a way... having been ousted to fend for himself at such a young age, he still acted like a stunted young brat. He had to care about something, didn't he? After all, he saved her from Crow—that beast of an Engineer more tech than human. Hare at least had the mental strength to combat a man three times his size as he tried to tear off her dress. Thank the Maker for that.

Hare stopped mumbling. "Hey, where's that Yonch Formulator at? I know he's here."

Damaetra gasped at the slur. And out came the stunted brat again.

"Do you want another broken nose?" Nico squeezed his fingers inward, and even the tiniest muscles flexed in his forearm.

The bathroom door slid open, and Jack stepped into the room. "I'm right here." The insult had no effect on his stolid features. No wrinkle, no furrow, no frown. He only adjusted the cuffs of his new sleeves.

Wearing an ordinary dark royal shirt with a stubbed collar and decorative epaulets, Jack resembled an associate of Audun... except for the circular sun lines surrounding his yellow eyes. The shirt complemented his form and was tucked neatly into a pair of tan trousers.

This was not the look of the creepy man she knew during captivity. The Yeunish Formulator could almost pass as handsome when not sneaking around wearing that disturbing stained lab coat.

Hare wrinkled his nose. "Gehenna, I can smell your dump from here."

Jack ignored him, continuing to adjust his sleeves. "Good news," he said, "storm is ending early."

"It is? Says who?" Nico asked.

"Seven Cities Union news." Jack held up his e-disk. Bright blue letters hovered over the black disk with the confirming headline.

The report made Damaetra's heart flutter. The more she thought about it, the more she wanted to go back West—back home. The sooner she could get home, the better. Still knowing she was that close to Mount Gehenna had given rise to a cluster of worms in her belly, and all she could think about were those black teeth... that rotting breath.

"I want to go home," she blurted. Nico looked at her with pity. She didn't like that.

"Well," Jack said as he pocketed his e-disk, "you'll get that chance sooner than we thought. Personally, I'm going to leave as soon as the first grain of sand falls to the ground."

"Where are you going?" Nico asked.

"I have business elsewhere."

Hare pitched forward, baring his teeth. "What about my Witis?" he demanded.

Jack smirked, nodding at Nico. "You have your brother now. He knows how to make it."

Hare cursed under his breath. As a Weggevens, he knew he wouldn't get far without that shot.

"Alright then." Nico clapped his hands. "Since it's the weekend and we still can't leave yet, what should we do in the meantime?"

Hare wriggled in his seat. "Oh, pick me! I have an idea!... You can let me go."

"Shut up."

Damaetra's stomach gurgled. The taste of stale metal agitated the back of her tongue, only increasing her hunger. "I could eat," she said.

"You know, yeah we could go eat. Surely Krik'tha has already checked Dill in. I can message him if you want to message Lor?" Nico had already pulled out his e-disk, drawing patterns over the surface.

Damaetra hesitated. "I, well... Can we meet them in thirty standard? I'm going to see what Krik'tha gave me," she said, tapping a finger on the clothing box.

CHAPTER 5

Ration Blocks and Revelations
Loren

The dining hall smelled stale. Too busy to work the art of food, no one cooked here. These rows of "food" consisted of opulent trays stacked with monochrome squares of rations. Vegemeal, protein blocks, and oatcress were made to look appealing by their display. Garnished with colorful strands of ivy and twinkling tech, Guild Central worked hard to make the bland standard issue slop from Audun look appetizing.

No one ever clamored to get their hands on the compressed chow bricks, especially Lor. Vegemeal reminded him of Luci. The protein blocks were gritty, and oatcress tasted like a stale belch. At this point, he only prayed there was at least a table for meat crackers and toast. He was hungry and would have to suffer the sustenance.

This was only his second time at the joint hall, and it was more crowded than the last time he was here. Gale stood next to him, sending messages from his e-disk to people at work, despite having taken time off for the entirety of the storm. The busy medic was hardly ever hungry, using food only as fuel and not a source of enjoyment. If Lor could channel that same energy, it might make him happier.

Ever since that night he had steamed red buns made by Val, he didn't want rations. His body craved something real and unprocessed. This was all he was allowed, and he readied himself to pretend.

Sharply dressed members of Guild Central roamed from table to table, socializing with each other in a formal slant. It made Lor feel like a kid in his dad's clothes. What did he know about anything? Krik'tha chose a pleasant set of clothes for him to blend in, but he didn't like the idea of wearing the blue and gold of Audun. The shirt was a tasteful deep blue, with a pressed collar and muted gold buttons. The fabric felt expensive but nice against his skin. At least on the outside, he appeared to belong. He would start to feel more comfortable when his friends showed up.

As he surveyed the hall, there were clear differences in each profession. Formulators clustered together in no distinguishable arrangement, favoring darker colors to wear, probably to hide the stains of their craft. Engineers were more orderly, walked stiffer, and favored greens and oranges. If he were to take an overhead view of their table, it would look like a tech chip ready to install. Shepherds stood out the most with their eccentric clothes and hair, talking in rhythmic patterns. Readers roamed around separately, choosing light and airy colors. Their movements were delicate and flowing... they moved in a way that Lor found eerie. There had to be a way to shield his mind from them. They were probably already listening to him.

None of the Reapers were in the hall, and Lor was thankful for that. In one corner, Lor saw a cluster of people he assumed were Weggevens, since one appeared to be a skin changer that had found a way to cross-morph like Fowler. Instead of a bird, this one was a woman blended with some sort of grazing creature. A set of small horns sprouted from her forehead. It was hard not to stare.

The woman looked up at him, and he turned away as fast as his reflexes allowed.

Why must you be such a weirdo?

More people like Fowler had to exist in a partial transformation. This one happened to be only the second one he had seen.

"Hey, nice threads," Dill said, poking Lor in the back. Dill wore a light green long sleeve similar to his, but with brushed silver buttons. The colors went well with his dark skin, and he could have fit in well with the other green-clad Engineers. That is, except the fact that Dill wasn't as stiff as week old toast.

Lor was about to say something when Nico came in with Hare, Jack, and Damaetra. Maybe it was because he hadn't seen her in a few hours, but Damaetra was stunning.

She wore a loose shimmering ivory blouse with sheer sleeves over fitted brown slacks. She found a way to pin her hacked hair back, and it made her look as if she owned the place. Their eyes met, and she smiled.

"It's been a while since I've worn pants. I mean, not a dress," she said with a laugh.

Lor chuckled and took her hand. "You look great."

"Pink? Really?" Dill said as he pinched Nico's shirt.

"Hey, I *like* pink," Nico said, swatting Dill away. His buttons were flattened pearls.

"Well, at least it looks like we fit in somewhat," Dill said, looking around.

"Except for your mod." Nico flicked Dill's visor, which made a dull plastic *thunk*.

"Hey, stop that! Why did you have to cover up your beautiful legs with long *pants?*"

Nico laughed and pushed Hare toward a table. Lor had forgotten about the twin for a moment, as he was quiet for once. Hare wore the same scowl but ignored everyone. Krik'tha got him matching clothes to Nico, which neither of them was happy about, and no one dared tease them about it.

After collecting their rations, Damaetra devoured a protein block before Lor took a bite. A diet of cave fungus had surely left her wanting, even for rations.

Nico pulled his lips back and took a toothful of vegemeal, wrinkling his nose. "I never could get used to these."

Hare glared at him, shoving an entire brick in his mouth, chewing frantically to create a thin green foam at the corners of his lips.

"Gross, dude," Dill said. "Hey, that reminds me, there was a new material delivered to Engineers that I might be able to use for our little... problem." He nodded at Hare.

"Can you get it done fast?" Lor asked. He wasn't usually in the habit of discussing a person in front of them, but for Hare, he didn't care what he thought anymore.

Dill clucked. "I've already started. I can get it done as soon as I add the new lock."

"So you *made* something in the few hours between leaving my room and coming here?"

"Can't stop greatness." Dill grinned and popped a hunk of oatcress into his mouth.

"Wow, I'm impressed. Has mechanics become your new girlfriend?" Lor nudged him.

Dill hummed. "As if. It's a worthy distraction, though."

"I hate to cut in," Gale said, clearing his throat. With as quiet as he had been, Lor almost forgot about Gale. He peered at the group over his glasses in that familiar look that used Lor knew meant a lecture was incoming. "We still need to figure out what happened in that cave. I've been trying to search database information but have found absolutely nothing through the network."

Everyone fixed their eyes on Jack, who sat silently picking at a ration block. Once he noticed their anticipatory stares, he raised his eyebrows. "What?"

"Well, *he* has been no help to us"—Gale motioned at Hare—"but you both used to..."

Gale paused. Lor had never known his stepfather to spare anyone of embarrassment or insult, if that was his intent stopping midway through his sentence.

"You knew Par," Lor said. "You knew her well. Now's the time to tell us what you know."

Jack huffed, cracking a sarcastic grin. "Hate to break it to you, but I don't know much either."

"Don't lie. You know more than we do."

Lor stared at his reflection in Jack's thick black goggles, knowing those yellow eyes stared back.

Jack shook his head. "I knew Maron was there."

Dill pounded a fist against the table, inviting glances from others nearby. "What in Gehenna, man! Are you talkin' *the* Maron Valoa'brenga?"

It was funny how he emphasized *the* as if Maron was a famous entertainer. Most citizens regarded him as a fable—only one that Dill still believed in. The mere mention of his name drew an image of Maron's face merging with the cave wall, dripping in gold as he was held in agony.

Jack hushed him. "Calm down, kid."

"Was that his grave? What did he look like? Was he really big? Or tall? Was he sexy? Did he have wings?"

Jack raised an eyebrow and laughed. "*Wings?*"

"He was alive down there," Damaetra interrupted. "Holding the breach closed... tortured."

Dill pounded the table again. "What? When were you going to tell us?"

She shrugged. "We never had the chance until now."

"Maron was the 'seal' I had to break for her." Lor pressed his lips into a line and furrowed his brow, pushing the man's pain from his mind. "He's actually still down there with her. Alive."

"I'm sorry... *what?*" Dill had stiffened, leaning forward with neck stretched so far that branches of tendons strained to hold his head in place. "We have to go back!"

"Not a chance," Damaetra said, squeezing Lor's leg under the table. For her, it would revisit a bad memory.

"What *is* he? Undead or someth—?" Nico paused, studying Lor. He cleared his throat, reforming his question. "How long do you think he was down there?"

"Something like a thousand standard. Or more," Jack answered.

Dill gasped and chuckled, leaning back and shaking his head.

The idea of it seemed fake. What could any of it mean? Who was Maron Valoa'brenga? Better still, who was Paerli Harea? Was there anyone on Roseaarde that could answer any of these questions?

"How can we possibly figure out what's going on when the tomes tell us nothing?" Lor picked at a protein block. His stomach rumbled, but he couldn't eat.

Nico perked up, raising his brow and parting his mouth with a finger in the air. He looked a little silly, but it was an expression Lor knew well when his friend had an idea. "I think I might have a thought," he said.

"That's a first," Hare grumbled.

"Remember Guide Horace at the program?"

Dill smirked. "Well yeah, who'd forget that guy?"

"I didn't tell you all this before because it wasn't my secret to tell. But..." Nico glanced around for any unwanted listeners. "...I overheard him talking to that Foscan—"

"Val," Lor interrupted.

"Yeah, that guy. I overheard him talking about his *condition*. One that requires a certain special *treatment*. If you know what I mean."

Everyone looked at Jack, who shrugged. "Yeah, so?"

It made sense, and Lor felt stupid for not making the connection. That day after their classmate's funeral, Horace was there at the small diner with Jack, receiving a wrapped package. A package certainly full of the silvery green syringes.

"So, what... is he a strongman or something? A runner? No way is he a skin changer," Dill spoke between more fevered bites of oatcress.

"No, he's something I've never heard of." Nico scanned the dining hall again. Ducking low and putting a hand to the side of his mouth away from Hare, he whispered, "He's a *two-mind*."

"What?" Dill barked out the word and drew the attention of the nearby table.

Nico hushed him. "A two-mind," he hissed. "I don't know what it means."

Jack tittered and clicked his tongue. "Is this entire group completely ignorant?"

Yes. Lor knew that much.

Dill pursed his lips. "Hey, we're still new at this. Would you give us a break, old man?" he said.

Gale looked up from his e-disk, having been absorbed again by work issues and miscellaneous news. Hearing the word "ignorant" must have triggered the side of him that was only too pleased to bestow knowledge. He lowered his head, returning to his network research.

"It's a Weggevens plagued by the dead," Gale said, not bothering to look back up from his e-disk. His fingers swiped mercilessly through holopage after holopage of articles, as if being stuck in Guild Central was depriving him of a life-giving connection to Audun.

"Plagued by the dead?" Lor rubbed his chin.

Jack folded his slender fingers and sat upright, exuding the familiar eerie posture and mannerisms of the one Paerli knew as "Cricket," only with a nice shirt and combed hair. "He has a spirit attached to him. It's the worst kind of Weggevens anyone could possibly be."

"Alright, so what does it mean?"

Lor envisioned Jack rolling his eyes under the goggles. "Children. All of you. It means he can't turn it off, and it's constantly draining him. Two-minds usually die not long after they're infected. In fact, Horace is the only one alive that I'm aware of. It's a terrible curse, with the only positive being the gift of information."

"Information! We can use that," Dill said.

"You can *all* use it." Jack shook his head.

Hare sniggered.

"We get it, we're ignorant. Just tell us plainly, please?" Nico wore his frustration well.

Jack leaned back again, relaxing in his chair and running a finger over the edge of a vegemeal brick. The corner crumbled, leaving a green stain on the pad of his finger. "A two-mind doesn't happen the same way as any other ability. It happens randomly to anyone at any time. Horace was already a practicing guide when his spirit latched on. Luckily, I had business in Secas when I found him near dead in the market alley."

He cracked his neck, then his knuckles. Lor didn't think this was a tale to get limber for, but Jack was Jack. "The signs of Weggevens death by draining are subtle but unique. It starts with dry skin at the hairline... it pulls and wrinkles as if the face is trying to detach. Then dark sunken circles surround the eyes before the lips curdle and crack..."

Jack detailed each facet of death with a disturbing amount of interest. Damaetra wrapped her arms around herself, sinking her shoulders low as if to hide. The marks on her wrist cast shadows in the depressions where Par tried to steal her silver in the cavern. It was a permanent mark, never to fade, never to heal. A wave of rage pulsed at Lor's temples.

"...Ultimately, the person turns into dried fruit skins in the sun. There is a point of no return where even my... *treatment* will fail. Horace was almost at that point."

"And what point is that?" Nico asked.

"The hint is in the eyes. They begin to cloud over, blinding the poor bastard before death." Jack pulled off a piece of the vegemeal and sucked it into his mouth.

It made some sense; Horace wore that signature pair of glasses. Were they necessary after what he'd been through? Lor put an arm around Damaetra, who remained stiff and folded.

"So what's the deal with the spirit then?" Dill asked.

"Well, depending on the nature of the spirit, it sometimes takes over... like a skin suit. But Horace has a good one that doesn't do that. It just spies for him—he always knows what's going on during the program."

Lor chuckled to himself. Right after becoming a Reaper, Horace told him he knew what he'd been up to with Damaetra the whole time. It all made sense now—he had a little help from a friendly ghost.

"Is that *all?*" Nico asked.

Jack tilted his head upward, as if he meant to find the answers in the ceiling techlights. "No. That's not all. At least, not for Horace."

"Alright, *and?*" Nico's patience waned as he beckoned with his hand for Jack to spit out the details.

"Think about it for a standard second... It's a *spirit.*" Jack stared at everyone, waiting for a spark of some form of critical thought. When it didn't come, he sighed. "Spirits have the secrets of the dead."

Dill sucked in a breath.

Secrets of the dead. History. Everything Lor ever could learn about the world and then some.

"It's best to keep this secret to yourselves." Jack pointed at everyone for each word.

"Um, hel-lo..." Dill jabbed a thumb at Hare. "The whole reason we still *keep* this jerk is because of a secret."

Hare narrowed his eyes at Dill. He opened his mouth to say something smart when Jack laughed.

"He has no reason to blab about a two-mind—no one would believe him. One might be hard-pressed to believe even one of *you,* but it's better to keep quiet about such matters."

"But that means Horace would know more about the breach, right? Because of this spirit?" Lor asked.

"Possibly. You'd have to ask him."

Lor sighed. As a resident of Heart Island, it would be expensive to ask Horace. No e-disks, and handfuls of plats to get a ticket for the ferry, whether it be for the program or the resort.

Pulling out his e-disk, Lor flipped to his bank account, seeing payment for two days of work at 5,799 plat. A trip to the resort was over 7,000. There was no way he was going to ask Gale for more of his money just on an off chance Horace would even talk to him or know anything about the breach. Or his immortality.

"Wish we would've known while we were there." Dill sighed and stood up. "I'm going to finish those anklets for our new friend. I'll message you when they're done." He chomped into his protein block, then tossed the rest on his plate. "See you later," he said, spewing a few crumbs.

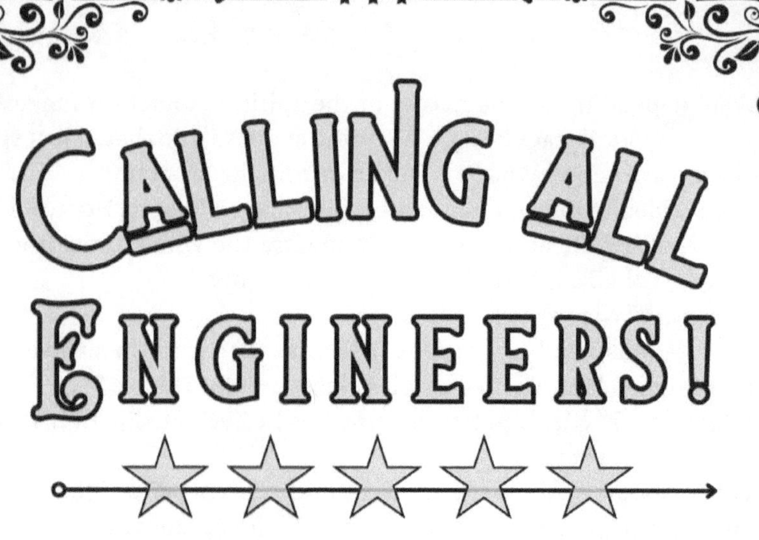

Have you tried **ID lock** yet? If you haven't, you're missing out on a fantastic opportunity to take advantage of a valuable engineering concept that just went off-license!

Get your hands on a material kit today! It contains everything you need to craft ID lock for your very own project.

Available at your local branch at a deep discount this week only!

CHAPTER 6

The Past is Dead
NICO

THE TEXT CAME AFTER A standard hour in Nico's room. Eager to replace the weakened ivy cords, Nico rushed downstairs with Hare to meet Dill.

"There, that ought to do it," Dill said while clasping the new shackles to Hare's ankles and threading a second set through the armrest to bind his wrists. The ankle cuffs were discreet enough to be covered by his pants, but Dill threw a small blanket over Hare's wrists. He leaned into Nico and whispered, "These will only unlock with your fingerprint... The one with the scar."

Hearing that, Nico subconsciously rubbed his thumb and forefinger together, feeling the deep ridge cutting through the pad of his thumb. It was an old grade school injury that was blamed on his rambunctious brother, even though it was definitely Nico's fault.

Hare bent over to peer at his ankles, toes turned inward, and frowned. "You know you can't keep me prisoner in your little luxury apartment," he said.

"I can and I will. For now anyway." Nico waved goodbye to Dill and pushed his brother through the Formulator atrium.

"What if I have to take a *dump*?" Hare's voice echoed through the hollow hall as he looked around at the other Formulators walking around. An older woman let out a small cry, and Nico heard her mumble to herself.

"Shut up, Niki," Nico hissed as he looked over at the gawking spectators. Showing off his best charming, dimpled smile, Nico nodded at his peers, waving and walking at a furious pace toward the elevators.

"Don't call me that," Hare said. He grunted and rocked back and forth in the chair, causing Nico to weave to prevent the chair from toppling.

"Stop it!" He smacked the back of Hare's head. "What are you, a toddler?"

Once in the elevator, another young man around their age was inside. Dressed in a pressed suit, he was stiff and poised with the posture of maturity. He wore a pleasant, minted musk fragrance and nodded politely at the brothers as they boarded.

Hare shifted his leg to the side and let loose the most thunderous fart. The man's expression curdled.

Hare tilted his head toward the man. "Hey... did you just *fart?*"

The elevator stopped, and the door began to glide open. The well-dressed man squeezed himself through the crack and hurried down the hall, leaving the faint trail of warm spiced fragrance in his wake.

"Sorry!" Nico shouted as the door slid shut. His face had become a bloody shade of crimson. "Honestly, Niki?"

"What? I can't help it if you feed me vegemeal bricks. They give me gas. And stop calling me that."

"You *chose* to shove the damn thing in your mouth."

The elevator stopped at their floor. As Nico wheeled Hare out, he gave the chair a jerk, whipping his head. Everything had to be difficult. Any compassion he had for his brother was fading fast.

"You know, if you don't stop acting like this, there's only one solution to this problem."

"And what's dat, bwover?" Hare stuck out his lower lip in a pout.

"Your death," Nico hissed between his teeth.

Hare giggled. "You don't have the sack to kill me."

"You're right, I wouldn't kill you. I'd let Jack do it."

"Right, ole Jack the Yeunish weenie?"

"Keep pushing it."

Hare sniggered and belted out in song, "He's a weeeeenie, a little weeeeeiner!"

Nico jerked the chair again just before another Formulator passed them in the hall. It was a young woman with a timid smile and a light flush in her cheeks as she hurried by.

They rounded the corner of the hall to the room. Once inside, the cool blast felt nice on Nico's hot, embarrassed skin. He pushed Hare to the table, making sure there was nothing he could grab or use.

"So where's the girl?" Hare asked, scanning the apartment.

"Her name is Damaetra, and she's trying to stay on her own tonight."

"She should be *here*."

Nico raised his eyebrow. "Tough. She's not staying with us tonight."

"Call your boyfriend and tell him to make her come here."

"No one can make her do anything, not me, or even *her* boyfriend. Why are you so worried about her, anyway?"

Hare clicked his tongue. "What can I say? She's hot."

"She's *taken*." Nico walked to the kitchen and flipped on the light to see Jack leaning against the counter.

Nico jumped back. "Maker, you scared the crap out of me! What are you doing in the dark?"

Jack grinned, rolling his neck around in a casual stretch, releasing a few pops in his spine. "Just waiting."

"That's not *creepy*," Hare spat.

"I made more of these while you were downstairs." Jack pressed a handful of syringes on the counter. "Try not to waste them."

Remnants of his work lay strewn across the counter, as small gray wisps rose from the hot crucible.

"I'll leave you two alone for a while," Jack said as he went to the front door.

"Where will you go?"

Jack shrugged and left.

Hare struggled in the chair, grunting and whining. "Just let me go, Nico. You don't even know me, and I don't care enough about your Yonch dork friend to snitch on him."

Even though he wanted to punch him again, it was the first thing Hare said that Nico somewhat trusted to be the truth. After years in the desert, his brother didn't seem to care about much, let alone Lor's heritage.

Nico opened a water can from the cabinet and plunked a straw into it, skidding it across the table for Hare.

"I spent my *life* thinking about you."

Hare rasped out a hoarse laugh that made him sputter and gag. "Aw, how sweet," he said with a tight throat, "but alas, Mom and Dad chucked me into the desert where I made new friends and gained *new* brothers."

He wasn't wrong, and Nico hated that. A hollow emptiness stung his insides. Ever since he learned that his brother was alive, Nico still hadn't reached out to his parents. It hurt—the whole thing hurt. Not only did they abandon one son, but they lied to the other. For what?

"Why are you so hateful toward me?"

"Why didn't you try to find me if you thought I was alive?"

"I was only thirteen!"

"Me too, *brother*. Me. Too." Hare tittered and looked away.

The only thing he could think to do was pull out a chair in front of Niki-Hare and sit there. Selfish—he'd been selfish. Poor Nico, missing his brother... not thinking about his actual brother.

Niki was so different. Bronzed skin with deep lines that sprayed from the corners of his eyes. Squinting during runs, goggles pressed against his skin, or just smiling with friends while baking in the hot sun could do that sort of thing.

As Nico sat there in silence, studying each pore in this new stranger, twin light blue eyes studied him in return. If it weren't for the wind-blown, slightly long hair that was unevenly cut and had gone ashy in the sun, Nico would have thought he was looking into a mirror of time. Oh, poor Nico, going to school, learning things, making friends, sleeping in a bed… That butchered hair was probably cut by some homeless barber that he no doubt called his true brother.

"I'm sorry," Nico said. "I should have fought for you."

His twin said nothing and continued to watch him, as if he still hadn't said enough. A subtle twitch lifted his lip, and for a moment it looked as though he wanted to say something but decided against it.

"Look, we both lost something that day. Don't you think I've paid enough with my legs?" Nico slapped the side of his knee and felt nothing. It was the part of getting them back he still couldn't get used to. They *looked* real, and if you cut them, the flesh opened and healed, but they were dead and cold. "I should hate you."

Hare tilted his head, studying Nico like a lost counterpart, or some historical relic. "Hate me, I don't care. You're only afraid of what I know."

"That's not true."

The accusatory glare… it searched into Nico's soul.

"It's only *half*-true," he corrected.

"And the other half?"

"Just wants his brother back." Half of him wanted his brother back. If only Hare hadn't literally sliced off his legs.

"Then take off these stupid shackles."

"You know I can't do that."

Hare rolled his eyes, bumping bound wrists against the armrests.

"Sorry, you hurt me pretty bad. You hurt Dill pretty bad—"

"And now you're fine."

"Maker, are you so cold that you can't even understand what you did?"

Hare pursed his lips. The length at which he could stare at Nico without blinking was unnerving. Instead of laughter, the lines around his eyes could have been crafted by years of resentment.

"Want to know what I think?" Nico asked.

"No."

"I think you're the same Niki, just angry and bitter. Do you remember that time when we were young, and there was that one stupid girl…" Nico snapped his fingers, forcing the memory. "What's her name?"

Hare snorted. "What stupid girl?"

"You know, the one you had such a crush on in first levels?"

"Tilly. Fat trunk on that one."

"Uh, yeah... Tilly. *Anyway*... remember how you spent a whole night rehearsing how you'd ask her out?"

"You're not helping."

"She was so cruel... Laughing and calling you an insufferable spaz."

"Nico, what is your stupid *point*?"

"Insulting you to your face was one thing—she had to spread rumors that you had a tiny crooked thingy."

"*Thingy*? Gehenna, you're such a baby. Yeah, I remember. So what? She was a slut anyway, trading favors in the bathroom for a street draught that was popular back then."

"Noxeine?"

"Whatever. We called it Klik. She traded tit for Klik."

"Did she actually? Or did someone start that rumor?" Nico spread his face into a wry grin as bait. Hare took it gladly.

"Ha, let me guess... *you* started that rumor."

It was a start. Trying to reach that inner Niki, the relatable brother Nico knew long ago... it was difficult.

"She hurt you, and I wasn't going to let her live it down."

Hare smirked, letting a small smile tug at the corner of his mouth. When he realized that, he leaned down to smother the look by taking his first awkward straw sip from the water can in front of him.

"I've always looked out for you. If you weren't acting like such a jerk now, I'd *still* want to look after you. We could be like our own private team," Nico said with a smile. Inside, he knew he'd always have to keep one eye open for his two-man "team."

It worked. Hare sat up and smiled back—the same dimpled smile that reflected his own. Had he finally gotten through to him? Were things finally going to change?

After a long moment of smiling, the silence got a little weird. Hare tilted his head to the side with the same awkward grin. "I have to take a dump."

Nico slammed his water can on the table. "Damn it, Niki!"

Wheeling his brother into the bathroom, Nico loosed the ankle guards to a length that was sufficient, then let the chair roll on its own, nearly spinning it completely around. Hare's wrists were extended as far as they could be from the armrest while he smirked in the dark.

"Good luck," Nico barked while sliding the door shut as hard as he could, "and if you make a mess in there, *Maker help you!*"

A subtle rap came at the door. Nico peered through the visitor's glass to see the top of a shimmering white-gold head. Once he opened the door, Damaetra's small frame stood there with her head down, eyes locked on her hands.

"I couldn't do it," she said.

Nico widened the door for her to come in. Face red and wet, she had a long tail of her own hair wrapped around her fist. He remembered seeing it coiled on the floor when going in there to get her things. He should have gotten rid of it for her.

Damaetra took in a long breath, taking the first steps back into his apartment. "It was on the floor of my room. I didn't think it would actually still be there." She held her hand out, holding the hair. "I guess since Krik'tha told them we were sick, no one came to clean the room."

"I'm sorry, I should have cleaned—"

"It's not your fault." She shook her head. "It's *hers*."

CHAPTER 7

The Snake
DAMAETRA

THAT NIGHT, DAMAETRA LET HER head sink into the pillow, looking straight up at the ceiling. The sides fluffed up around her ears, muffling the hum of the quiet room.

Against a wall at her feet, Hare relaxed in the wheelchair, having succumbed to a full, consensual dose of Lapis Evening. Jack sat in the corner armchair in silence. It wouldn't be a stretch to wonder whether he slept at all. Nico flipped off the light, and the apartment was nothing but blackness until her eyes adjusted to the tiny film of receding light at the high pencil-thin windows.

Guild Central was uncomfortable, she decided. The rules were weird, and she couldn't be near Loren, where she belonged. An image of the spreading red web over Loren's shirt after he was shot interrupted her thoughts. The overwhelming feeling of despair was an unwelcome guest in her head.

Turning to the side, she saw Nico on the couch. Too tall for the short two-seater, he had removed his prosthetics and had them jacked into the outlet overnight. Thank the Maker his lower half was covered by a fat blanket. All the horrid memories fought for her brain space. The bounce of Nico's flesh in the sand... the spray of Dill's face sinking into the grains... all of it haunted her. And all of it came at the hands of the man at the foot of her bed.

She had told Loren that Hare could be redeemed. Since telling him, she still hadn't changed her mind, but it would take work. She stared at the door, waiting for the scraping sounds to start. The noises didn't come. This was a safe place. A safe place with three grown men. Granted, one was thin enough to snap in two, and the other was bound to a chair, but three grown men.

She closed her eyes, asking the Maker for peace and some way to connect to Loren during their times apart.

She had just laid down for the evening, staring at the unread message she sent to Loren an hour ago with a frown. Her heart and her mind were at war—he could have been losing interest in her after learning about her lousy final marks in the program. Worse still, he shared a hall with Paerli, one of the smartest, most beautiful women she'd ever known. They were close... too close. And Par was all about Loren.

As her lids became heavy and the fading light patterns on the ceiling blurred, a faint scraping noise scratched at her door lock.

"Hello?" she whispered.

The scraping became a flurry of hooking, grinding, and turning until the lock popped and her door swung open, bumping into the opposite wall. A nightmare, this was a nightmare, she told herself over and over as she covered up with a flimsy sheer blanket and peered over the edge of it. The doorway was black with a hulking form, and she swore it was the darkness coming to claim her.

Her throat peeled apart in a dry swallow.

"Oi ma'am, she's 'ere," the darkness rumbled like distant thunder in a thick dialect she recognized from the far North.

A nightmare. This was a nightmare.

A second blackness slid inside—slender, graceful, and familiar. Like a dancer. Like Paerli. What little light remained in the room cast mottled shadows on the slender face, now nearly at her bed.

Wake up, wake up, wake up from this cursed nightmare! With a shaking finger, she pressed the sensor on the bedside tech lamp. Her intuition about the slender stranger had, unfortunately, been true.

"How did you get in here?" she croaked.

"Shh," Paerli hushed, looking behind her shoulder.

It was her, but not really. Not when she sauntered up to Damaetra's bed and yanked the cover away. Pale legs were exposed under the tech lamp, stretching out from under a long sleeveless shirt just a little too short to cover her underwear. The blackness in the doorway took great interest.

Paerli clicked her tongue. "This won't do."

Throwing the cover back, Par rifled through the cabinet. Not just a nightmare, a privacy violation as well.

"Here," Par said as she tossed Damaetra's lavender dress at her. It was the one she wore when she first started dating Loren. How quickly could a good memory go bad.

"Put it on," Par ordered.

This nightmare had teeth. As she pressed the dress close to her chest, she tried to remember the technique her sister, Cae, taught her that would let her control her dreams.

I am in a dream,

I am in a dream,

This is only a dream...

Par stomped toward her, letting the light hit her black eyes and cut creases into a worm-like face. "Put on the damn dress! I'm not going to ask you twice."

The survival reflex acted fast, sliding the dress over her head. Obey the worm and you will survive.

The carefully cultivated friendship she made with the worm flashed before her, reminding her of the things she told it that even Loren didn't know. Things about her real father. Things about her. In her memory, the worm became the snake, wrapping its coils around Loren, flicking his ear with its vile tongue. If only she could have saved him then. If only she hadn't been so blinded by the excitement of a new relationship that she didn't see the reptilian grip squeezing his neck.

"Come," called the snake.

The dress fluttered down Damaetra's legs when she stood. The dark companion to the snake licked its lip and moaned.

Maker save me.

The snake nipped Damaetra's heels, if only to make her scuttle faster to the door and toward the moaning shadow waiting for her. As her bare, sweaty feet protested against the marble, the breath of the betrayer blew hot in her ear, and she felt the forked tongue at her lobe.

"I'm going to mate with your man. And there's nothing you can do to stop me."

Damaetra tried to turn her head to cover Par with curses, but nothing was there. It had latched on to her hair, tugging her neck back as she strained to keep watch on the moaning shadow, now reaching out to her and rubbing itself.

The long white-gold waves of her hair disappeared inch by inch down Par's gullet as she unhinged her jaw and feasted on the strands. Every bite schup, schup, schupped *away as Damaetra opened her mouth to scream out nothing.*

She didn't mean to wake everyone. How loud was it? Nico sat on the edge of the bed by her legs as Jack sat upright in the corner chair. Even the effects of Lapis Evening were no match for her terror, rousing Hare from a drugged stupor.

How embarrassing. The weight of the dream filled her head with stones as she sighed and plopped her head back into the pillow. "Sorry. I had a nightmare."

"Do you need anything?" Nico asked.

Damaetra pursed her lips, shamed to act like a fool in front of an audience. She glanced at the closed door. No crude shadow. No cruel Reaper.

After her father died, she had slept in her mother's room for years. Many nights were interrupted by screams, and her mother, always the saint, provided her the comfort drink she always needed without fail. "Can I please have some water?"

Nico jumped up and went to the kitchen. There was nothing innately special about the clear, tepid liquid, but there was something about it that filled her veins with calm. It was no different at that moment when she took a demure sip, letting the ghast of her nightmare fade away.

"You're safe here," he said.

Damaetra took another swallow of the water, feeling its cool touch running through her veins to rinse out her bad blood. The two former members of Team Snake watched her from their positions. She couldn't tell if they were indifferent to her or pitied her. She wanted neither. "Am I?"

CHAPTER 8

It's a Dirty Job
LOREN

THE START OF A NEW week came fast, and Lor wasn't ready to reap just yet. If he wanted to make plat for his trip to Horace, it wasn't negotiable. A sour taste lingered on his tongue as he sat on the edge of his bed, feeling like he'd been crushed under a jumper sphere. Gale lay curled on the couch; it was still too early to get up.

Each night brought with it a new dream for Lor, and each new dream was a test of his reality. Last night's vision was hard to interpret. It had something to do with shadows and snakes. He hated snakes.

Time to get back into the habit. It took him pains to rise from the bed, but he succeeded. Minor triumphs. Nothing like going into a new workday, not having a single clue what the assignment would be. What sort of trash collection would it be on his first day back? Perhaps more blue... surely with the storm, waves of sea creatures scrambled to execute themselves on the shore. He would be in the Maker's debt if it was nothing but green—the easiest pull, even if the little cacti did numb his arms.

After a quick "see you soon" to a groggy Gale, Lor hurried to the atrium to meet his Reaper crew. The same Anglia girl gave him her signature frosty glance while the others stood apathetic under the weight of increasing yaslecha. It was a bitter consequence of his profession. After witnessing the effects it had on an immortal like Par, Lor told himself he would rather die.

Janice was the foreman that day. Gruff and pointed as she was, Lor appreciated the fact that she usually left him alone. Scanning the group, he found Krik'tha sulking nearby. It was odd. It could have been all the secrets he kept for Lor and his friends, making an awkward conversation more so... or it could be nothing related to Lor at all. Foscans did indeed hold secrets of their own, if their superstitious tales and strange rituals were any proof of that.

The ride to their destination and Krik'tha's supporting silence led Lor to speculate on all the "what-ifs" in his mind. Their cruiser passed under the colorful tree tunnel that marked the path to Secas. Lor watched as the branches swayed with secondary maelstrom winds, dumping handfuls of leaves to the ground in their own version of colored flakes of snow.

Would they pull purple this time? Orange? Lor had never done either. The prospect had his interest, but when glancing back at Krik'tha, he lost his confidence that it was purple or orange. Krik'tha returned Lor's glance with his one white eye, smiling only with the smallest corner of his mouth. The eye seemed concerned. Then they arrived, and Lor figured out why.

The morgue. It was the damn morgue.

This was a test. The Maker was testing him. Pulling silver had to be the fastest route to yaslecha, but Lor decided he wouldn't fail. Silver was a lofty order for a person who felt out of practice.

"I can help, if you ask," Krik'tha whispered.

Lor declined the offer, resolving to grow up. This was his life now.

Three whole phials, full to the brim, no exceptions. Three phials of silver for a few thousand plat. That should be enough to travel to Heart Island resort. Then he and Damaetra could escape Guild Central and never look back. If she wanted to.

The first corpse reminded Lor of Dill. A stiff Danashi man lay on the cold slab—his dark skin paled by death with Formulator preservation draughts swimming in his veins. The preservation was part of the pungent smell hanging in the place, and it didn't take long for it to give him a headache.

One day it *would* be Dill on the slab. As long as Lor lived forever, it would be Gale... it would be Nico... it would be Damaetra. Par would live on for eternity to torment him... but would Maron allow that?

Transparent skin-tight film clung to the dead Dill look-alike, ready for burial. Did he have a family? Brothers and sisters?

"Is easier if you don't think about them," Krik'tha said, as if reading Lor's mind.

He was right. Lor relaxed his fingers around the man's throat. The familiar electricity hummed in his palm. As easy as reading a book.

Hazy shapes developed into a forested roadway until the focus rested on a crack slicing outward from a hole in a cruiser windshield.

It was hard to breathe. A long, slender, and dark object protruded from his lung. Each inhale felt like a cactus rolling inside his chest. The object sucked backwards out of him, traveling perfectly through the windshield hole, closing it up as it passed, and landed back into the hauler in front of him. The two vehicles rolled backwards to full speed when the hauler popped over a stone on the road, jiggling the object back into position.

There was an anxiety there—he was running late again, and the hauler was moving too slow. His cruiser followed the hauler closely, hoping it would get out of the way. His wife would count the minutes, and he had taken too long with his mistress.

Silver pools collected on the slanted morgue table, rolling down toward a drain in the center. Lor watched the silver disappear down the grooves as he orally recorded his observations into the assigned V-note. No investigation needed—the man was in a vehicle smash-up, taking the blunt end of a howie rod to the lung. The roundsmen didn't need to know the *reasons* this man met his misfortune. So he kept that part quiet, making a mental note to purge it from his head into his own notes later. Maybe manually on paper so he could burn it. As despicable as the reasons were, leave dignity with the dead and peace to the living.

Lor sighed. Even a skin changer was better than a Reaper. One could be kind and ugly at the same time. Why trade a soul to stay somewhat normal-looking? He was determined to discover why yaslecha happened. Something told him the pull and purge had something to do with it. After all, why would he feel remorse about yanking out a person's essence when he couldn't remember doing it in the first place?

The drain whooshed and sucked the last squirt of silver from the table, and there was enough in the collection bin for one phial.

"Two more." Krik'tha's voice startled Lor. Two more phials, then he could wash his hands of the place and look to the future. Krik'tha offered again to help, but Lor refused, moving to the next cold slab decorated with a stiff Anglia.

Just a kid…

"Don't think about it." Krik'tha's warning was repetitive, but he appreciated it. Lor wrapped his fingers around the chalky white neck.

Small grains of sand and a motley assortment of pebbles pressed against his back. Black fuzz blurred many faces hovering over him. They blubbered and sobbed at his demise. At once, they picked him up, moving back to the salty water, laying him face down in its depths.

He fought the waves with cramps in his arms and legs while pressure squeezed invisible walls against his torso. Brine came from within him, returning to the sea. And then he stood, waving at a cute girl on the beach.

More silver dribbled from the boy, dripping into the collection bin. Lor wanted to cry along with the faces. There was no room for that here... he must press on. He spoke the events into his V-note, forgetting all of it the instant it was captured.

"Last one," Krik'tha said, pointing at a woman lying on the next slab.

The woman was completely stripped, and Lor flushed. Of course his first time seeing a feminine form would be by a woman who couldn't consent.

She appeared to be Mesaman, with curled dark red hair that made spirals over the metal slab. Her plump pale lips turned up into the smallest grin, as if she had been having the most fantastic day just before the Maker came for her. Lor frowned.

Once again, Lor declined Krik'tha's help.

Colorful pottery lined open shelves in a warm home, yet he saw all of this from the floor. He stared at the ceiling with a slowing heart as a slender shadow slithered away.

A jolt brought him to standing, but he was looking at a puncture in his leg. Turning back to the stove, a pinch nipped his calf muscle. The hum of an old song buzzed in his throat as he baked a batch of sugar horns for a special someone's birthday while letting in the comforting breeze from an open door.

The silver glugged into the collection bin.

"Life is cruel," Lor said to the woman's sunken smile.

Taking to his V-note, he recorded the details of the woman's brush with a deadly snake. Then he remembered his dream. No time to think about that. The recording must be made. As the words exited his mouth, the memory spilled from his head, along with the dream that got tangled in with the mix.

The snake, the snake... it was a worm. No, the shadow? Gone. Damn.

He rotated a pinky in his ear, as if it would bring it all back.

As if sensing that Lor had finished, Janice approached and demanded his V-note. Once she tucked it into her bag, she smiled at him. "Well done, Loren. Expect to see a raise in your box tomorrow for the... *child.*"

That came as a surprise. Guild Central wasn't as heartless as Lor believed, after all. Not that plats could make up for extracting a kid, but at least they recognized the deeper tragedy of it. Depending on the raise, it could be his ticket to Heart Island.

It had to have been his destiny to go there. Well, if he believed in that sort of thing. Which he didn't.

When the cruiser dropped off the Reapers, Lor spotted Damaetra pouring from Formulator Hall with waves of others. Holding her shoulders back, she walked with a marked change in grace and loveliness. The choppy white strands she had pinned back aligned in such a way as if she meant it to be cut like that. Her eyes met his, and she smiled.

"We got out early today," she said as she closed the gap between them.

Lor didn't need to ask why when he saw two roundsmen leading a downcast man wearing a black button-up and colorful bow tie decorated in swirls. Their conversation swelled and faded when passing by—something about a snake bite and condolences on the birthday tragedy. A flash of crystals clinging to his fingers while crafting sugar horns came and went, teasing Lor with information that he once knew but forgot.

"Poor guy," he said as the roundsmen accompanied the bow-tied man away.

Damaetra watched them go. "That's Mackie. He's a super friendly and talented Formulator who's been helping me get caught up. Apparently, his wife died today and their daughter found her."

The snake, the snake... the worm?

"How did she die?"

"Snake bite. Came right into their house. He was in such a good mood too because it was his birthday."

Lor narrowed his eyes, searching his brain. It sounded familiar, like he'd heard that story already, but that wasn't possible... he had just gotten there. "She's with the Maker now," he said.

Damaetra hummed. "Yes, she is."

Still searching, he remembered the howie rod man. He was going to write his indiscretions manually, then burn the memory. "We cleaned up at the morgue today."

"What? How morbid!"

Lor nodded, looking beyond her shoulder and still trying to piece together the snake story. "Yeah, I'm starting to understand yaslecha more."

"Yas-what?"

One of the more peculiar aspects of his gift and he hadn't even told her about it. Perhaps he was afraid to tell her...it might scare her off to know there was a possibility he could stop feeling.

"I'll tell you later," he said.

NEW!

FOR A LIMITED TIME!

Take advantage of Secas' special offer to take an all-inclusive luxury vacation at the beautiful Heart Island resort!

GET YOUR TICKET FOR HALF PRICE!

~~pL 7200~~ pL 3600!

That's right, you can enjoy a whole week of blissful relaxation, and you don't have to go alone! Only A few spots remain, so get your tickets today!

Get a discount booklet to use at any of the resort's extra amenities and shops!

Looking to find rare jewelry? Need an extra set of clothes? Or, do you just want to relax at the Rosaarde-renowned spa and salon? There's a coupon for you!

***Restrictions apply. Heart Island Resort is not responsible for any loss or injury incurred as a result of attendance at the facility or use of the coupons.**

CHAPTER 9

Run Rabbit
HARE

NIGHT HAD SETTLED IN, AND Hare was ready. The hot girlfriend of that dirty reaping Yonch stayed at her own place, and it was bittersweet. While he liked to look at her, she was innocent. Looking was harmless. What Crow tried to do… well, if he hadn't been a good beast, he would have died that night. An ultrasonic chop to the nuts first… then before the blood stopped vibrating from his sack, he'd find his eyes had gone missing.

At least she wasn't there to distract him now.

Using all the dexterity he had in his feet, he crept toward Nico's bed, still attached to the wheelchair. The slick tile protested against his socks. If Nico thought he'd be more comfortable sleeping without shoes on, he only made it harder to "walk" across the floor. The sinewy tendons serving his feet flexed, caving in the surrounding skin. An aching fire smoldered there, and the long days spent sitting in the damn chair made his muscles weak. Big toe first, then the rest—repeat and repeat until within reach.

The cursed wrist bindings weaved through the arm rest bars, holding his pulse points against the puckered and fraying leather. *Stupid Nico, gotta have control. Can't even let me wipe my ass.*

Just a little more… Once he goes through with it, there was no going back. Nico would never forgive him, and that would be that. He stared at his twin. A pretty face, an educated mind—it was looking into a reflection on the other side of a more glorious life. Even in sleep, he was perfect. What he wouldn't give to trade.

Tilly would be even more obsessed with Nico if she saw him now. It wasn't the rumors about his *thingy* that had him depressed for days in his room. It wasn't her mocking laugh that had him retreating for hours to listen to the metal licks of Electric Dead's *Suffering* album on repeat. No… it was the fact that she wanted the better brother. They always did.

Screw you, Nico.

A chain link shifted and made a faint *tink* against the exposed metal on the chair's arm. He held his breath.

Nico heard nothing. Lying on his back, Nico had his head tilted forward. They faced each other. The print he needed was on Nico's left thumb—the one with the scar running through it. He remembered getting in trouble for that for some reason, but he didn't remember why. All he knew was he was getting blamed for something that was actually Nico's fault for once. Mom and Dad just assumed it was the *naughty* brother.

Lucky for Hare, Nico's left arm was free, draped around the back of his head, palm up like he was a model posing for an ad for Sleepwise™ Underwear. Eyes perfectly closed, mouth perfectly pouty.

Glancing around, Hare's eyes had gotten so used to the dark that it was like seeing during a stormy day. After a quick look at the bathroom door, he saw it was shut tighter than his father's crack. Jack the Yonch couldn't take another night in the armchair with those long waterbird legs of his, stretching out in the tub like a spoiled princeps. He'd better not get up and catch him. It would ruin everything.

Hare checked the bedside table again, and the shadow of a syringe bundle humped over the surface. Everything would have to be quick. His socked feet would have to be quick. His skin would suffer, but he had to. They'd have heals for him where he was going, as long as he made it.

Nico jerked his hand. Hare ducked down in reflex. As Nico moved his hand up and down his perfect face, he messed up his eyebrows while tinting his cheeks pink... And back to posing for underwear.

Pearls of sweat swelled on Hare's upper lip. If he got caught, they would have that Danashi dork make another set of shackles. They would make sure he was completely strapped to the chair with ten-finger and ten-toe ID locks dotting the entire thing.

There was just enough slack in the wrist bindings that he could reach the lock to that thumb poking out over the side of the bed. It could be a graze. That Engineer was so cocky in his ability, he made the ID lock too sensitive.

The square pad received the graze and released the lock. The delicate chains pooled on the blanket right in front of Nico's face. It was a syrupy sound, quiet enough to keep his brother sleeping in his fancy pose. Hare only heard his blood washing over his eardrums. A cold, thin stream of relief came from Hare's lips, which played around in Nico's curls. He held his breath again.

With free hands, Hare reached for the bundle of syringes on the night table, gluing his eyes on Nico. Inching along the surface, his fingers wormed around, trying to find the bundle without help from his already occupied eyes. The plunger end greeted them, and he curled his fingers inward to pull the cluster close enough to gather them into his palm and set them on his lap over his *thingy*.

Once the bundle was secure, he prepared himself for the tricky part. Gripping the armrests and leaning back, he was careful not to make the wheelchair material squeak underneath him. Rock-hard runner's abs squeezed together, pulling at every fiber attached to his ribs as he raised his bound ankles, pressed together, toward Nico's still exposed thumb. This would have to be quick. He shook in silence as the burning ache hugged his torso.

Just... a little... more!

The squeaky leather softly complained under Hare's increased shaking. A twist and slight bend of the knees angled the lock at just the right position to accept the sensitive graze.

The ID lock opened, dropping its payload to the floor in a splintering *clang*. Nico's eyes snapped open, meeting his. While Nico was still under the spell of first waking, Hare had to take his opportunity.

Shoeless, he bolted.

Nico ran after him in only his perfect underwear.

The Formulator Hall atrium passed in a blur. He'd have to smash the front door to get out. That lame, pointy trophy from the assistant's counter would do the trick. He swiped it and chucked it at the glass, which gladly swallowed his offering, opening up a portal to the fresh outside air. Thankfully, it didn't set off an alarm.

Nico wasn't far behind.

Bare skin slithered from the broken hole as he wriggled around to avoid getting pricked. *Why, isn't he just a fine young man, coming through a broken door in his sexy Sleepwise™?*

"Where are you planning to go?" Nico shouted from behind.

The wind wailed over Hare's ears as he picked up speed. It didn't take long to develop a limp when the burn of sock fabric screeched over his soles.

"Just let me go!" Hare shouted back. The wailing wind cut into his eyes, making them water as he blinked in a fit. The one thing he forgot to grab as he sprinted from the room were his goggles. There they sat, plain as he remembered, on Nico's stupid table.

The stench of foam-crusted dead fish coated his nostrils as they passed Guild Central's shore. It made him choke.

"I'm sorry we tied you up!" Nico shouted. Playing the sympathy card to get him to slow down would not work. Nico caught up as they ran side by side. The Weggevens curse was no match for his brother's teched-out legs. That spiteful swipe Hare took at Nico in the desert only made him better.

"Don't be sorry! I'm free now!" The last word caught in his mouth when a tiny insect flew inside. It tasted of long grass and metal, tickling his throat and reminding him why he didn't talk and run.

Ditching Nico would be tough. Now that they were evenly matched, he had to find his weakness. He zig-zagged through Guild Central and burst inland onto the sand, with Nico at his side like a real parasite.

The storm had calmed, but an electricity still hung in the air, stinking of ozone and stirring up miniature sand funnels. The fine dust made them both cough, frantically using splayed fingers to wave a clearer path in front of their eyes.

"Please, Niki!" Sand curtains arced beside them as they barreled through it.

Hare's feet lit up like a campfire as sand friction merged with sock friction. The bundle of syringes pressed into his palm as he gripped them tighter. What to do, what to do...

He caught the flicker of illumination pulsing around Nico as he ran. That light was the key. He knew it. As he squeezed the syringes, he knew about his own weakness, and the fix was in the palm of his hand.

But what's your *weakness, Brother?*

With a quick slide of a drug barrel from the bundle, Hare injected himself on the go. "Stop calling me Niki!"

If his thinking was good, it would work. Raising the needle high, he thrust it downward into the glowing light, piercing the flexible coolant tube of Nico's upper right thigh. The force broke the cylinder open, spurting a jet of green eneris from the split. Each step Nico took forced more eneris into the sand in thick pulses until he became nothing but a shadow behind veils of miniature maelstroms in the desert storm.

"I still love you!" Nico's distant plea faded as Hare finally rid himself of his brother.

And that was that. As he made trails in the desert, the relief of freedom he expected turned out to be a lie. He was alone again, like always. No one ran next to him, and no one was there to spread rumors about a spiteful chick to avenge him. All because of what? A grudge that should die.

He slowed to a jog to save his feet as he got closer to his destination. The row of lights flickered in the distance as agitated yellow dust scissored through the atmosphere, and he frowned.

Don't hate me.

Chapter 10

An Actual Vacation
Loren

Niki escaped.

The message from Nico hovered over Lor's e-disk as it came through. It was still night.

Lor groaned and rolled over, head pounding. Losing him was inevitable—he knew they wouldn't be able to contain that guy. The illuminated message cast a halo on his bed table, catching the edge of Par's pendant. It shimmered red stars within the black stone, and Lor moved to grab it.

The pillow sighed when he lay back down as his head sank deeper into the down. He turned the pendant around in his fingers, staring into the stone's starry depths. The golden chain was thin but strong, dangling like a gilded spiderweb. Maybe Hare ran back to *her*. Maybe she would somehow give him that power he talked about.

The pendant's red stars drew him in as he stared into another world full of blood planets. Clenching his fist around the stone, he broke the hypnotic travels through it and closed his eyes.

Buzzing like tiny gee flies, there was nothing but confetti static under his lids as his colors had stopped cooperating. Too much noise in his head.

What if Hare did run to turn him in? He said a quick prayer to the Maker for protection for himself and absolution for Hare. There had to be some good inside of him like Damaetra said... right?

The stone remained cool in his palm, and he thought of his dream. It was Par again... with Maron. Far from the oozing dry husk he remembered, Maron was whole again. What strange magic kept him alive forever?

He slid the e-disk from his bed table and swiped open a blank quicknote.

"The night of one-fifty-three, year twenty-five eighty-five," he spoke into the dictation program, then cleared his throat. "I dreamed of Paerli.

"She was angry, like always... but this time, she was with Maron Valoa'brenga, the ancient Igni protector. He wants to see me, but she protests, telling him the world hates his kind. I don't think she's wrong, but there aren't any Igni on Roseaarde other than him. Would Audun even know what he is? He wants to see me. This scares me a little.

"Nothing changed about the breach—it's still a gross hole in the wall. Neither Par nor Maron talk about it, but Maron called her 'wife' at one point. Do I *want* to know more about that?

"They ate the pretty glowing plants inside the cavern. Maron cursed at her for destroying a large area of it when she came after us. There's definitely something special about that place.

"What I'm really not sure about is whether the next part was real. I transported to the middle of the desert in one of those renegade death camps. A group of seven adults and two children camped around the fire, but half of them slept.

"It happened too quick, but it looked like they were born out of the shadow when the bandits came on them. Two of the sleeping adults found the unlucky end of one of those telescoping clubs with spikes on it. Then a fight broke out between the two groups. It was shocking to see, especially with children. But it didn't seem to matter because the boy, calmer than Dill during a crafting session, grabbed the guy with the club.

"If it were me, I would have really peed my pants! But not these kids. The guy being held by the boy turned into a stone pillar, standing there and letting the boy hold him. It was weird, though... his limbs started to go all white and fuzzy, as if he were turning to ic—"

Gale fake-coughed from the bathroom door, flicking on the techlight. Lor spun around on the bed to face him.

"Hare escaped," he said before Gale could push any words out. The look on his face dissolved.

"Hare *escaped?*" Gale repeated, as if to make the statement make sense.

"That's the message I got from Nico. Hare got away."

Gale cursed under his breath, rubbing his face pink the way he always did. "He's going to turn you in."

Lor took a deep breath and furrowed his brow. His headache grew, and he pinched the bridge of his nose to help counter the pain. "What can we do about it?"

Gale sighed and shrugged. "Nothing. Not anymore. But if you were still thinking of staying here, I would highly suggest against it."

"I wasn't. I want to go home to Peakwood. Maybe I can hide in Audun like you said."

"That would probably be the right thing to do. Who were you talking to?"

The e-disk sat warm in his palm, the dictation software open and hovering over the surface. "No one, just taking notes about my dream."

"Anything useful?"

Lor swiped away the program and tossed the e-disk onto the bed table, where it wobbled. "No. It's still a confusing mess of things."

"Shame. Well, I'm up now, so I'm going to get something to drink."

Gale helped himself to the kitchen. Wandering back and forth between cabinets, Lor noticed he wore a pricey pair of long-style underwear that came down to his thighs, decorated in light blue stripes. A crisp white shirt fit snug against his chest and back, complementing his features well. Krik'tha had a talent for dressing everyone, turning even the most plain man in his underwear into something extraordinary.

Gale faced Lor and held up a tea packet. Lor nodded his approval, then let his brain drift back to the dream. Between Hare's escape and the strange renegade camp, it was more important than ever to have that conversation with Horace.

"I should have enough plats to go to Heart Island and have a talk with Horace," Lor said.

Gale had his nose deep in his teacup. Gale swallowed the hot liquid hard. "That's great." His throat rasped from the burning tea. "I came across this advert last night." He held up his e-disk, displaying a pink and white image of a sale notification. "Tickets are half off. I was thinking of going with you. You know, to make my time off an actual vacation."

Lor smirked. "How much time off did you have to use to save me?"

"All of it."

"Everything?"

"Yep. Everything for the rest of the year."

Guilt slapped his already pounding head. If he had just listened to Nico about Par, he could have ditched her. They never would have had their fight in the desert, he wouldn't have almost died, and Gale would still be in Peakwood doing who knows what things he liked to do for fun. Count med supplies and read newslite, he guessed. It was a miracle any of them still stuck by his side. Nico had fake legs, Dill fake eyes, Jack was there for some reason, and Damaetra was mistreated, but they were still there. Another bit of noise to add to his confused colors. He closed his eyes again, and there were the gee flies, colored and swarming into nothing.

"I'm sorry," Lor said.

"Hm?"

"I've been stupid and selfish."

Gale hummed and tapped on the counter in a disjointed rhythm. "Maybe," he said, "but you sacrificed yourself for Damaetra and your friends.

That's not selfish."

It wasn't much of a sacrifice if he caused the problem that needed the offering. It was a nice thought, and he smiled. "Stupid, though," he said.

Gale laughed and shook his head. "You can't get smart without a little stupid, son. What you did was noble... even if you'll suffer for..."

"Eternity. I'm going to suffer for eternity."

Gale's smile faded. He put the tea to his lips again as if to hide his frown, not taking a sip.

A knock tapped at the door. He must have woken up right at the time between a fully black night and a misty dawn since a small stroke of light painted the ceiling from the high window.

Krik'tha had come by, bringing with him another set of clothes for both Lor and Gale. Seeing the sleek boxes tucked under his arm excited Lor to see what new duds he'd be getting. As Krik'tha stepped into the room, Lor's payment box caught his toe and skittered across the floor, spilling out a few of the radiant plat tickets.

"Oh, oh!" Kriktha dropped to the floor, scrabbling to gather them back into the box. "Is heavy," he said, handing the box to Lor.

Between his dreams, Hare's escape, and the noise in his head, he'd forgotten he got a bonus for reaping a kid. Eneris money... like blood money but worse. It was a good thing he remembered nothing about what happened.

Krik'tha turned to leave when Lor called him back. The one-eyed Foscan seemed to know a great deal about rituals and tales. There was a chance he knew something about his curse. "Do you happen to know anything about immortality?"

Krik'tha's smile tilted and cracked down his face until it morphed into the same look he had on the day Lor asked about extracting his own gold. Not a good start. That was a fight he didn't want to pick, but it was happening.

"Why are you asking me this thing?" His voice had deepened into cold disappointment.

"I..." Lor looked at Gale, but he was not giving their conversation a speck of attention, poring over his e-disk news. That face wasn't expected. Disappointment, sure, but it was bordering on anger. His impulsive "why" spilled from his head, and he couldn't think of any smart way to get the conversation going in his favor. Krik'tha studied him, and all Lor could do was pop his lips open and shut as every scenario made its way to his mind-filter and got trapped. "...I made a mistake."

The white eye fixed on him. Krik'tha's face pulled forward into a mega-pucker. "You are cursed?"

A curse wasn't the word he used, but it was a good one. Lor nodded, and Krik'tha shook his head. "I am sorry for this, but I cannot help."

"Why not? You helped me with the ah... *extraction...*"

"I know nothing about curses. Is thing for member of cult. Ask them." He puffed out his chest, giving Lor one last grave glare, then left.

He had officially done another stupid thing.

CHAPTER 11

Touching the Void
LOREN

THE DESERT MAELSTROM CALMED ENOUGH for the stations to prime their trains for travel. Gale estimated they'd be running again shortly after their "vacation" at the island.

Jack didn't wait for the trains—true to his word, he left the moment it was safe enough for him to do so. It was a guess, but Lor assumed Jack went back to the Kanckette tents where he said he grew up. If traveling by foot, it would be days before he got there. He left behind several recipes for Nico, as well as the phials of chromatis Lor pulled from Fowler. A special package, wrapped in wrinkled brown paper, sat in Lor's duffel courtesy of the special Yeunish Formulator.

Standing at the ferry rail, Lor let the salty breeze rush over his skin, listening only to the torrent of humid air over his ears. He stood alone, gazing off into the blue horizon, remembering the first time he spoke with Damaetra on the pink shore. She was so different then. More innocent and naïve perhaps, but he knew right then that she was the one.

In fact, everything was so different then. Even his friends had changed in less than a standard year.

Dill and Nico saw them off at the ferry, opting not to spend the plats for the resort. Lor didn't blame them. Now that he was getting deeper into Engineering, Dill didn't want to spend a week without tech, and Nico... well, he was a wreck after losing Hare.

The blow he took to the coolant tube was the end of that leg for the second time. Only, there wasn't a runner/medic or supernatural Formulator there to collect his leg and keep it frosty for later. The damage had set in, so black and green in the dry heat that Dill couldn't save it. The loss left Nico hobbling with the use of a walking crook. Lor tried not to laugh at the idea of him hopping back to town in only his underwear. It was a little funny.

It would be no fun on a beach with just one leg, he told Lor. And it was a good time to have a conversation with his parents. No argument there.

Glancing over at Damaetra, Lor saw her gazing off in a daydream. She was only too eager to go with him, afraid to be alone again. After buying the tickets, he got a complimentary coupon book. A discount trip to the salon might make her feel nice. The only things that would keep her hair behaving were a hat or a handful of pins. She opted for the hat that morning, and the brim waved in the ferry breeze.

Pulling into the dock was like a wave of bad nostalgia. Less than a standard year ago, he was hopping off that same ferry and meeting Paerli. All sweaty and falling hard already. No wonder he wouldn't listen to Nico.

Jumper shuttles waited nearby, filling up with gaudy tourists, some complaining that their e-disks, V-notes, and watches got confiscated. One man had a shiny black techthetic arm that he handed over angrily.

"And what am I supposed to use to eat? Swim? I paid a lot of plats to get here!"

Well, mister, you should have read the fine print. Always read the fine print.

Gale rushed to the closest jumper he could find to reserve it before they were left waiting for the return shuttles.

"It's been a long time since I've been here," Gale said as they rode toward the opposite side of the island. They were the first spoken words between them since getting on the ferry. Lor tittered and smiled, having forgotten that Gale had been there once too. The program rarely remembered the people it considered failures.

The resort came quickly, and it was more resplendent than he imagined. During the program, it was only a glistening shadow in the distance, but up close, the cluster of buildings was crafted in shining glass and stone. Hard wooden beams decorated the trim, and each window was artistically framed with colorful beach rock.

Damaetra gasped, bending her neck to watch the towering structure as she approached it.

"Remember, there's no tech in here," Gale said, tipping the driver. "Everything will be manual."

Lor scoffed, thinking about the armless man. Did Gale think he was blind?

The resort side of the island was much closer to Mount Gehenna. How scarred and ugly it was on the outside. He knew what it really was... the petrified shell of a gigantic tree with a fight for life growing on the inside. The shell so resembled a mountain that the mount secret-bearers had everyone fooled. Those who held its secrets held them very close. That he even knew anything about it was a work of the Maker. Damaetra pondered it, reflecting on her prison for nearly a week. Gale didn't rush her, but she didn't take too long.

The inside of the resort was like a rustic Guild Central, but more colorful and pleasant. There was a smell in the air, like many tropical places... phillo blooms and hanso fruit. It was an instant assault to Lor's sinuses but a charming aroma. Hanso smelled better than it tasted.

A mosaic pattern embedded turquoise spirals into the floor, flanked by ivory and rich brown stones. Each step they took clacked over the surface, echoing through the wide-open lobby. A large mechanical clock tick, tick, ticked in tune with their pace, showing off its exposed gears and bobbing pulleys. It had been a while since needing to look at a manual device for the time. Lor reached into his pocket for his e-disk, coming out empty-handed and cursing to himself.

Glancing to the corner of the lobby, he nudged Damaetra. "Check it out," he whispered.

A cluster of void brothers gathered, talking among themselves and organizing stacks of papers in their hands. One brother fanned himself with a stack, rolling his eyes to the ceiling before catching Lor watching him. He smiled.

Lor ducked his head and planked a hand to his brow in a "casual" misdirect, but the void brother couldn't have been that stupid.

Damaetra scoffed. "How profane," she murmured. "I hope they don't bother us."

Lor dropped his hand. "I don't know why they let them hang out around here."

"Maybe they have some deal with the resort."

Lor hummed, pondering the idea of a strange business deal.

"Good morning, good citizens," the attendant greeted them with the whitest grin Lor ever saw. "Welcome to the Pink Palm Resort!"

Lor scanned the room again, rolling his eyes around to hopefully observe the group from the side without making direct contact. The void brothers passed out their propaganda to any sucker willing to get close enough to them. Not many people got within arm's length.

Dill claimed to have come across them at some point during the program, but his description of little midnight blood-suckers was only several distances off the mark. They wore long robes made of thick and scratchy fabric the color of wet pebbles. Some hid under hoods, others let their hair out in the open. Those robes had to have been hot.

"Loren, the lady asked you a question," Gale said with a stern shove to

Lor's shoulder.

"Oh, sorry! What was the question?" How long had he been staring at them?

"Are you interested in any activities the resort has to offer? We have a fine list of several excursions you can purchase for just a little extra plat." She handed him a list.

The activity menu was older, worn in the corners with a dark crease traveling down the center where someone folded the thing. Each activity had a price next to it. Underwater adventure, the runner's experience, mid-sea fishing... a campus tour.

"Oh, how about the campus tour?" Lor tilted the sheet to Gale and whispered, "We can catch Horace."

Proud of his plan, he grinned at the paper. The bonus was that it didn't cost as much either. He didn't reap a kid just to waste it on island nonsense.

Gale nodded in agreement. "Three campus tours then."

"Very good! This is a great time to visit campus, since there are no students yet." She pulled out three pre-made paper tickets, stamping them with bright pink ink and handing them to Gale. "You'll get to visit the classroom hut. And if you're lucky, the resident guide will perform the tour! He's so smart... his head is just an endless gift of knowledge!"

If only you knew, lady.

If Jack knew what he was talking about, Horace had some fetching secrets.

"Alright, you are all set for room five-oh-seven." She handed Gale a slender piece of metal with a series of twining teeth at the tip. "The pulley is just around the corner. Enjoy your stay!"

No tech meant pulleys instead of lifts. Growing up in a tech-rich city, pulleys were only mentioned in tomes. Riding one was not on his wish list.

At the end of the hall, a gated box waited for them. Similar in size to a traditional lift, the pulley had an operator inside. He greeted them with a wide grin and gripped the handle of a wheel spanning the width of the box that connected to his side panel.

The operator was meaty. Stuffed into a white shirt and pink vest uniform, he would have passed for a tropical sausage. Sausage. It had been too long since he had real meat.

The operator slid the door shut and asked for the floor number. Five. It was effortless for his bulk to spin that wheel and fly them to floor five.

"Are you a strongman?"

"Loren, that's rude," Gale interjected.

The sausage smiled and pulled the brake lever. "I am," he said. Not everyone thought Lor's questions were rude—only Gale. Seemed like some things never changed.

Their room was clean, and the air smelled like nothing at all. It was crisp, cooling the tip of Lor's nose as he pulled it in. A third bed had been slotted into the room for Damaetra. Each bed was so close to the next that it looked like one long white platform running wall to wall. The staff even remembered the standard decor of a sheer white canopy to hang over the extra interloper. The ghostly fabric waved in the stillness. Like a playground for ghosts.

"When's the tour?" Lor asked, dropping his duffel on the center bed. Damaetra took the one in the deepest corner farthest from the door.

Gale hummed, pulling out the tickets. Glasses propped at the tip of his nose, he squinted at the paper. "First thing in the morning, it says. Hour eight, we have to meet for the jumper shuttle."

"Good, we have time today," Lor said, smiling at Damaetra and taking her hand.

Gale pinched the bridge of his nose, then looked up at the ticking manual clock on the wall. "I'm going to rest a bit. I haven't slept well in a while."

"It is a vacation."

Gale climbed into the gauzy tent, awkwardly catching the delicate fabric on his foot. "Take the key," he said, motioning to the long metal object on the table, then rolling over.

Swiping the key, Lor left with Damaetra.

The void brothers remained in the lobby, peddling their propaganda with outstretched arms to guests scuttling around them. A woman walked by, taking one brochure to transport it to the trash bin right inside the door and within view.

"I don't know about you, but I'm a little curious about what they're trying to sell," Lor said.

Damaetra took in a deep breath and scrunched her nose.

He caught her look. "We don't have to..."

"No, we can. I just don't like it," she said.

"Are you sure?"

She nodded. "Maybe it'll be good to see what the other side is trying to say."

They tupped over the turquoise spiral hand in hand toward the same brother who smiled at him earlier. Alone, he fanned himself with his stack of brochures and a disinterested glance into a far corner. He was one of the few who had his hood down, exposing his Anglian white hair and spectral pale skin.

"Excuse me," Lor said.

The void brother stopped fanning himself and put on his salesman smile, pushing a pamphlet toward them. "Are you curious about the unknown? Is there a fire in your—"

Lor laughed. "I don't want your pitch. I want to talk to you."

The man stepped back and looked around. He leaned in to Lor and whispered, "Is this about that girl that works in the campus kitchens? I swear, she came on to me, bro—"

"No..." Lor interrupted, "this isn't about the girl in the kitchens."

"Oh good"—he blew out a sigh—"forget I said that. My name is Ancel. And you are...?"

Lor cleared his throat. "Ah, hm, I'm... uh, Tad. And this is Nariah."

Damaetra elbowed Lor.

"Good to meet you, Tad and Nariah. What can I do for you?" His eyes were the same color as Damaetra's, but with a ponderous glaze of dreamy congeniality. Ancel and Damaetra could have been siblings.

"What can you tell me about Mount Gehenna?"

Ancel clicked his tongue, and his face split into that same merchant's grin. "Ah, yes, the sacred mount of gifts and power. You can read about it in our comprehensive info packet." Ancel urged his hand forward again with his paper offering.

The once glossy black surface had dulled under several sweaty thumbprints that smeared their subtle rainbow grease along the edges. Glowing blue letters sat in the center that proclaimed: *The Maker's Magic.*

"I don't want to read your pamphlet." Lor waved his hand. There was no way he was touching that greasy brochure. "I want to know what you think about Mount Gehenna. Personally."

Ancel tucked the paper back into the stack and sucked his teeth. The slippery smile mask had fallen. "I'm just a peon, anyway. Unless a member pays out a bunch of plats over time for the privilege of knowledge, they don't tell us any more than what's already in here." He tapped the stack resting on his other arm. "What do you want to know?"

"Tell me what you think Gehenna is... And maybe what it's not," Lor said.

Ancel smirked. "It ain't a mountain, I can tell you that much."

Very clever, Ancel.

"So what is it if it's not a mountain?"

Ancel shifted, rapping two swift taps of his toe onto the tile. "You'd probably have to talk to a Foscan about their little superstitious fairy tales for that kind of information. And who wants to do that?"

Lor sighed. "So you don't have any theories?"

"Oh, I have theories."

Lor circled a finger in the air, rolling his eyes. Ancel was getting on his nerves.

"I don't think the Maker has anything to do with that place. It's the rot of

Roseaarde if you ask me... death from below."

It certainly smelled rotten. That putrid aroma was engraved in his brain, and thinking of it again drew it out of his memory, blessing him with the phantom scent of it. Part of it had to have come from Maron. For so long, he stuck to that wall, leaving his own twisted tree rings of dead flesh inside the umbilicus. The rest came from what? The breach itself?

"What makes you think that?" Lor asked.

Ancel smirked again. "There's an old history book. I read it a long time ago, but I'm not stupid... I remember the passages. I'm not sure if the book I had even exists anymore. Audun ordered all presses to stop printing it, and pretty sure it had all copies destroyed. I mean, that book was ancient when I had it back as a kid."

"But it has to exist on the network somewhere, right?"

"I don't have access to that here, but I would say no. Audun went through quite a bit of trouble to rewrite history. If they found you snooping around on the network looking for old dead history... well... just watch yourself."

"Point taken."

"Here... Take a brochure." Ancel handed the top trifold to Lor—a fresh one without grease smears. It was an honest ask, no slimy sales or conversion tactic. Lor took it reluctantly. "Read this. Learn how history and faith get lost in translation. Then you'll believe whatever they tell you because you have no choice."

"Who's they?"

Ancel hummed. "They are them."

"What do you believe?"

"I believe in truth."

Damaetra cut in, smiling at him. "It was nice to meet you, Ancel."

They turned to leave him when Lor spun back around and asked, "Why did you become a void brother?"

Ancel shrugged. "Got nothing better to do. Whole family's dead. Besides... I thrive in controversy. Have a wonderful afternoon." He winked at Damaetra and waved, fanning himself with the brochures again.

The warm, wet beach air draped over him like his own personal void cloak. Ancel couldn't have been the only person on Roseaarde who thought the way he did. There were Foscan fables and old forbidden history tomes. People had secrets.

"That didn't go as I expected," Damaetra said.

"Me neither." He reached down to take her hand, spotting the finger-shaped indents in her wrist.

Noticing his attention, she flicked her wrist around in front of her chest with a smile. "My new tattoo."

The sun caught the scars, shimmering over the silver that had been pulled close to the surface of her skin. Even if she wasn't bothered by it anymore, it bothered him.

"Ah, watch it, Loren," she said, grabbing his arm and pulling him back. "You're always tripping on these."

The ivory corner of ancient tech poked from the sand right where he was about to step. He knelt down, brushing away a ditch around it. Several lengths later and the tech still hadn't revealed its base. These things were buried deep... there was no telling how big these pieces were. Running his finger along its pitted surface, ravaged by salt, wind, and water, there was a smaller piece partially hidden within. It trilled in response, rattling in the ill-fitting hole.

"What's this?" he said out loud, though Damaetra wasn't listening. Her attention was on the horizon, eyes closed and most likely praying. She touched her "new tattoo," rubbing it back and forth in a self-soothe.

Back at the tech, Lor pinched the small piece out of the big piece. Pink grains clung to every pit and crack, wedging even into the finer details carved around the perimeter.

This little piece was like nothing he'd ever seen. Several rings intersected each other within a delicate framework of irrational design. He hooked his pinky finger through them, turning it back and forth, unable to determine where the intersections began and ended. It just was.

A cypher had been carved into the inner rings, which had a familiar, yet alien, look. Either the Maker was leading him to little clues about Roseaarde, or the world had fallen asleep. Who wouldn't be interested in such a thing? The real question, and probably the same question Ancel would have, was why didn't they care?

Lor pocketed the tech and prayed he wouldn't be caught with it. That night, he had another vision.

Secrets of the Dead
LOREN

THE SAND WAS A BLISTERING *fire under his naked feet. There was nothing in the vast openness to use as a cover. He had to protect them somehow, but the only suitable dressing he could part with were the strips of fabric wrapped around his head.*

The strips were wet with brine, and there was enough fabric to fashion a set of pouches to tie around his feet and ankles. Planking his hand over his eyes, he saw nothing but vast dunes. The sun scorched his unprotected head, soaking up heat through his black hair straight onto his scalp. He was going to die here.

A glimmer in the distance hovered just above the horizon. A mirage, nothing more. But what if it was more than that? It took all his will to move his legs, trudging forward.

Just as he crested the first hill, he was greeted by a resilient little cluster of squat cacti in the sand, as if gifted from the Maker for him to pull water from. If no water could be drawn from it, he could squeeze the life out of it for some green eneris. What he would do with that, he didn't know. A burn soother? Could he drink it?

A jet of sand spiked into the air, and he took a step back. Maelstrom aftershocks, no doubt... it smelled like electricity. For a moment, he imagined running into one to go soaring through the air only to strike his head on a rock. That would be better than this.

Casting the thought aside, he bent down to pluck out the sweet cacti. Spikes prickled his palm, but he didn't care. He pinched and yanked out clusters of slender needles before pushing his teeth forward to take a bite from the cleared flesh. Once that drop of moisture hit his tongue, a primal thirst took over, forgoing the removal of the needles in favor of more succulent meat. He devoured the little thing in three bites, regretting his choice not to remove the needles as he pulled them from cheek and tongue.

After finishing off the final cacti in the cluster, he stood tall, squinting toward the horizon from atop the dune's spine. He felt somewhat better, but a proper meal would have been divine. All he tasted was his own blood on his tongue.

Something distant flapped in the wind, like a flag of surrender... or an invitation. He made his way toward it.

The journey taxed his senses, and his head spun circles and hallucinations. How would an immortal die in the desert? Would it be total dehydration? Cursed to stare at first sun, second sun, and moon for endless cycles until a random desert crawler feasted on his bones? Would he feel everything?

He tried to find more gifts of cacti, but his eyes couldn't focus, and any treats in the sand were lost to vertigo... but the flapping object stood before him, beating on the breeze. It was a derelict canopy tent.

It must have been a death camp at some point, long abandoned for the brighter side of the dune. Whatever that meant. Most camps like this one contained bunker holes dug out for cooling down and protection. And his streak of luck evaded him— there were no bunkers here.

The pathetic shred of fabric would have to be enough until second sun to keep the burning rays from his head. He sat underneath it and sprawled out his legs, leaning back and staring at the sunlit pinholes worn out in the grayish material.

Wind whispered death into his ears as he watched more sand spouts burst into the air, followed by the hiss of grains falling back down and an electrical smell. Colors crept into his vision, swirling over stones in the sand and casting chromatic shadows underneath them. There were no more cacti to eat here... he didn't imagine experiencing a slow death to be such a trip.

A long shadow stretched over his modest little campsite and stood sentinel over him. He stared at it—a silhouette against the sun. In all the spinning colors and visions of the otherworld, he passed off the shadow as just another hallucination. That was until it spoke to him.

"Are you lost?"

Lor's eyes snapped open, finding himself in the same bed he lay in at the resort, cloaked in a veil of gauzy fabric. The analog clock ticked away, and he wished he knew how to read it. The darkness told him only that it was still night.

He glanced over at Damaetra's bed and saw her curled up to the side and nearly buried under her covers.

Lor wanted to fall back asleep and solve the mystery of the desert stranger, but he was afraid of missing his "meeting" with Horace. Cursing under his breath, he remembered he had no e-disk to record his dream. He slid off the bed to find something in the room to write with and on.

Lucky for him, there was a cheap resort-branded pad of parchment on the center table, with a writing implement hooked onto it. Documenting everything down to the taste of blood in his mouth, he wrote out six pages of detail. His writing callous ached, having gone soft again after leaving the program.

The dream had to have been real. He wasn't even himself inside of it—he walked in someone else's body. He knew from the long black hair and darkened skin. Pausing for a moment, he scribbled in the margin: *Par's past?*

"What time is it?" Gale said through layers of sinus blockage. Lor jumped, dropping the pen to the table with a clatter.

"Sh, I don't know," Lor whispered. "It's still early."

Gale sat up and squinted at the clock. "It's... almost seven," he whispered back and yawned again.

I'll have to ask him again how to read a timepiece. How pathetic.

Oof. Cold floor. Lor pattered over to the kitchen for something warm to drink. No powdered mix here, just a weird cylinder with a plunger.

"That's a press," Gale said, rubbing his face with a mighty yawn so wide Lor could peer into the pink recesses of his throat. He got up to take possession of it and fed it a large scoop of coffee granules. "Gotta heat some water."

Water sputtered from the tap through a spigot corroded by years of mineral assault. An earthy dirt smell followed.

"They've been making powder packets since before you were born," Gale said while heating the water over a proper fire in the box at the counter. "I'm not surprised you don't know how to brew coffee."

Lor hummed and watched Gale move about.

"We'll probably have to get Damaetra up soon. I hate to wake her," Gale said, grabbing mugs from the cabinet.

The kettle wailed, and he poured the steaming water into the cylinder with the coffee. The scent was nothing like any other coffee Lor had. There was an undertone of hanso fruit that hung in the air, and he wondered if it was a special flavor. The aroma of hanso was a theme at the resort. The only smells during the program were dust, paper, and chalk.

He sipped the hanso-scented coffee, glad that it didn't taste like the funky fruit, and glanced over to see Damaetra sitting up in bed, stretching her arms in front of her. She shook her head "no" after an offer of coffee.

"So, about your teacher, Horace." Gale propped the glasses on his head, patched with brownish stubble.

"He's not the type of person I can explain. You'll just have to meet him," Lor said.

As expected, few resort guests were interested in the campus tour. Only two couples joined them at the shuttle line. Both couples had wide grins barely contained on their youthful faces, and Lor wasn't interested in talking to them. They were naïve. He supposed he shouldn't have been so judgmental considering his own experience, but their trip was business only, and his time at the program felt like a generation ago.

Their hopeful voices buzzed in the background while Lor closed his eyes. The colors remained static, interrupted by lines of black that jiggled when the couples talked.

"They say this is the ideal location for the program because of how far it is from the city," one man said in a squawking pertness Lor found insufferable.

"Or how close it is to that place," said one of the women with an equally shrill tone.

"Well, if I can get in, I hope I can get Shepherd." The third male voice was more pleasant, streaking light blue through his colored static. A color! It was a start.

"What about Formulator?" The shrieking woman.

"Or what about Engineer?"

What about the cost?

Their jabber had Lor rethinking his own first day again. The jumper shuttle rolled to a stop near the ferry dock.

Gale nudged him. "Did you bring Jack's... *gift?*"

Lor patted a stuffed-looking pocket with a curt nod.

They stepped onto the sand, and Lor chucked himself to the side, dodging another piece of ancient tech and nearly twisting an ankle. Damaetra giggled at him, and he flushed.

A silhouette jogged toward them from one of the main buildings, with the familiar disheveled tuft of hair. Lor smiled, recognizing the gait and funny bobbing mop.

Lor leaned in to Gale to whisper, "That's him... That's Horace."

Sand kicked up around his feet and slowed to a halt when he planted himself in front of the group and tilted his head at Lor and Damaetra.

"Mister Turtingas... Miss Praes..." he addressed them, holding out a hand to Lor. "Why, I admit I'm perplexed to see you on a campus tour."

Lor smirked. "Are you, though? This is my dad, Gale," he said with a quick test of Horace's sincerity and a firm handshake. "We were hoping to have a talk with you."

Horace glanced at the rest of the tour members, who waited expectantly with those same simple grins spread over their faces. He glanced back at Lor, scanning him. He felt naked under that gaze, knowing that his friendly spirit was feeding him everything.

Horace called over another staff member to take over his tour responsibility, then turned back to them. "Come this way," Horace said, leading them toward the rows of housing units.

Their destination was the last house in the row closest to the dorms. While he had never visited or been inside before, it definitely belonged to Horace.

They stepped inside the modest home. Similar to the classroom, the floors were covered in sand and the walls were made of wood, dimpled by the ravages of salt in the air. The faint scent of mildew that radiated from brown-colored fabric furniture and damp air created a greasy film on Lor's skin.

Horace directed them to sit. It would have been rude *not* to sit, but the threat of a wet seat and dank smell that would follow him out was real. Damaetra tugged at him, and the choice was made. A plume of funk dusted up as he relaxed into the cushion. Funny, that particular aroma would have been noticeable on someone who lived in it, but Lor never smelled it on Horace. He had his own smell that, once Lor learned about his need for Jack's drug, he attributed to that.

"So, what brings you back?" Horace asked. He picked at an orange patch sewn on the arm of his blue puffy chair.

Gale cleared his throat. "We have a few questions we need to ask you. We've run into a bit of trouble."

"Oh? And what can an old, lowly guide offer to you in these troubling times?"

Lor smiled at him, giving the odd bulge in his pocket a squeeze, making the paper underneath crinkle. "But you're *not* just a guide, are you?"

Horace paused. "And what makes you say that?"

"Because I've learned that you're a two-mind."

Picking at the patch with more intent, he twisted the threads between thumb and forefinger, pursing his lips. "That's quite the *rumor*, Mister Turtingas."

"Maybe. Or maybe it's not a rumor, and you already knew we were coming." That was a guess. If he was wrong, then he was not very good at this sort of thing.

"You're an intuitive one, Loren. I'll give you that."

"So, will you help us?"

Horace tutted and sighed. "If you know what you know, then you are aware of the cost of helping. I'm sorry, scratch that. The cost of *living*."

"Yes. And I brought you something." Lor pulled the package from his pocket, rolled up in wrinkled parchment, then placed it on the conversation table.

The signature crumpled brown paper and spiraling twine holding it all together lit him up. It was old-fashioned, nondescript, and ordinary... it was a package Horace had procured many times over during his trips to Secas. He sank back into his chair with a smile. "So you've become better acquainted with Jack, I see."

Lor smiled. "He saved my life," he said, curling a fist over the spot in his stomach that took a punch from Crow. The scar twitched, thrumming a deep tic in his gut that could have been a response from his organs or gas.

"Jack is a modest man," Horace said. He laced his fingers across his belly as he leaned farther back. "I, too, have found myself at his mercy."

"So I hear."

Gale shifted his legs in the hard chair and nodded at the syringe parcel. "So, would this be enough to help you for a while?" he asked.

Leaning over the syringes with elbows on the table and steepled fingers under his chin, Horace studied Gale. "Do I... *know* you?" he asked.

Pink flushed Gale's cheeks, and it was all he could do to contain his discomfort. It was always a power move for him to straighten up and find a way to "look down" at the situation. That moment was no different from the thousands of times Lor had encountered it. "I-I don't *think* so."

A long pause from Horace caused Gale to fester into humility. Horace seemed to ignore that. "No, I think I know you from somewhere." He watched Gale for another moment before a glimmer twitched at the corner of his eye. That glimmer set his face to relax and carry on with the issue in front of him. "Ah, anyway, how is it you came about the knowledge of my *special affliction*?"

"My friend, Nico, overheard you talking to Val," Lor said.

"Yes, well, my thanks to your friend *Nico* for not telling the world about it." He gave one more glance at Gale before boring into Lor. "Have you done it yet, Mister Turtingas? Surely, as a member of Guild Central, you've paid the toll... Have you reaped silver?"

Lor went quiet. All he remembered were the human husks. The result of a full squeeze. He did that to them, and he didn't remember their stories... only the slow, agonizing descent into yaslecha. Of course, Horace already knew the answer.

"You ask me, but you know already, don't you?"

Horace picked up Jack's package, and the paper crackled in the silence. Pulling out one syringe, he turned it sideways, letting the liquid inside slop to the end. It swirled with silver, like a child's glitter stick—the kind that if turned back and forth, sparkling motes curled in response, reaching with their shimmering tendrils.

He pinched the plunger and stretched the barrel toward Lor, with the needle pointing at his face. "Beautiful thing, that," Horace said. Then he remained quiet for some time, admiring the swirling glitter drug. "A cure for the living made from the dead. And by a *Yeunish* Formulator no less."

"So you know Jack's secret then."

Horace tapped his head with a grin, the way he had in the program. That funny quirk finally made sense. He couldn't *help* but know things. Nothing was hidden from a two-mind.

"The Yeunish are a fascinating people," Horace said, admiring the syringe, "forbidden from practicing Guild abilities when they're just so *good* at them." He looked at Lor with an expression he couldn't translate. It was possibly a mix of glee and fear. "I bet Audun would be terrified of *you*."

That was something that had crossed Lor's mind. The hope Gale had of having him hide behind the walls of Audun with a Mesaman face and Guild ability might be the death of him if the city ever knew.

Continuing to turn the syringe in his hand, Horace clicked his tongue. "Being a two-mind is not a common thing, I'm sure you've been told. Most die within days of discovering it." The syringe cap popped from the needle and skittered across the table when he flicked it off with his thumb. "Two-minds can't turn it off, you see. Little parasites they are. I wouldn't be surprised if I were the only one alive. It's very unlike a skin walker, a strongman, or..." He narrowed his eyes at Gale. "...a *runner*."

Gale folded his arms and looked down into his chest, yet peered up at Horace.

Horace chuckled at the embarrassment he caused. "I *like* my life on the island. It's humble... ordinary. The Seven Cities don't recognize a two-mind, reasoning that those like myself are politically dangerous. They're not wrong."

"But Readers—" Lor interjected.

"Wear a nice accessory," he interrupted, holding up a hand, "assigned by Audun, and made of gold. I'm sure you remember where yours once was."

The crescent scar cutting through his forearm itched at the mention. Lor ran his finger across it, feeling the soft and textured tissue, still dark pink from healing. "But why would you let me implant myself, knowing that I am *Yeunish*?" He whispered the last word. There was no telling what kind of person might be on the other side of that window, listening to all of their secrets.

"Oh, for the same reasons you've been told by your father. But it's probably best you no longer have it."

Damaetra made a soft groan, looking down at her own arm with the bulge still sitting there, unperturbed.

"Alas, their tech can't control the uncontrollable. Which is why I prefer to live as I am in secret, if you get me." Horace's hand trembled when he put the needle up to his arm. Several pocks littered his skin from years of using Jack's drug. Plunging the Witis treatment into his muscle, he sighed. "Sometimes I wonder if any of this is worth it."

"Maybe there's a better solution for you," Gale said. "I'm a medic... I'm sure there's something that the colleagues in my field can try."

Horace tittered. "You know, you remind me of a man whose story started before I was a guide here on the island. It's quite fascinating if you'd like to hear?"

"Sure," Lor said. "I mean, at least I want to hear."

The old guide smiled and relaxed again. "Very well. There was once a young man who came to the program. Class of nine-ninety, I believe. He was brilliant, with a bright future."

He paused and gazed upward at the thatched ceiling cobbled with bubbles of dried mud.

"I know what you're thinking," Horace continued, smiling. "You're thinking, 'what does this have to do with anything?' Well, trust me, it's important.

"This man, see, he was incredibly intelligent, like I said. He wanted to help people. Maybe he would be an Engineer, or maybe a Shepherd. No matter what the Maker gifted him with, he would always use it for the greater good. Interestingly enough, the Maker sought fit to bless him on the very ride over to the program, before even the first day of classes. Can you believe that?" Horace laughed with nostalgic mirth at the memory.

As Horace chuckled to himself, shaking his head, Lor noticed a shift in Gale. He looked uneasy in a way Lor had never seen in his stepfather.

"It was an easy transition for him, of course. A lot of things came easy to him," Horace continued, picking at the armchair again, "but it was not what he expected at all—no, it was all wrong. What would he tell his young wife? Or, when she came of age, his infant daughter?

"Well, did I mention how smart he was? He decided he would continue the program. I don't know how he did it, but he found a way to avoid the nudge entirely, rejecting the little golden lie the program tells its recruits every turn, knowing that it's not responsible for gifting a Guild ability. Brilliant. No need for amateur surgery behind the dormitory." He smirked at Lor, whose face went hot all the way to his hairline.

"While in the program, this smart, special man met another student, and they became instant friends. Although, this smart young man always did maintain his secret, even from his best friend, Greg. Hiding in plain sight, the clever boy pretended to leave the program Guildless, forsaking his 'blessed gift' as a Weggevens runner for a life of medicine."

Lor shot a look at Gale, who had twisted his face into wrinkled regret.

"Greg was the only one truly Guildless between you two, wasn't he?" Horace traded picking the patch on the chair to tapping the arm. "You both enrolled in Peakwood Academy for non-Guild professions together. Only, *you* went into Health—for him, it was Law.

"Rather unfortunate... that accident that killed him. Too young, I say, but practiced enough to have known better. But as with all second chances, the conditions were just right for him to find me on an ordinary shopping trip in Secas."

Horace bent forward again with fingertips pointed under chin, regarding Gale directly. "Greg says hello."

CHAPTER 13

The Most Important Thing
LOREN

"So THAT'S HOW YOU RECOGNIZED me, I take it?" Gale said, not angrily but not kind.

Horace chuckled and shrugged. "Life is funny, and I'm still human after all. Greg has his fun in my noggin'."

"So what does it all mean? My dead friend is living inside your head now?"

Tired and weary, with dark, watery circles under his eyes, Horace sighed. "Strange, isn't it? How we all seem to be connected in some way."

"Maybe it's the Maker's doing," Lor suggested.

Damaetra took his hand and squeezed it. The silvered ridges on her wrist flexed and crawled over her bones.

"Perhaps," Horace said, running fingers through his wild hair. "Now that you are well acquainted with my secret, you must understand that allowing Greg to reveal his knowledge will drain me that much faster. With that in mind, quickly now, what is it that you want from me?"

In the silent pause, Damaetra nudged Lor. "Oh! Uh... I'm not sure where to start," Lor said.

"Start with the most important thing," Gale said sharply. The situation clearly had Gale irritated, but in a different way. Having his long-dead best friend living inside the mind of some stranger probably had something to do with that. In a small way, Lor felt bad... a little guilty even, for putting him through that.

And what was the most important thing? They were all important. The breach, his immortality, Maron... Par. All of it.

"Did you know Paerli Harea was an ancient?"

Horace grinned. "Of course."

"But you let her into the program."

"Letting her in is not how I remember it. Even Greg is sometimes subject to the power of... persuasion, if you understand."

Lor chewed his lip and thought about that for a moment. Then he remembered Par's other victim. "You mean... a Reader?"

Horace tapped his nose. "Well done."

Livia was the Reader on Par's team. For all her faults to support Par, Lor couldn't be mad at her. Damaetra had found an ally in the dark with her, and in a way, she helped keep her alive. With an uncommon gift of the push, she hid well as a dumpy and plain woman wearing thick-rimmed glasses that made her eyes appear twice their size.

"And you didn't say anything to anyone?"

Horace tittered with a small grin. "Not if I wanted to keep my secret."

"But Val knows your secret. Did you not tell him, a Foscan, about her being an ancient?"

"What would he tell me about that? I knew her intention, but who am I to raise the alert? Again, it would just draw attention to me, and I won't be made a spectacle in Audun."

Fair enough. Lor sighed and leaned back. The only rational next question he thought to ask was, "Who is Maron Valoa'brenga?"

Rolling his head to the side in his chair, Horace seemed bored with the query. Or just tired. Barely moving, his chest rose and fell. "He's a fairy tale, Mister Turtingas."

Damaetra made a small cry in protest, which Lor responded to with a squeeze of her hand. "You and I both know he's not just a fairy tale, Horace. Who is he?"

Horace waved his hand to the side as if batting away the festering smell of mildew. "Just another ancient."

"No, he's not just some ancient. He's an Igni. What is an Igni?"

Rolling his head back toward the trio, Horace grinned again. "Ah, yes... the Igni. Your ancestors."

"Ancestors? You mean the first humans?"

"No, Mister Turtingas... I mean *your* ancestors."

Raising a brow, Lor tilted his head and studied Horace. "What does that mean?"

Something was wrong. Horace sat up and ran the back of his hand across his lower eyelid, blinking repeatedly. A silver smear painted his index knuckle.

"I'm sorry, Loren... I told you the drain happens fast. This may have to wait for another time." Another swollen drop swelled at his tear duct, shimmering in the warm light. "As you can see, I'm leaking."

"Oh Maker," Damaetra said, reaching for another syringe and bringing it to him.

The gesture made Horace chuckle. "You're a sweet young woman, Miss Praes," he said, uncapping the syringe and hovering the needle over his arm. "In a way, I wish I *had* said something. About Miss Harea... or should I say, Mistress Valoa'brenga. It was an awful thing she put you through."

Plunging the drug into his arm, he grimaced as Damaetra flushed. She rubbed at her "new tattoo."

"I'm sorry, Horace. I didn't even ask the most important question," Lor said.

Letting out a breath and placing the syringe back on the table, Horace sat down with a look that told Lor he already knew. "What is the breach?"

"Y-yes. That."

"You've opened it."

Lor cleared his throat. Greg must have been very active, diving deep into every secret place and thought, feeding knowledge into Horace as his silver spilled from his eye sockets. "Yes. I opened it."

Sighing again, Horace soaked the last drop of silver from his face with the corner of his collar. It left a black spot—something Lor didn't expect from silver. "You did a noble thing," Horace said, "by saving her." He nodded at Damaetra.

"To what end?"

"Now that is one loaded question." He pointed in Lor's direction in the same flamboyant way he used to during the program, which made Lor wistful.

"Horace, what exactly did I do when I opened it?"

"Nothing that wasn't already starting to happen," he said. "Maron was worn out. He held on to that corruption for far too long. It was only a matter of time before the leaks got bigger."

"What leaks?"

Horace smirked and hummed. "Have you ever taken the time to question? Why do we do the things we do? What is our purpose? Who do we answer to?"

It might have been a rhetorical slew of questions, but Lor opened his mouth to answer anyway, finding nothing but a grievous sigh coming from his throat.

"There is a reason, I think, that a two-mind suffers so much," Horace continued. "There are things of this world that we aren't meant to know. Things that the Maker protects us against."

"Like what?" Gale asked after a long bout of silence.

"You are aware that I hold the secrets of the dead."

"That's what I understand a two-mind to be."

"Then you must know that it's a burden to know things. Good things... terrible things. If I were to share this burden with the whole of Roseaarde, what do you think would become of us?"

Silence. Not even sure what to say, Lor folded his hands in his lap. Ancel's brochure crinkled in his pocket as if to taunt him.

"Of all people, Mister Turtingas... You should be the most concerned about the future. Or have you forgotten already?"

He had, and he had not. As his mind spun from one thing to the next, a random word or thought would bring him back to reality, facing the fact that he was immortal. In a way, he felt responsible for the future. At least, he thought as much. The fact was, he was afraid he'd become like Paerli. Years of living with a reaping ability was a guaranteed flight into yaslecha.

"The breach is another secret, guarded by the city," Horace continued. "No one was meant to find it in the way you did. I mean, of course the ancients would know how to access it. But there is an offshoot of Audun citizens that want to help. They want to seal up the leaks for good. Even Princeps Renae is unaware of their efforts. Now that it's open, well... their plans have been expedited."

Lor groaned. "So, Horace, I'm struggling to understand what the breach actually is. This is all great information, but what is it?"

"One final answer before I must stop, or Greg will suck the life out of me." Horace gave a weak smile.

"It was created a very long time ago... the breach, that is," Horace said with a sigh. "In times dead and gone, even before Miss Harea was born, there was a war between the North and East. It was the very war that now litters our beaches and whose materials confound our researchers..."

Pausing to glance out the window, Horace folded his fingers together, cracking the middle knuckles on each hand. Little was known about the East, and no one really talked about it. The most he'd ever heard was Dill once going on one of his tales about how it was guarded by sea monsters.

"The objects in the sand have eluded our Engineers for hundreds of standard years. There's something about that tech, something they can't duplicate, that was powerful enough to punch a hole between worlds right at the root of the tree of life. The tree that you know now as the burned stump of Mount Gehenna.

"Interestingly enough, that opening introduced our world to something different. Something we weren't ready for. About a generation later, Guild abilities showed up, making their way through the first of the post-war settlers. Well, back then, they didn't call them Guilds. Maron Valoa'brenga was one of those hosts... along with his wife, Miss Harea."

Everyone inside Horace's muddy hut went silent, with only distant laughter coming from the beach outside.

"So..." Lor hummed for a moment to think. "So... wait. Let me see if I understand. There was a war—a war with a fictional land, that left all those annoying pieces of junk in the sand, which I've nearly broken every single one of my toes on, and that was responsible for the breach? Because it somehow found its way to the root of Gehenna, tearing a hole into what... another dimension? A dimension with Guild abilities?" His voice cracked over the last two words, making Damaetra giggle. At least she found this funny.

What a lame story. It was so absurd it could have been ripped from the pages of one of Eva's silly fiction books about other planets and beings from the sun. Nonsense.

"Hard to believe, I know," Horace offered. Then he narrowed his eyes and lowered his voice. "But I wouldn't look at the breach as just another dimension..."

The room dimmed slightly when a group of extra swollen clouds passed overhead, blocking out the sun. The dip in temperature was enough to raise the bumps on Lor's skin.

"What do you mean by that?"

"I mean... something dark. Something... evil. Greg won't tell me any more." A full silver drop slithered down his cheek, dropping to the armchair with a wet *plip*!

After the third syringe, the questioning had to end. Lor wasn't about to kill Horace for Greg to feed him more fairy tales.

The barrel squelched new drug in Horace's arm. "My advice for you at this time would be to find the two ancients, Maron and Paerli, if you can. I know she hurt you as well."

Damaetra's look hurt Lor. There were no secrets in that room. Finding Par and Maron was the last thing he wanted to do. Maron could have been a murderous psychopath for all he knew.

Hey, how was the last millennium bound to the stinking bowels of an alternate dimension? Did you meet anyone cool?

No, there was no way that guy would be normal. All he remembered were his eyes. There was a vacant determination to pull Par back into the depths with him. Calm and unnerving. Par was wicked, but wicked he at least understood.

"Thanks, Horace, this has been interesting," Lor said, standing up and holding out a hand to Damaetra. "We have a lot to think about."

"One last thing, since I know it's on your mind." Horace got up to open the front door. "He's no threat to you. The brother. Take care now."

They left Horace, letting him know that if he couldn't get in touch with Jack, he could also reach out to Nico. *What a team you all have become,* he told them.

Hare was no threat, and that was some comfort, even if the rest was unbelievable. At least Gale seemed to relax a little.

Lor glanced down at a piece of ancient tech peering up at him from the sand. An orb-like bulb was embedded into the side, crushed out like a plucked eyeball. A war with the East... what a load of nonsense. Everyone knew the East didn't exist.

ACTIVITY IN THE DESERT

Current activities in the desert have Audun working tirelessly as law enforcement attempts to investigate increased renegade death camps. Visits to the Kanckette tents are prohibited until further notice. Units have been deployed to watch over the residents.

HELP WANTED

Attendant needed for Guild Central's Formulation Hall. Must be focused, and professionally trained in non-Guild social class. Position requires many hours of sitting, reaching, and problem solving. Weekly pay: pL 5,500

Laid back, tech-dry Resort Admin wanted for beautiful Heart Island. Don't let the opportunity to live and retire on the famous eastern island to pass you by! Housing and meals included. Weekly pay: pL 2,000

Readers needed for Audun! Were you blessed as a natural Reader? Princeps Renae wants you! Duties include but not limited to: questioning, maintaining ethical order in the Seven Cities, and possibly the influence of specific stakeholders.
Paid daily! PL 3,300

The Ethics Committee is expanding! Seeking dedicated citizens with a love for the Law and moral standing to work with current administration to create new, and uphold existing laws. Call for details:
01-7C-0010.

CHAPTER 14

Wherever He Goes
LOREN

GALE SAID LITTLE TO ANYONE the rest of their time at the resort. He muttered to himself every once in a while, between reading printed news articles on the beach and pacing in the kitchen. The words he uttered were quiet and out of reach, but Lor heard him say *law* once, and *stuck*.

He probably thought his friend was trapped, unable to *move on*. If it were Nico or Dill, Lor would have felt the same.

A violent death, only to be sent into a stranger's head... the spirit would have all the time in the world to come up with fancy stories to feed into his host. A ghost's boredom made fools of them all. The breach was just a smelly hole at the bottom of a rotting tree, and there was no power to be had. In her own weird way, Par just wanted her husband back and lost herself along the way. Lor blew out a breath. There was nothing for him to do about it but enjoy the rest of his very expensive vacation, starting with a gift to Damaetra for a trip to the salon.

While waiting for her, he hoped to run into Ancel again to pass the time over theories and laugh at the new nonsense Lor had heard. The lobby was empty, so Lor paced the beach hoping to see the void brothers. Nothing. Restlessness set in, aching his mind, but he chuckled to himself at how things had changed. His whole experience in the program taught him to avoid the cult members. Krik'tha even raged about them, spitting on the ground and making weird gestures. Now here he was, searching for them.

Maybe they were just misunderstood. No one in their right mind would worship a rotting hole in the wall, but they really weren't so bad. Lor sighed and glanced beyond the water, thinking about Horace's "war of the East." If there *were* an East, Heart Island would be the place to see it. He would have seen something, or heard something, right? He shook his head. It was stupid.

The hazy, empty horizon reminded him of the first time Damaetra showed him how to talk to the Maker. It had been a while since his colors made sense, and he didn't think about them much. The same static fizzed there when he shut his eyes. Bored like Greg, he attempted to reach out to the Maker once again to pass the time.

Maker...

The word bounced in the hollows of his mind, repeating until it faded.

Are you still here?

The words again plopped into his river of thought, rippling outward and fading. As the echoes died, the slightest flicker of white gold vibrated to the surface.

"Loren..." Damaetra touched his shoulder.

Finally! His eyes slapped open, and he spun around to see her new style.

"What do you think?" she asked, tucking some of the neatly trimmed strands behind her ear, with a coy smile lighting her blue-violet eyes.

No one was as stunning as her. She used to hide her face with that long hair. It was gone, revealing all rawness and awesome splendor. She was her mother's daughter... her mother, the queen Thea, and she, a queen to be. A beauty that makes a man weep and thank the Maker for something so wonderfully miraculous. The white violet, dressed in pale gold, stood there, requesting a mere man's approval.

Who am I to utter blessings upon a literal creature of God? She had to know how her light blinded me, and I craved it!

"It's short," he said.

Damaetra frowned. "You don't like it?"

Burn out my eyes with that light, and I will have it. Let me always live in the warmth of your beauty.

"It looks good." Lor pinched the bottom strands and smiled at her.

"I guess it's alright," she said with a sigh. "It's been weird getting used to shorter hair."

"It'll grow back."

It wasn't just the haircut, not really. Seeing her in that new way drove him into a wild sort of madness that only had one solution. The ring! The little piece of interlocked ancient tech still sat in his pocket, buzzing for his attention by rubbing at his skin from the small hole that had been scratched away along the side of the fabric. Withdrawing the tech, he turned it around in his fingers. The interlocking rings were smooth. Smooth enough to wear.

"Hey," he said, "I found this the other day. Do you like it?" He extended the tech toward her, and she held out her hand.

It was almost the color of her bright alabaster skin, yet the edges glinted under the light. Pink stains from ages buried in the sand ran along the rims.

"I've never seen a piece like this before," she said, turning her palm. Transfixed, she watched the light hit at different angles, casting a tease of blues, greens, and yellows. "Normally, the tech has sharp edges. This one's pretty smooth."

Lor took the tech back and replaced it with his hand in hers. "We've been through a lot, you and me," he said.

She looked up at him, surprised in the change of tone. "Yes, we have."

"There's nothing I won't do for you."

She smirked. "Nothing at all?"

"I would travel to the pit of Gehenna for you."

That made her giggle. "I don't know how much farther down you could go than what you already did."

"I would die to protect you."

"Whoa, Loren… I don't want you to die." She took a step back, eyeing him. "You almost did that already."

"And I would do it again."

As the dainty tech sat in his open palm, her expression tensed, washed with suspicion. She bit her lip, nodding at it. "So, what do you intend to do with that?"

He was a man possessed. His thoughts, his words, they weren't his, but they felt right. They *were* right. Everything they had been through. All his feelings for her hammered inside of him at once, as if the tech itself compelled him. It slid easily over her middle finger.

"I mean to make a promise to you," he said, "to be your protector. To love you forever. Would you allow me to do that?" The tech spoke for him. In no universe was he ever so eloquent.

She gazed at the tech wrapped over her finger. While unconventional, it was a perfect fit. It wasn't pitted or scratched, as if it had waited for thousands of years buried there, just for the right moment to be found by a bungling clod. She wore it beautifully.

Please say you will…

"I-uh, Loren, this is unexpected…"

Please say you will.

No one would ever hurt her again.

Damaetra still gaped at the interlocking rings. A couple walked past with their footfalls delicately *piff piff piffing* in the sand as their conversation about plat investments faded away. The longer she stood there with no answer, the more his knees quivered over bony calves.

"I'm not sure what's come over you, but the truth is," she said, pausing. In the silence, she frowned, staring at the ring.

Could she have done a better job emotionally punching him in his groin?

Too much? Too fast? It had been a year. Surely she knew whether she wanted him forever. A *Yeuni*. The thought he'd forgotten stirred his knees again, spreading to his jellied spine.

A short sniffle and a sigh broke her silence when she looked up at him. Then she smiled. "The truth is, Loren, wherever you go, that's where I want to be."

It had been too long since he'd kissed her. Fighting the urge to throw up, he kissed her. The blood finally warmed up in his limbs, bringing the feeling back, and hardening knees and spine again. With a tear in her eye, the future Mrs. Turtingas laughed.

CHAPTER 15

Seasons Change
LOREN

"DON'T FORGET THAT," GALE SAID, pointing at the notepad Lor used to write out his dream at the resort. He was pacing a lot that morning, curt and bothered.

After their visit to Horace, Gale spent most of his vacation alone. The deepest conversation they had involved the plans once back in Peakwood. He agreed to let them stay with him for a while after getting married, but cautioned that *Eva will stay for a while* as well.

Guild Central in general was good to him, but Lor was glad to leave it. The entire apartment hall reminded him of Par, and he wasn't about to listen to Greg's advice to go find her.

He glanced at his e-disk. Damaetra, Dill, and Nico would be waiting for them at the fountain soon. Word finally traveled about Fowler's death, and Guild Central was more than willing to allow all four of them to leave. They might have had a little persuasion from a certain Reader at the front desk, but Lor wasn't sure if Livia was behind that decision or not.

The morning air had the aroma of petrichor from a light post-maelstrom rain shower. Dewy mist stuck to Lor's hair, weighing it down. Both Nico and Dill waited at the opposite side of the fountain with Damaetra, as an idling jumper waited across the driveway.

Lor punched Nico's shoulder. "How did your parents take the news?" he asked.

Nico tittered and swung his bag over his shoulder. He wore a pair of new slick black legs made by Dill and fashioned entirely of tech. They fit as if he were born with them. "Oh, they took it as well as I imagined they would. Which was not well at all. They were mad I even tried to connect with Niki again. And they were... rather upset that he cut off my legs."

"Well, duh."

"They paid me well for these new ones, though," Dill cut in with a smile, "even though I wasn't chargin' nothin'. I couldn't say no to a wad of plats."

Nico chuckled. "After calming down, they were fine with me moving out West."

The brothers' relationship with the Dicuses was only paper-thin. He glanced at Gale, who angrily shoved bags into the jumper while Damaetra tried to help. So many years he defied Gale, rolled his eyes, dismissed him. All those years pressing Gale, and he could have gotten rid of his problem for good and thrown his bastard stepson into the street. Not even a stepson, really. Just some bastard kid of his coworker and slave.

Stupid AND selfish...

"I know that look on your face. Stop it." Nico flicked Lor's shoulder.

"Ow! What look?" Lor rubbed the sore spot.

"That look where you go all distant, thinking less of yourself. I said stop it."

How well he knew him. Lor laughed.

"Besides," Nico continued, pausing to nod at Damaetra, "*she* thinks the world of you and agreed to *marry* you! I hope you can see yourself the way we all do someday."

He was right. Too much time was spent regretting his past actions. All he could do was forgive himself and just be better.

"You're right." Lor smiled. "Here's to a *new*-new beginning."

They loaded all the bags into the jumper and climbed inside, ready to look forward to the future and put their short time at Guild Central behind... and to put Par in the past.

The jumper ride to the station was weird. It was only just over a standard year ago, he came to Secas alone with Gale, now returning with three more people he loved. It was a new life, and he couldn't imagine living it without Damaetra, Nico, and Dill.

"You know, I haven't even checked my messages since we got back from the resort," Damaetra said, pulling out her e-disk and turning it on.

While she checked her messages, Lor turned to Nico and Dill. "I like the new legs, by the way. You sure know how to churn projects out fast, bud."

"Well, you know... you're dealing with a genius," Dill said with a smirk. "Seriously, though, I think I just do best when someone needs me. And Nico needed me *so* bad."

Nico jabbed Dill in the arm. "I was doing just fine hobbling around with my cane and having a blast trying to use the bathroom with one leg."

"Can they go fast too?"

"Oh yeah, I greased these stumps up like a roast at classic holiday."

Lor groaned. "Don't remind me of food... I haven't had anything good to eat in so long. Nothing but ration blocks."

"Hey, Loren," Damaetra murmured as the notifications on her e-disk buzzed one after the other. Each holochat flashed by too fast to read before the next one loaded. "I'm not sure what's going on, but I'm probably going to stay with my family for a little while when we get back West."

Once the messages stopped rolling in, she flicked through them. Caella, Eloria, Cae, Cae, Eloria... The black disk held several messages from her sisters. As she scrolled through them, the tone shifted from concern for each other, to arguing with each other, to blaming each other, and her e-disk served as mediator.

"I can't make sense of what they're saying," she said. Her face scrunched inward as she squinted at a message from Eloria rambling about Cae's state of mind and her own increasing headaches.

"Do you want me to come with you?"

Damaetra opened her mouth to answer when a zone-wide alert chirped through everyone's e-disk.

> **Breaking: New reports out of the Span show increased Weggevens activity on the outskirts of Kanckette. Incoming visitors are encouraged to avoid the area until local roundsmen can assess the issue and determine the appropriate course of action.**
>
> **Tent resident, Zane Gamboda, 10, was found dead during the 14th hour following the conclusion of the annual maelstrom. Roundsman investigation suggests unstable and rapid Weggevens onset of unknown origin. Developing story.**

Just a boy!

Greg was right... Maron really was holding back the disease. And Lor had widened the gap.

PART 2

Chapter 16

Desert Scum
Ayala

Second sun was close to setting, and the shimmering stars revealed themselves through the inky sky. Warm yellow lights flickered on, radiating from within the thin tent skins dotted along the underside of the train tracks in Kanckette's desert.

Ayala crouched beneath the tent flap, peering right and left for signs of any late stragglers returning to their derelict homes. Taking a hesitant step forward, she glanced down, searching for Mother's "gift" for any would-be intruders.

An electrical trap drew a thin line around their tent in the mustard sand. It buzzed in front of their entrance about the distance of two of her feet. Mother rigged the thing to keep out brigands with her skill in engineering.

Ayala was no fool. Even at her young age, she knew how to disable Mother's machines. Ayala watched her in secret during her bouts of creation to learn the right technique in shutting them down. A few quick thumb flicks of the internal switches with a turn of the coarse knob and the faint hum in the sand hissed into silence. Ayala had never seen the trap work, but Mother said it would stop a man's heart. The shadows of the desert were home to all kinds of men with hearts...

Once she rendered the trap a harmless line in the sand, Ayala took her first steps out into the cooled air. She had been severely bothered the day before—namely with the death of her late best friend, Zane. It wasn't the first death she'd witnessed, but it was one that rattled her core. Mother took it harder. Their bunker became Mother's grieving pit, and she shut herself down there for the evening.

Ayala wouldn't be long. She just wanted a short stroll alone, without question after question from the others. She didn't know what happened—it was so quick. One minute Zane was Zane, the next minute he was dead. Not just dead but burned up and ashy.

Something about that day made Ayala's belly go funny, as if she were being pulled somewhere. And then Zane died. Before seeing much of anything else, she ran away from him with her friends. Some say he just exploded, but Ayala overheard Mother telling a friend that Zane's skin turned to coal before splitting open and spilling out fire.

She didn't know anything about his skin, but she knew *her* skin crawled, sending tingles to her fingertips. The lingering scent of that cursed "fart" they smelled right before still sat in her nostrils, as if she could never smell anything sweet ever again.

Continuing her escape, the camp became a string of techlights behind her the farther she wandered into the desert. She lifted her hand. In the beds of her fingernails, Ayala observed an unusual dim orange radiance. The heat in her hands and the curling warmth swirling in her veins thrilled and nauseated her all the same.

The black of night was best to stare at them, away from tents and rings of techlight aiming at camp from the track spotter beams.

Was the stinky fart smell related to Zane's death? Even stranger... her glowing fingernails?

She rubbed her fingertips together, feeling a sort of liquid spreading like jelly under her skin, soothing out the tingling as she continued to wander farther from her tent... from Mother.

She knew better than to stray from the group, but she needed to think. Unknown terrors lurked among the dunes, and not all of them had to do with the weather. Predators lay in wait for any unsuspecting party to wander past to pilfer from, whether it was cash or flesh.

Not long before the incident with Zane, Ayala had her tenth birthday party with all her friends. Zane gave her a stone he found shaped like a shell and painted it in shades of purple and yellow, her favorite colors. She forgot to ask him where he got the paint in this place. Thinking about it made her sad.

The birthday party was when she realized all the boys crushed on her, including Zane. She took after Mother with her curves showing young. Mother said it was in a boy's nature to admire that which was beautiful, and that she, Ayala, was an object of beauty to them.

Be careful not to let them take it from you, Mother had warned. She didn't know what that meant but always wondered if it had anything to do with her father. In her imagination, Father was a handsome Danashi leader of a band of do-gooders that fell in love with Mother at first sight while stopping through camp. They fought for her affection, and Mother chose him out of all. He was smart, funny, and adored Mother until the day he died during a particularly wild maelstrom season in the desert. That was what she told herself.

Mother fussed over her constantly. She cared what Mother thought—she really did. But casting that aside for a moment, Ayala still chose to sneak out from under her nose. She only wanted a better look at the recent change in her body that she didn't think came with simply growing up.

She didn't tell Mother. Telling her would worry her more, and she was still mourning Zane. Ayala still mourned Zane, but not with tears, with her own mild version of rebellion. If she died, hopefully Mother wasn't the one to find her ash in the sand.

Blackness swallowed the light after she wandered far enough out that the row of tents was a distant glow under twinkling train lights. The lightless sky gave the yellow-orange in her fingertips a spotlight. It was enough to illuminate tiny capillaries on her finger pads like liquid fire. She swooshed her hand through the air, watching the light trails, then switched to wriggling her fingers to see the bright balls of her fingertips dance in front of her.

Too cool! She wriggled them some more and laughed, pressing her fingers together and watching the liquid fire squish and squeeze through them. Zane must have been too weak to handle it. That was the only thing that made sense.

She frowned at her dancing fingers.

Thinking about him made her sad again. His purple stone sat next to her pillow, where she held it at night. Sometimes she held it so tight the shell pattern dug into her flesh, taking almost a standard hour to go away in the morning. Mother would be worried for her now.

This is stupid. I should go back.

Just as she turned a heel to return to camp, a darker, slinking shadow crawled up her back and chilled the air around her.

"What'dwe have here, I wondeh?" a deep drone of a Northern drawl came from behind her, followed by the familiar sound of sand shifting beneath several pairs of feet.

Ayala swallowed and spun around to face the rounded belly of a man more than twice her height and three times her girth. Three other men stood behind him, snickering offbeat while stalking forward. This was not the story of love at first sight, like Mother's.

Ayala took a small step back, nearly tripping over a grouped set of mature cacti in the sand. The misstep made one of the other men chuckle louder. He was bony and short, with gaps spread throughout his mouth. The teeth he had were blackened to rot.

"Go away," she barked while continuing to back away from the men.

"Actually, I fink ye should come wif'us," the massive man said. A disjointed babble of agreeable grunts and sniggers came from his band of thugs.

Each backward step she took was overwhelmed by two of theirs. The warm air dried out her throat, choking any protest Ayala was desperate to utter. There were no friends here.

"N-no. I don't want to." The liquid in her fingertips swirled, feeling like needle points under her skin, and a burning sweat collected under two loosened chestnut buns atop her head.

The man laughed at her. "Oi, but ye'd *love* ta spen' the evenin' wif *me...*" The man stepped forward again, and the small techlight he carried cast a shadowy mask along a grizzled, fat-filled face. One of his eyes was covered in a hazy white film, the other a solid black iris. He used the black eye to scan Ayala's tiny maturing body and laughed.

Ayala whimpered, and a tear crawled down her face. *Stupid! Stupid!* It was stupid to leave the tent... and not worth the price Mother had warned her about. She imagined the trap stopping this man's heart.

"'Ey, I saw 'er first!" the man with rotted teeth said, tugging at the large man's arm.

It was a minor distraction, but she could use it to run. Everything in her body was hot and pumping, but her limbs froze. The men continued to argue while the others took sides and joined the fray.

Sprint, sprint, sprint!

If she could only unlock her joints, she could sprint toward the tents, get Mother's attention, and get the weapons.

Turning a foot, she readied herself to bolt. The oversized man snatched her wrist.

"She's mine!" he growled. With a sharp yank, he coiled his arm around her. The smell coming off his skin was like a rotting corpse—a smell she was too accustomed to out in the desert slums. Stinking sour sweetness, and the knowledge of what it was, never sat right with her. In reflex, she gagged.

After a few dry heaves, she knew her time was coming to an end. So she mustered every corner of her lungs to belt out a powerful scream. The sound coming from her slight frame pierced the air far and wide, like chitter birds in the early hours that always woke nearly every soul in the desert. If only she were a chitter bird.

The brute lifted her up, taking her farther from camp. She squealed and kicked, but a bite-sized girl like her was no match for a towering hulk, wrapping his stinking flesh around her. The men laughed at her struggle.

"Oh, I'm gonna love this one," the man said, belting out another laugh.

"Momma! Momma! Mommy!" Ayala pulsed her screams until her mouth filled with flesh squeezing over her face. The prickly hair coating his arms tickled her nose.

No, no, no! Mommy!

Ayala took in a deep breath and sank her teeth into his thick arm, locking her jaw shut until she tasted hot iron.

"Mother fu—!" The man dropped her and winced at the new bloodied crescent carved into him. "You stupid little bitch!"

The man shot out a clawed hand to grab her again, yanking her to her feet. Ayala dug her heels into the sand. Summoning the chitter bird within herself, she let out such a shriek that her would-be captors shrank back, covering their ears. She wouldn't... she *couldn't* stop screaming. Thick saliva pooled at her lip, mixing with the blood on her chin.

The tent line came to life with a wave of techlights flickering on and bobbing up and down toward them. Fresh panic stirred the burly brigand to attempt grabbing her again. If she could stand her ground against him for just a standard minute...

Ayala stumbled forward in his direction, but her wailing didn't skip a beat. It had to have been a reflex. In moments of fear or danger, Mother told her a person could do extraordinary things to survive. For Ayala, her body moved for her, as she welcomed the man's hold on her in a wrist-grip handshake.

The fire of her fingers seared into the thin skin covering his tendons. Orange light ignited, pouring from her nail beds, and wrapped curling ribbons of flame around his forearm.

"What in Gehenna?" the man said, dropping her wrist and backing away as the flare traveled up his arm. The thick hair coating his arm withered inward just before blackening the malodorous flesh into coal.

"Ayala!" Mother's voice cut through the din, reaching Ayala's ears like a song. She came with a line of people running toward them. Their lights danced over her as she stood in front of the burning man.

His chest heaved as he uttered profanities and swung an orange-and-yellow arm around in a frenzied oval.

Mother grabbed Ayala's arm, yanking her into the safety of her shadow. The blaze brightened Mother's face, and they backed away from the scene, jaws open. The formidable man was reduced to a squealing mass, writhing under Ayala's flames.

"He tried to take me, Mommy! He tried to take my beauty like you said!" Ayala cried, gripping the hem of Mother's skirt.

Mother wrinkled every inch of her face in an explosive fury before whipping out a small engineering piece to aim it toward the offender rolling around in the sand. If he hoped to smother the flame, he was too late. Ayala watched his flesh sizzle and burst.

A bolt barb popped from Mother's chamber, implanting itself deep into the meat of his leg. He jittered in place, no longer trying to put out the fire. His teeth pressed together as every muscle tightened and buzzed under Mother's barb. After the electricity ran its course, the man stopped, giving Ayala one last glare with his black eye before erupting into a volcano of scarlet and organs.

The lackeys scattered. Mother grabbed Ayala and pulled her into a gallop while shielding their heads from the red rain. Other campers yelped and ran with them, shouting to each other in a mess of words Ayala was too frenzied to understand.

"Baby, what were you doing out there? You know better than to wander after second sun!" Mother huffed back toward the tents with Ayala in her grip.

"I'm sorry, Mommy, I'm sorry!" Tears carved tracks down Ayala's dusty cheeks.

Mother sat her down inside, taking one last look out of the tent. Ayala knew she was disappointed in her. She didn't make it secret with exaggerated side-eye as she turned the coarse knob and flipped switches in reverse order to re-arm the trap. The tent light dimmed briefly as energy coursed through the reactivated trap.

"What were you thinking, turning off the trap? Where did you *think* you were going?" Mother crossed her arms.

Ayala only whimpered, her attacker's blood dried and flaking around her mouth.

Mother reached over to a dented can of water that sat tilted in the sandy floor—a "gift" of charity someone from the tracks above had thrown below. Cracking it open, she handed it to Ayala. "Wash out your mouth."

Ayala didn't argue, sloshing it around her mouth, then spitting into their waste bucket. "Mommy, I was curious, I'm sorry," she said.

Mother took a rag and wiped at Ayala's mouth. "Curious about what, baby?"

"About these, Mama." Ayala jabbed her hands out toward Mother like spears. The orange glow persisted at her nail beds.

Mother examined her daughter's fingers, turning her hand side to side. She hummed, running a finger over the strange nails. "They're very warm," she said, pressing one finger over Ayala's middle nail. "Hot, actually. What is this? Are you hurt?"

"I don't know. I don't think so. They been like this since being with Zane and the fart smell."

"Fart smell?"

Ayala twisted a knuckle over her eyelid and yawned. "Yeah, we all smelled it. Then Zane died."

Mother looked at Ayala with that same expression she didn't like. She was getting too tired to care. Unnaturally tired.

"What about your other friends that were there with you that day? Quint, Betta, and Treece?"

Ayala bit her lip and folded her hands in her lap, feeling the heat of her palms. "Um, well… Quint has hands like mine, but white. I don't know about Treece, but I know Betta's eyes are kinda *weird*. Like a cat."

Mother drew her daughter in and held her.

"Mommy?" Ayala said into Mother's shoulder.

"Yes, baby?"

"What's wrong with me? Is this what puberty is?"

"No, honey." She shook her head.

"I'm so *tired*." Ayala yawned and swayed. Her face paled, with wrinkles rippling at her hairline.

A tear streaked over Mother's cheek as her lip quivered.

"Just lie down, sweetheart. We'll get some rest and figure this out in the morning."

CHAPTER 17

Mother, Engineer
JACK

LINES OF HEAT WIGGLED INTO the atmosphere, like ghostly fingers rising from the dunes. Extra hot days were quiet, with most residents seeking the shade of tents and bunkers. Jack shuffled through the arid yellow grains, leaving a long dragging trail behind him that was swept up by the hot breeze.

The tan desert coat flapped behind him, blending into the background, leaving only his face, hair, and black goggles visible. A stranger would think he was nothing but a floating head.

It was a shame what happened between him and Par. They met here, not long after his parents died, just a dirty kid in the sand whom they called Cricket. Par never aged a day as he got taller, lankier, and more eccentric. She was like a mother to him. Pride was never an issue for him, but for some reason, it was pride that tore them apart. If she had just kept her mouth shut about the Yeunish, maybe things would have been different.

There was no sense in crying about the past... a force beyond his reckoning compelled him to shun her that day. And that was that.

Hazy dust particles were forced apart by a whomping gust pulsing from the first of the post-storm trains overhead. It revealed a group of children running around in the distance, laughing with each other.

Jack smiled at the wild children as he advanced on the camp. The closer he got, the more visible he became, until one small girl with short black hair noticed him walking toward them. She stood stiff-legged and staring. The other children noticed their friend stop and copied her, turning toward him.

They all screamed in unison, loud enough to rouse anything in a fifty-metre radius. In a panic, he scanned the field for signs of residents coming to check out the fracas. The last thing he wanted was to cause a scene. He tamped his hands down, hoping to calm the children.

"Jack! Jack! Jack!" their voices carried through the camp as they ran to him, each wrapping their tiny arms around his legs and giggling while pulling him toward the tents. He stumbled stiff-legged in their grasp, trying not to laugh.

"We missed you, Jack!"

"Yeah! Where've you been!"

"Is Niki with you?"

Jack patted the head of the girl with short black hair. "No, I'm sorry, Niki's not with me."

The girl's eyes were strange and animalistic, forcing him to double-take as she smiled up at him innocently.

Don't stare at the poor girl.

Jack grinned, then put his arm around her shoulder for a light squeeze.

"Well, look who finally came *crawling* back." A voice he knew all too well approached from behind, and he smiled to himself. A rhythmic hiss of bare feet made bold steps through the sand, getting closer and closer. He spun around and saw her.

A deeply curved woman in a long tan skirt cinched at the waist caught up to him. Her loose white linen blouse shifted when her arms swayed at her sides. Desert life had been kind to her when he was away, deepening her copper glow. Wavy red-brown hair trailed behind her, swaying in the breeze.

"Hello, Jack," Mother said as she planted her feet in front of him. The grin she wore reminded him of the ones she made when they were kids, as she cooked up a bit of mischief.

"Verena." His voice cracked, and it made her giggle. Pale cheeks flushed crimson, and he tried hard to be nonchalant about it. "Where's Ayala?"

Verena's sly grin soured at the mention of her daughter. "She's lying down right now. In fact, I'm glad you're here. Can you come see her?"

"Is everything alright?"

Without answering, Verena nodded toward the group of children. "Jack will visit with you all very soon, alright? I need to take him to visit with Ayala."

The children moaned and murmured, running off to where they came from. Jack took in a deep breath as Verena led him toward her tent near the end of the row.

Only their feet raking through the sand made a sound under the breeze that whistled over Jack's ears. Verena wore the mask he knew too well—a steadfast shell of strength she intended for the sake of the children hid a troubled mess underneath. Something was definitely wrong.

The daughter his childhood friend bore alone made him soft, as if the girl were his own. Had he been able to protect Verena, perhaps life could have turned out different. Verena could have been his... but any child she would have borne him would have been cursed as a Yeunish freak.

The day Ayala was conceived was the day Jack met the monster inside of him when he crushed the desert rapist's balls in the sand. They popped like gory water bags as the man screeched louder than carrion fowl. The sack-less coward crawled back to his hovel in the middle of nowhere, leaving Verena half-dead in the sand and filled with the last of his seed.

It took more than a standard month for her to heal as he fed her through tubes and mended her bones with under-baked formulations. Tireless days passed before Jack finally sowed ingenuity during his frantic war to salvage Verena's life and the one growing inside her.

A formulation, crafted from desperation, and unlike any before it or any since, became the salvation to any Weggevens. A bit of green and white blended with a touch of human silver... his own silver.

The draw marks still made their impressions into the back of his right arm after asking Paerli to pull *just a little* during one of her visits. It was for Verena.

Then it didn't work.

The real cure was a simple step away. The silvery-pearl green formulation was only a precursor to the ultimate flesh renewal: *Verdigris Mend*.

All it needed was a splash of gold.

At the time, Jack never asked Paerli where she got the gold, but the formulation worked, and he didn't care. As he thought about it, the chances were strong that the gold came from a weak and helpless Maron while stretched over the breach.

The green miracle formula had Verena on the mend, yet mostly bedridden as her belly continued to swell. It pained him to watch her grow another man's child.

The day Ayala was born, she was quieter than the dunes at dusk. Rather than scream, her huge hazel eyes over fattened cheeks trailed over the medic, and attendant, and everything in the room before settling on Jack... and she stared at him for an age. Any hatred or envy he carried vaporized, and his only wish was that Ayala was his daughter.

Verena pushed the tent fold to the side and ducked to enter. Jack followed, heart pounding.

"She's been sleeping, mostly." Verena's smoky voice hit him hard after the bout of silence.

Jack hastened to kneel next to the girl lying on a thin mat. The buns she wore at her crown were messy from tossing in sleep. Despite the heat, she had not one drop of sweat on her copper-colored skin.

Putting a pale hand over her cheek, he fought to make sense of what he saw. Wrinkled hairline, scaly flesh... he pried open an eye to see a hazy film. "She's a *Weggevens*?" he hissed.

Verena nodded, biting her lower lip. "Not a kind I've ever seen before."

When Jack lifted her hand, light filtered through her skin, showing off hundreds of little capillaries and veins. As he held on to her, the heat became so unbearable he recoiled, dropping her hand.

"They're hot, aren't they?" Verena knelt next to Jack, putting the back of her hand on Ayala's forehead.

Jack frowned and craned his neck to make sure the tent was closed to curious outsiders. Once satisfied, he pulled a silver-laced syringe from his utility pocket. The remedy Ayala needed would send him to banishment. No questions asked.

Sliding the needle into Ayala's arm, he injected a full adult dose, which made her stir, grunting and rolling to the side. After a moment, the light and heat crawled back down to just her fingertips.

"The heat was consuming her. What happened?"

Verena put her face in her hands and shook her head. "I don't know." Her voice was muffled against her palms. "There was an... *event*."

"What kind of event?" Jack stood, observing Ayala's small twitches as she lay there. Her mouth parted as she sank deeper into sleep.

Verena struggled through her explanation of Zane's death—the spontaneous combustion that rocked the community and changed her daughter. Despite leaving out the messier details, the strong shell she wore cracked.

"He was Ayala's best friend," her voice quivered. "I couldn't even tell you what happened, I was doing the damn laundry. I should have been paying more attention to them. To her."

Jack hummed. His non-answer wasn't much consolation for Verena, but it was the breach. It had to be. "She'll have to learn how to control it."

Jack patted Verena's shoulder awkwardly, willing himself to show compassion when he didn't know how, even if he loved her. The man she needed was in him somewhere. If only he could just be normal.

Verena brushed a tear from her cheek and nodded, putting on her fake plastic grin.

"There aren't many Wegs out there that know *how* to control it. And she's just a girl," she said.

Jack wrinkled his nose and rubbed his chin. "I have doses for her until she does. The same ones I used to give Niki and the one I gave her now."

"How's Niki doing?"

Jack shrugged. "Don't know. He betrayed his twin and ran off."

"Niki has a twin?" Verena raised an eyebrow.

"Long story." He glanced over his shoulder again to make sure the tent flap was sealed, then pulled the goggles from his eyes to rest them on his head. He blew out a puff of air and rubbed the circles that had formed around his eyes. How little she really knew about the bugger that was like a little brother to her.

Verena closed the gap between them and brushed sand from his cheek. "It's been a while since I've seen your face," she said. "Look at these circles around your eyes. Let me get a cool towel."

Without letting him speak, she went to the back of the tent and opened a hatch in the floor only large enough to fit one. As her head disappeared below, Jack thought it would be better to go down there with her.

The bunker itself was the same width of the tent but deeper, allowing more clearance for his tall frame. He was hot, and the cooler bunker would feel nice.

Yes, that was the reason.

Descending the splintered ladder into the bunker, he heard her humming to herself at the opposite side. Verena opened and closed a series of chest doors and drawers, making a symphony of squeaks and squeals as the hinges protested. Searching for the perfectly cool towel, she hummed the lyrics to the song he recognized at once.

> *Voe`sh ka dessniah`h*
> *Kalech voe ani`e*
> *Oma`sh en kash o`shtei*
> *Zandea ban`toi ey...*

Old Yeunish. A long dead language, hundreds of years before the decline of Foscan. She knew it because he knew it. The song was the last he remembered of his real parents, burned in his memory.

As children, she swore to keep his secret. As teens, he taught her his lullaby. As an adult, she sang it with perfection.

It put him in a trance, watching her, remembering the day he told her about himself and teaching her the song. Why did she sing it now?

He wanted to say something. He wanted to march up to her, spin her around to face him, and tell her how he felt all those years. All he did was stand and watch her as a graceless clod with throat trembling in conflict with his mind debating whether the words should come out.

Why am I like this?

"Oh, you came down," Verena said as she slid up to him with a tatty gray cloth in her hand.

"Y-yeah," he muttered.

"Here, let's take a look." She patted the chilled cloth along his eyebrows and temples.

She was so close. The cloth did feel nice pressed over the goggle lines in his skin.

"I rigged my water reservoir with a coolant sleeve," she said while examining his face. "It's pretty simple really, but the material wasn't easy to get, otherwise I would have made one for everyone."

Beautiful so close, it was hard to believe Verena was an Engineer.

"It's nice," Jack said.

"Well, it's been a lifesaver on especially hot days, that's for sure." She continued to pat his face with the cloth. The other hand pressed into the hollow of his cheek, where his bad habit of grinding his teeth created a tough ball of sinew. She was so close.

"I love you," he blurted out. Verena froze and tilted her head. "I mean, I l-love your coolant sleeve."

Idiot.

She lowered her voice and smiled, continuing to pat his eyes with the cool cloth. "It's pretty great, isn't it?"

"Mm-hmm."

"My favorite thing about it is how... *reliable* it is."

"A-and it will always be there for you," he said.

"Yes, I can count on that. And I can depend on it to help protect me and my daughter." Her eyes, her lips, her face were so close.

"Always."

"Ja`*k*aeyur," she whispered.

It had been so long since he heard his real name. He'd been starved of hearing it spoken for too long, and coming from her lips did something to him. Only Verena knew it and used it in secret, pronouncing it perfectly as if it were her own language.

She draped an arm around his neck and kissed him. A grown man who spent tens upon tens of standard years of his life in hiding, dodging curious strangers and trusting mostly no one, had never been kissed. Despite the harsh desert winds prone to crack even the most supple skin, her face was soft. He didn't know what to do.

"There you are!" the child-like squeal came from above as Ayala's face poked down into the bunker.

Jack jumped and spun around while Verena flipped her hair back and brushed wrinkles from her blouse. The little girl's face spread into a wide grin the moment she spotted him.

"Jack! I had a dream about you!" She tumbled into the bunker and ran to him, slamming hard enough into him to make him stumble back. She wrapped her arms around his slender waist and squeezed. The drug worked fast through her.

"I missed you," he said. The taste of Verena's mouth lingered on his lips.

"You won't believe it, but I can make fire from my hands!"

That news hurt his heart a little. She had no idea what it meant to be a Weggevens... the careful planning and pains that came with a life draining out. She was just a girl.

"I heard," he said. "How are you feeling?"

"I feel so good! Like I just had the best nap ever!"

"Yes, well, let's get you something to eat," Verena said, tugging on Ayala's arm to pry her off Jack. "Go on up and I'll be there soon."

Ayala bobbed her head sharply and crawled back up the ladder. Verena turned back to Jack.

"We have a lot to talk about," she said.

"Yes, we do."

Verena clicked her tongue and grinned, strolling up to him and planting her mouth over his again. It was a fleeting moment, but one he would tuck away next to his parent's lullaby.

"Then we'll talk," she said as she pulled away to follow after Ayala.

Once Verena had fully made it up the ladder, Jack heard Ayala ask, "Is Jack going to be my dad now?"

Allowing Ayala her space to eat lunch while avoiding any awkward "dad" conversations, Jack ducked under the tent, stepping back into the open desert. He laughed to himself at the thought, but his mind held on to that moment. The two most important people in his world had accepted him back.

The heat squeezed at him, causing even his first knuckles to sweat. He didn't like the heat, or the grit, which stuck to every sweaty surface on his skin. A filmy haze persisted in the air, coating silhouettes of the children playing in the distance with an ochre-colored veil. The bunker was much more preferable than this.

Jack sighed, squinting through the haze as he scanned the area. While the goggles were good at hiding his eyes, they weren't great at staving off smudges. A few tents down, a smeary figure stood, heavily cloaked, the tail hem undulating in the agitated breeze.

Something about the stranger's stance was familiar. Twitchy. The stranger was engaged in conversation with the residents of that tent while using erratic hand gestures. The more Jack watched, the more he understood.

Of course he came back.

Tent city was his home, and now that Par was lost to Gehenna, he most likely felt obligated to return. Jack wished he hadn't.

He allowed his gaze to linger too long when Hare turned and spotted him. For a moment, there was a subtle flinch of a foot—a momentary bid to flee. He stood firm, locking eyes with Jack for a stretch of time that could have been a standard hour. After an eternity of staring each other down, Hare relaxed his posture and made a wicked grin, turning around as if Jack weren't there. The edge of his cloak disappeared into the neighbor's tent.

STRONGER TOGETHER

NEW JOB ALERT

Wall roundsmen for evening shift. Must be alert and focused, ready to defend against con-men with Guild abilities. Applicants 35 years and younger only. Weekly pay: pL 10,000

EXCLUSIVE

As the maelstrom calms and travel opens, Audun reminds all citizens to stay vigilant, and report any ill health to your local emergency medic.

While the Seven Cities work on a solution to the Weggevens epidemic, we want to thank you for your continued support. It is important to remember to report any strange activity, or stray Yeuni to the authorities.

The current bounty on the Yeunish has increased to pL 80,000 due to the likelihood of their involvement in the above mentioned epidemic.

Stay proud, stay alert, and Audun wishes you all the best for you and your loved ones.

The Wind Through The Tree
Loren / Gale

THE HOUSE SMELLED THE SAME, but different. A lingering aroma of Gale's tea hid under a cold, stark emptiness.

"Nice house!" Dill said as he gaped around at the walls.

Lor took a lot of things for granted. Dill certainly never knew the kind of luxuries Lor didn't realize he possessed. Gale had been great to him.

"Thanks," Gale said, flipping a switch and waving his hand at the sensor in the upper corner.

After signaling the sensor, the house lit up.

Dag the Small, Lor's actual mother, trotted into the room, bowing at Gale with her usual quivering stance as if she was terrified. Gale glanced at Lor and sighed, then nodded at Dag. "You can stop acting, he knows."

Instantly, her shoulders relaxed, and she put her hands up to her chest.

"Dad! You couldn't ease her into it?"

"Why drag it out?"

Lor sighed. He couldn't look at her. Not right away. He felt her eyes boring into him—those white, eerie eyes that he knew used to watch him at night. He couldn't blame her for keeping the secret. After he learned the truth about her, he imagined all the things he would talk to her about: everything about his real father, his heritage, their history... he even had a few conversations with Nico and Dill about what he would say... but he found himself choked on embarrassment. It must have been hard for her to watch him grow up, treating her like an ordinary servant. A *slave*.

A conversation picked up between Dill and Gale, droning behind him as he continued to refuse to look at his own mother. Not long after, the front door swung open, slapping against the opposite wall as Eva hobbled inside with three large bags. Nico rushed toward her and grabbed two of them, standing there frozen with the two large bags in his hands. The interruption was a perfect excuse to draw Lor's attention toward something other than the awkward reunion with his mother.

"Thanks," Eva's voice rasped from her throat as she dropped the last bag to the floor. "I'm Eva, Lor's sister." She held out a hand toward Nico.

Was he flustered? A blush swelled over his cheeks as he continued to hold the heavy bags and stumble through his own introduction.

"You can put those down, you know," she said, still sticking her hand out.

Nico plopped the bags to the floor to shake her hand in an awkward exchange typically reserved for Lor. If Nico was lucky, she only found it adorable.

Life in the cities had been good to Eva. Padded curves in all the right places from actual food found in Audun, and the most radiant she'd ever been... Though he didn't say it, his face said it all; Nico was obsessed.

All curves and bouncy hair, she went down the hall as Nico watched.

Lor leaned in and said, "Was your hand all limp and sweaty when you touched my sister?"

"What? No!" Nico turned a deeper shade of scarlet that gave him a boyish charm.

Gale's house was modest, with two extra rooms aside from his own. Lor had the basement level where he'd stay with Nico and Dill, Eva had her room to herself, and Dag stayed in the other. As long as he remembered, they never had that many people staying at once. Things would get better once Eva went back to the cities and everyone else found jobs.

Leading Nico and Dill to the basement, Lor stopped for a moment to see the flashing holopics on the wall. None of them had changed... a colorful one of him with Gale, Eva, and his "fake" mother Surai at the cold beach flashed by.

"Just put all your stuff down there." Lor pointed down the stairs, pausing to watch the images scroll.

"You sleep in the dungeon, do you?" Dill smirked, tromping down the steps, forcing groans from the cracks in the wood as he went. Nico followed, leaving Lor on the landing.

It was *this* frame... he plucked the one three spots to the left from the wall and swiped through until the image of him and Dag popped up. Holding his index finger on the projected image to keep it from moving past, he pressed down on his own baby chest. He was so ordinary. Nothing like any Yeuni he'd seen. Even he struggled to believe it. But Gale wouldn't lie to him. Par was clearly disgusted with him when she spat it in his face.

There she was—his Foscan mother holding him, feeding him, and gazing at him in a way he imagined a mother would. Either that, or the truth was that they had a Foscan servant weirdly obsessed with him. He laughed at the thought.

So what now? There was no way he'd be able to have children. They'd all be cursed. Or at least, there was a chance they'd be cursed. If he did the math, they'd have a seventy-five percent chance of having Anglian children and a twenty-five percent chance coming out Foscan. The rules of Yeunish genetics didn't follow normal patterns. It wasn't a very interesting topic either. Maybe a ten percent chance?

He snapped the frame back to the wall, watching their picture cycle to Gale at a medic awards ceremony. Leaving the holopics behind, he followed his friends downstairs to lay out the rules of his room before anyone claimed his bed.

Second sun sank below the horizon, casting the last of its purple hue through the crack in Gale's top window. He sat in bed, reading a book with his readers propped over the tip of his nose. After all the things he learned in the past month, his mind wasn't really on the text. Loren's near-death experience, now getting married, work, lost time off... Greg. There was nothing he could do for his old college friend anymore, but what new revelation lay in wait, threatening to sink his world all over again?

Rubbing his face in reflex, it was a bad habit, he knew, but the tingling warmth of blood flushing back into his cheeks moved his sinuses. They were perpetually tight, giving him nasty headaches. The dust in the air, always floating around and triggering allergies—he made a note to ask Dag about the home filters.

The book *whumped* closed in his fist, and he stared at the cover. As he studied the gilded lettering on top of the loaded medical tome, there was a demure rap at his door. It was about time. He slid his readers to the top of his head and cleared his throat.

"Come in," he said.

The little Foscan servant poked her nose through a crack in the door, white eyes gleaming in the dark slit. Gale waved her inside and sat up.

"Els'daegal," he said, smiling.

She stepped inside, turning to glide the door shut. It clicked quietly in place. Loose linen fabric swayed as she slipped toward him, draped over her features and buttoned up the front with pearly clasps. Her black hair cinched into a thick tail, brushing the top of her perfectly round fundament.

The only light in the room came from a soft yellow glow of techlight at his bed table. Her teasing curves in the dim light were simply inappropriate. It had been a long time, and he hurt just to look at her.

She leaned across him to pull the thick wool covering across his waist. Every fiber of that blanket ran itchy fingers across his legs. The scent of her neck as she passed over him had the crisp note of summer snow under a pale caryopsis tree. It intoxicated him.

"Vous'h cau oesle'te?" she asked in a smoky whisper.

Guests were in the house, and the walls were thin. Yet, he ran his thumb and forefinger along the hem of her loose shirt, tugging it ever so slightly. "Cau oesle."

Those eyes found his wandering hands, but he couldn't help himself. Every word he read in that medical tome flew from his mind, and all he felt was the burning in his chest.

She hummed and brushed his hand away, only for it to slither over her backside.

"Now?" she asked, pulling open the top drawer of the bed table to grab a small blue box.

He didn't answer with words, only with his hands as she swatted each one away with a giggle.

"Mae'guae haer," she said while drawing out a silver ring from that blue box and sliding it down Gale's middle finger.

Gale reached up to her pearled clasps, thumbing them open. The shirt hung over her curves, exposing her pale stomach.

"Mae'guae haer."

"Mm-hm." She smirked, kissing the coarse stubble covering his head before ripping his shirt off and tossing it to the floor with his readers.

That was the first good bout of sleep Gale had in a while. He stared at the ceiling wearing a satisfied grin. Dag stirred next to him, her hot thigh brushing up against his. The logistics of getting her out of the room before others woke up weren't at the forefront of his empty head.

Dag settled into him again, half-asleep with her long hair pooled around her in a shiny black puddle. The tie she used to gather it back shimmied down the tail during their nightly activities. It sat on the pillow.

"Gans'te?" she asked in a groggy stupor.

"Is that what you think of the first thing you open your eyes?" he teased, pulling her closer and pretending to grind her leg.

"Oh, *Master* T." She drawled with feigned hysteria. "Master T, you are more beast than man!" She giggled and hid under the blanket.

Lor woke up to the sound of his toilet activating. For a moment, he forgot where he was, but his eyes finally focused and told him he was in his bedroom.

Nico had abandoned his padded slab on the floor for an early morning pee.

Snapping on the techlight, Lor found the shadowed curl of Dill in the big red chair facing his bookshelf. He would have offered to share the bed, but Dill kicked in his sleep. The last thing Lor wanted was a cracked jaw.

His e-disk sat on the nightstand. As he went to grab it, that same book on Law sat there where he left it before leaving for the program. Things had changed so much.

Picking it up, he thumbed through the pages until he saw a single paragraph on the Yeunish.

> As a class of people known for their propensity toward chaos and
> disorder, it is the roundsman's responsibility to secure the safety
> of citizens by aiding in their capture. Proper encouragement
> of peers to do the same is a requirement, and to do otherwise is
> considered insubordination.

"Chaos and disorder, huh?" Lor whispered to the pages. "I think you have it wrong, *book*." He slapped the tome shut with a soft *whump!*

The real curiosity was whether society actually believed passages like those. Audun had a grip on the citizens, he knew that much. A grip tight enough to squeeze out any risk of defiance.

Lor stood and slid the book into the shelf quietly, opting to pull out the green bound book on Guilds, the spine of which he'd never cracked. Just as he was about to find the chapter on Reapers, his stomach rumbled, and he put the book down in the same spot on his nightstand where the Law tome used to be. A cup of coffee with breakfast would hit the spot. Then he could read.

Throwing on a black tee with a pair of lounge pants, he pattered upstairs to the kitchen. The house was quiet and dark, with only peeling sweaty feet stepping across marble making any sound. The first light of day sprayed an overcast haze of gray light into the halls. Flicking on the overhead lamp, he opened a cabinet to pull out a small white coffee mug that had the emblem for Peakwood Academy printed on the side.

No coffee packets were left in the drawers as he patted around in them, and he didn't remember how to make coffee the "long" way. Gale could show him again. This time, he would remember and do it himself the next time.

At the end of the hall, Lor made his way toward Gale's bedroom. When he tipped an ear to the door, he heard the faint bumping and rustling noises of a man awake and moving around.

"Hey, Dad, do you think you can show me how to make cof—" He slid Gale's partition open.

In the dim light of the room, Gale sat upright on his bed, holding on to his mother—the servant. They hugged tightly. Very tightly. Lor had never seen so much bare skin.

"Loren, don't you *knock?*" Gale shouted, grabbing the wool blanket to sweep over Dag's indecency. She dipped her head below the covering.

Lor dropped the mug, and it shattered on the dark wood floor. He bent to pick the shards up with shaking fingers.

"Get out!" Gale scolded.

Lor jumped and slammed the partition shut, catching a shard under the bottom and slicing a gouge into the wood.

He huffed down the hallway through the flickering holopics in their frames, catching random flashes of Gale in various poses and smiles, and all he could think of was his stepfather banging his mother. The wide grin of triumph... it mocked him.

Nico poked his head from the basement door, yawning and stumbling into the hall as Lor passed.

Running fingers through his perfectly curled hair, he muttered, "I heard a crash. Is everything alright?"

Lor cleared his throat and let out a loose chuckle. "I'm pretty sure I just walked in on Gale *doing* my mom."

Nico stopped and gaped, fingers still twined through coils of dark blonde hair. "Oh?"

Lor shook his head sharply with a quick grunt, then continued toward the kitchen with Nico slogging behind.

"I guarantee he'll want to talk to you about that later." Nico yawned again with a chuckle, taking a seat at the island.

"Maker, I hope not." Lor fumbled through the cabinets again, searching for a new mug. Hopefully not one that had Gale's achievements or associations painted on it.

After finding a plain blue mug with no labels, Lor went to the ration panel. His shaking fingers finally found the trap activator, and the doors in the counter hissed open, raising an empty plinth. Of course. He sighed with a throaty edge.

"I guess my mom was too busy *humping* Gale to order the breakfast rations," he grumbled. Nico eyed him curiously as he paced around, swinging the empty blue mug. He wasn't really that mad. At least, not at their *fun.*

Puke. Doing what he did in a house full of people, and Lor was the lucky one to find out. It made the task of reconnecting with his real mom that much weirder.

The slicing sound of Gale's partition sliding open made the hair on his arms stand up. It was Dag scuttling through the hall with a handful of white ceramic shards in her palm and a web of sweaty hair laced across her forehead. She wore a green striped robe with the initials "GAT" embroidered on the left breast.

"I'm sorry, Loren," she uttered, dumping the shards in the bin and darting over to the panel to order breakfast rations. "You want coffee, yes?" With quick and shallow breaths, they were the first words he'd ever heard her speak... and it was *beyond* awkward.

"A-ah, yes, please... M-mom," he said, closing his eyes to avoid looking at her. Their undulating shadows pulsed over his color static.

Ugh. His eyes snapped back open.

Gale sauntered into the kitchen as Dag made the final ration orders in the wall panel.

"Loren," he said, clearing his throat. "Can I have a word?"

Nico shot a look at Lor. "Uh, I'm gonna check on Dill," he said before springing from the chair and disappearing down the hall.

Dag bowed toward them out of habit and scurried to her actual room.

Gale craned his neck to watch her disappear into her room and *whap* the door shut. When he was satisfied they were alone, he glared at Lor.

"What are you looking at *me* like that for? *You're* the one stuffing my mom."

"Don't talk *filth* like that," Gale warned.

"Sorry, I don't know what else to call it."

"You could have said nothing at all." His face was pink even before rubbing it with his rough hands. "Anyway, I'm sorry you saw that. We hoped we could tell you about us *after* you got married."

"Why wait at all? Why didn't you tell me when it started?"

"Loren"—Gale moved over to the cabinets, searching for a mug—"you were too young to understand."

"Too young? What are you saying? Was this going on when Surai was still alive?"

Gale choked. "Maker, no! Never. I loved Surai... we *both* did." He patted a hand around the shelf and frowned. "You broke my school mug," he muttered.

"Sorry."

Gale sighed and pulled out a different white mug with a green plus sign. It was a work mug that Lor also wanted to break, but by throwing it. And not by accident. A newly installed hot water spigot near the sink splashed steaming water into the cup.

Lor watched him and furrowed his brow. "So you've been having a weird affair with Dag—whom I now know to be my real mom—ever since I was a kid? Does Eva know about it?"

Gale poured tea crystals from a dry packet into his hot water and stirred. The spoon struck the sides in a rhythmic clanging that reminded him of funeral bells. Gale smirked. "It's not an affair if you're married."

And there it was—the glint of silver wrapped around Gale's middle finger. Had Gale said nothing, it would have gone unnoticed.

"You and Dag are *married?*"

"Going on thirteen years." Gale sipped the hot liquid.

"Gee, Dad, did you even wait for Surai's body to go cold before putting your hands all over my mom?"

Gale slammed the mug down, sloshing light brown liquid onto the white marble as the spoon abandoned the cup altogether, clattering to the floor. "Don't you *ever* talk to me like that again!"

"There's the Gale I remember." Lor rolled his eyes. It was in his nature to poke at the danger... a stubborn habit that he was too weak to break. He flinched, waiting for the wicked punishment for his "smart mouth," but it didn't come.

Gale blew out a whistle, rubbing his already red scalp. He tempered himself and drew air in through his nostrils in a slow, steady breath. "I understand why this would upset you," he grumbled through clamped teeth.

"Do you? Everything I've known my entire *life* has been a lie. Where was my real dad while you two were busy *screwing?*" There it was again.

"Loren, by the Maker, if you talk to me like that again..." Gale flared his nostrils. His skin was red enough that Lor thought his brain might boil in the cauldron between his ears.

That was enough. The beast had been sufficiently poked. Lor dropped his arms on the counter and pressed his forehead into the dark shallow of his folded elbows. "Sorry." His voice came muffled through his arms. The mug scraped against the counter, followed by a careful slurp.

"I didn't lie to you about your father. He died before you were born," Gale said after a scratchy swallow.

Lor turned his head in his arms, staring off into the living area. He didn't even know his real dad's name. The story they told him was that he was just some guy Surai knew from school, and that he was a Shepherd who volunteered to transfer to the mountains of the far north. The lie he believed growing up was not that he was dead. That was a nugget he learned not long ago when he found out who he really was. Everything was a lie... Gale had to know how horrible that felt.

"How did he die?" Lor mumbled with a vacant gaze in the opposite direction. His eyes traced the fireplace mantle, with carved marble ivy laced around it.

The mug scraped against the counter surface again. "He had a genetic wasting disease. I couldn't do anything for him, and he couldn't help himself."

"Did I inherit it?"

"Thankfully, no. I had you checked."

"So who was he?"

"His name was Haedrian. Haedrian Vasei. So I guess technically your name is Loren Vasei."

Lor heaved a sigh and turned his head toward his stepfather, still laying over his arms. "No," he said, "it's Loren Turtingas. Even if it's not as pretty."

Gale chuckled. "I'm sorry you had to learn all of this... like this."

"How did my family end up at your doorstep?"

Gale pulled his lips inward, then sucked his teeth. "Haedrian was a medic at my office. He really was a smart guy. But you got your stubbornness from your mother."

Lor couldn't help but smile. He tried to picture the meek servant as a bossy back-talker that put Gale in his place many times over thirteen years. And yet, he still loved her, apparently. Foscans weren't a race he personally was very attracted to, but there had to be something about Dag that would make two men risk their livelihoods and their *lives* to be with her.

"Was my mom Haedrian's servant, or did they meet through some sketchy dating e-net to make a Yeunish transaction for the thrill of breaking the law?" Lor sat up and pointed at himself.

Gale tittered. "You're not a... Yeunish *transaction*." He sipped the tea and closed his eyes. "But you are so much like your mom. And yes, before you ask, we butt heads sometimes. But you were right the first time—she was his servant. Somewhere along the way, they fell in love and made you."

"It's forbidden for them to do that. Everybody knows."

"Yes, it is, I'm fully aware. But your father and I were friends. I even knew them before she got pregnant with you—which is why Surai and I were the only ones he trusted to keep it quiet. And I did... even from you."

Lor put his head back, face down. "If she's your wife, why do you call her a slave's name?"

Gale swallowed his tea hard and laughed. "What, Dag? That's short for Els'daegal, her Foscan name. I added 'the Small' as a formality for the Seven Cities. She thought it was funny. You know... because she's short."

"Ellzdegel?"

"You'll learn how to pronounce it, eventually."

"Dag is a weird nickname."

"So it is. But it's hers."

Lor opened the ration trap again, happy to see the order completed with stacks of breakfast blocks and his favorite sarga fruit next to packets of coffee.

"So, how did you get away with marrying her?"

Gale picked up the newslite that came with the rations and plunked it in front of him. "Everyone has their secrets."

"Why the act, then? Why hide it all?"

Gale smacked his lips and leaned back in the chair. "We made a plan. Thinking about it now, it almost seems silly, but we thought it was best for you."

"So just keep Lor in the dark and all is well..." Lor said, scratching his chin mockingly.

"Here's the thing, son. I'm sure you're aware that your heritage is a... problem."

"Yeah, I get that."

"How well did you understand that as a boy?"

Lor chewed his lip.

"Exactly. We hid your heritage from you and hid our relationship because we didn't want anything to happen to you. I promised her I would protect you."

"So... why were you mean to her again?"

Gale pushed his lips forward. "I was only mean to her in front of you and Eva. It was all a ruse. Trust me, I always made it up to her."

"Gross."

"Is it really that gross to you?"

Lor clicked his tongue. "No. Not really, I guess. I guess it's better that she's with you than some other random jerk. Does Eva know any of this?"

"Not yet, but I think she's suspected us for years. Either way, I'd appreciate if you didn't tell her."

Lor put his hands up and shrugged.

"Anyway," Gale said, blowing out a heavy breath and raising his eyebrows, "I have to get back to work. Someone has to pay for this house full of people."

CHAPTER 19

Slim Silver

JACK

THE FRESH YOUNG WEGGEVENS SEEMED to respond well to her new ability, even if it had the potential to kill her. Verena thought it would be a good idea for Jack to stay with her for a while as they "figured out" what to do about Ayala's condition. No mention of their brief kiss, but he knew it was on her mind. It never left his.

It was windier than usual, blowing hot grains of sand everywhere. It collected around the seal of his goggles and irritated the surrounding skin. Ayala was unbothered by the weather as she ran around laughing with her strange friends.

If Verena allowed him to, he would like to brew some more Witis Rejuvenate for Ayala in the bunker. There were only a few syringes left, and his silver supply waned. As much as he didn't want to, he debated finding Par to get more. On his way home from Guild Central, he didn't expect anyone from camp needing the formula, especially one of his two favorite people. Who would?

Hare had come out and talked with him briefly that morning. *No hard feelings*, he told him. Jack knew he was just trying to get on his good side for more of the drug. The problem was... he didn't have more.

His sand-colored coat tails flapped in the breeze as he stared off into the undulating dunes. Beyond those dunes was the cavern where they left her. How long would it take to get there?

A warm presence approached him, and the hem of a light blue skirt waved next to his legs. Verena leaned her head against his shoulder, her hair smelling of the ozone that leaked from her engineering crafts.

"Ayala really loves you," she said, staring off beyond the dunes alongside him.

Jack sighed, pressing his molars together. He loved that little girl like his own. That Weggevens sickness couldn't have chosen anyone else at this cursed camp. It had to choose her. It was his duty to take care of her... to make sure she didn't die by it.

"She should have been *my* daughter," he said, not thinking too hard about what he was saying. He'd grown tired of holding himself in. Strange, gawky, and wooden, just because he felt a certain way, it changed nothing about himself on the outside.

Verena stood upright, stepping in front of him. The blue skirt billowed and blew in the breeze, twining with his coat and tugging at them.

"She *is* your daughter," she said.

Jack glanced over at Ayala, still running circles with her friends in some game he didn't know. The soft pressure of hands slid around his waist as Verena's cheek came to rest on his chest. He held her, taking in the smell of electricity in her hair.

"Am I interrupting?" a familiar drawl poured out from behind Jack. Verena popped her head up to look and her face brightened.

"Niki! You're here!" she said, giving him a tight hug. It was the first time Jack had seen "The Hare" smile with joy—real joy. Not the kind that came from sarcastic remarks and insults aimed at his brother.

"How is the new job?" she asked, brushing sand from his hair.

Hare looked up at Jack and shrugged. Joining up with Par was his "new job." Too bad the position was eliminated.

"Eh, it just wasn't for me," he said, shooting Jack another glance. Jack sniggered and rolled his eyes.

"Well, we're glad to see you," Verena said. It was wise of her not to bring up his brother, even if Jack didn't agree with the "glad to see you" part.

"What do you want?" Jack asked. The edge in his voice made Verena raise her brows.

"*Tsk.* Can't I just revisit old friends?"

"I don't have any of it left," Jack said, patting his pockets and pulling the insides out to show nothing but lint and sand collected inside them. It was a small lie. He had five left.

Hare clicked his tongue. "Why, I'm insulted that you'd think I just wanted something from you."

"Is that right? How many do you have left?"

Narrowing his eyes, Hare sucked his teeth. "Three."

Jack tittered. "Stop running then."

Hare sighed. "It's good to see you too, Verena," he said, giving her another hug, then wandered back to the same tent Jack found him at the first time. It was the one belonging to the Freely family. They had a young son, Quint, and another on the way. Their charity to Hare was rivaled only by their poverty.

"Is he still tent hopping?" Verena asked. "Someone should build him his own."

"Maybe." Jack considered him for a moment. If he could squeeze an ounce of trust for Hare... just enough for one task, they could use a couple syringes for him to travel round-trip to Par. She could get him silver and bring it back to make more of the drug. Perhaps a mountain roundsman would make a generous donation. As payment, Jack could build Hare his own tent. And if he was feeling generous, maybe even dig him a small bunker inside.

As he daydreamed about his plan, one of the children screamed.

It wasn't Ayala, or anyone in her group—an older girl wailed in the distance, crouched low next to a figure lying in the sand. Jack and Verena ran toward them. The girl was Anglian, known in camp as "Ness." Pink burns coated her blanched skin. The desert was no place for an Anglia.

As Jack closed the distance with Verena on his tail, he saw an Anglia boy about Ness's age writhing in the sand in front of her.

"Oadeus! Please stop, Oatie!" Ness tried to put a hand on his shoulder, but the boy was inconsolable.

White froth had accumulated in the line of his lips. Blue irises were half-moons in his eye sockets, shivering their way to the back of his head.

"Back up, Ness!" Verena shouted, pulling the girl to her feet and holding on to her.

Jack scooped Oatie up from the sand, recognizing the rapid onset of Weggevens death immediately. The boy was small, but his throes were fierce, rocking Jack on his feet as he attempted to run him to the privacy of Verena's tent for treatment.

"I k-know your s-secret-t-t," Oatie stuttered through chattering teeth. A long groan pulsed from his throat as he threw his head back again, squeezing Jack's hand tight enough to overlap his fingers and crack the middle knuckle.

Jack ran harder toward Verena's tent. Oatie's body bounced with each step, but his limbs were rigid. The crowd had grown thick, running after them and shouting offers to help. Any chances of calming the boy's convulsions in private were getting slimmer and slimmer.

How many syringes would it take? Two... maybe three? That would leave them only five left between his stash and Hare's. There was no telling how willing Hare was to share his either way.

"Back up!" he shouted at the children that had collected at Verena's tent. They scuttled backwards with mouths hanging open, allowing Jack entry.

He laid Oatie onto the floor, and Verena ducked inside alone. "Is he turning?" she asked.

Pointing at his Formulator chest, he grunted as he held the boy's head.

"He's already turned."

With the syringe passed to him, he flicked the cap from the needle. He plunged it into Oatie's arm as Jack held his breath. The tiny hole left by the needle filled with a minuscule drop of blood. Jack watched, waiting for the calm that came with his drug.

Oatie continued to tremble, when the Witis seeped from the needle mark, snaking its way through the cold bumps coating his arm and dribbling into the sandy floor. Rejected, as if his whole body refused help.

"Damn," Jack hissed.

Oatie writhed, arching his back in an unnaturally stiff bend. His pallid flesh went waxy, pushing out an oily sheen and trapping the sweat inside. There were only four syringes left. It was risky attempting to use another if his body would purge it. It didn't happen often, but just like with Verena's spontaneous kiss, Jack once again didn't know what to do.

As if reading his mind, Oatie popped his lips a few times before finally stuttering, "Y-you're almost out-t-t of your c-c-cure. C-an you us-s-e me when I d-d-ie?"

"Don't say that," Jack lied. Oatie's condition was beyond his help. At the moment, he almost missed the fact that the kid seemed more knowledgeable than he should have been.

Oatie grinned, his eyes closing into thin slits. "I t-think my silver would-d-d be a g-g-good gift. F-for A-ayala." His words softened before he shuddered, taking his final breath in Jack's arms.

Verena made a small cry, covering her mouth and running from the tent. It was too familiar. The withering, the weakness. Oatie was too young to handle the stress. Maybe he had an illness or something else that made him more feeble and unable to handle it. But Jack had seen it before. A long time ago during a routine business trip to Secas. Rare, and usually fatal, the boy had become a two-mind.

Jack stood and stared down at Oatie, now still from his convulsions. First it was Ayala and her friends, now it was Oatie. Who else would fall victim to the breach? Perhaps it was best the poor kid didn't live out a hard life as a two-mind. Whoever infected his mind was bent on taking someone down with them. A shame.

Ducking under the tent, the high sun cut through the tint of his goggles and gave him a headache. Verena's tent was surrounded. Several children waited, mouths covered and eyes wide as more adults jogged to meet the group. In their silence, Jack heard the sand beat against all the flapping fabric tents.

He shook his head.

"Oadeus! No, Oatie!" Ness cried. Her shoulders heaved, and the boy,

Quint, comforted her.

Jack sighed. Beyond the crowd of tent residents, billows of sand blew from the tips of dunes in the distance. Mesmerized by them, he studied them to take his mind off the child that had just died in his arms. It was then that he noticed a burly silhouette standing beyond the crowd, watching the grief circle. Jack squinted. A desert brigand, maybe? Any brigand had better stay clear of Verena's tent lest his stomping foot get itchy again. As Jack stared the figure down, it turned and disappeared into a veil of swirling sand.

Chapter 20

Getting It Over With

Loren

It hurt. It continued to *hurt. The electric pangs zapped his spine, and all he could do was groan. There was no light—merely the dim illumination of dark adapted algae and fungus. How long had it been since the fire?*

Time was irrelevant here. Sinew had molded to the structure, and nothing could save him. He would eventually die here, and no one would know. That was, if an endless could die. Somehow.

The worst part was the loneliness. Sometimes he snuck into her mind to see what she saw. It was the closest thing to living he could do. If not living through her, he slept. Days... months... years. He was overdue for a long nap. It was time.

Was it now? A thousand years asleep, and he couldn't stay awake for long, no matter how much she screamed. That woman was a stranger to him... full of rage and lust. She had to be saved. The new one could help him. The three of them locked together in mind and spirit.

She screamed again. Why did she hate the people so? Everything from her mouth was a lie. Could he trust what she said about his kind? Was he the last?

But the bloodline was strong... together, they became strong. It made little sense. He was sent to save them from the writhing corruption. His pain, his loneliness, his suffering... was it all for nothing?

"I must go," he said to her. It was no surprise that her response was more shouting.

"The Roseaarde you knew is gone!"

"I must go see what damage you've done by releasing me."

"No, you won't! You can't!"

The misuse of her ability ached him. The life growing in this place was trying so hard, and she wasted their essence across the walls with each word and flick of her wrist. If she meant to make a point with him, it only made him angry.

"I must go and find food. You keep destroying ours." Despite the growing anger,

he maintained his ability to remain calm.

"Where do you think you're going to find food? I told you, the Roseaarde you knew is DEAD! You won't find wild giltberries or saxeroot... it's all ration blocks and manufactured shit!"

The words confused him. "What is this...'shit' you speak about? What does it taste like?"

The face she made was strange—puckered inward, as if she had eaten a sour sarga. "I told you that you have no idea what Roseaarde is anymore. Let me go with you."

"No."

"You can't stop me!"

"No, I can't stop you, woman. But you will not be coming with me. He is set to be married, and you are not welcome."

At that, she was silent.

"I don't *care*, it's illegal!" Eva shouted upstairs loud enough for her rage to muffle itself through the floor and snap Lor from his dream. He rolled over and stared at the dark ceiling. "Does it not matter to you at all what happens to us if Audun finds out?"

"Lower your voice," Gale shot back. While he didn't yell back, it was a rumble loud enough to hear between the wooden planks separating the basement from the kitchen above.

"You don't know what I've seen in the cities, Dad!" A frantic pacing creaked over the ceiling. Eva's footsteps marched around the kitchen.

"Are you *trying* to wake up the entire house?"

Lor chuckled to himself, imagining Gale sitting at the table with his plinth of rations and newslite, calm and cool as Peakwood waters, while Eva threw a fit. He knew it had to be about his marriage to Dag.

"She sounds sexy when she's mad," Nico said from the floor. He had also woken up and rolled to his back, hands behind his head and lying casually with ankles crossed.

It was the goofy grin on his face that did Lor in. "Ew, shut up," he said, chuckling. Drawing the e-disk across the nightstand, he opened up a quick note to jot down his new dream. It seemed so real... a connection with the Igni himself. No time to marvel at it. A message from Damaetra projected from the base.

DAMAETRA: You guys should come to Audun and get registered soon. Miss you!

If his work consisted of nothing but pulling life from things, he was already ready to retire. But she was right. They would have to go there soon.

Going back to the quicknote, he swiped several details about the dream.

"What are you doing?" Nico had propped himself up on an elbow.

"I'm recording my dream."

"Nerd. Why?"

Lor chuckled, thinking of the right way to word his strange visions. "Well, ever since Par and I"—he shuddered—"*swapped* eneris, I've been seeing things at night that I can't explain."

"Tell me about them. Maybe I can help?" Nico sat up cross-legged on the floor. His posture was impeccable.

"A-ah, sure. I'll try..." Lor explained everything he saw in his dreams—from wandering in the desert, to meeting "Karl," and this most recent one. The tale was interrupted a few times by Eva's tantrum upstairs, and Dill waking up to listen. Once he'd finished, Nico tipped his chin to the ceiling as if it had the answers.

"Well, that last one had to have been Maron, don't you think?"

"I mean, it almost seems obvious," Dill said, yawning.

Lor sucked his teeth. "The thing is, I'm not sure if these visions are even real. Are they real?"

Nico shrugged. "The last one, the one possibly with Maron, seemed to line up with what we already know, so... maybe?"

"Oh man, that means he's gonna come find you!" Dill sat up. The purple light on his visor seemed to brighten, as if the dead hollows of his eye sockets widened underneath it.

A loud thump hit the floor above. "Dammit, Dad! I'm sorry, Dag." Eva's voice trailed off as her footsteps faded down the hall. The door slammed to her room.

Lor sighed. "I'd better check on that."

Upstairs was quiet, with inaudible murmurs of conversation between Gale and Dag. He didn't want to know what they were talking about. After running into them the day before, it was probably something he didn't want to hear. Rather than look his mother in her strange white eyes, he wandered into the living room to the fireplace.

"So Eva knows now, I take it," he said.

"You heard that, did you?" Gale rustled his newslite.

"Everyone heard that."

"I'm sorry it woke you. Have you contacted Seven Cities yet for your career?"

"We were going to do that today sometime." Lor ran his hand along the mantle. It was clean, freshly dusted. The reason? Something new sat there, propped up in a display clip. "When did you get this?" He took the object from the clip. It was dull with age and sort of resembled a silver shooter, similar to the ones Dill made. It looked ancient.

Gale cast his newslite to the side and stood, making his way to the mantle where Lor held the shooter. "Be *very* careful with that," he said, gently taking it from Lor's grip. "This is very old." He rested the shooter back in its display clip. "I got it after I dropped you off at the program. Seemed like the right thing to do."

"But *why* did you get it?"

Gale ran a finger down the handle. "Remember that arrest we saw at the train station? I wanted something just in case."

"Why couldn't Dill make something for you?"

"You don't understand," Gale said. He grinned, but nothing in his face expressed joy. "This is very old tech. It uses a long-lost form of propellant and projectiles. These aren't like Dill's needles. These are completely fatal."

The wound in Lor's side tingled. He felt the dimpled entry point. "Like the Crow's device? The guy that shot me?"

"It's a little different, but sort of. These bolts will always work. Yours was a dud, thank the Maker."

Lor bit his lip. "So... do you carry it around? Just in case?"

"Not yet." Gale led Lor back to the kitchen. "I want to practice with it a bit first. Get familiar with it before sticking it in my pocket like an idiot."

Dag smiled at them while sitting at the table, waiting for them to join her as Lor considered all the ways to break into that relationship. None of the ways he thought of avoided her connection to Gale. Then all he could think about was how Gale still had her dusting the mantle.

"So how did Eva find out? The same way I did?" Lor said, pulling a chair from the table.

Gale glared at him from over his glasses.

Lor raised his hands. "Sorry, just curious."

"Anyway," Gale drew out the word, rustling his newslite again, "Eva can take you to Audun to register while I'm at work. That will give her time to cool off."

Lor stuffed a piece of dry toast in his mouth, snagged a sarga fruit, and then pushed away from the table. Taking the fruit with him, he left the kitchen to talk with Eva.

"Don't get juice on the floor," Gale called out as Lor hiked down the hall.

A quick rap on the door followed by an irritated "come in" prompted Lor to peek through a crack into the room. Eva paced, throwing things in and out of her suitcase.

"Leaving already?" He stepped inside, leaning against the doorframe and taking a bite of the yellow-skinned fruit.

"No. I'm just annoyed."

Lor didn't have to ask why. "Dad said you can take us to Audun."

"Don't be dripping everywhere with that nasty fruit," she said, chucking a light top with black and white stripes into her bag.

"You sound like Dad."

She rolled her eyes. "Do you even know what he did? What he's *been* doing?"

Lor took another bite, slurping up a loose drop of juice from his lower lip and wiping his face on his shoulder sleeve. "He married Dag, yeah."

Freezing in place, she put her hand on her hip with her mouth open. "You *knew*?"

"I don't want to talk about it."

"Oh-ho-ho, please, *do* tell, baby bro. How exactly did you find out?"

The tone was just like her, silly but dead serious. If he didn't indulge her, she would put him in a headlock and rub her knuckle into his scalp until it burned.

"Don't do the thing," he said, wiping his mouth again as she advanced on him, fingers clawed and flexing with a mischievous grin. "Alright, alright! I walked in on them yesterday... You know... Maker burn my eyeballs."

Eva roared so loud her throat clenched, pushing out hoarse laughter.

"It's not funny!" He tried not to spit out fruit. No matter his protest, she continued her wheezing, bending over to take in a breath. "I'm probably scarred for life seeing my... *that*, thank you very much!"

Choking on the words "my mom," he stopped himself. Even if Eva knew about Gale and Dag, that didn't mean she knew about him. It wasn't something he could keep from her forever... and when she learned about his heritage, he hoped only a few dishes would suffer her wrath.

"Alright, alright, so will you take us to the Seven Cities or not?"

After a good hearty laugh, she wiped a tear from the corner of her eye. "Yeah, whatever, I'll take you to the stupid cities. And stop hovering there, holding that slimy pit. I'll come out in a few." She slammed another fistful of clothes into her suitcase.

The sarga pit squished between his fingers as he fought to catch the dribblings. Not wanting to make her any more irritated, he left her to taking clothes in and out of her bag.

The kitchen was empty, and he was glad for that. Facing Dag in any way by himself was not a thing he wanted yet, especially in the wake of finding her and Gale like that. There was time... thanks to Par, he had a lot of time.

"Is it safe?" Dill called from the hall before poking his head around. Once he saw they were alone, he and Nico shuffled in their socks toward Lor.

As if he couldn't get any more perfect, Nico was dressed in his sharp pink button-up with pressed black pants. Not one perfectly coiffed hair was out of place, and his teeth sparkled.

"You make us look bad," Lor said, grabbing another sarga from the table's plinth.

"Speak for yourself," Dill teased, brushing wrinkles from his shirt. Holes dotted the hem where his belt rubbed.

They agreed to go to the cities when Lor suggested it, with Nico taking a special interest in the fact they'd ride with Eva there.

"Speaking of which." Lor thumbed over at Eva as she rounded the corner to the kitchen.

"You jokers ready to go to the cities?" she said, grabbing a dry tea packet from the spread.

Nico shifted and sat upright, clearing his throat in with a noticeable warble.

"Let's do it," Dill said, hopping from the chair.

"You sure you want to go looking like that?" Eva tipped her empty mug at Dill's chewed-up shirt hem.

His face soured. "What's wrong with my shirt?"

Eva didn't have to say anything because her face was loud enough, and that was part of her charm. Dill got the idea and left to change. When Lor thought about it, he remembered Surai was a lot like that, too.

Once they got outside, Eva's all-terrain cruiser sat at the curb. As an Engineer and the only person in the family who knew how to drive, seeing the cream-colored jumper hybrid wasn't much of a surprise. To Nico, however, he was dumbfounded, and most likely even more flustered. The cities paid well, that's for sure. Although, why Eva needed something that could tear through the desert was beyond him.

A ride with Eva was different—Lor had never been her passenger, and he was a little interested to see how her driving compared to Damaetra's. While they weren't going to ride through the sand anytime soon, he was curious.

The ride to Audun made him want to zone out. Dill was distracted, and Nico's attention was on Eva. She even let him sit in the front. Lor closed his eyes, hoping the colors would align.

Ghostly traces swiveled like smoke—a very different look than the static. He chuckled to himself at the thought of the sheer trauma of seeing his mom with Gale, which slapped them into shape.

The smoke pulsed to Eva and Nico's conversation about the Engineering city, Ascendia. Bright yellow like the skin of his favorite fruit swirled with a green the shade of verdigris, twisting and spinning in a curious dance. The yellow belonged to Eva, and the green to Nico. The more he watched, the more it felt like voyeurism.

A thick violet spike pulsed through the citrus smoke when Dill excitedly said, "Look, it's the spire!" Lor's eyes snapped open.

There it was—the great white spire impaling the cloudless sky. Distant specks of tech floated at the peak, resembling lazy insects orbiting a bleached bone. Cameras, detectors, scanners... he only imagined all the tech that surrounded that place.

Cruisers whizzed by as they pulled up to the building. They hopped out with assurance that Eva would come get them later and were then swallowed by the crowd of people making their way to and from the surrounding buildings.

The space was a dizzying mess of glass and metal, threatening to knock Lor over with the sheer size of it all. He swayed, staring up at the spire's towering height. Gleaming white stone and glass made up the capitol building, standing out as a ghost among the darkened buildings that surrounded it. The entire block was intimidating. There was no way he was staying in a building with over four levels. All of these were twenty-plus.

"Watch it," a man who side-stepped Dill grumbled as he marched toward the building.

They stood out in the crowd—lost, confused, small...

"Let's get this over with," Lor said.

CHAPTER 21

My Son
LOREN

LUCK FAVORED THEM ALL WHEN applying to the cities. Although, without the implant, only Damaetra snagged a higher paying role. It was a bit of the Maker's favor that there was an implant shortage at the time of application. After two standard months, the cities had forgotten they didn't have them. No one asked, and they didn't volunteer to tell.

The Reaper city, Obsidia, had Lor sorting phials, which came as a respite from pulling people...especially children. Over time, the different types of eneris fascinated him. Each phial he shimmied into place made Lor remember how it felt in his hands and through his soul when he pulled.

Blue felt like drowning, white like flying... the green that he pulled from hundreds of desert cacti stung him mercilessly, and the red was electric. He swirled a phial of silver, watching the highlights dance with the shadows in a shimmering routine of random beauty. Silver didn't have names, but they should.

Another standard month and he was dispatched as a collector in the morgues. The cities had many morgues and not enough Reapers who wanted the task. As the low man in the hierarchy, he had no say in the matter.

Recording his pulls made him feel empty of memories, but a single seed in the most primal part of his mind told him what he did for them was wrong. Reaping was wrong. Small mercies allowed him to forget the people he pulled, yet sometimes at night, he howled awake from someone else's dreams. Lines blurred between the nocturnal connection he held with Maron and the people he harvested for Audun.

Obsidia deposited his plats directly, and it was a good wage for *custodial* work. Each daily delivery brought him closer to building his future with Damaetra, even if it was soul-burning cash. At least Damaetra's pay came from honest work.

Daily, he watched his account climb higher and higher, with the occasional accolade from Gale telling him, "well done." They'd come a long way.

Eva's short stay at home turned into a permanent solution for her dwindling numbers. Too much high life and not enough savings placed her at Gale's mercy. It didn't matter to him. He was happy to have his daughter around, even if it did come with excessively frequent visits from Nico.

Another standard month and the nightmares returned, with one especially nasty one that had Lor screaming, *cirv`e!* into the night. Good fortune or very good timing led to his mother racing down the stairs to wake him.

The under glow of her eerie white eyes reflected unseen light in the room, yet having her there put him at ease. That night, four standard months after returning home, they sat in his room and finally talked.

She was a Reaper, but unpracticed and safe from the descent into yaslecha. Remembering what Val told him at the end of the program, that *to reap was natural to Foscan*, he decided he inherited the influence from her. Whatever cirv`e was, it brought the two of them together, even if she wouldn't tell him what it meant.

Is not Foscan, she had told him, which sprouted his idea to learn her language from her. After another standard month, he could recite the Foscan alphabet, count to fifty, introduce himself, and ask for the toilet. She giggled at his pronunciations but never hesitated to correct him. Even Gale side-eyed his progress, offering minor grins under his morning newslite and toast tips.

Things had gotten comfortable, and Lor found it harder and harder to leave Dag's language lessons for morgue pulls. They were comfortable enough that even Gale openly kissed his wife when he left for work, while Eva lost interest in her anger toward him. If Lor were to guess, Nico had a lot to do with that shift in her. He was the hot new thing in her life, and that demanded most of her attention.

One standard month left and Damaetra would be his wife. She claimed the drama of her family had died somewhat, but mostly her sisters were silently leery of each other. It made the occasional family night awkward and was a real test of Aedras's patience with Cae and Eloria. Lor had begun to appreciate his future father-in-law, yet despite that, dreams of Damaetra's real father plagued his nightmare one night, and he worried himself over how that was possible.

Dag stayed with him that night when he summoned her comfort. He hoped that by telling her the dream, it would erase itself from his memory like reaping people did.

After describing in great detail the brutal murder of the poor Anglian working man with Damaetra cowering in terror as the criminal ransacked their house, the memory of bursting flowers from their decorative vase burned their image in the black parts of his mind. It haunted him, and it didn't go away, bestowing its fresh horror onto Dag. *Why would the memory stay this time...* he had asked her, but Dag, unfamiliar with her gift, couldn't give him a good answer. She touched his hand—Reaper to Reaper—and there was something there. Outside of Par constantly fussing over him and ultimately groping him, he realized he had never touched the skin of another Reaper for longer than a standard second or two.

Holding on to Dag's hand had a fuzzy sort of magnetism...an electricity that buzzed between them. The walking current was enough to raise the finer hairs on his arms, and he laughed at the mild tickle. The gold eneris that fed his being shivered near hers, and she opened her mouth into a perfect circle when she felt it too.

That moment drew a small tear from her eye as she looked at him.

"Mae'guae haer," she said to him, lower lip quivering between a frown and a grin, "I love you, my son."

CHAPTER 22

The Start of Something
JACK

ANOTHER ONE LOST. BEFORE LONG, the camp would be so thin that he'd be the only one left with his wife and daughter. It was such a cruel waste of silver. The bodies burned differently when it was still inside them. The breach hadn't yet "blessed" them with a Reaper, so what could they do?

The moldering pile of ash and bone sat like a black island at the north boulder. When squinting, it could be mistaken for a mirage—an oasis in the barren desert. Ayala refused to venture out there any longer... she said it was cursed.

Verena had set up a nice workbench for him in the bunker to make more phials of Witis for Ayala, Quint, and Hare when a nondescript package arrived following the death of Oadeus. Three large phials of silver lay within, courtesy of Horace.

It had been pooled from the six or so students of class 1010 that succumbed to the curse, and pulled by that scrawny Foscan, Val. The late student's parents wouldn't miss a scoop from each when they received phials of their loved ones' remains. Hare didn't have to visit Paerli after all. Jack said a quick thanks to the Maker again for that fact.

Hare appeared next to him in a cloud of yellow sand. "What do you need?" he said. The disturbed air tossed around Jack's coat and hair. The runner had proved useful in the last standard year, running errands and finding materials... or stealing them. He visited Secas market often—most likely to see if he'd run into his parents.

"I'm running low on green. Can you get some?" Jack passed two syringes to him without so much as a glance.

Hare tucked the syringes in a side pocket. "Can I get some... what kind of question is *that*?" he taunted just before disappearing in another burst of sand.

Jack flipped open his e-disk for the time. He'd have his supplies by midday, as long as Hare didn't tarry. Trust hadn't been fully earned yet, and Jack would be watching the clock. The Yeunish bounty seemed to increase every month, and it wouldn't be long before Hare would cash in on his head. The runner swore he didn't want it, but Jack kept one eye on him, regardless.

The ash pile was no longer alone. For the past several months, Jack had caught occasional glimpses of the stranger watching camp. The stranger didn't come often, but when he did, it unnerved him. A part of him worried it was someone coming to claim the bounty on his kind. The other part of him worried for the general safety of his family. More "death camps" had sprung up in the distant dunes, eager to take advantage of the weakening tent city. Weggevens of all flavors cropped up—from elementalists to volatiles, and he'd seen more than he cared to.

He'd been able to craft a few phials of Fowler's Last Grudge before giving all the chromatis back to Lor, but he'd already had to use two of them. It was enough to threaten the death camps, but they still made their attempts, and Jack knew the city wouldn't protect them. The curious figure that watched them hadn't made a move yet. It was only a matter of time.

After the first few sightings, Jack worked with the Freelys to dig out a safe bunker for Hare, despite his mild distrust in the skittish runner. As prickly as the little speedster was, Jack didn't wish for him to die by death camp.

Verena poked her head from the tent. "Come inside, Jack. It's windy," she said. She withdrew without noticing the man on the horizon.

Turning his body but not his head, Jack kept his eye on the blocky shadow kneeling next to their dead. He ducked under the tent's freshly reinforced frame and let the flap slap closed. Ayala sat at the table, doing her numbers and swinging her legs while humming a random tune she made up. Jack kissed her on the head between her two russet-colored buns, and she giggled between hums.

"That tickles!" she said, scratching out her first level equations on wrinkled parchment.

"I sent Hare out for some green," Jack said to Verena. She busied herself at the tiny cook table.

She side-eyed him with a smirk. "Aren't you glad you made up?"

"I still don't trust him."

She tittered. "In time. *I'm* glad anyway. Without the upgraded material he brought back, our coolant sleeve would be puttering out by now."

"You know he's probably stealing that stuff, right?"

Verena peered at Ayala, who was busy with her numbers, not paying attention. She shuffled through the sandy floor next to him and leaned in to whisper, "Just evening it all out… we've been spit on too long down here."

Jack kissed her pursed lips and smiled. "You're right."

"Besides," she said, going back to her cook table, "more people are needing your remedy every day. Is there anything you can do to… *reformulate* it?"

"Reformulate it how?"

"You know… so it doesn't use…" She mouthed the word *silver* in silence, motioning to a vein in the bend of her elbow and watching Ayala.

Jack shrugged, pointing toward the bunker for a private conversation.

The coolant sleeve hummed in the background under the patter of Jack's footsteps on the sandy floor.

"The more people that turn, the harder it's going to be to hide what this drug is," Verena said as she climbed down the ladder.

"We need to come up with a better solution," Jack agreed. "I just don't know what that solution is."

Verena bit her lip and nodded. "I've been meaning to ask you. Why hasn't that Reaper friend of yours visited? We really could have used her help taking care of our people."

It had been a while since Jack considered Par. After their exchange in the desert, he'd had enough of her. The truth was, he had no idea where she was anymore. Perhaps she was living her immortal life away in the desert. Perhaps she moved on to the next band of gullible suckers to buy her lies.

He shifted, tucking his hands in his pockets. "I haven't really talked to her in a while."

"That's odd." Verena narrowed her eyes at him. "She was like family to you."

"Not anymore." The descent of Par's madness echoed in his mind as the image of their partner, Bat, crumpled beneath her fingers. She was so willing to murder a member of their crew, and Jack's fear of what she would do to him if she knew… His tolerance finally snapped when she openly mocked his kind.

"So what happened?" Verena urged him.

Jack told her everything. From meeting her in childhood to following her in adulthood. The only thing he couldn't tell her were the *reasons* he followed her. Even he didn't know.

"She just *killed* a guy? Were you friends? With the guy?" Her eyes were a warm golden in the dim light of the bunker.

"Not really, no."

"So this 'job' that Niki had… the job was to act as one of her goons?"

Jack's heart pounded at the look of disgust on her face. He had just started to get along with Hare again and didn't want to wreck it. "Don't think less of him for that."

"Well, it's hard for me *not* to... he really hurt people for her. Could have killed them too. His own brother! That we didn't even know he had, by the way."

"Yes, I know."

"Thank the Maker you had the good sense to help them."

Jack nodded, rubbing at his eyes as the fine sand motes from the air found their way onto his eyelashes. One righteous act didn't right all the wrongs he had committed under Par's leadership.

Verena crossed her arms, still wearing disgust on her face. It was bad timing for Hare to come back from his errand, but the announcement from Ayala came from upstairs anyway. The deep drone of Hare's voice carried across the bunker opening, followed by Ayala's light chatter with him.

"Don't say anything to him, please?" Jack said, gripping Verena's hands and holding them to his face.

She curled a lip. "I'll try."

Once upstairs, Hare grinned and tossed a wrapped box at Jack. Not the most agile, Jack jerked to the side, watching the box bounce off his chest and *piff* into the sand. It forced a laugh from Ayala.

"Nice one," Hare said with a chuckle. "Good thing those phials are plastic."

"How much?" Jack asked as he picked up the box and thumbed open his e-disk. His balance was still decent, but it was shrinking. Par's support had been cut off, and Hare claimed that stealing plats got harder with each new tech upgrade.

"On the house." Hare grinned. "I ran into my rich, regretful parents."

Checking the time, Jack raised an eyebrow. "And you didn't stay longer with them?"

Hare shrugged. "I got what I needed from them for now. Dad about had a heart attack when he saw me. I got these for you, Verena." Thinking twice about throwing the package, he held it out to her like a gentleman. She took the package with a half frown that wasn't lost on Hare.

"Thanks," she mumbled, picking at the adhesive sealing it.

"I thought maybe you could do something with these... as an Engineer. I saw someone make something with it before."

When Verena unwrapped the package, several uniform pieces of pearly ancient tech rolled into her palm. They were small, carved with strange symbols, and lightweight.

"You've seen an Engineer work with ancient tech?" Skeptical but intrigued, she raised an eyebrow.

A twitch snagged Hare's lip. Nico's leg adapters had ancient tech in them. He only knew that it was possible, not that he watched his *good buddy* Dill make them after he slashed out his eyes. Was that a twitch of guilt on his face? Very curious.

Hare nodded at her stiffly. "It's not much," he said, "but I thought maybe of all Engineers, at least you could figure out how to make them useful. Especially since you're good at electrical stuff."

Flattery was not in Hare's handbook. It was his way of serving penance... to create a little good in someone else's life to deposit toward the terrible he caused in others.

"I appreciate that, Niki. Thank you. Maybe someday I can meet the Engineer that could work this material."

Jack and Hare glanced at each other. "Ah, sure. Maybe someday," Hare said.

Have a special vacation at the classic and rustic Sunset Springs Inn, where your Foscan hosts take special care of your every need! Only standard seconds away from the largest field of springs. Soak in the healing waters while watching second sun set through the ivory forest. It's truly a magical experience you won't forget!

COLD AIR, HOT WATERS

Pohay'an's hot springs are fed by the wintry mix and heated by an underground fault of unknown origin. The citizens have enjoyed use of the hot springs for a thousand years!

★★★★★ *"Vast o`esh lish teo Mae`g haur. Wie`faur kalech teo jaulene`lien."*
~Foreign Visitor, Yor`ikur "Rik" Bileu [*Beast Tamer*]

OPTION 2

ONE WEEK STAY

pL 1400⁹⁹

LIMITED TIME OFFER

A Pohay'an vacation means:
- All inclusive stays
- Quaint rustic lodges
- Access to hot springs
- Beautiful nature trails
- Magical Ivory Forest
- Technology forward
- Wedding bookings!
- Foscan Servants

BOOK NOW

OPTION 1

WEEKEND EXCURSION

pL 599.⁹⁹

A Pohay'an weekend means:
- Partially inclusive stays
- Quaint rustic lodges
- Access to hot springs
- Beautiful nature trails
- Magical Ivory Forest
- Technology forward
- ✗ Wedding bookings
- ✗ Foscan Servants

BOOK NOW

CHAPTER 23

Minor Inconveniences
LOREN

IT WAS A GOOD DAY to sit on a train doing nothing. An overcast shade of slate covered the sky, and the mood was brooding. Not long and Lor would be a married man—a strange thought considering not two standard years ago, he was living alone in Gale's basement with no friends. A reputation he earned from the humiliation he endured at the hands of grade school Luci, no doubt.

Suck it, Luci, and your nasty green mouth.

A proper suitcase lay propped open on the bed with a hodgepodge of half-folded clothes packed inside. Not one for fashion, they mostly consisted of plain shirts and ordinary slacks that most likely had rips somewhere in them. It was a vacation, after all; he didn't need to dress up for anything other than the very small wedding, and Eva promised to take care of that.

The train ride would be longer than the one to Kanckette. The little town of Pohay'an was quite far north, where snow blanketed the earth year-round and molten pools of mineral water broke through the crust to be warmed by Roseaarde's core. It sounded mystical. Lor's only wish was no delays from the increasing number of Weggevens transformations or train car heists. The possibility of more arrests also loomed ahead, and if he was supremely unlucky, he'd get to experience all three.

"Hurry up, Loren!" Gale's voice called down the stairs.

Piling the rest of his things in a heap on top, he closed the case. With a quick fix to his freshly cut hair, he raced upstairs to join the rest. When he reached the top of the stairs, he heard the buzz of conversation in the kitchen. Eva fussed with Nico's collar while Dag spoke with Gale and smiled, touching his cheek.

"Dill's meeting us at the station," Nico said with a glance at Lor. Eva brushed at his hair with her fingers. "He's bringing Emilia. Remember her?"

"Emilia? No kidding?" Lor dropped his case on the floor as it rolled slightly behind him.

All he remembered of Emilia was how high-maintenance she seemed with her string of pearls always clasped around her exposed neck. That, and Dill's mild obsession with her.

"Yep," Nico said, smiling as Eva sauntered away toward her room. "Apparently they reconnected in Ascendia. Remember, she became an Engineer, same as him?"

"Oh yeah, that's right. It seems so long ago."

"Doesn't it? Eva knows her too."

"I know *of* her," Eva said, coming back up the hall with her case. She smiled. "She's alright as far as I know."

Gale cleared his throat in a booming, attention-seeking way. "Everyone ready?"

Lor nodded with a grunt and glanced at the mantle. The antique shooter was missing from its clip, as Gale had grown accustomed to carrying it more often. Hopefully he didn't need to use it, but it was good to know that his dad had become adept at using it if they needed him to.

The station was a cluster of activity. With all the waves of Weggevens transformations, new medics and roundsmen were hired to help control the chaos. Their jobs were especially difficult, as some Wegs were not the usual flavor. Elementalists and volatiles were two new ones. However, without Jack's remedy, they easily killed themselves by using their ability.

It was a surprise that the cities hadn't figured out the drug yet, and it was a surprise that the new Wegs continued to kill themselves knowing the risks. It had become more of a nuisance than anything, and Lor was frequently dispatched to take care of the silver. Grunt work for the grunt.

The usual panhandlers and buskers worked their corners as crowds of people showed up to take their long-needed rides to other parts of the country. As they snaked through the crowd, Gale kept one hand on his utility belt, trigger finger at the ready.

"There she is—with her family," Lor said, pointing toward Damaetra and her family wandering toward the ticket gate.

"Loren, please don't just wander off," Gale said, following close behind.

Smiling to himself, Lor sniggered at the fact that Gale still hadn't stopped being the overprotective dad to his marked son, even as an adult.

After a handshake from Aedras and a hug from Thea and Cae, they all headed to the train. Eloria had been cold toward him, and he didn't know why. Instead of brooding over it, Lor chose to deal with it another day—one that was far away from his wedding day.

The bank of jumpers poured more people into the station, including Dill with his date. Grinning wide under the purple glow of his visor, he helped her from their jumper. Lor chuckled to himself, as Emilia hadn't changed at all—she was all grace and snobbery with a string of pearls clasped around her slender neck. The one difference was her new fondness for their energetic friend.

Dill grabbed their two bags while Emilia hung on to his arm. It was a sight to behold... the proper and the improper, clasped at the side as a flower might cling to wet bark—it somehow worked. Lor smiled as they approached.

"Nice to see you again, Emilia," Lor said with a handshake. "Ascendia treating you well?"

Taking his hand in response, her grip was firm and rough, completely unlike what he imagined.

I love being an Engineer were words he never expected to come from her, but she proved him wrong with a genuine smile.

"And I'm so glad to have reconnected with Dill." She gave him a smart peck on the cheek that he received with a cocksure grin.

They had to have fallen into some alternate universe. Barely able to contain the look on his face, Lor hummed.

"It's all a lie!" The hoarse bellow echoed through the station. Lor jerked his head to see where it came from, and Gale pressed his hand over the shooter's bulge in his pocket. Emilia let out a small cry, craning her pearled neck above the crowd.

Another Yeunish arrest. The man was being dragged by a type of shackle set Lor had never seen before. They were fully wrapped metal gloves clamped around his hands, bound by chains to connect them together while pulling him forward. The man stumbled on lame feet, wearing dirty clothes with brown stains over the front in a spatter pattern. The pattern looked as if he'd been punched in the mouth, but a while ago.

As they got closer, the man gazed up at Lor, messy black hair covering one golden eye, and he grinned. Lor didn't think it was meant to be sinister, but the gaps in his smile made it so. Closing his eyes to avoid the wracked grin, Lor pulled his lips inward.

The colors under his lids swirled in a mix of hues until a green pulse spiked through them when the Yeuni shouted, "The cities are a *lie*! Viev`le Igni!" His voice faded at the end of the station.

Igni?

That was a word Lor knew. It wasn't lost on Dill or Nico either, as they glanced at each other in a trio of suspicion.

The Igni lives.

A simple sentence, but he shouldn't know it—the language was not Northern Common. It was foreboding, a reminder of the many dreams in which Maron advanced on his position. He tucked the thought away, peering over at Damaetra, who still had a hand on her mouth.

Gale relaxed his tension over the shooter, nodding for them to move forward onto the train.

"I never get used to that," Damaetra whispered to him. "I can't help but think of… you know."

"I know," he said, drawing her close.

Because one day it could be him. That was her concern. After all that time following Hare's escape and he still hadn't been arrested, well… he stopped worrying about it. Wherever he was, Hare was harmless, like Horace said.

They boarded the crowded train. Once inside, all heads were down, fully enveloped in their e-disks. It was eerily quiet for such a crowd, and Lor felt too self-conscious to speak. Rather, he settled in next to Damaetra and closed his eyes to welcome the colors that had returned as smoke. There was no reason he could think of for the switch, but he was happy to have them back. The train hummed, sliding forward until reaching full speed.

Only one delay. Lor hardly took a deep breath when the train announced an emergency stop at the first station.

"Everyone freeze!" A roundsman burst into the train car with a pair of local medics.

The car's passengers groaned as a woman near the front convulsed in her seat. Shoulders sagging and neck bobbing, she almost fell to the floor before the first medic caught her. They must have seen her before the other passengers.

Another Weggevens curse. The only thing to watch for at that point was whether the woman survived.

Lor flipped open his e-disk to check the time. It would be second sun before they got to Pohay'an. He sighed and plopped down into the seat as other passengers did the same.

The Weggevens victim moaned in the background while he played a quick game of Gehenna's Pass. She had no loved one to hover over her and wail, and for that, he was glad. It would just be a matter of waiting it out until the roundsmen could get her off the train and they could move again. Two of three delays now. The odds of getting the third were increasing as his luck seemed to be going down.

The woman's noises faded as the roundsman removed her from the train. After a few moments, the train lurched forward, onward to Pohay'an.

Damaetra rubbed her temples with a sour expression and eyes closed.

"Headache?" Lor asked, running his hand in circles over her back.

"Actually, no…" she said, eyes still closed. Her ancient tech ring glimmered under the artificial train light. "I just feel strange. I feel like something is trying to invade my mind."

Lor craned his neck to look around. There weren't any other infected people turning that he could see. "A Reader?" he asked.

"No, I don't think it's anything like that. It wouldn't make sense... I'm no one worth reading."

"I don't know, you've got a pretty dirty mind."

Damaetra clicked her tongue with a playful whap to Lor's shoulder. He put her in a head lock and kissed the top of her head as she giggled in his armpit. Once he let her go, he caught eyes with Eloria a few seats away. She turned away quickly, but her face was pale and sickly. The look bothered him—she seemed troubled.

"Is Eloria feeling alright?" he asked.

Without looking at her, Damaetra sighed. "I don't know. She hasn't been acting herself for a while now. I couldn't tell you."

It was a touchy subject. Damaetra had a few fights with her sisters in the past few months. He wasn't interested in dredging it up for her or getting involved. It was something they would need to work out as sisters.

The long ride would be made longer if he let it bother him, so he didn't, choosing to catch up on his winning streak in Gehenna's Pass while occasionally checking out Dill and Emilia's odd relationship. She leaned into him with her slender tan legs bent and pointing toward him with ankles crossed. The strappy blue heels on her slim feet pressed together, relaxed at the floor and bouncing together with the beat of the train movements. Emilia fawned over Dill, and he was loving every second of it.

Lor laughed to himself and closed his eyes to ride out the rest of the journey watching the chromatic smoke of conversation.

Nestled in a patch of ivory forest, Pohay'an station cut through the cream-colored trees. The train slowed to a stop, and groggy passengers rolled from seats to gather their bags between yawns. The station was clean and crisp as it hit Lor's nose, unlike the stuffy heat of the trash-ridden Kanckette station. Second sun was close to rising, and soon the scene would be bathed in purple hues.

Taking in the scene, Lor lingered behind, amazed at the steam rising from several hot springs surrounding the station. Red signs with tall white letters said: Not For Public Use.

If the town weren't so far from civilization, Lor would want to live there. When he looked up, he saw the familiar Foscan, Val, waving from the station exit. Once he and Damaetra had decided to get married in the small town, Lor took out Val's old letter to him and reconnected with him. Val was more than happy to help them secure their wedding venue and even offered to cook for their reception. The kindness made Lor wish Val was allowed to take payment, but it would only go to his owners.

"It's good to see you, Val," Lor said, holding his hand out to greet him, but Val bowed instead.

"Here I am called Vox the Fragile. But it is good to see you. I hope travel was good."

Another slave name. It made him grateful that Horace allowed Val to use his real name during the program. While on the beach Val rarely wore shoes, in Pohay'an, he wore thick boots and covered himself head to toe in padded brown clothes with fur lining the neck. Slick black hair was pulled into a tail and tucked under the fur collar. His white eyes glimmered over a cordial grin.

Behind him stood an older Anglian couple that appeared on the verge of needing Lor's silver extraction services. Val affirmed he belonged to the pair, who were called the Gammelhaens. It was their courtyard they would be married in. When Lor shook the patriarch's hand, he feared he broke it when a knuckle popped. Mister Gammelhaen paid no mind, praising his *friend*, Vox. His wife stood next to him, bobbing her feeble head side to side in warbled agreement with a stuttered hum coming from her throat.

Following pleasantries, the group gaped at the transportation the Gammelhaens brought to take the entire group to their "humble" estate.

CHAPTER 24

Wedding Cirv'e
LOREN

CLUSTERS OF WHITE HYACINTHS SPECKLED with violets formed the crowns around Lor's and Damaetra's head. Her hair had grown back enough that Eloria spun squat curls in it that formed a white-gold halo around her head. Val had out-done himself when helping to arrange the ceremony.

They married during the first split, where the weather was just perfect enough to display new life in the buds of branches, yet a cool deterrent to pesky gee flies and other insects. More hyacinths and violets decorated the guest aisles, giving the scene a view like a floral cloud. It was perfect.

Two custom vows and a kiss later, and Lor and Damaetra were husband and wife. The small audience erupted in cheers, mostly from Dill and Emilia. Hearing wild whooping coming from the pearl-studded proper girl had him choking back his own laugher.

He stared at his bride, skin pale in the white of the sun, eyes half-violet in the light, lit not just by the glimmer of day but also her wide grin. The dress she wore draped across her shoulders like webs of silk.

Beyond her laced shoulder stood a shadow in the trees—bulky and still. Another glance and it roamed away, deeper into the ivory forest. Perhaps a wandering vagrant stumbled onto their venue, realized their mistake, and left. It stirred a pit in his stomach nonetheless.

They strolled down the aisle hand in hand as their short guest list celebrated them.

The Gammelhaens' celebration hall was quaint but lavish, half indoor and half out. The patriarch, Boeris, made his fortune the old-fashioned way with grit, determination, and three different non-Guild positions related to entertainment. Illea, his wife, worked two non-Guild roles in education. Together, they rarely saw each other, and Boeris lamented to Lor how little time they spent together in their youth, and to "not make their mistake" with his new bride.

Lor promised he wouldn't, losing himself in Damaetra's eyes as she stood there with him. The couple had grown very old together, with no children to share their lives. It struck him that in his relationship, only Damaetra would be the one growing old. Watching the Gammelhaens' heavy heads bob on weak necks with deep lines cutting through every inch of their skin as they spoke brought him down, and he made an excuse to wander elsewhere.

Val made real food for everyone with the help of a few other Foscans in the area. The array of choice overwhelmed, but Lor found the demure tray of red buns steaming next to stacks of glossy sarga tarts.

Gale made a friend in Aedras, sitting at a table outside near the tree line in animated conversation. Gale should have had the person he loved next to him, and Lor protested their agreement to leave Dag behind for appearances. The fact was, he wanted his mother there.

Damaetra was rapt in conversation with Emilia and Nariah, whom Lor was surprised came to the wedding. Leaning against a thick white tree, he took a generous taste of the sarga tart, feeling the sour bite in the sides of his jaw and savoring the feeling.

A chill crept across his shoulder when he felt the cold presence of a shadow.

"I should congratulate you," a deep voice rumbled from behind. It felt foreign, with a slight uncanniness.

Lor fumbled the sarga tart into the patchy grass before spinning around, coming face-to-face with the one soul in all of Roseaarde he didn't expect at that moment, in that place. The timing couldn't have been any less impeccable.

"M-Maron," Lor choked as he stared at the imposing ancient standing before him. An oversized pair of sunshades obscured his eyes, a tip Lor could only assume was given by Par. He glanced around for signs of her. "Y-you're alive?"

"That was a question," his voice rang deep, rattling between Lor's ribs.

"What are you doing here?" Sweat filled the lines in Lor's palms the way it did when he was a younger...when he was pathetic.

"I told you I would come."

Small flashes of Maron's renewed face hovered in the deeper corners of his memory, muddled with all the other memories forced on him by the city's variety of morgues and silver death. Maron's intended presence at his wedding in that moment was delivered to him in the most bizarre set of dream sequences that couldn't have possibly been mistaken for a wild imagination.

"Was that you standing in the forest?" Lor asked, referring to the shadow he witnessed between the trees.

Maron tilted his head toward the trees with a stony expression. "I have been just here the whole time."

A vagrant then—nothing to worry about outside of the fact that he was now talking to an *ancient Igni* in the middle of his wedding. Lor's heart thrummed—a feeling he hadn't experienced since leaving the cave last year. It was the connection he learned way too late that tethered himself to Par, the second beat pushing his. It made him nauseated. She had to be nearby.

"Where is she?" he asked, putting a hand over his heart, attempting to act nonchalant about the nausea.

"You mean my wife? She was not welcome here."

Lor tilted his head. If Par wasn't there, why did his heart beat out of sync? Fingertips dug deeper into his shirt as he hoped to control the offbeat cantering. Then it struck him—it was Maron. It had to be. Lor was part of their twisted inner circle of accidental immortals, and the three of them were connected. He seemed to be the only one debilitated by it.

"You're right," Lor said, throwing his shoulders back and standing tall, "she was not welcome. So why are you here?"

"I have come to ask for your help."

"And what can I possibly do to help?"

"You and your kind are important."

"That makes no sense and didn't answer my question." Lor's heart skipped again, causing him to bend over briefly and catch a glimpse of the sarga tart on the ground taking on crawling insects. He clicked his tongue in disappointment.

"No. I suppose not."

"Alright then, how am I important?"

The Igni didn't answer. Rather, he gazed off beyond Lor's shoulder to someone standing behind him.

"*What* in Gehenna's language was that?" Nico asked, holding a glass half emptied of light tan-colored liquor smelling of spice and berries. Eyes wide, he fixed them on Maron, not having the slightest idea just who stood in front of him. Nico's alcohol perfumed breath hovered between them, and he subtly swayed. It wasn't too surprising he didn't understand him with his dope-addled comprehension.

"I asked how I was important," Lor repeated.

"That is *not* what you said. It didn't even sound like Northern Common *or* Foscan."

Lor eyed Maron.

"We speak the language of the Maker," Maron stated, his gaze harder than winter stone.

"There! There it is again!" Nico pointed toward Lor. "I know I'm not *that* drunk. Who is this anyway? Aren't you going to introduce me?"

"A-ah," Lor stuttered, putting a tentative finger up to his own lips as if it would shush him. He scanned the venue for eavesdroppers. "This is... This is *Maron*." He whispered the last word. "You know... the Igni we left in the cave?"

Nico stood upright, brows frozen halfway up his forehead and jaw locked. Knocking back the last of his spiced alcohol, he let out a small hiss and cough. "Oh Mak—oh Gehenna... Holy—"

"Shh!" Lor shushed him for real, putting a hand up to his mouth.

"He can't *be* here," Nico mumbled under Lor's hand.

"Well, he's here. I'm trying to figure out why without making a scene." Lor turned to Maron. "Well?" he said.

Maron coughed, attempting the patchiest version of Northern Common Lor had ever heard. "We must work together. She is seduced by the evil one. My Paerli... desert gem turned desert terror."

"Where is she now?" Lor shot a glance at Damaetra, who was unaware of their secret meeting with an Igni, completely engrossed in conversation on the other side of the venue.

"She is with tree, to confer with the unspeakable. It is the vile creature, the zlae` duch cirv'e."

Cirv'e...

Maron paused, features unmoving, but Lor could see he searched for the most appropriate translation as it cycled behind his eyes.

Cirv'e!

It was the foreign word he called out one night—a puzzle even his mother couldn't solve.

Maron's neck trilled up and down, and a low grumble came from his throat. "She *speaks*... to the worm."

Instant bumps prickled in a wave up Lor's arms.

The silvered eyes slithering toward him and the vibrations of the guttural voice telling him, *gotcha!* culminated into disbelief. "That's... not real... Cirv'e isn't *real*," he whispered only to convince himself. If he declared it out loud, it wasn't real.

"The wha-at?" Nico asked with a hiccup.

"Foul thing. I must return. I have already seen how much damage cirv'e has done, and my safety is at risk. Find your kind and come. And bring pendant." Maron called the last part over his shoulder when he had already begun walking away. Before Lor could protest, Maron disappeared among the ivory trees.

He turned to Nico with a sour face. "What am I supposed to do with that?"

Nico shrugged, swaying and rattling the ice in his cup. "Maybe you're not

-hic- ready to know yet."

"Why would he travel all this way in all that time just to leave me hanging about cirv'e? And what, find my kind? What does that even mean?"

"You're asking the wrong pers-hic-son."

Nico had greased his nerves with the spiced liquor, rendering himself conversationally useless. Lor sighed. Find his kind... he could only assume Maron meant other Yeunish people. The only one he knew was Jack, so where did he expect him to find more?

As the thought made its way out, he got that dreadful realization that most Yeunish were in the Southern Morass. The morass was a one-way ticket by manual boat ride, and as far as he knew, they died there. It was possible, he supposed, that a few had escaped, and they were the ones being arrested in front of him. But there was no way for him to know, unless he volunteered to go there.

Forget it. It was his wedding day, and an issue he would deal with some other time. Maron chose the worst time to pay him a visit.

Stop thinking about it.

Lor chuckled at his friend swaying there and flashing Eva a goofy grin. A blast of wind raked his back, throwing his hair and pressed shirt into chaos. Spinning around, he saw nothing out of the ordinary, only that the wind had stolen some food from the table.

CHAPTER 25

Watcher

IT WAS A TWINGE OF jealousy, nothing to get worked up over. It just wasn't fair. The white clouds of flowers and decor filtered through the tree branches. Hare wobbled on two tired feet as he crouched in one of the ivory canopies.

The young black leaves had started to bloom, giving him a little cover to watch the wedding from up high. He dug his clunky third version e-disk from his pocket—a *gift* he found in the sand from the station above the tents—to let Jack know he'd be a little longer. Jack didn't need to know why, even when he asked.

The curly-headed, no good brother sat with another woman, whispering to each other with plastic smiles on their faces.

It wasn't fair.

Jealousy was a foreign feeling for the runner who claimed to not care. He found himself wrestling with the worms flopping around in his midsection— the envy in his brain telling him to feel sick. He wouldn't give in.

If Nico wanted to leave him behind, so be it. If he wanted to move on with his new friends and his new girlfriend, who was he to protest anyway? A curse-addled *twin* brother? Bah! The blame was squarely his, and he knew that after escaping him all that time ago.

I still love you, Nico's declaration after getting stabbed and left in the desert repeated itself like a guilty mantra in his head. How? How could he?

...Did he still?

They used to be so close that no one could ever tell them apart. Hare sighed. Now look at him—dusty, musty, covered in sunburns and lines... looking old and used up. They'd definitely be able to tell them apart now. Nico was a perfect color of tan, no burns. He had a perfect smile, no missing teeth. The curls on his head were perfect and shiny, a shade of dark blond that no hairdresser could duplicate, not stringy and bleached from hours running here and there, tossed by the wind. Hare hated him for it.

It wasn't fair.

They were so evenly matched before that the kids just called them "Niki-Nico" as one amorphous human. One of them would respond—to them, it didn't matter who. If he hadn't been in his room during the night of his unfortunate transformation, his own parents probably wouldn't have known who was who.

Sitting in the tree, under cover of baby black leaves in the majestic ivory forest, Hare pictured a different life had he not turned early. He would be sitting there with his brother. Maybe with a girlfriend too and enjoying a nice wedding in public with friends. Instead, he crouched in a tree like a sicko, watching a world he missed out on.

He was a pioneer, really. So many kids turning in the desert, too early. Too young. Back then, it was a shame for a wealthy family to have a Weggevens child. He supposed he couldn't blame his parents for the pressures of society... but he did anyway. Now, were these early transformations being cast away to be forgotten? Nope, they weren't. At least none that he saw in the desert. In the desert, everyone died.

It wasn't *fair*.

Jack's message still hovered over the screen in his palm, asking how long he'd be gone. As much trouble as he gave him, Jack really wasn't that bad a guy. After he nearly bit his tongue off from the shakes, Jack found him lying in the sand near death when his parents abandoned him. Hare was lucky to be found by the very man who had just discovered the Weggevens treatment.

Brought back to the tent of an unconscious, pregnant Verena, Hare recovered next to her with the Witis drug. Feeling re-energized, and after years of practice becoming capable of controlling his buzzing legs, it was through Jack that he finally met Par. Beautiful and awful, with sweet words of power and revenge in her mouth, Hare was instantly smitten with her.

Long, dry spells would pass without her visits, and each time he prepared his strategy to win her over. Why she chose that bumbling idiot, Hammer, he'd never know. He didn't care to know any more than the resentment that festered and formed a ball of energy in his insides. Resentment toward Hammer, toward Par, toward Jack for even introducing them in the first place, then his family... especially Nico.

As he watched his brother continue to whisper to the woman next to him with smiles and not a care in all of Roseaarde, Hare thought he'd be overwhelmed with rage. Rather, in a strange twist, he felt remorse.

Nico sat there... just *happy*. After everything Hare had done to hurt him and he was still happy. Legless, but content... betrayed, yet surrounded by loved ones.

It just wasn't fair.

The desire to impress Par… to serve *cirv'e*… the moment he chose to cut out the little one's eyes… even that dude was happy, and the remorse burned. The hatred he felt to see his brother again and the desperate attempt at evening the score with violence, well, it meant nothing anymore, and he felt small for it.

Maybe Nico was right. Maybe this was why he didn't have friends. This was why his brother broke his nose, and why Jack *still* didn't trust him.

Glancing down at the syringe in his hand, he jiggled it between his fingers to see the silvery wisps swirl in the barrel. Nico said he knew how to make the drug. He wished he didn't have to rely on it. Tucking it back into his pocket with a sigh, he glanced back up to see the final wedding kiss.

The Anglia's hair had grown somewhat, and she was even hotter than before. She had filled out from the last time he saw her after being starved by Par. It was a petty thing for Par to do… why she cared about that Yonch enough to do something like that when she had the team… She had Hare.

From the corner of his eye, Hare spotted a shadow among the trees, watching the wedding from the ground. He ducked his head and held his breath, whispering a short prayer that his foot wouldn't slip.

Who was that?

Staring at the figure for what felt like ten standard minutes, it left, shuffling back through the forest to the line of cruisers parked by the small inn. The way it sauntered toward the vehicles reminded him of the same shadow that stalked them in the desert. It was familiar. Familiar enough that he wondered…

Eyes trained on the stranger, Hare narrowed them to focus his vision. The bulky figure folded itself into a regulation cruiser fitted with a strip of emergency tech along to the top. Tilting his head in confusion, there was only one thought that nagged his mind.

Was that a roundsman?

The surprises didn't end when Hare spotted another figure advancing toward the wedding. Slender, tall, scary… it wasn't one he was wholly familiar with, but the smallest hint of recognition sparked a memory. It was the memory of traveling through the umbilicus with Par to see the source of "power" she promised Hare. It was a man stuck to the wall—a grotesquerie dripping gold and groaning.

It couldn't be… could it?

He waited and watched. The man found the Yonch. Surely the man Par called "Maron" would tell him secrets. There were many secrets surrounding Maron… and Par herself. A part of him thought he should be lucky to have known some of Par's secrets—even ones she wouldn't tell her supposed "match."

It wasn't his fault they weren't his secrets to tell. He certainly paid for it with a broken nose and an extended detainment. The thing was, Par wasn't always so angry. She said she was in love once... deeply in love with the ancient glued to the wall.

Humanity had failed their world, inviting the blackness of that dimension to spread its rot. The curse that Hare carried... the curse they all carried. Maybe Maron would tell him about the... *Yeunish*.

At that moment, Hare told himself he'd stop saying Yonch. Habits were habits, after all.

He ducked his head behind the branches, watching them talk until Maron left. While the *Yeuni* was distracted with Nico, Hare shimmied down the tree and plunked into the damp grass.

Pulling out the syringe, he stuck himself with the drug and his stomach rumbled. It had been too long since he had anything so decadent as the array of hot sweets, meat buns, and candied fruits piled up on the lacy tables before him.

He propped open his pockets and readied himself for the heist before blasting through the venue and topping them up with as much as he could carry.

Ayala would love the sarga tarts.

CHAPTER 26

Steamy
LOREN

"I'VE NEVER BEEN IN A hot spring before." Damaetra stuck a toe in the water, testing the warmth. She shivered in the crisp night air. Her wedding curls swelled around her face in a platinum halo.

Steam puffed from their hole, filling the air with a salty mineral aroma. Lor went for it, slipping his body inside up to his throat. The sudden change in temperature raised the hair on his arms and he shuddered. Damaetra tittered and eased herself down the salty steps.

"Oh, ouch!" she said, rubbing her hands. "It's burning where I bite my skin."

"That'll teach you to stop putting your fingers in your mouth." He smiled, wading in her direction.

She splashed some of the water at him. "So we're married now," she said with a grin.

"That we are."

The thought of being married was something he never considered when living life as a hermit in Gale's basement. If things had changed so drastically in the last few years, how much more change would he need to anticipate? Where would they end up living, and would there be pets? Children?

That reminded him... "Hey, I should have talked to you about this before we got married, but..." He bit his lip, leaving her hanging. Eyes wide and anticipating the smack of horrid news, Dametra's mouth pressed in a thin line tight enough to whiten the pink of her lips. He sighed. "We probably shouldn't have children."

She relaxed a little, letting the color flush her mouth again. "You're afraid?"

Fear was absolute. In his case, fear was necessary.

"Aren't you?"

Her posture relaxed, and she shrugged nonchalantly. "Why fear what we can't control?"

A wave of steam warmed his neck. The mineral pools had a magic to them, the way they reflected the silver moon, casting an aqua glow in the water. Wading to the other side of the pool only large enough for four, he sat on a salted ledge and gazed at her. Her eyes were closed with a smile on her lips as she stretched her arms to either side, resting them there. The blue-green water's glassy reflection shimmered motes of white light across her nose like blanched freckles. Lor could stay in that place forever.

"We had a visitor today. At the wedding." Bringing up Maron wasn't on his post-nuptial to-do list, but he couldn't ignore it.

She giggled, keeping her eyes closed as dew clung to her eyelashes. "We had a few visitors today. Who do you mean?"

"Someone *not* on the guest list."

She opened her eyes and studied him with a half grin. "Alright, I'm interested. Who?"

"You won't believe it." To keep his thoughts straight, he stalled for just a moment. Damaetra flicked water in his direction, and a rogue drop plunked in his eye, bringing the salt fire.

"That burns!" He rubbed at it.

"Tell me who, Loren. *You* started this." She played with him.

Rubbing his salted eye, he used the good one to peer up at her. "Don't get upset, alright?"

She sat upright, dipping her hands into the water and resting them in her lap. Lines sank into her face. "Alright..."

"I'm only bringing it up because I think we need to talk about it."

"Loren, just tell me already—who did you talk to today?" Her spirited grin fell.

"Alright, alright. It was Maron. You know... Valoa'brenga."

She choked on a snicker, as if trying to swallow a dry capsule, then openly laughed. "Very funny, Loren. Maker, you had me worried for a minute."

As much as he liked hearing her laugh, it wasn't the time, and he frowned. "I'm serious. It was Maron."

Her closed-mouth smile morphed into a grimace and a head tilt. "Come on, you're joking... Maron is dead."

"No. He's immortal, remember? He can't die." He felt like such a fraud. Here he pointed out another man's immortality and continually forgot about his own. It wouldn't surprise him if Damaetra forgot too.

"How? He was nothing but mush! Did a blob slither here and visit?" She still didn't believe it.

"No, he wasn't a *blob*..."

"So he was whole? I mean, he looked normal?"

"Well…" Lor shrugged and looked up into his brow as if it would conjure Maron's face in his mind. The only word he could come up with was *otherworldly*, which Damaetra cocked an eyebrow at. "It means he didn't look like fruit jelly stuck to the wall."

She shuddered. "Ew. I was hoping to forget that."

"Sorry," he said with a chuckle.

"So what did he want?"

It happened too fast with words Lor didn't understand. Something about his people and… cirv'e. The worm. He hadn't told her about that first dream, and he didn't remember the one that made him scream out the name. "He wants me to find my people and come to the tree."

"No way are you doing any of that," she said, leaning back again.

"Why not? It's not every day an extinct race visits on your wedding day."

"Loren, we escaped that place. Why would you ever want to go back there?"

"Well, the part about an extinct race? We could learn so much about how life was in his time. Doesn't that interest you at all?"

The white reflections danced over her nose as she shifted to peer at him. "And what would you do with that information? The past is the past, and we have to think about the future. Besides, if he's the last of his kind, it's not like we can do anything to bring them back."

"I just feel like I have a bit of a responsibility to—"

"Just let it go." She tilted her head back and closed her eyes. It was the first time they really disagreed on anything, and Lor wasn't about to push it on his wedding night.

Closing his eyes as well, he stretched his leg out to see if he could reach her with his foot. When his skin made contact with hers, the white-gold smoky fractals appeared beneath his lids, still laced with faint cracks. Rethinking any plans with Maron was best—she was right. That place created those cracks in her life, and it was stupid to think about dragging her back. They were in a good place, had a whole future ahead of them, and he could just forget the whole thing.

As his foot touched her leg, she didn't try to push him away, so he kept it there, watching the colors and not knowing what to look for. Maybe he wouldn't see anything. After all, not everything had to be some complicated message.

CHAPTER 27

Feelin' Breachy
ELORIA

MONTHS OF NONSTOP NOISE. CAE'S constant yapping had Eloria on edge, and she feared she would snap. Morning, afternoon, evening… even while sleeping, her voice pierced through the walls.

It was nothing special or anything secret, just constant activity. Looking at Cae irritated her to the point where she just *stopped* looking at her. Cae didn't seem to mind but occasionally pestered her until she was acknowledged. It was a weird feeling to gaze upon a person who wore her face and be struck with the desire to punch it out of existence.

Like some sort of animal, Cae behaved like a creature of the night. Eloria found peace in rising early when her sister tired out.

The morning following the return from Pohay'an, Eloria was somewhat glad to be back in the city. More city sounds meant more noise to drown out Cae. However, a little over a month later, and even the sounds of the city were a nuisance.

She didn't know what to do anymore. Was it just hormones? Was she going through some weird bodily change unexplained by medics? Her sleep suffered, and it sallowed her already pale complexion. The long golden white hair she used to wear in loose waves became flat and greasy.

A low growl hummed from Caella's room. Another day, another nightmare. They'd been more frequent as of late, and the last time Eloria could stand to talk to her own sister, she recommended a visit to an adviser. Damaetra's new father-in-law, being in medicine, surely had connections to brain medics. Cae wouldn't hear of it—she swore Eloria was the one with the problem. And that was the end of it.

Sipping on a hot cup of bean water, she closed her eyes and hummed. The unkempt white hair tickled at her nose, and she told herself she ought to get a trim, but only a trim. When Dame had her hair chopped off, it came as a shock—she always loved her long hair. But it wasn't until she overheard Dame talking about it that she knew. It wasn't her story to tell Aedras, but Dame should tell him at least. He'd be furious. Hell, it still made Eloria angry. Whoever this "Par" person was would find the hostile side of her knuckles. Right in the damn kisser.

The why's made her feel inadequate... why wouldn't Dame talk to her about it? Why did she have to overhear her talking about it to someone else? Openly on the train, no less?

At any rate, she overheard a lot of things lately. Whatever hormone issue she was having made her hearing overly sensitive. That's what she told herself when listening to all the horrible banter on the train. The cute one, Nico, just freely talked about his feelings for that Eva chick. She was sitting right there, man! Maybe she liked that sort of obsessive talk—feeding her ego or some such crap. The little one, Dill, talked about things that made Eloria debate therapy. Why couldn't they just shut up and shove it down? Citizens had more respect for people who weren't so emotionally raw in public. Who was she kidding... *Eloria* had more respect for respectable people. *Silent* people.

A shuffle and the sound of a tome falling to the floor thumped in Cae's room. Eloria cupped her face in her hands and sighed at the sound of Cae getting up too early. Tromping into the kitchen, she brought her noises with her... blah, blah, blah.

The sounds gave her a headache, and she rubbed her temples, hoping to stamp out Cae's voice. She had learned to despise it and become irrationally angry at it. By pressing her temples, she could force a low ambient drumming in her ears that helped.

In Cae's case, it was nonstop. When she went to the plinth for morning rations, it was *toast, toast, toast, toast*, then *fruit, fruit, fruit, fruit*. A random growl, then a return to repeating herself. Even the drumming struggled to pound it out. Cae sat across from her muttering *eat, eat, eat, eat*.

At once, Eloria raked her fingers down her face, leaving angry red lines down her cheeks. "Caella, by the Maker, for once would you just *shut* the *hell* up!"

Cae stared at her sister in silence, eyes wide and brows raised almost to her hairline. After a moment, she narrowed them and pursed her lips. "I didn't *say* anything."

Tending to her toast, she spread fruit jelly over the top and took a bite. As she chewed, Eloria heard her ruminations. *I wonder what the weather's like, I wonder if they have a handsome friend I could meet, I think I should wash my clothes today...*

Mouth closed, she sat chewing while playing on her e-disk to avoid

Eloria's glare, yet the words continued. She couldn't have said anything—not with her mouth closed. But Eloria heard it. How was it possible?

After a minute of glares from Eloria, Cae actually opened her mouth to speak, looking up and rubbing her stomach. "I haven't been feeling very well since the wedding," she said. Her repeated pattern morphed into *meat, meat, meat, meat.*

Shocked at the new desire, Eloria never knew Cae to eat meat. However, she herself never turned away a good slice, and a sleeve of red crackers sat at her place at the table. Testing what she heard, Eloria slowly wrapped her fingers around the sleeve while watching Cae. It crinkled under her grip, which stirred her sister's interest. Her eyes, black with hunger, watched Eloria's hand as it held the precious stack of meat.

"Is the toast not sitting well in your stomach?" she asked. "Or how about the fruit jelly?"

Meat, meat, meat, meat.

Cae stalked her sleeve of red crackers like some sort of night cat. Peeling back the sleeve and plucking a cracker from inside caused Cae's head to bob and weave to watch. She licked her lips.

"Do you want one?" she asked.

Cae nodded feverishly, and when Eloria tossed her the meat cracker, it disappeared between sharp teeth. Eloria blinked and rubbed her eyes. She must have been seeing things. Cae's teeth were normal, lodged with bits of the red flesh. The noises had crescendoed into sloppy wet sounds as her sister relished the salted meat with hums and moans. It was obscene.

Flipping on her e-disk, she set a reminder to make an appointment with a medic regarding these insufferable hormone shifts.

So ridiculous. Eloria wrapped her jacket closer to her body as she walked through the streets of Audun. It was so damn loud.

Normally, street sounds were a slight comfort to her, but everyone and everything had to make noise, and it had to be in her ears. The medic was available immediately, so she took the appointment. If she had to endure any more of Cae's wet noises, she was afraid she'd disfigure her sister's face.

Missing a day of work had her on edge. She loved her job and didn't want to imagine the wrong-think some substitute would try to program into her young students' minds. It was paranoia, for sure, but it persisted nonetheless.

The ivory capitol building came and went as she passed by, and her ears felt ready to explode from intersecting pandemonium.

It had to be hormones. There were capsules for this type of thing. Before she knew it, she'd be in and out of the medic with a script for some herbal that would either cure her for real or blanket her in placebo. Either way was fine with her as long as the noises just stopped.

Her feet hit the ground in rhythmic steps, but she could only feel the pressure of the walk. The external din overwhelmed any other aural trigger.

If she had to shoot up with some Formulator draught that cost a hundred plat a pop, she'd do it. Anything to stanch the noise.

The medic building was black with an ugly green trim around windows and doors. The ugly beacon made her quicken her pace to get inside.

The waiting room was warm and stuffy, setting off her sweat glands from the rushed walk inside. Taking off her jacket, she fanned herself with it, inviting stares from other sickly patrons. She ignored them. Fortunately, the assistant called her name quickly.

"Miss Praes, what brings you in today?" The medic swiped around on a V-note he cradled in his elbow. He uttered a grunt of irritation as the holo buttons projected from the screen glitched over the wrinkles in his shirt.

"I'm hearing everything. I think it's hormones," she said, trying to maintain a serious face. It was hard to stay serious when festival rave music played in her ears. She glanced around for speakers or some source playing the music. Finding none, she tried to focus. The medic was wickedly handsome.

"Hearing everything? Hormones don't do that, Miss Praes." He strolled toward her to check her vitals, and the festival music bumped harder.

It was the type of music weekenders listened to while rubbing up against each other and taking pills or shooting up sketchy draughts. Not a very professional track list for a medic's office.

As he pressed fingers into her wrist and listened to her heart, she could feel his thoughts as if they were her own. Standing deceitfully close while asking her to take deep breaths, the artery in his neck pulsed to the electric beat. He didn't fool her. His eyes were fixed on her cleavage.

Sweat rivulets danced down her temples in the dark room full of laser lights, holo icons, and intoxicated dancers undulating with the tempo. The pressure on her wrist sent electric pulses into her spine when she took in the scent of baked pheromones radiating off the medic's neck. She closed her eyes and bit her lip, moving in just a little bit closer...

"Well, Miss Praes." He jerked back, swiping notes into his tablet. The sterile room had returned, and the music stopped. There were no dancers or lights—it was just them. "Have you visited, or been in contact with, members of the desert?"

Still reeling from the weekender party in her head, she blinked and cleared her throat. "N-no? Not that I know of."

More swiping on the V-note. "Have you experimented with or habitually used the unlicensed Yeunish drug known as 'audioxine'?"

Just some street drug she'd never heard of. Eloria prided herself on keeping her body clean. Did someone slip it to her?

"Gehenna no. I don't do drugs."

The medic eyed her. The look was charming—green eyes under hooded lids and a swarthy complexion. Heat crawled up her neck.

"That's good to know." He focused on her chart again, swiping in more data. "One last test... this is very new tech, and I'd like to try it out on you if I have your permission?"

The electric beat crescendoed again, thumping party music in her ears. When she spoke, her voice fought with the fluids in her head. "What is it?"

"It tests your blood for specific markers that can tell me frmr fmlwomolgil..." His voice sank into the vortex of bass beats. The dull pink of his mouth moved in rhythm as his attention drifted from her face to a gadget he pulled from a drawer. Sweat collected at her upper lip. "Are you paying attention, Miss Praes?"

She dragged a sleeve across her mouth. "Yes, go ahead and use it."

It was a small finger draw that sucked her blood into a blue-gray device plugged into his V-note, which she had to press her thumb into. The device registered her print, loading the holo image to hover over the screen in full 270-degree display. The medic pinched and spun the print around, zooming in on specific areas in the labyrinth of lines while her blood numbers ticked away underneath it.

The scrolling values oscillated like a gambling game, and she held her breath. The first value appeared, and it meant nothing to her. Then the second, then the third... all values ticked into place until three neat rows of ten lined up under the hovering thumbprint. Some values were green, some were blue.

The medic hummed. "Very interesting," he said, turning her arm back and forth.

"So what's wrong with me?" Little bumps raised on her skin as his touch lingered there.

"Nothing is wrong with you at all... you're perfect," he said with a wink. "You're a late bloomer is all."

She didn't like the sound of that. If he meant to make her feel young and small, it worked.

"A late bloomer?" she asked.

"It doesn't happen often, but your opportunities just got so much better." He shrank the data down into the V-note, swiping more notes inside. "Based on my assessments, and a positive result from the G-scan, it appears that you have developed into a Guild."

His endearing asymmetrical smile should tell her to be happy, but she was confused.

"No. I'm non-Guild. I'm in arts."

Even his laugh made her knees weak. "Yes, you certainly are. But now, if you so choose, you can move to Celerity city and work with the other Readers. I'm a little jealous, to be honest."

It made sense. It made complete, total, utter sense. This was her life... forever bathed in the thoughts, feelings... and *music* of others. Never would she relish a moment of peace again.

"I don't understand." Of course she understood.

"Are you interested in working in the Seven cities? I'm sure you can find a community there. Like-*minded* people to commiserate with." He chuckled at his bad pun.

"I don't want to be a Reader. I'm in arts, remember?"

That decadent laugh again. "Yes, of course. But you must understand that whether or not you choose to work in Celerity, you still have to register with the cities."

Her heart thumped in her chest. City registration was a life sentence of being tracked. As an arts member, no one cared about who she was or what she was doing, and she liked it that way.

"Listen, I-I'm happy where I am. I don't need to actually register anything, do I?"

As he slid the V-note on the counter, he looked at her with pity, making her feel like a child again. Moving to a different set of drawers, he withdrew a golden button the size of her fingertip. "Unfortunately, you need to be registered with this diagnosis. You're a *natural* Reader, which Audun would find very interesting... and useful. Especially one so powerful as your numbers suggest."

"No thanks," she said, collecting her jacket and bag, preparing to stand. The medic stood up before her, holding the golden implant.

"No choice," he said. In that moment, his charm wasn't so charming, and his mannerisms were just patronizing.

Again, her heart raced. She fluttered her lids and straightened herself, arranging for her last resort—a seduction. In secondary school, after her body pumped curvy hormones throughout all the parts that mattered, she used her wiles in ways that got her out of a jam many times over.

The medic was handsome, and perhaps immune, but she would try her former ways with him. Earlier, she felt him checking her out, and wanted to use that to her advantage. And use it she did.

Big blue-violet eyes gazed at him under the long, thick white lashes. She was sweating at her nape, so she flicked her thick white-gold hair behind her shoulder so he could get a whiff of her scent. Thick lips curled into a saucy grin as her fingertips found the hand that held the implant.

His skin was cold, but she felt the tiny bumps rise under her touch. As she caressed his forearm, the hairs stood on end, flushing blood into his cheeks.

"I don't want to be a Reader," she whispered into his ear. At her words, his body stiffened.

"I hear you don't want to be a Reader," he affirmed. The shift to a stiffer tone was unexpected, but she used it.

With another whisper, "You can put that implant away then."

The golden button slowly disappeared beneath his closing fingers. "I'll go ahead and put this away."

He broke away from her stiff-legged and moving on auto, to plunk the implant back in the kit where it came from. Turning to her, he smiled. The smile unnerved her—it was rigid and compliant. The color of his eyes had darkened, and he stood across from her... as if waiting for his next instruction.

She backed away toward her escape route, slowly watching him as he watched her. "Goodbye," she said hesitantly.

He waved in staccato swipes. "Goodbye."

Leaving the exam room, she marched down the stark white hall, hoping not to be stopped. She pulled out her e-disk, ready to swipe her fee to be let out of the building.

That vacant stare, the blind repetition of her demand... that was not physical appeal that persuaded him. She stared at her hand. Nothing about it had changed, but her touch did something to him.

The e-disk beeped at the door, withdrawing her fee, then unlocked to let her free. Once she stepped onto the pavement, she ran. The blood in her legs pumped fire as she sprinted down the street. Jumpers whirred past in high-pitched wails as the murmurs of citizens assaulted her mind. Just as the noise about tipped her into madness, the breeze whistled songs across her ears in a welcome white noise.

Focus on the wind. Just focus on the wind.

The more she repeated the mantra, the more the chaotic noises dissipated, until nothing but the breeze remained. She grinned to herself, feeling at peace for the first time in months.

Their apartment appeared at the eighth block of running, and Eloria caught sight of Dame and her new husband getting out of a jumper taxi in front of it.

"Dame!" she shouted. Both of them turned to her as the jumper pulled away.

"Elo-lo, great timing!" Damaetra said with a smile.

"What are you doing here?" She slowed down and bent over to draw in heavier breaths. She wasn't interested in hearing dirty thoughts about her sister from her new husband.

"Cae called. She was hysterical, so we rushed over here."

"She was?"

"Well, yeah. I mean, she's been acting strange for a while, but this time it was different. More real and less exaggerated."

Eloria guided them inside, taking the lift to their apartment. When they opened the door, Dame swooned.

"Whoa, it really stinks in here, Elo," she said.

"What? I don't smell anything. Do you?" Eloria motioned to Loren. He just shrugged and shook his head "no."

"Caella!" Eloria shouted.

"It's like... It smells like an animal in here. Did an animal get in your apartment?" Damaetra plugged her nose as she spoke.

"No, I told you I don't smell anything, Dame." She called for Cae a few more times until a faint cry came from the bathroom.

The echo of her voice sounded in Eloria's mind while she was still in the bathroom. "Elo-lo, what is going on?" Cae whimpered, strutting into the room on four white velvet paws to sit at Eloria's feet.

The blue-violet eyes of her twin stared up at her, under more white down and long white whiskers. Her pointed ears twitched, listening.

Damaetra cried out, putting a hand to her mouth.

Loren pressed his palms toward the floor as if it would stop the transformation. "Don't move, and don't change back. You need Nico's help."

DON'T BE A VICTIM!

A new Yeunish drug has hit the streets and has the youth addicted!

Help Audun rid our country of the illegal formulation known as "AUDIOXINE"

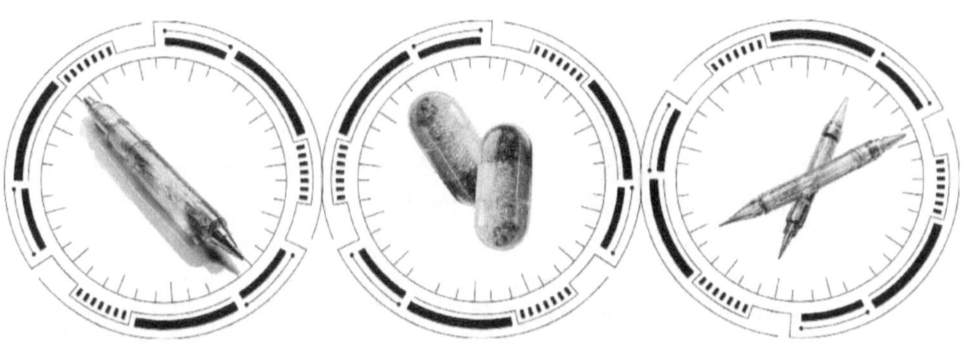

YOU MAY HAVE ALREADY RUN INTO IT!

Symptoms include, but are not limited to: excessive thirst, seeing the world in shades of orange, hearing voices that aren't there, an irrational desire to slam your head into a hard surface, and a sore throat.

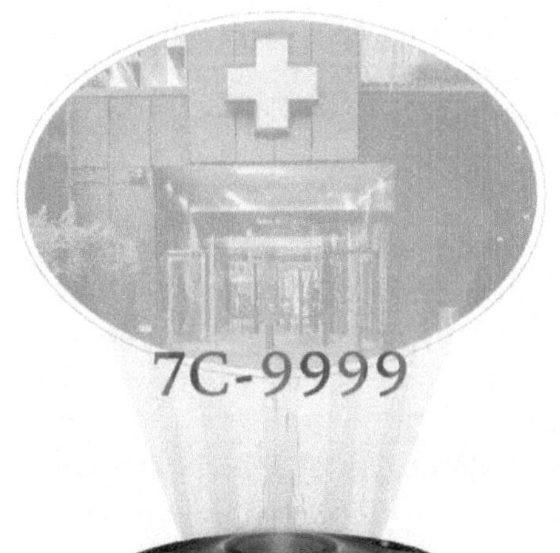

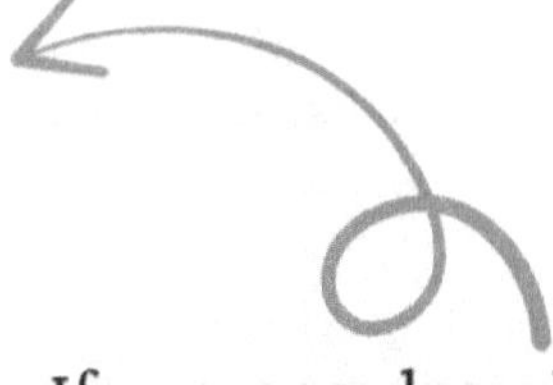

If you or a loved one has been affected by audioxine, please reach out to the Audun rehab hotline at 7C-9999.

CHAPTER 28

Guild Rot

STUPID. IDIOTS. THEY WERE EVERYWHERE. That old man who lit up and stained the marble inside the spire... it took the Foscans two full days to scrub most of it out. Guild rot... all of them.

Just the other day, three people turned in the market. Three! These jerks can't help but interrupt a man getting rations without fainting like a woman. Gehenna.

Wearing the blue and gold of Audun, the roundsman stood to his full height with the ivory crumbs of oatcress and protein rations flaking from his uniform. The older woman who sat next to him on the park bench glanced up with milky eyes and smiled in a kind of fear that anyone could have mistaken as an anticipation for rain. No, not a rain cloud, it was only his wide shadow, spreading over everything it touched.

The lingering taste of the protein block's savory sweetness lingered in his mouth as he brushed off the remaining crumbs, then strutted to his city-issued cruiser, taking his shadow with him. He parked in front of the no parking placard, because he was a busy man. Sliding into the slick interior, the material groaned.

The front panel lit up when he pressed his thumb to the ID lock, showing several yellow dots lazily moving around on the screen. His job was special—the Guild crime unit. Each implant represented a sorry sap moving about their day in a trackable yellow circle at his fingertips. One particular dot held his interest day after day.

It used to travel to and from the Formulator city of Milaris and the outskirts of Audun during business hours. Lately, it traveled from Milaris to Peakwood. Rumor had it this particular Formulator married a Yonch. He was all too pleased to spread that rumor, which gifted him the authority to keep an eye on that dot. He was determined to find that Yonch and collect the bounty.

It wasn't about the plats, really. It was about sending that bastard to the Southern Morass. He dragged his nubbed fingernails over a jagged pink scar, scratching that deep itch that never went away. As he did, his foot got heavy on the accelerator.

As he raced down the road, a Danashi jumper driver pulled out in front of him, slowing down once they realized they just insulted a roundsman. He grinned at that, satisfied at their discomfort enough to not immediately issue a citation.

Their bumpers nearly touched as he followed the jumper. He liked how it made drivers sweat, imagining all the stupid thoughts running through their stupid heads. *What did I do? Am I speeding? Did my numbers expire?* While trailing the terrified driver, his intestines rumbled.

Must've been a sketchy oatcress bar.

He belched the flavor of bland grain with another squeaky undulation in his gut. Sighing, he flipped on his blue and yellow emergency lights. The Danashi skittered out of the way immediately, giving him the freedom to press harder on the accelerator. More vehicles parted in the warmth of his emergency beam. *Yes, obey the law, insects.*

Watching the road split for him made the blood pool in his groin, and he adjusted accordingly as the already snug city-issued uniform got tighter. He sped through the rift, blowing street litter in a twirling trail of degraded paper and discarded bags.

CHAPTER 29

Little Ones
ELORIA

"YES, A CAT. UH-HUH," LOR told Nico over a call. The small holo image of Nico's bust hovered over the e-disk. He occasionally looked over his shoulder, at whom, Eloria couldn't tell.

"I can be there in about twenty standard," he said.

"Awesome." Lor flicked off the image and tucked his e-disk away.

Eloria paced the room with her thumbnail pressed between her teeth. When they filled her in on the nature of Jack's creation, she didn't take it well. Those poor souls... "You know, the cities make a medication for Weggevens."

Damaetra lounged on the couch, holding a hand to the left side of her back. "Yeah, but their medication is expensive, with too many side effects. *This* treatment is—"

"Illegal," Eloria finished.

Damaetra sat back, scrunching her flushed nose.

Caella mewled as she curled up on a chair across from Damaetra, then let out a low growl. Beneath the animal sounds, Cae's faint plea called out in frustration. *What do I do* was the most Eloria could make out.

"We're working on it, Cae. Just be patient," Eloria said.

Damaetra tilted her head at her, pursing her lips. "Is that a twin thing or something?" she asked.

"Is *what* a twin thing?"

"The thing where you knew what she said just now."

She already forgot. No one knew about her reading ability. "O-oh. Uh, no. Not really."

"You speak cat then?"

Just focus on your own heartbeat, Elo.

It was just barely enough to drown out Dame's incessant head noise.

Eloria stopped pacing to lean against the wall without an answer. Dame glared at her, waiting for an explanation.

"No, I don't speak *cat*," she said, folding her arms. "Why can't she just change back, anyway?"

From the window, Lor gazed out at the street and spoke to the glass, fogging an oval over the pane. "Do you *have* a Weggevens treatment from the cities?"

Eloria huffed, burning a hole in the back of his head. "Of course I don't have it," she said.

"From what I remember, transforming back and forth is what drains a skin changer," Lor continued, coming into the room, "and with nothing to help her if she did change, it could probably do some damage."

Cae growled again. Rather than answer, Eloria held up a finger at her feline sister.

The motion didn't go unnoticed by the prying Dame. Eloria rolled her eyes, waiting for the incoming questions. "Seriously, though, it really seems like you know what she's saying. How?" Dame asked.

The noises swelled again—a messy racket of Dame's grumbling, Lor's humming, and Cae's whining. Resuming her pacing, Eloria focused on the only sound she could somewhat control. Her heart beat fast, but not even loud enough to drown out the tiniest fraction of dissonant sounds.

An echoing cadence of Dame's same question drummed louder, and louder, and louder still: *Tell me how. Tell me how. Tell me how. Tell me how.*

Persistent brat.

Eloria clutched her head and made a deep rumbling groan through her throat, rising into a bark. "I'm a Reader, alright? I'm a Reader, and I need you all to just *shut up*!"

It was the first real moment of peace she had in as long as she could remember. If only she had a handy pocket full of surprises to announce every time she needed to shut the inner mouths of everyone around her.

"You're a *Reader*?" Dame's voice was a whisper. "I mean, I know there've been a lot of Weggevens changes, but not high-class Guild abilities. When did this happen?"

"I don't know," she whined, "a while ago. I was diagnosed today."

"Did they tag you?" Lor asked.

Eloria held out her arms. "The medic tried, but I convinced him not to."

"You convinced him, or you *pushed* him?" The leery look on his face made her feel naked, and she hated him for that.

The gift of the push was prized in Audun. The way the medic lusted after learning what she was—eager to implant her and turn her over to the cities. There must have been some finder's fee for turning in someone that powerful. Thinking back on it upset her, and a tiny crack of a smile twitched at the corner of her mouth when she remembered how pliable the sap was when she easily convinced him to let her go.

"I guess I pushed him," she said, "but I ran out of there so fast, I didn't even get anything to help with the noise."

Damaetra sighed. "I'm sorry, Elo. I guess—"

There was a knock at the door, and Nico's face pressed against the frosted glass insert.

"I had a couple left, but I'm going to have to make more," he said as he strolled inside wagging a small leather roll. "Where is she?"

Caella had moved to the dark wood floor. She whapped her tail against it, sending wisps of white fur into the air and it collected in whorls around her. When Nico saw her, he tried not to laugh.

"Well, if anything, you can always find a home with the cat colonies in Secas," he said, getting a hearty hiss in response from Cae.

"Alright, alright, go ahead and change back." He pulled out a syringe, flicking the barrel.

Cae stretched out, pushing her tail into the air. She whimpered, sitting back down and tilting her head. No one had to know how to speak cat to realize she wasn't sure what to do.

"I guess just concentrate on being human," Nico said with a shrug.

Eloria tittered in amusement, as if such a sentiment was all it took. If only reading was like that.

Cae stretched again, furry white legs elongating in front of her. The mantra *human, human, human*, repeated in her mind clear as any word spoken out loud to Eloria. There had to be more to it than that. It wasn't until Cae really started describing herself, or what she thought of herself, that the change stirred.

Pores in her skin slurped up the fur. Once the velvet down retreated, her hands grew to normal size, but rather than her claws retracting, they spread over her nail bed to form human nails. Pointed ears slipped down the sides of her head, rounding out and smoothing the plush fur to reveal bright, snowy skin.

At least Loren had the decency to turn away when Cae lay there, bare-assed on the floor. It was too much to ask Nico not to be a pervert.

"I'm completely naked!" Cae cried, rolling to her side, both hands darting back and forth, trying to decide which private area to shield. The couch blanket was just enough to cover her as Eloria left to get her some clothes.

Shuffling through Cae's drawers on the other side of the flat wasn't distance enough to drown out all the head noises. Cae being the loudest, she worried most about not having control over herself. With no medication, would she wither and die?

A back-and-forth exchange fired up as Nico offered to let Cae stay with him to give Eloria's "reading" a break, which Eloria found rather thoughtful for the guy who not moments ago was peeping her sister's breasts. He also offered to supply her with his special back-alley injection that she thought abhorrent.

Fisting a wad of clothes for Cae, Eloria marched back into the room, tossing the crumpled fabric on top of her prone sister.

"I think it's a good idea to take Nico up on his offer, Cae," Eloria said.

"That's not going to get annoying at all, you hearing *everything*," Cae said, slipping on a long shirt as the men continued to avert their eyes.

"I was only in the other room, and you're loud. He's right, though. I need a break from the noise."

Cae tittered and finished dressing, giving everyone the all clear to look at her again.

Underneath the toxic waves of Cae's self-doubt, Eloria heard the smallest whisper: *What do I do?*

Dame muttered in her head, and it was just audible enough to hear as a whisper through a closed door: *Loren was right, we never should have tried for children... oh Maker, what do I do?*

Eloria gawked at her baby sister, and she gawked at her in return. "Dame... are you pregnant?" she barked.

Lor's eyebrows climbed his face, and he shot a look at Dame, mouth open. Eloria realized her mistake, covering her mouth and uttering "sorry" into her palm as Dame's goofy gawking crumpled into an annoyed glare.

Nico held out his fist for a bump, but Lor just stared at it until loosely rapping his own closed knuckles against it.

Chapter 30

Patchy People
Jack / Hare

About a week had passed since the Freely patriarch became a Shepherd. With the surge of Weggevens curses, it was a nice change to see a Guild ability that didn't require illicit treatment. Jack had grown tired of making it. It was not lucrative work, and it began to consume most of his time.

Verena hit wall after wall in her pursuit of creating something useful from the ancient tech Hare brought back. After many requests to meet the Engineer Hare mentioned who could manipulate the material, the truth of his relationship with Dill finally came out.

The following month was an irritating season of passive aggression between Verena and Hare that Jack was eager to get through. Although, since no one hardly talked to each other during that time, he was able to dedicate himself to experimentation, finding the right mimic for silver by mixing purple with white and a touch of obsenis forturum, the plentiful and cheap black eneris. Once purified and rendered, the ratio was able to sustain the formula without using dead people.

No one he knew understood what eneris truly was, which got him thinking more and more about the implications of using such a material in his formula. Maker forbid it to be their soul... how many people had he damned to exist in the veins of a random Weggevens? No tome explained it either, leaving Jack to simply wonder, then push it out of his mind.

The new formula gave him a little respite, knowing that he no longer had to rely on illegally sourcing silver for shady dealings. However, obtaining the purple was no easier. Because of that, Jack didn't question Hare when he brought some back.

Down in the bunker, Jack held a few freshly minted alt-silver pearls in his palm, rolling them around to hear the dull clinking sounds they made when smacking together. If he could spare one or two, Verena could use them in her pursuit of crafting a permanent Weggevens cure from the ancient tech. It would revolutionize the market and also make Jack's job easier.

As he rolled the pearls in his palm, Verena stuttered down the ladder into the bunker in a rush.

"I have an idea, and I don't want to lose it," her voice warbled from the hurried steps down the ladder as she rushed toward the drawer that stored the collected pieces of ancient tech.

The drawer got stuck on opening, full to stuffed with the pieces of tech Hare had brought back from his journeys.

As she fussed with the pieces, lining them up on the counter, she turned to Jack. "Do you have any more silver to spare?"

The alt-silver pearls still sat in his palm, and he considered them. "Actually," he said, pausing to pluck one from the cluster, "try this if you will."

Handing it to her, she took it with a raised eyebrow. "I need to try—"

"If it doesn't work, I have a few silver beads left."

She studied the replacement piece and nodded. Without another word, she went to work.

Jack left her to pursue her idea for several weeks. The alt-silver pearl supply diminished, and Hare had to acquire more purple somehow. The runner claimed to receive it through his parents' guilt plats, but either way, Jack didn't care how he got it. At one point, Verena requested an errand to fetch more ancient tech.

Over time, as Verena worked and Hare got her the materials she needed, she stopped being passive aggressive with him and stopped thinking about the whole matter of his violence against people. As long as he felt his remorse, it satisfied her.

It fell even further from her mind when she had a breakthrough with her experiment. Without divulging her secret, she worked tirelessly for several more days until she finally emerged from the bunker, several shades lighter and several pounds thinner. Jack frowned when he saw her shrunken curves and shapely dress drooping in all the good spots.

"I think I did it," she proclaimed, holding a pebble-sized square, thinner than parchment. Little angry spikes protruded from one plane, while the other had silvered symbols shimmering on the surface.

"What is it?" Jack asked, reaching out to observe the piece. Verena withdrew the new toy and held it instead to Hare.

"Will you try it for me?" she asked as Hare took it from her and turned it back and forth. "If it does what I programmed it to do, it will replace Jack's treatment. Permanently!"

She clasped her hands together at her mouth, pressing her front tooth on a knuckle.

Hare chuckled. "Hell yeah, I'm going to try it—what do I do?"

Verena picked the piece from his hand and aimed the spikes toward his arm. "It sticks to you. Like this."

Without warning, she jabbed the spikes into his arm as he let out a yelp. Ayala giggled when his voice cracked.

Hare's shaking fingers danced around his skin where the new implant affixed itself. "A little warning next time?"

"Sorry, sometimes you just have to go for it. How do you feel?"

There was nothing remarkable about the implant. It sat there, hooked into his flesh, and did nothing but pinch. "I don't feel anything."

"Oh! It has to be activated, hold on." Verena took his hand, pulling out a finger to extend it. Then she guided his finger along the side of the implant, gliding it down until the symbols embossed with alt-silver lit up like some sort of ancient magic. Ayala awed at the change, moving closer to examine it, then standing on her toes to get a better view.

"I recommend only activating it when you have to run, but it should keep you safe from life drain. Want to take it for a spin? Give it a test for Ayala?"

"Yeah, I can be the test Hare," he said sarcastically .

"Good. Because her friends Quint, Betta, and Treece need them too."

The new patch clung to Hare's skin, an itchy irritation at first, then just another part of his arm, flexing and bending with every movement. He ran a finger around the edge where it responded to his touch. The engravings that framed the little patch illuminated a soft ivory glow, sustained by his own blood at the surface where it touched the alt-silver filigree.

In the time it took Hare to grow used to the new extension, Verena had crafted an abundance of the little things, intended for other tent residents. He was able to snag a few from her drawer.

The instructions were to activate it only when he needed to run. He intended to run. There was a small errand he wanted to make.

A new pastime of his had become ritually stalking Nico. Every time he found himself at his brother's apartment complex, he froze. Daytime, nighttime... he knew the routines and watched Nico's silhouette behind gauzy curtains. He blamed the stalking on the "twin thing." Really, he knew it was more than that.

Laughing to himself, he thought about how easy it was to find Nico in the network street codex. Only the Maker would find Hare, as no person in their right mind would purposely allow their location to be stored there. But a city worker drone would.

Were the thousands of plats worth it to trade his whole identity to the cities? Hare sighed and looked down at his worn shoes. Maybe it was. If he'd been raised right, the Weg city Pandemonia could have been his future. He could deliver packages to rich jerks for hot meals and a real roof over his head instead of fabric and sand.

Jack did good by him, though, getting him his own tent. It was cozy, in its own way... not like Nico's building, tall and lifeless metal gleaming against the sky and absorbing light. Standing on the other side of the street, Hare bent his neck back to find the window of apartment 333. A faint light cast its glow from a deep inner room, revealing the open balcony door. Gossamer curtains breathed in and out from the opening.

The night was temperate, perfect for open windows and the comforting aroma of lingering sunlit surfaces. A sweet aroma of distant rain came in subtle waves as Hare glanced around for any strangers watching him. He swiped in a quick message to Jack, letting him know he'd be back in a standard hour and that all was well. Jack, a man of few words, responded with a thumbs-up.

Scanning his surroundings once again to confirm he was indeed alone, he hooked a foot into the first of the fire escape loops.

After Nico's favorite buddy's marriage, it wasn't much of a surprise that he would choose to live with his *second* favorite buddy. The little tech-eyed freak liked his sleep, and Hare made sure to set his e-disk timer to Dill's bedtime.

Hand over foot, he arrived at 333. It was the closest he'd ever got to being inside the apartment, and his fingers shook. Yeah, Nico said he loved him, but that was a long time ago. It probably wasn't true anymore, and he was here, on his balcony... a complete stranger his brother might be inclined to call the roundsmen on.

What did he expect by showing up uninvited? Open arms? A hug and forgiveness? A relationship? What did he even want from Nico? He hesitated on the ledge, watching the curtains lick the door like hungry tongues looking for a morsel.

The pair of Weg patches clinked together in his pocket. He meant to make amends with his brother through Verena's tech, but he was afraid it wouldn't work. After all, his gift was only valuable to the medic, old "what's-his-name."

It didn't feel right... he wasn't nailed with about a hundred knockout needles by that group to expect a warm handshake and a hearty hello.

He said he loved you...

One foot turned on the rail, he hesitated as he peered down at the distance needed to climb down.

"Hey, what are you doing out here this late?" The soft voice sent chills up the back of his neck. Whoever it was that snuck up on him had been quiet as hell. When he turned, he almost fell from the rail, but her quick hand grabbed his shirt, pulling him back to safety.

"Wait, you're not Nico... Am I seeing things?"

He jumped to the solid security of the balcony, brushing wrinkles from his shirt. "Who are you?" he asked, realizing that was stupid.

She made a dismissive laugh. "Who are *you*? And why are you on the balcony?"

"I was about to go... sorry, I didn't mean to upset you—I'll be leaving now." He turned to pull himself back over the rail.

"No, wait," she said, clutching his shirt sleeve and tugging it toward her. Her nails were painted a bright shade of orange. "Are you Nico's brother or something? I didn't know he had a brother."

It was no use lying to her. Despite all his physical flaws, he still looked like his brother. The grip she had on his shirt was tight enough that even if he tried to run, he'd leave his shirt behind, still clenched in her dainty fist. And he didn't have a lot of shirts. She kept her grip on his sleeve, and her light bluish eyes pierced his face, scanning him up and down. It made him feel completely exposed.

"I-I'm his twin. Please don't tell him I'm here."

The fabric slid from her orange-tipped fingers. "Wow, Nico has a twin too? I'm Caella. Everyone just calls me Cae. What's your name?"

"Uh..." He hesitated, not used to attention from other women. Especially beautiful ones. They either ignored him, laughed at him, or occasionally spit at him. The only ones that treated him like a friend were Verena and Ayala.

She stood there, waiting for his answer with an upturned brow and folded arms. A smirk followed rhythmic tapping over her bicep. What name should he give her? Surely he couldn't give her his real name. Or his runner name. The desert Hare was a code name, but he no longer cared for it to be his identity. Par gave it to him, and she lied to everyone.

This woman was a fresh start—he could give her any name he wanted. Hell, he could call himself Tito and she wouldn't know any different. Then they could run away together and disappear completely.

"You still with me?" She snapped her fingers in front of him. It was remarkably loud. "I can't just call you 'Uh,'" she said with a giggle. "Or, I suppose I *can* if that's what you want to be called."

Still cycling through options, he swallowed, telling her the first thing that came to mind. "Sorry, my name is Niklaus."

Cae cleared her throat and straightened her shoulders, sticking out her hand like a law-minded militant. "Well, Niklaus, it's just a pleasure to meet you, randomly, in the dark, on Nico's balcony."

Taking her hand, he tittered. There was something familiar about Cae he couldn't put his finger on. "What did you mean by, 'Nico has a twin *too*'?"

Glancing over her shoulder into the dim apartment, she turned back to him with a grin. "Well, I just happen to be a twin myself. Would you look at that? We already have something in common."

A smile crept across his face, exposing his missing canine.

"Look at that dimple," she said with a giggle, "you *are* Nico's twin."

The blood rushed to his cheeks, and her words made him feel sweaty. He couldn't remember the last time he was compared to his brother. Probably before he turned. It was nice to feel equal to him again.

"Ah, hm, well," he stammered, "don't tell him I was here."

Putting a hand on her hip, the blue hue of night cut a shadow into her figure, and she tilted her head. "Are you two not on speaking terms? Is that why you're sneaking around on the balcony?"

It was way more than not being on speaking terms. Betrayal after betrayal would have surely had Nico on the defensive, unwilling to give more chances after the third, fourth... fifth? Cae didn't need to know any of that.

"Not really, no."

She grinned at him. "So, why *are* you here then? The mysterious, handsome Niklaus?"

Handsome. The blood flushed his cheeks again and he looked away, hoping not to reveal how affected he was by her charm. "I'm, well... I came to give him something to give to a Weggevens friend."

"Oh? It wouldn't happen to be for *me*, would it?" A swift breeze played at a string of her short hair, and it shimmered in the low light of the apartment.

"Ah, uh, are you a Weg?"

She smirked and brushed the little hair back, straightening wrinkles from her night shirt. The starlight blue shirt clung to her features, draping down to her mid-thigh and swaying in tandem with the curtain. Pale light illuminated her white skin. She could have been a mythical night spirit. It made his heart quicken, and he backed up a little more in the safety of the shadow.

"I'm a new one, but yeah," she said.

The Weggevens patches itched his thigh from inside his worn pocket. It would be a shame to leave here without giving one to her.

He cleared his throat, standing upright and forcing down his nerves. "Would you look at that? We have something *else* in common," he said with a smile.

"No way, really? What are you?"

He twisted around to lift a foot and show the worn and yellow stained soles of his shoes. "I'm a runner. You?"

With a low whisper, she confidently stated, "Skin changer."

Intriguing. Beautiful and a Weg. That tiny sliver of a connection—he held it close. It didn't hurt that she was clearly flirting with him. All he could do was utter "Wow," as he stared at her pouting lips with his mouth open.

"Well, don't look at me like that," she said with a playful shove to his shoulder, "I've only changed once so far. Nico says I shouldn't do it too often unless I learn how to live in limbo."

"Limbo?"

She giggled. "Yeah, I don't like the sound of it either. It's living halfway between human and animal... and I don't want to be half-cat."

That strange man they killed in the desert must have lived in limbo. Crow shot him down. While Hare wasn't technically responsible for the man's death, he felt responsible. *Interfering with a medical emergency*, or some such nonsense rule the Ethics Committee pumped out. Still, he shouldn't have interfered. The thought made him frown.

"Uh-oh, do you not like cats?" she asked, bending down to get a look at his downcast face.

Waving a hand in dismissal, he shook his head. "No, I love cats. Especially ones that turn into beautiful women."

The last time he had tried flirting with anyone was with Par, and she friend-zoned him hard and fast.

"Handsome *and* slick," she said with a giggle.

Lost in Cae's flirtations, he couldn't remember the last time a woman showed any interest in him. He looked at her, ghostly exquisite in the moonlight... but she lived with Nico. It would be Tilly all over again. "So, why are you staying here with Nico? Are you dating him or something?"

"What? No!" She stepped back with a hand to her chest. "He's dating his friend's sister. I'm just here because..." Her voice trailed off as she moved her hand to a very familiar spot on her arm to scratch it.

That itch was undeniable. It was the first choice of injection spot, until it became too scarred to use and the needle moved to other parts of the body, forever marring them in pocks.

"He knows how to make the *good* treatment," he said, feeling a little like a jerk. She only nodded, giving a meek smile, with her hand still clutched at her arm. "I'm sorry, I didn't mean to—"

"It's alright. You didn't know."

Verena's patch poked him through his pocket again. He jammed his hand inside, feeling the sharp corner, and pulled it out. The engravings along the side filled with alt-silver caught the moonlight, reflecting it in her eyes.

"You should have this," he said, handing it to her.

She took it, turning it over in her fingers, admiring the delicate silver work. "This looks expensive," she said. "What is it?"

"It's a new thing for Weggevens. I have one too. See?" Lifting his sleeve, the cracker-shaped tech stuck to his arm, inactive but with the faintest glow radiating from the etchings.

She poked his skin around the tech, sending prickles over his flesh. "What does it do?"

Running his finger along the edge, he activated the implant, lighting up the symbols and warming the area on his arm. He felt the blood move to the area, rinsing itself over the spikes from the implant buried under the skin. "It's more of a permanent solution to that treatment Jac—*Nico* makes."

Her eyes widened, then she jabbed the implant back toward him. "I can't take this from you," she said. "I only just met you."

Plucking the implant from her palm, he moved to her side, lifting up her sleeve. "No, really. They're meant for people like us. Someone like you." Without giving her the opportunity to protest, he pushed the tech into her skin the way Verena did to him, where it latched on. She hissed through her teeth as the spikes punched into her muscle.

"That stung," she said with a chuckle.

"You activate it like this..." He pretended to run his finger around the perimeter of his own patch. She mimicked his movement on her new implant, and the symbols lit up.

"It's warm."

"That's how you know it's working." He wanted to smile in the same way that got a reaction out of her before, but since he thought too hard about it, the smile came off as awkward.

She giggled at the attempt and wrapped her hand around his forearm. "I'm really glad I met you tonight. Even if sneaking around on the balcony was a bit creepy."

He deflated. "I'm sorry."

"Don't be. We all have our issues, and you're clearly Nico's family. I still don't think I can go home yet, even with this new tech."

"Really? Why not?"

She hummed, snickering between thoughts. "Well, my twin... see, we live together and..."

Pausing for an eternity, he leaned so far forward he almost tipped over.

"Well, she's a Reader, and apparently I'm noisy," she finished with a shrug.

"O-oh... Oh!" was the first thing to come from his mouth. He blew out a quick prayer of thanks that her sister wasn't there to read *his* noisy head.

"She just has to learn how to quiet her mind. Once she does that, I can go home."

"Do you live nearby?" he asked. Sure, asking for her address wasn't even creepier. Though he kicked himself for it, she didn't seem bothered at all.

"Actually, no. I live close to the Audun spire. Here..." She pulled out her e-disk, motioning for him to do the same. When he did, she made a few swipes, then hovered hers over his until the street map with her apartment beacon projected over his along with her phone number. "Now you'll always be able to find me." She winked and tucked her e-disk away.

This chick had guts. Even if he thought of himself as harmless, she didn't know that for sure.

"I-I probably have to get going," he stuttered, stowing his e-disk and holding his hand over the pocket that held her information. He guarded it, as if at any moment it threatened to disappear.

"It *is* late," she agreed. "Come visit me sometime. During the day."

"I wouldn't miss—of course—wait. I couldn't... I can't wait."

Smooth.

She giggled and kissed him on the cheek, sticking a finger into one of his dimples. "Stay adorable, Niklaus."

Lifting his shoulders and grinning wide, his gaze lingered over her heart-shaped face and ghostly complexion in the moonlight. He ached to leave her, and the lingering touch of her pink lips heated his cheek. The cold breeze of the travel home almost took it away, but it tingled there the rest of the night.

CHAPTER 31

Wicked Encounter
LOREN

TWINS! THEY RAN IN FAMILIES, and it was somewhat expected, but it still came as a surprise when the medic examining Damaetra told Lor what to expect. Thanking the medic for her expertise and guidance, they left the office, never to return.

It would be dangerous to return, Gale had told them, referring to Lor's Yeunish heritage. He couldn't tell them what their odds were of having them with only one parent hiding the genes, but it was risky to have a city-appointed medic delivering the babies. Gale volunteered, mapping out a plan for the due date and reading more books on the subject.

As her belly swelled, Lor petitioned the Maker more and more, beseeching through his colors and finding nothing but the smoke of others gabbing in the room. He couldn't focus on anything.

One strange evening, five standard months after he learned he was going to be a father, he found an anomaly in his colors. While his eyes were closed, a portal lens manifested from the smoky spirals of color, a sight he hadn't had the pleasure of since pulling Maron from the wall. In his excitement, he gladly entered the portal, looking for the quiet presence of the Maker. When he thought back on it, he should have paid closer attention to the coat of blood and ash.

Inside, he trembled. The vast chill of that inner chamber ran needles into his flesh, and the smell of sulfurous rot was acid in his nose. Reaching a spiritual hand to the "walls" of his surroundings, his fingers returned coated in thick blood. Immediately, he wanted out of that place.

Spinning around, the doorway had shut, leaving him floating in the hellish realm that swallowed him whole.

Maker? he called out, only hearing an echoing drip amidst the silence.

The Maker was not in that place.

An aching sense of dread swelled in his stomach when he frantically spun circles to see nothing but blood and bones clinging to the walls.

He fell to his knees, a squelch into rotting mud, then cried to himself. A slow, *shuff... shuff... shuff...* slithered deep in the darkness, squirming louder and louder as he sat in the sludge, frozen in grief and terror. It called to him... with each slither of flesh against congealed blood, and the squish of bones plunking into the mud, releasing from whatever hall it traveled through, it called his name.

While it crawled to him, the voice mocked and praised him in the same breath, reaching inside the deepest parts of his mind, making him feel the most vibrant parts of life while desperately wanting to die. The deep masculine timber of a voice lined with the feminine—extreme on both ends—whispered promises and pleasures. They converged on him, wrapping delicate tendrils on and through him, squeezing slow and delicious around his neck.

He groaned as his heart thrummed and his thoughts sank into that night with Par grabbing him and feeling him. The apple scent in her hair aroused him. He felt her tongue on his and his body responded, even when he first tried to shove it down. Nothing but carnal bliss numbed every sensitive piece of him, and only the most meager fraction of his soul cried out for his wife.

Your flesh is weak, the voice cooed from the pit with a soft gurgling chuckle.

A dark mouth wrapped itself around him, sucking and sucking while he alternated between groans and tears. It was the most painful lust he couldn't have conjured if he tried. He wanted to tear through his flesh, and he didn't want it to stop—all memories of his world before the portal faded into darkness. Gold leaked from his pores, running rivulets down his arms, raining into the rotting mud that he felt deep down were piles of feces. *Cirv'e*. All he remembered was pleasure, and all he wanted was pain.

Lor wanted to cry, but the stinking hole dried his tears as his precious gold mixed with rivers of shit. He squeezed his fist, hoping to hold on to his life force as it rose between his knuckles and coated his fingers like a thin gold glove.

Then he felt it. The familiar tremor that stood his hair on end, filling his veins with warmth he thought never possible again in that place. Intense carnality traded itself for familial love, and he remembered Damaetra. Gale, Nico, Dill... their faces came back to him, and he darted blind, wet eyes around for the source of it all.

The memory of holding her hand and feeling that special touch vibrated harder still as the malevolence in the dark slithered faster toward him, calling to him in a foul language he shouldn't have understood.

He relaxed into the magnetic vibrations when he knew what it was. Gold on gold—it was his mother's presence.

Loren? He shook when her voice called him, then he gave into it, arms relaxed in the tainted mud with back hunched in submission. Traces of the tendril around his neck remained, yet fading.

The hell hole trembled, and the voice inside of it shouted blasphemies as it raced toward him.

Momma... he cried.

And there she was, holding his hand. Lor lay on the living room couch, facing the ivy-carved fireplace as Dag held on to him. Actual tears had coated his cheeks, and at first he didn't know where he was.

"I fear you wandered into the den of the beast," she told him while stroking his hair back. It was a Foscan euphemism for having a nightmare, but he wanted so desperately to tell her how right she was.

Embarrassed, he sat up, raising his hands and expecting to see endless smears of gold in the cracks of his palms. Nothing was there.

"You saved me," he told her.

CHAPTER 32

A Most Unwelcome Surprise
JACK

"You just had to, didn't you?" Jack gritted his teeth. "Was it worth it to sell out to Audun?"

Hare swallowed and peered from the tents. "I swear it wasn't me! I don't know who told them," he said as his eyes darted between everyone. "I'm sorry, Ayala. I'm sorry, Verena."

Those were Hare's last words before he was nothing but a sand trail leading away from the tents.

"What a coward. Always running." Jack flung on his coat, then gripped Verena's face, standing with her, nose to nose. "Take Ayala and hide in the bunker until I'm gone."

"Jack, please," Verena pleaded.

"Do it. They'll come for you because of me."

A swarm of roundsmen descended on the Kanckette tents, stopping at each one and ripping people from their tables and beds for questioning. Shouts and murmurs spread down the line, but no one gave him up. It didn't matter if they did—it was only a matter of time before they reached their tent and dragged him from it.

Their tent flap whipped to the side as a hulking roundsman poked his square head inside. Ayala jumped and ran behind Verena as the man's eyes zeroed in on Jack. He grinned, turning his head back outside.

"Yo, he's in here! At the end of the row!" he shouted.

The rest of his body slithered inside, and he unfolded in the tent, nearly brushing his head against the peak of fabric.

As the roundsman slid out his baton, Jack held out his hand. The roundsman snatched Jack's wrist.

"No, please, he's done nothing wrong," Verena pleaded with him, stepping forward, Ayala clinging to her skirt.

"This is none of your business, *whore*." The man swung his baton and struck Verena across the face, sending her sprawling into the sand. Ayala wailed and ran to her. The paper she held curled under the heat of her fingers and the rudimentary math she had scrawled there flaked and chipped.

"Ayala, *don't!*" Jack warned. She whimpered as the roundsman wrenched Jack's arm behind his back.

Jack shouted curses, struggling under his grip. There was one phial of Fowler's Last Grudge in his Formulator chest he could use to turn the man into red pulp… but it would rip through everyone—even himself. Ayala cried in the background as Verena sat up in the sand, looking to Jack in surprise at the hit—strands of her hair had laced across her face. She felt at her nose with a shaking hand, fingers dancing over the bloody split on her bridge.

"You bitches are lucky we ain't pressin' charges against you fer harborin'," the roundsman taunted them, twisting Jack's wrist harder, forcing him to bend deeper and stare at his knees.

A rage-red cloud encroached on Jack's vision, but he tempered it. The safety of his family was in jeopardy, so he prepared to comply. The roundsman sniffed out the weakness in Jack's resolve like a crazed blood fish and struck him across his clenched jaw. The hollow thump of knuckle on bone rang out in a sickening peal, and he felt the edge of his teeth cut into flesh.

Ayala screamed, "Daddy, no!" and cried some more. Water formed at the corner of his eye. It was the first time since he married Verena that she had called him Dad.

The roundsman chuckled, cuffing Jack's wrists behind his back with ID lock shackles. "Ja`kaeyur, 'Jack,' Ilun`amaen, or however you pronounce that Yeunish shit… you're under arrest for hiding your identity, aiding murder, and practicing formulation without a license or legality. Any words?"

Jack frowned, tasting the blood in his mouth and locking eyes with Verena on the floor. Her lower lip quivered when she mouthed "I love you" just before he was yanked from the tent.

The man led Jack away, while members of camp trembled and shrank at their passing. The crowd of roundsmen abandoned their search, loading up into their Law jumpers and pulling away. All except one jumper remained, parked near the first tent.

Quint Freely, whom camp had nicknamed Snow Man, stood outside, fists down and freezing over. The Weggevens patch on his left arm bloomed with illuminated engravings. He glared at the roundsman taking away his friend's "dad." For a snow man, Quint had a hot head, not bothering to look to Jack for the obvious cues he gave the kid not to do what he was about to do. But he did it anyway.

Quint rushed the roundsman, grabbing his wrist. Blue and white rime crawled up his arm as he stood there like an idiot, processing what was happening. The standard issue Law jacket cracked open like an egg, showing off his pale skin underneath, splitting open with crystals of hoarfrost.

"Stop that!" he yelped. With the other hand, he beat Quint across his scalp with his baton. It was enough force that he let go, but not enough to knock him out. Snow Man rolled to the sand, snuffing out his icy fists.

Holding out a trembling arm, the roundsman turned it back and forth, watching as the midday sun warmed the gash in his flesh, sprinkling melted blood into the grains. Quint would face some trouble attacking a roundsman like that, but Jack smirked under his bloodied lip.

Serves you right.

As the roundsman shook his frozen arm, Quint crawled toward him with his own head wound leaking a hot trail behind. Standing as if ready to push a boulder, the roundsman waited for Quint to catch up for another hearty blow to the face. He jerked back, arching his spine with a screech when Betta leaped onto his shoulders, raking claws across his forehead skin.

"Son of a—" Distracted with Betta, the roundsman lost track of Quint's advance as his ankle, then calf, turned to icy stone.

From between the crowd that gathered, Treece emerged with a sinister grin. Verena had trouble fitting that girl with a perma-patch, and whatever she had planned made Jack nervous. She was a volatile, and there was no telling what would happen. She could die.

"That's enough!" the roundsman shouted, using his baton to fling Betta to the sand, where she landed on her feet. She shook yellow dust off her striped brown coat. Quint took another blow to the face from the baton, and the roundsman turned to face Treece, who continued her advance.

"No more!" the Freely patriarch stormed from his tent, calling a cloud of chitter birds to descend on the kids and the roundsman.

Several of the little black birds formed protective shells around the children while the rest rushed the roundsman. Their wings tickled Jack's head and neck as they pecked away at his captor. Swinging a semi-frozen free arm while maintaining his grip on Jack's bindings, the roundsman jerked him around, nearly causing a twisted ankle.

Once the children retreated to safety, Mr. Freely called off the birds. The roundsman was covered in ragged purple nips and splashes of white crap on his pressed blue uniform.

"Yer all going away for a long time, you hear me? Stupid desert dung holes!" The roundsman pointed at each of them with his baton.

Held back by the Freelys, the Weggevens children helplessly watched as their attempts at helping Ayala failed. The roundsman jerked Jack's arms, forcing him toward the final desert jumper idling in the "no vehicle" zone. The Audun colors of blue and gold flashed on the roof, and the tinted window descended halfway.

"Those brats getcha good, did they?" a familiar voice called from inside the cruiser with a gravelly chuckle. Shadows covered his face, but it wasn't hard to tell that his captor's partner was a massive man, crammed in the driver's seat. A single tooth shone under a cut of light.

No. It was impossible.

"Surprise," the man said, widening his grin.

CHAPTER 33

Haunting of the Past
LOREN

A STEADY DRIP, DRIP, DRIP PLUNKED from the leaky faucet into the white bathtub. The bluish water blushed to pink the more Damaetra pushed. Lor couldn't watch anymore, leaving the details to Gale. After all, he was the professional medic who sort of planned for this.

Upstairs, Nico and Dill waited to welcome his children into the world.

The sight of Damaetra's pain offered a more nuanced effect on his ability to remain conscious. Cutting out his implant during the program was more like a stroll down the beach in comparison.

"Be prepared for what you might see," Gale said. He moved about the bathroom with skill that looked as if he were made for that work. The warning he gave Lor wasn't about the mess of childbirth. It was the fact that not having the tech to see into her womb left the heritage of their children's birth a complete surprise.

Lor swallowed, attempting to push back the swerving nausea that threatened his balance. "How long has it been since you've delivered a baby?"

Gale tittered as he continued his pilgrimage through the room, gathering random medical objects. "It's been a while," he said.

"How *long*?" Lor relented and sat, his back leaning against the tub near Damaetra's head. He could still smell her violets among stale minerals in the water.

"Not since you were born."

Damaetra whimpered behind him, and he wanted to whimper too. Instead, he tasted the salty coating on the back of his tongue right before a good vomit.

"Loren," she cried, stretching out the "n" until letting out a screech.

He squeezed her hand, and she huffed in short bursts. Gale moved into position to catch the first one.

The little white head emerged, hazy under pink water. Gale lifted up his first grandchild, cinching and slicing the umbilical cord before wrapping the newborn in a thick blanket and handing the little Anglia child to Lor.

"It's a boy." Gale grinned before rushing back to catch the next one.

Lor looked into his son's swollen and pink face as he was ready to let out his first squeals. He wanted to show him to her, raise him up like a prize to the masses. An Anglian boy—perfectly perfect! And not Yeunish! Damaetra gripped the sides of the tub and groaned, pushing out baby number two.

Gale performed his ritual cinching and slicing before wrapping the second one in a tight towel. A breathy sigh and tempered grin spread across his face as he closed his eyes.

"It's a girl," he uttered.

A girl!

Damaetra sighed in the water, relaxing her arms and grunting as she shifted to look.

Terrified and thrilled, Lor imagined life with a daughter. To balance being a protector to a little girl, teaching her to be strong and love herself as he and her mother did—he wanted the world for her.

Gale's grin turned to dust when he held up the pale bundle. Her tiny head was coated in a thick swath of curled hair, not a cry uttering from her lips. She loosened an arm from her wrappings, touching her plump cheek with swollen pink fingers. She rolled her eyes open, locking them with her father's. They were beautiful, haunting, and yellow.

Fuck.

She curled her fingers at her cheek as her eyes closed again, no wailing and no tears. Her innocent moon-shaped face was round with fat and crowned in black.

Finally feeling the cold room, her brother curdled his chin, opening his mouth into a wide, gummy cavern and bellowed.

"Loren, can I see them?" Damaetra held out eager, dripping arms.

He handed the pink and white squall to her as the boy's arms found their way from the wrappings and clawed at his flushing cheeks.

The movement jostled his daughter, who remained content with the racket and made a slight rosy grin under chubby cheeks.

Gale moved about again, scurrying from one area to the next as Damaetra held her son, still sitting in the blush-colored murky water. White squiggles of hair stuck to her forehead, plastered there by sweat and the water's warm humidity.

His Yeunish daughter rested in his arms, completely unbothered by her brother's screams and ignorant of her own cold birth of a marked life. Gale's voice droned in the background, muffled under water of racing thoughts. All he could hear was the weak attempt of sound penetrating liquid.

"Loren!" Gale hissed.

Snapping his attention back to the present, Nico and Dill stood in front of him. Nico's cheeks had drained of color, while Dill fidgeted, darting his gaze back and forth from the baby in Lor's arms to his face.

"Roundsmen just pulled up," Nico whispered. A band of sweat beaded over his lip.

"Why are there *roundsmen* here?" Gale asked.

Nico shook his head, swallowing. "I don't know, but I have a bad feeling about it."

"Where's my mom?" Lor asked. "Where's Dag? Get her down here!"

"She went to the front door to meet them there and ask if—"

Bang!

Everyone jumped. Gale sprinted from the room, tossing aside his medic's coat decorated in Damaetra's blood. His footfalls blew up the risers as his runner legs carried him on the wind.

"Watch Damaetra and the babies. Hide—don't let them down here!" Lor handed his daughter to Nico and bolted after Gale.

His friends didn't say a word. Or if they had, Lor didn't hear it. Running up the stairs was like running through waist-deep water as his blood pumped heavy through sluggish veins. He cracked the door open to peer down the hallway. There was no one there to see him, but deep wails pealed from the kitchen.

Closing the door behind him, Lor slid down the hall with his back to the strobing holo frames on the wall. The pungent tang of electricity and blood hit his nose, and that was when he realized it was Gale who screamed.

A giant square of a man stood with his back to Lor but had Gale's arms pinned while he struggled to break free.

Lor blinked. Then he blinked again.

A flash of his descent into the nightmare realm of cirv'e spread before him before he realized his mother was on the floor in a growing pool of red. Her long tail of black hair swirled next to her face, swallowed inch by inch by the encroaching liquid. Eyes closed, face long, lips slightly parted.

Momma...

Gale shook and made guttural moans under the roundsman's grip, screaming for *Els'daegal* while cursing the intruders.

No... it is a trick of cirv'e. Just a trick.

Momma...

Gale continued to shake and wail as the roundsmen wrenched his arms, nearly popping a shoulder out of its socket. A second roundsman stepped in her life fluid, flicking his foot in disgust.

Just a trick. Lor blinked again, but nothing changed. Each scream of his stepfather faded in the swelling water closing Lor's hearing. A trick...

Momma...

A tear stung his eye, and the memory of magnetic vibration of gold on gold overwhelmed. There was nothing like it—she saved him. She *saved* him.

"Momma!" Lor cried out.

Gale whipped his head toward him and cried, "Loren, no!" His face was a deep shade of scarlet, with eyes already swollen and black.

Just beyond him stood the other, disgusted roundsman with Dag's blood on his boot. He was a mountain of a man, bigger than the one holding Gale. Crossing his arms, he cracked a grin. Thick scars littered his face, and Lor was struck by a weird sense of recognition from a previous life. A life that felt far away, yet not that long ago. A single tooth in that sinister grin glimmered under the window's pale beams of a partly cloudy day.

"There you are, you slippery Yonch," he said in a voice like pebbles grinding over each other in a deep well of mucus.

Under the dark blue and gold of Audun that decorated his uniform, there were circular patches of pink wrinkled skin over tanned hairy arms. Stretches of scar tissue banded across his face, but his grin was unmistakable. The meaty brute holding Damaetra hostage... Paerli's paramour... the strongman.

Hammer.

"You're dead," Lor whispered, his voice skipping from his throat. Hammer didn't hear him. He barely heard himself.

It shouldn't have surprised him that there were other Weggevens hiding their identities from the cities. Gale did it. Horace did it. Of all professions to choose to hide in, it had to be Law. He was just the type of man that would love to lord power over the citizens under the badge.

Jack's Red Mash concoction made the trail of blushing scars all over Hammer's skin. Lor prayed he didn't remember his friends, or Damaetra. He wasn't there for them. He was there for *him.*

"Loren Benedict Turtingas, you're under arrest for being Yeunish *piss.* Any words?"

Lor's throat tightened, and the only utterance was a pitiful squeak when he glanced back down to his lifeless momma.

Gale leaped up and down again, struggling against the other roundsman. "You son of a bitch! I'll have you discharged and banished! I'll go to the princeps *himself* to—"

Hammer socked Gale's mouth hard enough that a tooth skittered across the kitchen floor. A long string of blood and saliva poured from his lip as his knees crumpled and he coughed.

No.

The strongman pounded his fist into Gale's face again and again, knocking out more teeth and splitting open his cheek.

No!

Lor stumbled forward, heart racing and knees shaking. "Leave him alone! You want me, so *take* me!" He presented his wrists to the pair, exposing them for shackles.

Hammer tittered and nodded at the other roundsman, running his knuckles over his uniform pant leg. "Glove him. This little prick is a Reaper."

Hammer's partner sucked in a breath and glared at Lor, pushing Gale to the ground and kicking his ribs. Gale grunted and coughed again, rolling to the side and pressing his split mouth on the cold tile. Blood ran from it as he groaned.

No-name partner pulled out a stiff pair of metal gloves from a dark blue pack on the floor decorated with golden embroidery. The gloves connected at the cuff by a multi-link chain. Very hard to break... even for a strongman.

"Why they let a Yonch become a *Reaper*, Milo?" the partner's voice squealed from his throat like a young girl in first levels.

Hammer's real name is Milo. Check.

"Shut up! They didn't just *let* him, moron. Glove the bastard."

The cold metal brought him back to when he first entered the chilled depravity of cirv'e, and he shivered. A slight pinch pierced his flesh when they closed, and a mild burning simmered at his wrists. Hammer strolled up to him, casting his shadow over him as a towering bulk of meat. In school, in his circles, Lor had always been the tall one. But as a lanky twig, he was never very intimidating. Hammer was a monster—all height, muscle, and hair. The circular scars over his arms could rest on Lor's scalp like a wrinkled pink halo, and they covered most of his skin.

The same cocky grin crept over his face as he loomed over his prize capture. "Like what you see?" He bent an arm to flex it for Lor, making the scars dance. "That red shit in the cave did a number on me, that's for sure. But beauty fades eventually, innit right?"

Hammer's red-brown eyes scanned Lor, set inside a gruff, wide face. Twigs of unkempt, wiry gray facial hair framed his blocky chin.

Lor slowly turned a wrist, feeling a sharp stab in the pad of his thumb. He hissed, and a strangeness crept over his flesh that was more than just bleeding.

"Ah yes"—Hammer flicked one of the gloves, and it twanged—"see... these gloves here are special." His whisper blew hot breath into Lor's face, stinking of old protein blocks mixed with stale spit and chewing grass. The dirty clicks in his throat and grumbling warble had Lor craning his neck back to avoid hearing it. But Hammer's filthy mouth hovered just over his ear.

"They slowly leak out your gold."

Another vision of his time in the realm of horrors flashed twirls of his gold dripping into the scat. That burning was unmistakable. It was the same sensation he felt during the ritual of self he performed to extract it himself—a sucking pull that came from the darkest, and most hidden depths of his body. He did it to save Damaetra then, and he would do it now to keep her and his children safe. He would go with them and get them out of his house.

In silence, Lor faced the floor. Hammer wrapped thick fingers around the back of Lor's neck, forcing him toward the front door. As they moved through the kitchen, Gale crawled toward his wife, arm over elbow, leaving a blood smear on the gold veined white marble. Tears burned in Lor's eyes.

Everything he used to hate about his stepfather were all parts of a strategy against Audun to protect him for the one he loved. By going with them to banishment, Lor's babies would eventually hate him too.

Gale was a good man—an incredibly intelligent creature of the Maker, at the mercy of a Weggevens strongman. Lor's heart ricocheted off his ribs as he considered the cruelty of existence. Gale was no match for Hammer. Even if he did have the strength to run, he'd sap his life if he tried.

Hammer shoved Lor toward his partner, then bent down to poke Gale's back as he slithered over the tile to Dag. Gale flattened himself to the floor, wrapping his fingers around Dag's lifeless arm; his silver ring glittered on his middle finger, flecked with red. He uttered something inaudible.

Hammer leered at him. "I'm sorry, what was that?"

With a grunt and a wince, Gale rolled toward the monster, still holding Dag's arm. Swollen welts crowded his eyes and lips as they wept black blood.

Gale wheezed. "Maker... help... you."

Hammer stood and turned toward his partner to laugh. The partner also chuckled with a squeeze to Lor's neck.

Clicking his tongue, Hammer touched a fist to his hip. "Why, don't you just have the *nerve*," he mocked, a sinister grin planted on his bulbous face. Stretching his neck, he tilted his head and pointed at the twin silver rings around their fingers. "Would you look at that? I'll just go ahead and break up this dis-*gusting* marriage while I'm here."

Raising a fat foot, he punched his heel into Gale's nose, knocking him to his back.

"Dad!" Lor screamed. The partner whapped his fleshy hand across the back of Lor's head.

Lying on his back, Gale clutched Dag's arm as Hammer scanned the pair. Crouching and tilting his head some more, he stood after too long and shrugged.

"Looks like he's dead," Hammer said.

No.

Lor squeezed his eyes shut, the watery sting heating up his eyes like an unquenchable fire. A red-hot lens pulsed under his eyelids, inviting him inside. He knew what was in there waiting for him. It wasn't lust... It was rage. He wanted to puke.

I'll kill you! I'll kill you! Maker help me...

The partner pushed Lor's head forward, and it made his hands twist inside the gloves, inviting that jab and follow-up sting of eneris leaking. A rending pain burst through his arm, and that sucking pull of gold slithered from inside it, pooling into his palm.

He imagined it swirling into the muck again, a wasted stream of living icing over cirv'e excrement. A momentary flash of Maron narrowing his yellow eyes at him cut him to the core, and he tasted earthy petrichor. Electricity buzzed in his veins, and it reminded him of his mother's touch. He turned his head to see them one last time, lying on the marble tile of the kitchen.

Hammer burst through the front door, pushing Lor's head forward and sending the outlined image of their lifeless bodies to evaporate into the sun when he stepped outside.

CHAPTER 34

Listen to Their Cries
NICO

THEY COULDN'T HEAR ANYTHING.

"Screw it, I'm going to try listening at the door," Nico said, making a move toward the stairs.

Dill grabbed his wrist. "What if they're still here? You can't just toss a phial of Last Grudge in Lor's house."

"Who said anything about using a phial?"

"What else would you defend yourself with?"

Nico ran his tongue under his lower lip. Dill was right. He had more skill with health phials, leaving himself with nothing offensive other than the chromatic fury of Last Grudge. He couldn't unleash a miniature razor storm in the middle of the kitchen.

"We've been down here for hours. We can't stay down here forever." Nico went to Damaetra, who sat on a pile of blankets in the big red chair in Lor's bedroom. Her arms were stuffed with amazingly quiet newborns.

The Yeunish daughter watched Nico as her brother slept in the other arm. Damaetra's eyes were heavy from the pain killing draught he gave her, and her arms threatened to go slack.

Nico reached for the daughter, and he found it odd when she broke an arm free from her swaddling to jerk it toward him. He passed it off as mere reflex and picked her up. Dill went for the boy, and as soon as he had him secure, Damaetra's arms flopped to her side when she passed out.

"How long do you want to wait?" Nico whispered.

Dill rocked the baby boy and shrugged, nodding at Damaetra. "Let her rest for a bit, then we'll check."

The girl in Nico's arms continued to diligently study him. It was as if she was trying to memorize all the lines in his face and every curl in his hair. He smiled at her and stuck a finger toward her rogue hand. She took the gift of his finger happily in her fist.

"Do they have names?" he asked.

"I have no idea. I'm just going to call this one *boy*, and that one *girl* for now." Dill grinned under the purple light of his visor.

Something felt off, and the small hairs on Nico's neck prickled up. He thought about reaching out to Eva but wasn't sure what their situation was. The last thing he wanted was for her to come home to a confrontation.

Blowing out a breath, Nico readjusted the daughter and rocked her. The room was a mess—blankets and clothes tossed throughout, with an old glass on the nightstand half full of water and a patina of dust on the surface. The boy in Dill's arms started to fuss.

"Is there a soother piece around here for him?" Dill whispered.

Nico craned his neck and searched around the room, scanning the shelves and the big pack-sack on the floor. "Check in there," he said, nodding to the bag.

As Dill searched the dozens of pockets in the yellow striped baby bag, Nico moved to the night table, opening drawers. The top drawer had a couple books inside.

As he shifted the books, a few cables, a random pair of buttons and a remote, the glint of red and gold caught his eye.

"What's this?" he whispered to himself, picking up the small pendant. A black gem dangled from its golden holster, oscillating back and forth with glittering red stars from the inside. It was familiar, and he was drawn to it.

"Got it," Dill said, nuzzling the soother into the boy's mouth. "Hey, that's Par's pendant."

Nico rested the gem in his palm, and he remembered. "That's right. This is probably important. Better not lose it." He stuffed it in his pocket as the girl continued to watch him with wide, curious eyes.

Listening for any upstairs noise, Nico craned an ear upward, hearing nothing other than the little cooing noises Dill made at the boy.

Nico scanned the room, searching for a safe spot to lay the girl down. There was a playtech mat by Damaetra's feet. A little mature for the babies yet, but Nico laid her on the mat and nudged Dill. "Hey, watch her for a bit. I have to check upstairs. It's too quiet."

The purple glow under Dill's visor brightened. Whenever that happened, everyone assumed it was him widening his eyes. But he relented, holding the boy tighter for a moment, then laid him down next to his sister.

"Please don't die," Dill said.

Nico cracked the door to peek through, thankful the hinges were suitably greased and silent. The poor angle only showed him glimpses of the cycling holo frames on the wall. He spread the door wider, tilting his head this way and that for signs of the roundsmen or anything at all.

Silence.

The light was off in the room down the hall, illuminated only by the frosted slits of light filtering in through the front windows. All Nico could see were the hallway walls surrounding him with smiling holo images of his best friend's life poking out from their frames.

He didn't wear any shoes, which worked in his favor as he shuffled his way down the hall in slippery, silent socks. Around the corner, he wasn't prepared for what he saw.

Gale and Dag lay in smears of blood on the kitchen floor, with no sign of Lor anywhere.

"Oh Maker..." he choked.

No shadows or evidence of anyone still in the house lurked in the corners, but he still crouched low to tiptoe his way to them.

"Gale," he whispered.

No answer.

He knelt next to him. Sprawled on his stomach, Gale's hand loosely cupped Dag's arm. Her stone-cold skin had turned blue, and one eye remained open in a tight slit, reflecting a dull white iris in the glossy blood.

Oh God.

Gale was pale but warm.

"Gale!" Nico hissed, pushing on his back. There were no lessons he remembered on how to move a critically injured person. Nico bit his lip, undecided on where to place his hands, settling on cradling a palm around Gale's neck, and pulled his shoulder with the other. Dead weight was heavier than he thought.

Gale turned in Nico's attempt at being delicate, but once the momentum caught, his body flopped over onto the hard floor. The man he'd come to adore was unrecognizable.

A bluish black mask covered his eyes and swelled them shut. The thick reader frames Gale always had propped on his head somewhere had cracked in two in the middle of the kitchen floor with shards of glass lenses mingling among broken teeth slung like player's dice. A jagged split cut down his right cheek, which filled with fluid. The rest of his face was a confetti of lacerations.

"Oh Maker..."

He put two fingers against Gale's throat for a heartbeat. A dull thump knocked back, slow and steady. He did the same for Dag in reflex, even knowing she was dead. Some fatal shooter device got her point-blank in the chest. It went straight through her small frame, opening a red, toothless maw in her back.

Nico had only ever seen a real dead person once. The corpse was the resident corner-hopper that plagued Secas's open-air market. Homeless and alone, the man often tried to make conversation with passers-by, but no one wanted anything to do with him.

It hurt every time his family walked on by... he was sure the man had some stories to tell, and a family that loved him once. Years later, after Niki's incident, the man had slumped over at the corner of Rosa's Jewels and Sweet Meats Eatery. The gee flies had found him first.

Gale sputtered and coughed, spraying blood in aerosol droplets over the front of his shirt. Nico about pissed himself.

"Gale! Holy sh—*don't move...*"

Nico snatched his Formulator chest from where he left it in the living room. There were four phials of Verdigris Mend in there, but it was all he had left. He didn't have the gold to make any more, and Lor was nowhere to be found. Jack's formula was a powerful resource, and Nico thanked the Maker he knew how to make it.

The slick floor slipped under his socks, sending Nico skidding on his hip and nearly de-pantsing himself toward Gale. He held the chest high as he fell, safe from cracking open and spilling everything. The phials were in disarray as he flipped open the doors. One green phial lay on its side, threatening to uncork itself and vomit the precious healing draught over the velvet-lined case. He snatched it with shaking fingers.

As he stared at the phial's green solution sparkling inside the facets, he realized that Jack had never taught him how to actually use it. Time was wasting, and Gale's injuries were profound.

"Gale, how do I give this to you?"

Dark slits split through swollen eyelids, and a small peek of brown irises found Nico's face. Gale pawed at him with a groan, grasping the sleeve of his shirt. Loose swatches of gauze sat at the bottom of the chest, and Nico remembered how Jack soaked them with the solution when treating Hare. It was a start... He coated the swatches in the sharp-scented, goopy green draught and placed a square over each of Gale's eyes.

"Hold still," he said, "I'll be right back."

Nearly tumbling down the stairs, Nico's feet slid several steps at a time until falling to the floor of Lor's room. The noise woke Damaetra and she trembled while looking around the room. Her son cried, and her daughter studied the adults.

"Where's Gale's med kit?" Nico asked.

"What? Why? Who's hurt?" Dill rocked the baby boy.

Ducking into the bathroom, Nico emerged with the kit, making for the stairs. Damaetra reached for her son, and Dill obliged so he could follow Nico.

"Oh Maker..." Dill whispered when he saw Dag's body.

Gale lay face-up with the soaked green squares over his eyes. Nico lifted a patch to see that his eye wasn't quite healed but had started to work enough to bring down some of the swelling. A brown iris swam in red where the white used to be, and it rolled toward Nico.

Gale's hands wandered toward the med kit, grasping the handles. He attempted to sit up.

"Whoa, hold on, do you think that's a good idea?" Dill asked. Gale grunted and sat up anyway.

All elbows and knees, Gale struggled to stand. Stubborn rage etched his face. The med kit scraped across the floor when he finally stood, and he limped toward the hall bathroom, still holding a patch to one of his eyes. Dill shot a glance to Nico with his lips pressed inward, and Nico left to follow Gale.

Gale had busied himself sewing his face closed when Nico caught up to him in the bathroom. Each hook and swipe tugged his lip as he worked, and deep scarlet drizzled down his face. Eyes wild with fury, he relentlessly pulled each stitch through jagged flesh.

"They took him away," he mumbled through a dry throat. "They murdered my wife." A pinkish tear wobbled at the corner of his eye before free-falling into the white basin. The final stitch cinched in place, and he tied the knot while grinding teeth between parted lips.

Silence clouded the room. Nothing in the world taught Nico how to handle a situation like this. A million thoughts raced through his mind: *What now? What about the babies? Damaetra? Eva? Will Lor ever come back?*

The swelling had gone down enough to show the deep brown irises now crazed inside red whites.

Nico rubbed the back of his neck and tried to look away. "Maybe we could—"

Gale screamed at the mirror, taking a sharp swipe at a decorative vase on the vanity. It shattered against the wall, sending a shard across Nico's eyebrow.

As he dragged fingers across his slashed brow, Nico watched Gale stand upright and straighten his collar, as if preparing for an interview. Then he bolted from the bathroom with Nico trailing close behind.

Dill sat at the table, head cocked to one side when they came into the living room. Dag still lay there, still as stone and just as cold, and Nico readied himself for another outburst. Instead, he chased Gale to the mantle where he kept the antique shooter.

Gale yanked it from the clip and shoved the barrel in his mouth.

"God, NO!" Nico ripped Gale's hand back, nearly knocking him over. The discharge nicked the top of Gale's ear and blasted a hole in the ceiling.

"Get *off* me!" Gale shouted, wrestling Nico for the shooter as fresh blood dribbled down his neck, staining his collar. A second blast delivered another hole in the ceiling. Plaster dust trickled down, coating the conversation table.

"No!"

Gale grunted as he fought for the shooter.

A distant wail came from the basement.

"Listen to that! Don't you hear?" Nico shoved Gale to the floor and stashed the shooter.

"That's your grandson, Gale. Your granddaughter..."

The Yeunish girl didn't cry really. Nico knew it was the boy, startled by the shots. Dill sat dumbfounded in the corner, pushed deep into the cabinet doors, trembling.

Gale's lip quivered when he scanned everyone in the room. It was then he openly wept. Hands crusted with a mix of his and her blood, he rubbed the top of his head until it was as pink as the gash in his cheek.

PART 3

CHAPTER 35

It Must Be Love
NICO

WHAT A DAY. NICO TOOK the stairs to apartment 333. A death and a near-death. Two births. Their best friend had been banished. What in Gehenna was happening?

Banishment meant forever—and even if it weren't forever, no one knew what waited for them out there. They'd never see him again. Even worse, Lor would never know his children, and Damaetra had pretty much joined the widow's club at only twenty-six. What a damn day.

Rubber soles squeaked in the stairwell along with the mechanical whir of his knees every time he bent them. They needed greasing after all the sitting he had done in the past week at work.

Work. The cities didn't seem the same to him anymore.

A ratcheting click came from the left knee. He was lucky the knee joints hadn't locked up completely. Otherwise, the day could have ended with Gale decorating the living room. He shuddered. Just another thing to traumatize him.

When he opened the door and searched his brain for where he stashed the joint lube, a crisp breeze slammed it shut behind him.

"Cae?" he called out.

"I'm in here," her reply came from the center room.

He marched through the dim entry hall. Blank walls and a pathetic braided fake plant passed by until the space opened to the central room. Cae sat on the couch, ankles crossed to the side and hair tossed around in a wind-blown swirl. The last soul he ever expected to see again flanked her side, turning a toe into the carpet.

"Are you kidding me right now?" Nico dropped his e-disk with a soft thump into the same carpet.

"I didn't know where else to go," Hare mumbled. Cae reached up and took his hand.

"*This* is the guy you've been seeing this whole time?" Nico shouted. He rarely shouted. "Are you actually kidding me?"

They glanced at each other stupidly, and it looked like Cae would say something, but she didn't.

"Do you even know who he is?"

Cae opened her mouth again and peered up at Hare. "Well, I—"

"I mean, how the hell did you even *meet*?"

Their glances at each other looked more like guilt that time.

"Forget it. What can I do for you today, *dear brother*? Am I lucky enough to get one more betrayal?"

"Nico, I'm sorry, I—"

"See, it's been such a great day so far. My best friend was arrested, I watched a man nearly blow his brains out in front of me, and I helped bury someone. But hell, why not let me just go ahead and serve *you*!"

"They got to him, too?" Hare asked, eyes wide. Cae's lip quivered as tears rolled over colorless cheeks.

Nico flopped his Formulator chest on the counter and slumped his shoulders with a sarcastic side-eye. "What do you mean, '*too*'?" he said.

"I mean that Jack…"

"Oh, great. So now what?"

"Nico, my sister—is she alright?" Cae asked softly.

Her eyes glimmered with the onset of tears, and Nico felt bad for scaring her. For all she knew, the person he helped bury was Damaetra.

He sighed. "I'm sorry, Cae. I didn't mean to scare you," he said. "Dame is fine. She's with Gale and Dill, taking care of the babies."

Cae let out a long breath, darting her eyes back and forth as if calculating who the tragedy could have been.

"Lor's mother died today," Nico said, squeezing the bridge of his nose. "And now that you know, I'd rather not think about it."

They both nodded in silent agreement. The image of Dag lying there had him sick. Her face mirrored in red, one eye glazed open… he wanted to puke. She truly was small—and the bundle was light when he carried her to the black cruiser for extraction and burial.

An unfortunate casualty of the arrest…besides, she was just a Foscan, was what he was told by the attendant with a minor shrug and cruiser door slam. Just a Foscan… Did no one care? About *anything*?

"So, what do you want, Niki? I'm sorry… *Hare*?" Nico rolled his eyes.

Cae glanced at Hare and tilted her head. "Hare?"

Hare flopped his shoulders up and down. "Cuz of the runnin'," he said.

It wasn't hard to see that he was avoiding her look, and Nico sought to capitalize on that. "You know he's responsible for these, don't you?" He flicked his metal leg and bit back the pain in his fingernail. "*And* Dill's face?"

Cae sighed with a slight nod. "He told me, yes."

"And you *still* chose him? Unbelievable, Cae."

"Now wait just a second," she said with a furrowed brow.

"He's just so sweet and *adorable*, I think you'd like him." Nico pitched his voice to mock Cae. She frowned.

"I told her not to tell you," Hare said, "so blame me, alright?"

"Oh, don't worry... I *do* blame you."

Hare took a hard step forward. "Nico, I—"

"I had to use my own dead leg as a *crutch* to get back to Guild Central in the middle of the maelstrom when you stabbed it. Do you know how humiliating that is?"

"Nico—"

"And Dill couldn't save it, oh no... it was too hot and rotten. Do you know what it's like to carry your own stinking and oozing leg? In your underwear no less?"

"Nico, stop, I—"

"Not to mention all the years I spent grieving you, just to get them cut off to begin with!"

Hare threw his arms down at his side, forcing Cae to sit back on her seat. "I'm sorry, alright! I was in a weird place!"

Nico crossed his arms and sighed. The look his brother gave was a mix of anger and guilt. The remnant of chapping over dry cheeks sat under goggle lines and wild blue eyes. It wasn't fair what his parents did to Hare. It wasn't fair what Hare did to him.

Sins of the father.

Rich golden light filtered through the open balcony door, ready to give way to second sun. It cut lines across the floor to point at the couch.

Hare shrank back, wringing his hands as Cae continued to look up at him from her seat. "Truth is," he said, "I didn't stop thinking about you either. Even if I hated you."

Nico tittered and crossed his arms. "Is that right?"

"I get it if you changed your mind."

"About what?"

"You said you still loved me. When I ran away." He glanced up from under his brow, waiting for an answer to a non-question.

But Nico did say it. And he meant it. It had been almost two standard years since Hare left him for dead in the desert, and he remembered every grain that whipped his eyes and invaded his nose. The joints of his useless leg had locked in place, making a decent crutch until reaching a small house with green shutters and a roof in bad need of repair. A Weggevens skin changer lived there—modest living for a modest life.

The guy who owned the hut told him a similar story of being disowned—no twin involved, but tragic all the same. The way he talked, the way he moved, his story... they all reminded him of Niki. Every Weggevens reminded him of his brother.

Nico looked off beyond the window into the fading sky. He tried not to show it, but he stuck out his lower lip in a pout. "I haven't changed my mind," he said.

"Tell Dill I'm sorry," Hare mumbled.

"Tell him yourself."

"You'd make me face him?"

"If you're really sorry, you will."

Hare sighed. "Fine. Because I am." He relaxed and plunked down on the couch by Cae. "So now what?"

Chapter 36

Again
Loren

Humiliation... Audun's tool to shame the Yeunish. And for what? Did being born by Anglian and Foscan roots make him a criminal? Just the thought of a Foscan sank his heart, as all he pictured was his mom. They killed her to get him. They killed Gale. Only the Maker knew if Damaetra, Dill, and Nico were safe. And his babies... oh God, save his babies. Bitter salt stung his eyes.

"Quit daydreaming, *Yeuni*." An old woman with an engineering prod sneered and poked Lor in the back. The tip buzzed his flesh, forcing him forward in stuttering footsteps through mud. She grinned when he shook, showing him her red gums and wrinkled upper lip.

Lor obediently shambled toward the bank as Hammer followed them. A rickety smallboat bobbed in the water ahead, tied to a pier rotted by watery slime and time.

No one ventured here. Not only was it heavily secured by Audun, it was also where the banished were sent to die. A gray haze choked the air with a hint of green the color of puke. A figure waited for them in that boat, wearing a heavy black cloak. Lor couldn't see their face. It looked like death itself.

Closing his eyes as he shuffled through the bog, Lor saw nothing but vast emptiness. No smoke, no hell portals...not even the chaotic static from before his unfortunate encounter with cirv'e. The only image he could muster was of his mom's and dad's lifeless bodies as they lay in a pool of blood.

The coast boasted a bleakness that even light wouldn't penetrate—only a smoking bog haze of malodorous funk and the sad dreariness of first sun trying desperately to pierce through the fog. The zone was mysterious enough that no one knew what happened to it. A casualty of the ancient war? There were so many questions he regretted not having the foresight to ask Horace, and it was too late. He'd never see him again.

Lor winced at a second prod to his shoulder, and the gloves took their share of his gold. The sticky eneris squeezed through a gap at the cuff and chafed when it dried.

Twigs snapped to his left when another Yeunish man stumbled at the prod to his back. They both wore the same uncolored rag for clothes. Stripped naked underneath and forced to live in a scratchy grain sack, every part of Lor itched. The same material covered his feet, straining to keep the sharp shreds of rotted bark from entering his heels.

Cold and sticky, they marched ahead...one, two, and a third, no, a fourth Yeuni collected in line, each a formless shape under a ragged weave meant to haul grain. That's what they were—nothing but cargo to be shipped to its destination. Each bag followed by a prod to push it along.

"Move it," the old woman said, sticking Lor again in the meat of his butt as the buzz jerked him forward.

"I'm going," Lor snapped back.

"Shut it, or I'll smash it!" A different roundsman marched toward him. It was a woman, hair the color of Kanckette sand, and wider than she was tall.

Even the women roundsmen were built like bricks. If he hadn't been forced into the program, *he* would be the one corralling the unclean, sending them to their deaths in a scratchy bag. Gale had saved him from that fate, and the thought of his smart, amazing dad returning to the ground made him fight the urge to spit in her face.

As if reading his thoughts, she held up a sleek rod the width of his forearm, similar to the ones he'd seen connect with Yeunish skulls. Lor shrank back and shut his mouth.

"Hey, Josie!" An Anglia dressed in a white suit stood at the bank of the bog, near some sort of podium and not far from the smallboat. He waved at the stout roundsman who had the beat stick.

He looked like a ghost. All white fabric, white skin, and white hair blurred behind the grayish haze. The closer they got to him, the more Lor realized why he was there. The four exiles lined up for their brand, which he pulled from the podium and held with a pinky out. A dapper wraith.

The symbol burned red-orange at the end of a rod. It was nothing but the letter "Y" with two hash marks crossing through the stem. Josie the brick pushed the Yeuni next to Lor, and he stumbled toward the podium.

The brand sizzled on the Yeuni's forehead, but he kept quiet under a stretching mouth that gaped in a silent scream. A loose clump of his long hair had singed off where it hung along his forehead and caught under the brand, leaving him with a melted fraction of hair dangling there.

The cruel old woman with the prod poked Lor toward the front of the line. Up close, the podium stood firm against the ravages of salt and mist, framed with metal and built of carved wood. The guts were lined with tech capable of heating a Yeunish head decoration to flesh-melting temperatures.

When they approached, the Anglian twisted his lips and tilted his head to the side. His vibrant green eyes cut through the mist, searching Lor's features. "Are you sure this one's Yeunish? Doesn't look it."

"Got a witness and a scan. The markers are off the charts," Josie responded. Using the fat rod, she tapped him on the shoulder right on the bone, sending a spike of pain through his arm.

The Anglia shrugged. "If you say so. Which one is it?"

"Loren B. Turtingas."

He didn't like the way his name came from her mean, puckered mouth.

"Got it." The Anglia ghost swiped through a V-note fogged over by moisture in the air. "Step forward."

Lor obeyed. His gloved hands hung in front of him, heavy and full of sticky gold. Someone pushed his head forward with enough force that it could only have been Hammer. A deep chuckle hummed behind him.

The Anglia glanced at Lor's metal mittens and sucked on his perfectly white teeth. "A Reaper?"

Josie scoffed. "An *abomination*."

It took everything in Lor not to swing his heavy metal hands and catch Josie right in her square head. He fantasized her striking the mud with a bloody gash across her wicked eyes, and he would run. He would run all the way to Peakwood to his wife and babies, stealing them away back to Pohay'an where he could watch the motes of hot spring's light dance across Damaetra's face forever.

Instead, the salted sting of foul air burned in his nose, and the old woman with the prod cackled at him. Lor dipped his shoulders and bowed like the obedient garbage human they thought of him.

The glowing "Y" advanced toward him, blurring out of focus as his eyes crossed to follow it. Once the heat radiated just above his skin, he closed his eyes.

A cold snap of nerves curled and died, spreading from brow to temple, and he, too, wanted to scream. The sound wouldn't come from his throat, only the sound of the moisture in his skin boiling to bursting. A pair of silvered eyes shimmered in the blackness under his lids, grinning red in the dark.

"Sorry, pal. Capitol's orders," the Anglia said as he stuck the rod back into the hot tech.

Lor flexed his jaw and snapped it back into place. "If you say so," he mumbled.

The Anglia didn't hear him, but Josie gave him a good thump on the head with her beat stick. It was more menacing on the outside. Her punishing thwack pitched his head forward only at a slight angle as his skull echoed in the swamp. The thing was hollow on the inside.

"Now *this* bastard, I have no doubt about." The Anglia nodded to the next Yeuni who stood in line, waiting to be crowned the next king of the bog.

"This one's Jak`aeyur Ilun`amaen. It goes by 'Jack.'"

Lor perked up, twisting his head to the side to see the old Formulator tucked inside an identical brown bag with his head so low he could have kissed his ribs.

It had been a while. He'd gotten scrawnier since Lor last saw him. In a selfish sort of way, he was glad to have someone he knew with him in that place.

When the brand touched Jack, he didn't even move. It seared its "Y" into his flesh, like arms reaching to the heavens, and he wouldn't flex a muscle for them. It stole the joy out of the arrest for Hammer, who took it upon himself to strike Jack across the jaw.

"Whoa, chill out, man!" the Anglia hissed. He stabbed the brand back into the podium and stuck a finger out at the small boat. "Take them."

The old woman was too pleased to prod Lor toward death-in-a-boat. Jack had his own nasty herder—a thick and bald Danashi man. They made a game of it, shocking their charges in a rhythm with each other and laughing as Lor and Jack stumbled forward with each electrical kick.

The faint taste of green eneris coated Lor's tongue. It was the thick flavor of mildew and long grass mixed with an earthiness of mud after a good rain. When he got his next gentle push, he smacked his tongue to the roof of his mouth to make sure he wasn't already losing it.

"Hold up." Josie stopped them and shoved Lor's shoulder back. Beady black eyes studied him under a protruding brow that made her look like she crawled from the swamp. "Where in Gehenna is your damn brand?"

Before Lor could say anything, she swung his shoulders back toward the Anglia in the fog. He shrugged at her.

"You didn't push hard enough!" she shouted, dragging Lor by the elbow back toward the podium.

The pain memory lingered on his forehead. How was there no mark?

The Anglian observed his face with those piercing green eyes. If he wasn't about to do what Lor knew he was going to do, he might have thought they were nice. He hummed.

"I know it was hot... Here, let's just do it again."

God no...

Josie pitched Lor's head forward by the neck, and the Anglian whipped out the rod faster than a runner. Cold, searing snaps of nerves broke and coiled under his skin, sending fiery tendrils into his brain. The gloves twisted, taking their tithe of gold, and all he saw in the underdark of his lids were the slithering worms of his own essence falling into a slurry of cirv'e slop.

That time, he howled.

"Don't be a wuss," Josie spit, pulling his head back to verify the presence of an angry "Y" made of blisters and burnt flesh. She nodded in satisfaction and yanked the chain between his gloves to lead him back to the boat bobbing with the three other passengers staring back at him.

She didn't drag him fast enough. The taste of green flavored his tongue, and he knew he'd pay for it.

"Again!" she shouted after spying his smooth forehead.

"Josie, I got it *twice* now—"

"Again!" She shoved Lor forward. Even the Anglia hesitated... but only for a moment.

Pain.

"Again!"

This was what hell felt like.

"Again!"

"Josie, that's enough." The Anglia sheathed the rod and crossed his arms. "I don't know what kind of dark magic it's doing, just get it out of here."

With a grumble, Josie yanked his chain, but the boat was a blissful retreat, and Lor bolted for it. Her stumpy legs rushed after him, and he climbed inside before she could grab him again.

The boat rocked when death started the small engine. In silence, the green and gray shore drifted away, with the two blockheads Josie and Hammer disappearing beyond the pale mist.

No one talked. No one could. Lor couldn't even shut out the world anymore, forced to either stare at the defeated faces of his people or close his eyes and travel to the pit of hell, where some vice waited to consume him.

The Maker had abandoned the Morass.

One day he would fight to make his way home. One day he would see Damaetra again. At least, he hoped he would break free from the South before a thousand years of immortality passed.

The engine purred in near silence as they moved through the water. Death's face remained shrouded, buried under thick shadows. While listening to the ripple of mildewed water under their prow, a distant sound carried on the breeze. A gurgle, then a faraway wail in alien harmonics bellowed out there somewhere. It was enough to run shivers through Lor's torso. The only Yeunish woman with them let out a throaty cry, twisting here and there to find the source of the noise.

There was something out there, he knew. There was a chance it was his own death. But he couldn't linger on that thought because one day, that sad, frightened woman riding a boat to her watery resting place would be his daughter.

CHAPTER 37

It Stirs
LOREN

THE BOAT BUMPED AGAINST LAND. It wasn't solid, nor was it liquid, but a slurry of waterlogged grass and mud too thick to carry on, so land it was. The woman had whimpered the entire ride, letting out a hiccup when the boat hit the murky shore. The other stranger snorted awake, and Lor envied him. He didn't want to even close his eyes in that place.

Death's cloak faced them—an empty void. No light passed through it, leaving them to wonder who was behind the black. It pointed a finger toward the endless swamp.

First out of the boat was Jack. He wobbled a little on the slurry as it sucked with his first few steps. On his fourth, he sank in a hurry, falling waist deep. The woman had only straddled a leg over the side when she stopped and cried again.

"Watch your step..." a deep, watery drone spoke from the cloak, then chuckled. The laugh carried on too long with its grating rasp. It wasn't funny.

"Here, I got you," Lor said to the woman, holding out his rounded metal mitts. She gaped at them before grabbing on to his arms and letting him pull her with him into the slurry.

They plopped with a squash, followed by the last man. Death lingered for only a moment before steering the boat back into the mist. Lor thought he heard one last laugh fading with it, but that place was rumored to play tricks on the mind.

"What's your name?" Lor asked with a gentle touch to her arm. She glanced up at him, pearls of water at the corner of her deep golden eyes the color of first sunset. Black hair curled around the back of her ears in a stylish short cut that had been tossed around during the journey, and the scarlet "Y" on her smooth forehead had a pinprick of dark, dried blood at the bottom of the stem. She was a good ten standard younger than him.

"I'm Zary," she said with a sniffle. "It's short for Al`zaerya. What are them?" She nodded at Lor's gloves.

"These are…" He held them up, looking between them. A prison within a prison. "They're to keep you safe. From me, I guess."

"A Reaper," the singed-hair man said. He squelched toward them while Jack climbed out of his hole, resting on all fours and dripping with detritus. "Name's Brit. Short for Lob`aerit. And you are?" The short width of hair tickled the top of Brit's brand, and he tried to swat it away. He had a heavy Northwestern accent.

"Loren…that's it. I don't have a Yeunish name, but you can call me Lor." He pointed down at the man who once saved his life and now lived in the same predicament while hunched on all fours in the sludge. "And that's Jack. We know each other."

"Jak`aeyur," he mumbled to the mud.

"Well, Lor, Jack, Zary… I'd say nice ta meet you, but that'd be a lie. Maybe if we had fun at a club, or at a holofilm or somethin'…" Brit swiped at the hair again.

Lor appreciated Brit's directness. Their new home was a sprawling green sludge with unknown horrors lurking in the distance—not the best place to meet new friends.

"We can't just stand here," Jack grumbled, "we have to find a place to survive the night."

Zary stuck out a quivering lip. "S-sur-*vive*?"

Jack finally stood, giving everyone a look from under the green flecks covering his face. Without another word, he turned and began to walk away. Lor motioned for everyone to follow, so they did. The water rippled from same sinkhole Jack slipped into, so Lor hopped over it as the rest followed his lead.

"So, where you all from?" Brit asked.

"You first," Jack said, not looking at them. He squinted into the distance, scanning the horizon.

"Alright, well, I'm from Vesta Coast. Ever heard of it?"

Jack sidestepped another sinkhole, and they all followed. "You're from the Southern Morass now."

Brit tittered and ignored the jab. "It's just north of the cities by Peakwood Academy. Anyway, I lived with me uncle."

"So what happened?" Zary asked, skipping away from a small leaper in the mud, its skin slick with slime.

"Was livin' with me Anglian uncle," he repeated while avoiding the same leaper. "Somethin' happened to 'im, and he never got right again, so I was takin' care of him till 'e died."

A distant howl bayed beyond the boggy miasma. Zary shuddered, sidestepping a touch closer to Lor. For a teen, she was already quite tall, the top of her head nearly able to brush against his nose. In fact, it seemed most Yeunish were on the tall side. Both Jack and Brit were within two finger-widths apart in height, with Zary not far behind. The tall and lanky genes must have been all Lor inherited from the Yeunish. A pity really... the Yeunish had a strange beauty to them.

"I could'a lived in the house for the rest of me life on the runnin' plat me uncle left," Brit continued, "but of course when I was fillin' out the yearly paperwork, there was a glitch in the system and I had te go in person to fix it."

"You *had* to know you'd get caught, right?" Jack scoffed.

Brit chuckled. "Seein' me uncle had money, he got me some tech lenses that went right over these yeller buggers." He swiped a finger at his eyes. "Amazin' things if I'm honest. Some a them back-alley Engineers really got talent. Coulda had any color I wanted with 'em."

They hopped over another sinkhole.

"Anyway, since our peepers are a dead giveaway, I thought coverin' 'em would get me through. As I was there talkin' to the lad, I had a sneezin' fit somethin' awful. I din' think there'd be some irritation in a capitol office, but I'll be damned if one'a the things din' just fall right out!"

Zary gasped as they dodged another hole.

"The kid called the roundsmen quick as you like. And now I'm here."

"That's awful!"

Zary seemed like a sweet kid. The Seven Cities were cruel sending her here. Lor ached for his daughter, picturing her innocent, round face resting in the mud, waiting for some howling cryptid to snatch her away. Her parents had to be sick about her arrest. He would protect her for them.

"How did you get here, Zary?" Lor asked. A foot went ankle-deep into a watery hole, and he stumbled back to catch himself, rotating his imprisoned hands for stability and feeling the pinch. She grabbed his elbow.

"My boyfriend betrayed me," she said, looking off into the distance.

Ouch.

Jack turned to look at her. "I don't understand how someone that claims to love you could do something like that," he said.

"Well, he clearly didn't love me," she said, casting her eyes into the waterlogged reeds. "I lived in the Southern coastal village called Corl. Most people never heard of it. You?"

They grunted their "no's" as they skipped another mud hole.

"It's a small fishin' village, far from the cities. I'd be surprised if Audun knew it existed if it weren't for the taxes they nabbed from us without nothin' in return."

Jack pointed toward a faintly visible bank of trees in the mist, and they all turned to head that way.

"We didn't have much," she continued, "but my dad was one of the local fishermen for the town. Mom took care of the plants. But I love livin' on the beach. The smell of foam on the sand in the morning, fat waterbirds circling and calling out to us, the stars so bright they lit up the evenin' creepers like somethin' out of a fantasy…" Zary waved her hand across the sky, smiling into the misty glow of first sun struggling to pierce the haze. Her smile fell, and she stuck out a lip ready to cry.

Lor put a hand on her shoulder. "It sounds amazing."

"Yeah, well, *Pieter* didn't think so. He wanted a taste'a city life when some famous storyteller came to our village. She was a pretty Danashi lady in some big holofilm I never seen, takin' a vacation away from it all. After meeting her, Pieter wanted to be where the fancy people were. He wanted more than fish and vegetables…"

What a stupid kid, that Pieter. To trade real food for city life and bland ration blocks—a child's ignorance.

"When he heard he could get some plat by tellin' on my skin, he did it." Zary folded her arms, wrinkling her face in disgust. "Dad hated him. I should'a listened to him. But I guess he'd turn me in if I dated him or not. It just hurts more this way. The prick ran off to Trega's Sky over on the West Coast where they make a lotta them holofilms. Still not city, but closer to all the *pretty* people."

She stuck her lip out again, grabbing the stomach of her brown bag dress and twisting it between her fists.

"Screw that guy," Jack said as he lifted a bundle of drooping vines to let her through the tree bank.

The water was shallower, giving the fabric around their feet room to air out and breathe. Yellowed long grass poked out from the water in humps of soggy solid ground. Brit stopped to lean against a tree, asking for a break.

"We can't stay long." Jack warned. "In case you couldn't hear, there's something in the morass. We need to find other people… and quick."

"Alright, alright. How 'bout you tell us *your* story, then we'll go." Brit pointed at Lor, then picked at his teeth. "Like, how 'bout you start with how that brand disappeared from your head?"

In reflex, Lor put a hand there, bonking himself in the head with the metal glove. A flash of hot pain seared his memory, and the taste of green nectar filled his mouth before sealing his wounds. It took two standard… it took *that* long to discover the mechanism of his immortality. It was life bubbling up from the deep corners of every cell in his core that reacted to injury. Where it came from, he couldn't say. He *wouldn't* say.

"I couldn't tell you," Lor said with a shrug and eyed Jack, who eyed him back. Only he knew his secret.

"Dark magic it is then," Brit said with a chuckle. "I'm not here to judge ya. I mean, we're all banished anyhow." He brushed the stubby swatch of hair.

It was only the day before, but it felt like a lifetime. There was nothing Lor wouldn't give to go back to the steamy mineral-and-violet-scented bathroom to hold his babies again. The yellow cast in his stubborn daughter's eyes, completely comfortable and unbothered by her birth... she took after him, he could tell. If they had only made sure Hammer was dead in the bowels of Mount Gehenna... It was a pricey mistake.

He glanced at Zary, her eyes wide and waiting for him to tell them his story.

"I'm from Peakwood," he said, "and I lost everything..."

Detailing his path through life, from entering the program, meeting Damaetra, getting married, having twins, and the death of his parents, Lor watched Jack's face contort into a symphony of expressions with each new life experience until ultimately, he softened, looking down at his own bagged feet. Lor spared them the details about his immortality and cirv'e, but Zary's posture stiffened at the mention of Maron's resurrection.

"He's real?" Her question held all the markings of a girl reading tales as a kid, not thinking much other than his existence as a character in children's fiction.

"I'm sorry about your family," Brit said, putting a hand on Lor's shoulder. "We'll find a way to get you back t'your wife and kids. There's gotta be a way."

Brit was right. Two instances that Lor knew of had Yeunish renegades at the train station. Why they risked everything just to get snatched again was another mystery hiding somewhere in this bog.

Jack remained silent, offering Lor a slight nod and crooked half grin. "We should keep moving," he said.

"Right. You're right." Lor turned a foot, catching his toe on something hard in the earth. He sucked in a breath and hopped once, bending down to see what offended his foot. "What is that?" he asked, motioning at the pale stone sticking from the mud. Holes littered the surface, with jagged foramen opening to a hollow inside like a cracked piece of glass.

Jack knelt to examine the artifact, using his fingers to dig around the brown sludge. Hooking all ten fingers through the shattered hole, he pulled up with a sick sucking sound as the object stared at them with lifeless sockets.

"Oh Maker, that's a human skull!" Zary cried when a worm wriggled from the nose hole and plunked back into the disturbed mud. "I'm going to be sick..."

Jack's hands shook, dropping the skull to the ground with a soft *splish*.

"We're going to die here," she whispered, scanning the trees with wide yellow eyes.

"We're going t'make it," Brit said. "We just gotta get movin' and find the—"

A shrill roar pealed through Brit's sentence, freezing everyone solid. Their thin tree cover wasn't enough to shield them, and when turning his attention to the place they came from, Lor spotted their tracker.

In the open distance, not far beyond the trees, a shadow lurked, hulking and wet. A slithering whip curled from the side, undulating as the beast groaned in inhuman gurgles and clicks.

"Run!" Jack shouted.

Lor took off to the east with Zary at his heel while Jack zig-zagged off to the west, trailed by Brit, and disappeared into the mist.

"I'm scared, Lor!" Zary practically attached her hip to his as they jogged through the trees.

Their forest haven came to a sudden end when they ran into another wide-open clearing.

"Damn!" Lor whispered, trying to take Zary's hand, only knocking his glove into her knuckle with a clang as the creature bellowed. There was no telling how far it was from them, but it didn't carry on the breeze as it had before—it felt a stone's throw away. She grabbed his arm, and they ran.

Splosh, splosh, splosh, splosh, jump, splash…

A wet gurgle and shriek from the shadow beyond.

Zary's breath came in whimpered heaves with an occasional frantic turn behind her. Her hand on his arm clamped on, sweaty and slipping, until Lor dropped into a sinkhole up to his chest, knocking his face into the slimy water.

He spit out a mouth full of rank liquid and stood upright. "Run, Zary!"

She hesitated, stuck out her pouty lip, and turned heel to disappear through another patch of trees dripping with fetid ichor.

The creature growled behind him, ever closer still but not visible. A slithering squish of mud burbled as it closed in on him, and when he closed his eyes, all he saw was the bloody grin of cirv'e.

Heavy water crushed Lor's lungs as he trudged aggressively through it. Not even his first day in the morass and he was going to die. Swishing with bound hands, his abdominals ached. Right, left, right, left, right, left… the fabric tied to his right foot sucked into the mud. Then the left. Barefoot, he half swam in the mire.

A toe jammed into soft mud, and he scrabbled up the semi-solid to get better footing and made off toward Zary's trail. It was no place for a young girl to be alone.

"Zary!" he hissed.

"Lor, over here!" Her shadow beckoned from behind a thicker trunk. He ran to her, his oat cloth garment wet-slapping against his thighs, and ducked into the thicket. She whimpered again when he crouched next to her. "What do we do?"

"We survive," Lor said, craning his neck to find their pursuer.

It was no real consolation, but he was determined to get them out of there. A man's scream rang out across the Span. Whipping their heads in the direction of the sound, Zary wailed.

CHAPTER 38

The Drop Off

NICO

Back in Gale's house again. The inside was cold, different. Standing in Eva's room, Nico watched her softly cry on the bed. Everything in him wanted to be the stronger man and tell her that everything was going to be all right, but he knew that was a lie. Shock still hadn't worn off, and he wanted to cry too, but his body wouldn't let him. It was cold... different.

He did the best thing he could and sat with her, wrapping his arms around her as she pressed her wet face into his shirt. She was warm against him, the heat of grief radiating from her scalp and warming his neck. Everything was falling apart—all their plans, their future...gone.

Sure, Nico could move on. He could heal from losing his best friend, walk away from the Turtingas family, and start fresh back in Secas. The colorful summer market, the crystal blue salty sea, his parents—he could lose himself back to where he started.

But he wasn't that guy. Eva was the love of his life. Lor and Dill were his best friends. He squeezed her a little tighter as her sobs grew more intense.

There were children he felt responsible for. He felt responsible for Damaetra. He closed his eyes, taking in the scent of Eva's sweet hair and the perfume of her salted sweat.

One thing he never tried was to petition the Maker. He seemed like a faraway concept... a watcher of the creation. Surely Lor and Damaetra would ask for help. If he added his voice, would it make it stronger?

It wouldn't hurt. One last deep inhale of Eva's sweet scent and Nico's voice echoed in his head.

Maker, wherever Loren is, please watch him.

LOR

The man's scream barked into the atmosphere, and Lor's heart sank. It sounded like Jack.

"What do we do?" Zary asked. She cowered next to Lor and shook.

"Come on, we have to find a way out of here. Like Jack said, we have to find more people." While confident in his words, he wasn't confident that he could lead Zary to safety. Or himself. And there was a very real possibility that Jack was already dead.

"Look!" Zary pointed at another tree cluster across a short span of watery death traps. A light bobbed away deeper in the thicket.

"Maybe it's another person," Lor said, stepping forward and squinting through the darkening haze. "Let's follow it."

Zary agreed and held on to his arm as they took their first tentative steps into the mire. They were open bait for the creature. Its howls had gone silent, but the longer they waited, the darker it would get. So they ran.

Mud squeezed between his naked toes as he darted and dodged watery traps. Zary kept pace, looking behind her often, nearly twisting an ankle just before ducking within the new set of trees. The bobbing light had disappeared, and Lor held his breath.

It had been a while, but he closed his eyes. The colors raged under his lids, chaotic and furious, begging him to crawl through the pulsing portal lens dripping in hues of blue and black. The smoky swirls sucked inside it as if attempting to pull him along, but he knew what wanted him in there... it waited for him.

Maker, please watch over us.

DILL

Twirling a small spanner between two fingers, Dill found comfort in his Engineering fidget. The movement was a welcome distraction for the constant images of Lor's dead mother on the kitchen floor.

The babies slept in their cribs with the soft rocking module switched on while Damaetra slouched in the big red chair, facing the bookshelf with tears streaking her zombie face and sleeping. She had stopped talking to him. She stopped talking to anyone, really. Between exhaustion and depression, she cycled through sleep and sobs, never leaving the chair.

The image of her body blurred through his visor, and he used the spanner to tighten it with a sigh. If he didn't fix his visor properly or build a new one soon, he'd go blind, and that was another issue to add to the growing turd.

As she came into focus, the white-gold strands framing her face appeared greasy from neglect, and she wore the same clothes. Before long, she'd probably start to stink. The only way he felt he could help was by making sure her children didn't die.

Emilia promised to come by and help in the morning, and it was the light in his day he most looked forward to. While she helped with the babies, he could make his plans.

"Loren!" Damaetra shouted awake before descending into sobs again. The Anglia boy startled from her scream and began to cry with her.

With another sigh, Dill picked up the boy and cradled him until he calmed down. Once the boy fell asleep again, Dill closed his eyes.

Maker, please save my friend.

LOR

"There—there's another tree patch." Zary pointed to the west.

They could run to it, but there was no telling what direction they traveled. He chewed a lip, losing faith that there were any other Yeunish people in the morass. Death probably dropped fresh loads of banished people off every day, and this was where they would die. Black specks decorated the hem of his grain sack, and he shivered at the thought that it could be the rotting remains of generations disintegrating in their watery graves. But there was the light... bobbing its way through the next tree line.

"There it is! See?" Zary said, tugging on his arm.

First sun was yielding to second sun, and a deeper gray cast broke through in a depressing ashen glow. "We need to catch it," he said.

They stepped into the open area, looking both ways for signs of the beast. Nothing.

It was getting harder to spot the sinkholes in the lowering light. Zary nearly took a spill before hooking her arms hard in the crook of his elbow, nearly dislocating his shoulder. The pull put some torque on his wrists, as they gave their tithe of gold to the torture gloves.

"I'm sorry, I'm sorry!" she said as he pulled her up.

"It's alright, let's just keep our eyes open for the light."

She nodded, and Lor tried not to wince at the burning pain. The green flavor touched his mouth, and the pain simmered.

In the next block of trees, he closed his eyes to the same frantic maelstrom of color sucking into the void.

Maker, please save us.

DAMAETRA

Proper ladies must mask their fear and show strength of resolve to the public. All she wanted to do was disappear. The tears wouldn't stop coming, and her face felt three times its size from inflammatory grief.

The room was dim, but the silhouette of Dill had his back to her, rocking her son. Nico and Dill were such good friends. Without them, her babies would probably die. They didn't even get to pick out names for them before they snatched her husband away.

Aedras and her mom had no idea. All they knew was she was due soon. She should have called them, but she couldn't find the will to speak the words. Speaking them made them real, and she wasn't ready to face it: Loren was gone. Possibly dead.

The thought tried to bring fresh tears to swollen and gooped-up eyes. All that came forward was a dry burn. Now she had a Yeunish daughter to worry about. A very obvious Yeunish girl. The burn fired up again, and she wanted desperately to get up and shower, but her limbs were stone.

As soon as she could muster the strength, she would make Hammer pay. She would make Par pay. They would regret crossing *this* proper lady. Because this proper lady had Yeunish formulations up her sleeve. Formulations that would obliterate them.

She closed her eyes again, lulling herself back into dreaming with a petition.

Maker, I haven't been the best at talking to you, I know that. I come to you today, broken and in need of you. If you can spare my husband the Southern Morass, please send help.

LOR

"I think we're going in circles," Zary said. Her lip stuck out and quivered.

She said what Lor was thinking. Dusk was coming with the fading second sun casting its final lavender hue across the water. He looked at her—long pale face and thick black eyelashes dotted with moisture. Beyond her shoulder, the same mote of light bounced in a sprint through the next patch of trees.

"Look, there! Let's go," he said, offering his elbow. She grabbed on, and they bolted for the next cluster as Lor prayed for no sinkholes.

The Maker was good—no sinkholes. But his foot found the pointy end of a jagged twig and he howled, rolling to the ground. Everything burned—his foot, his wrists, his rage.

Zary crouched down and yanked the twig from his foot, and he cried out. The herbish flavor of green filled his mouth and nostrils again, and he rose to hobble into the trees with her.

"That hurt like a bit—" he started to say when he stopped to look at the ground where Zary fixed her attention.

Half a face, mixed with dried blood and debris, sat in the mud like a discarded mask. Yellow eye open and staring into the void, its light snuffed out. The left arm of the Yeunish brand reached out to touch the singed hank of hair tickling his brow.

"No..." Zary sobbed.

Lor looped his chain around her to hold her, and she buried her face into his armpit to cry. A low growl rumbled outside their patch of trees.

Maker, please send help!

GALE

The long shadow of Gale's torso stretched into his bedroom as he stood in the doorway. Second sun was setting, creating an especially dark outline onto the wood planks.

The bed he shared with Dag sat against the wall like a cold grave. Her silver band cut into his finger, and he rotated it with his other hand, feeling it drag his skin. The echo of her voice was embedded in the walls, and her ghost moved about, cleaning, caring for him, and sassing him with her sly grins.

Her image faded. He frowned, reaching up to the pinched cut on his cheek, sewn shut by his own hand. Verdigris Mend had sealed the wound faster than any city prescription could.

Glancing down at the floor, the light-colored gouge that marred the threshold where Loren had shattered Gale's school mug cut deep into the wood. Gale bent down and ran his finger over it, remembering the look on Loren's face in the doorway, and he chuckled wistfully over it.

That man... the one called Hammer... he did this. He destroyed his family. He used his hidden strongman ability under the authority of a roundsman to kill them.

One thing he vowed to himself was that he would make sure Hammer died—and painfully. He would pay for his hubris.

Gale's petitions were few and far between, but he closed his eyes, seeing the image of his wife smiling and reaching out to his face. He would use every breath of the rest of his life to make sure he kept his promise to her.

Maker, please... please save our son.

LOR

"No, God, no!" Zary whimpered at the beast. It raised its black, neckless face to the sky in ululations that sounded like laughter.

Like a spirit on the wind, Jack burst into their hiding spot, grabbing one arm each of both Zary and Lor, dragging them from where they stood. Lor limped furiously to keep up as the stick wound on his foot continued to close.

The creature darted through the mud in chase, slapping slick tendrils in the water in heaving splashes. Voiceless, they ran. The stink of earth and slime caught up to them, and a terrible chill nipped their heels. Just one look.

Lor turned to see the creature just behind them, red mouth open and readying for a bite. His heart vibrated and he fell to the ground.

Oblivion came for me...

Lor closed his eyes, preparing for the sting of his head separating from his shoulders when a voice called out.

"Back! Nazagora, back!"

A fiery whoosh blared nearby as Jack tugged Lor to his feet. The fire tipped a torch, being jabbed through the air by a Yeuni holding his other hand out. He strolled toward the beast, who shrank and simpered.

A second man, a short Mesaman, came through the woods with his own torch. He lowered it to cast orange light over the group.

"We're too late," the man said, nodding back east, "for your friend. Sorry about that."

Lor glanced toward the patch of trees, trying not to picture the mess the creature made of Brit.

The man shrugged and turned back to everyone. "Well, it ain't the first time, and it won't be the last. Come. You've officially survived the drop-off."

CHAPTER 39

New Recruits
LOREN

HUNGER PANGS JOLTED THROUGH LOR'S sides as they walked with the two strangers. The creature he came to learn was called "Nazagora" offered a limb for their dinner.

"They grow back," the shorter Mesaman stated, weaving through the trees. "A small price to pay for killing your friend. The name's Karl, by the way. You?"

Karl. The image of the pack-sack with the bold black letters scrawled on the fabric fluttered in Lor's memory as the same bag bobbed across Karl's back.

"I'm Zary, this is Lor, and Jack," she said with a smile and a tiny side-skip between steps. At least someone was starting to adapt.

The Yeuni who tamed the beast called himself Yor`ikur, or Rik for short. The dripping limb slung across his shoulders bounced with each step he took. "I am a beast tamer," he said. "We were looking for you but came a little too late."

"Looking for us?" Lor asked.

Karl spun around, walking backwards through the wet grass. "We get word of a drop-off, and we come collect. If we don't, Nazagora collects."

"And you said you were late this time?"

"Our communication channels can be flawed. But we do what we can."

As they traveled deeper into the thicket, a faint call of merriment echoed in the distance. Lor looked to Jack, who looked back at him with a shrug.

"Don't worry, you'll join them soon enough," Karl said. "For now, we eat."

They stopped at a small camp in a drier part of the bog. Trees encircled a cobbled stone fire pit like sentinels around the spot as if it were created just for camping. Rik slapped the Nazagora limb against the stone, then got to work setting up a spit.

As much as Lor appreciated real food, the look of the slimy black tendril lying there in its thick juices had him craving an oatcress bar.

"I can't unlock your gloves yet"—Karl nodded at Lor's hands—"but I can cut the chain between them." He pulled out a small Engineering cutter that whirred at the fulcrum as he opened it.

It was a start. Lor held out his hands, and Karl snapped the chain.

"It's been a while since we've seen a Yeunish Reaper out here." He stashed the cutters.

Lor sat on a thick stump, resting his useless, clunky hands in his lap, palm up. "I'm not the only one?"

Karl chuckled. "Well, you are at the moment. Sadly, Adan died about a standard year ago."

"Sorry to hear that." Lor frowned, deflated to learn he was still alone, and remembering Gale and Dag.

"S'alright. He was pretty old. But I'm excited to see what you can do."

Lor raised an eyebrow. Everyone already knew what a Reaper could do that he knew of. Zary took a seat on the stump next to Lor, offering him a chunk of Nazagora with her fingers. The smell was unexpected for a place like this. Savory, sweet, and smoky. He opened his mouth, and she poked the meat onto his tongue. In a small way, he felt pretty good about eating part of the creature that tried to kill them.

It was a lot like fish—flaky and salted with a hint of the sea. It was glorious.

The fire crackled in the pit, releasing the woodsy aroma with a hint of mint. Everything about this place was different than the North.

More cheers erupted in the distance. It was a small comfort to know there were actually living people there. Lor glanced over at Jack, who picked at the fishy tendril, taking small bites in silence. That night was the second time he saved Lor. The fire illuminated yellow across Jack's hands as he picked his food, and a light-colored band of skin wrapped itself around his middle finger.

Lor tilted his head and squinted at it. "You were married?" he asked, motioning toward it.

Jack turned his hand over to look at the band, then frowned and nodded, taking another picky bite.

"What's her name?" Zary asked, poking another cube into Lor's mouth.

Jack huffed, curling his lip into a half grin. "Verena," he said.

"Is she safe?" Lor asked with the meat crammed in his cheek.

Jack nodded and shrugged. "I think so... I *hope* so." He paused and took a sidelong look at Lor. "I'm sorry about Gale and your mom. Gale was a nice guy."

Nice wasn't the word most people used to describe him, but he *was* nice. He was great.

"And good work on the babies. I hope Damaetra is well," he continued.

"I hope so too." Lor tried not to let the water come from his eyes, and he smiled.

In between bites, Jack filled him in on what life in the desert was like for the past two standard before Karl interrupted.

"It's late. We'll set up camp here for the night," he said, handing Jack and Zary a couple pinches of blue-colored leaves. "And if you want, you can chew on these to clean your mouths from dinner. Works better than those fancy gadgets up North."

After Zary fed him the leaves, Lor crushed them between his teeth. They tasted like nothing, but his mouth did feel cleaner.

Karl turned around from helping Rik set up a small tent. "Swallow or spit, it don't matter," he said, then continued stabbing poles into the ground.

The first night of banishment... and there was no telling how many more nights there would be. At least Lor wasn't alone.

That morning, less fog obscured the area, and more light filtered through. Lor yawned, grazing his head with the hard glove. Zary wedged herself between him and Jack, lying on her stomach, facing him with mouth puckered open and breathing heavily with sleep. Their new companions had already left the tent, cleaning up the camp site.

"I can't thank you enough for your help," Lor said as he crawled out from the tent with a yawn.

Karl turned and chuckled. "Don't thank us just yet," he said, leaving it at that.

Odd.

Perhaps because they still hadn't made it to their destination, but Lor didn't want to press it. He was too worn out and depressed.

Once they left the site, it didn't take long to reach their destination, which was fortunate since Lor knew he was still recovering, and if he was still trying to recover, he couldn't imagine what it was like for Jack and Zary.

They came to a clearing, covered in lush green grass and a small body of blue water being fed by a nearby waterfall. It seemed so out of place in the middle of the morass. Stumps dotted the perimeter, and a crowd gathered in the middle.

They walked toward the people—old, young, tall, wide... more than just Yeunish, everyone was represented there. Everyone who acted as a Yeunish sympathizer, along with the "offending" race. There were grins, frowns, heads tilted and turned away. They formed a circle around the main clearing, but Lor couldn't tell what they had been looking at.

Karl cupped his hands around his mouth and shouted, "New recruits!"

The declaration was followed by cheers and jeers, akin to the shouts they heard in the distance the night before. Zary shrank behind Lor, and there was a strange foreboding about it all.

Two Yeunish men emerged from the circle, one with a split lip and the other with a split eyebrow, to join the rest of the circle as it opened up to swallow the three newbies. A stocky man, bare-chested with a loose black bun on top of his head, stepped in the center, beat his chest twice with his right fist, then crossed his arms with a smirk.

Karl patted Jack on the shoulder. "Alright, no spitting, biting, hair pulling, or crotch jabs, and respect the tap-out. Let's go!" He shoved Jack toward the circle, and Jack turned back with a furrowed brow.

"Just go with it," Karl said, taking a seat on a nearby stump.

The crowd began to grunt in a chant, pumping their fists and staring directly at Jack.

Hoo! Hoo! Hoo! Hoo! Hoo!

"Go on, now." Karl shooed at Jack when he didn't move.

Jack opened his mouth to speak, but Karl shooed him again, saying something along the lines of an *initiation*. With that, Jack turned to meet his new opponent.

They shuffled closer to each other, the stocky man bobbing his fists.

A look of surprise and fury came from Jack as he ducked away from the man's flying fist. The crowd erupted in jeers.

Lor hummed and leaned toward Karl. "So... what exactly is going on here?"

Karl leaned in to respond, eyes focused on the ring. "They're fighting."

"Yes, I see that, but *why*?"

"Call it a little... *ritual* we have around here."

The crowd chanted: *Niv`onar! Niv`onar! Niv`onar!* It must have been the name of Jack's rival, who happened to be giving poor Jack a severe beatdown. Lor hissed when Niv`onar's knuckles connected with Jack's chin.

After taking the strike to the jaw, Jack fell to the ground and rolled to his back, shielding his eyes with his arms. Niv'onar laughed and stuck out a hand to help him up. Jack accepted the offer, and Niv`onar turned to the crowd, raising his arms in triumph to a hearty cheer from them.

The circle opened again, waiting for its next victim to enter the ring as it purged Jack from it in defeat.

Niv`onar jogged from the circle toward Karl, and they slapped hands in greeting. "They survived, eh?" he said.

"Just barely," Karl said. "Nazagora claimed one."

Niv`onar sucked his teeth and tilted his head toward Lor. "Sorry about that. My intel was jacked. Name's Niv`onar, in case you couldn't hear. But call me Ivon, please." He stuck out a beefy, rough hand in greeting, then pulled it away when catching sight of the gloves, patting him on the shoulder instead. "Oh, another Adan? Great!"

Everyone was so excited to have him there, but Lor seethed at the fact that not one of them offered to take the damn gloves off. Jack finally stumbled back to them with a feathered red smear running up his cheek.

"I'm Loren," he said to Ivon.

"You're Mesaman?" he asked. "Are these your Yeunish friends?" He pointed a finger back and forth at Jack and Zary. Jack rolled his eyes.

"I—No, I mean, yes, they're friends, but I'm also Yeunish. Like you."

"No kidding? Sure don't look it. Ain't never met a blond Yeuni with... *gray* eyes."

"He is what he says he is," Karl interrupted, coming to a standing squat to push Lor toward the circle before plopping back down. "Now get in there!"

"Wait, I—" Lor held up his gloved fists.

"They're waitin' for ya."

Hoo! Hoo! Hoo! Hoo! Hoo!

Ivon wrapped a sinewy but deceptively strong arm around Lor's shoulder, leading him toward the ring and the crowd, hurling their insults.

> *Weak little baby!...*
> *...He's gonna piss his pants!*
> *Momma's baby boy!...*
> *...Sissy!*
> *Go home, dirty brat!...*

Kill that quivering and mourning child and step up, Lor.

"Don't worry," Ivon said. "They don't mean it. Or maybe they do. But mainly they don't."

A sacrifice must be made to the ring...

Terrified, he stepped forward. More jeers and insults flung his way, but the most tuned ear could hear the faintest of support—mainly from the women.

"Come, baby exile! Come earn your stay in the bog!" A slender man, taller than himself, strolled into the center, beckoning Lor forward with a crooked grin.

Lor shuffled forth, turning to see Zary, who would possibly have to undergo the same ritual. Maybe they were softer on the women and the young. He hoped as much.

A swift jab buckled Lor at the waist after his adversary punched him in the gut. An involuntary grunt blapped through his lips, and he took a step back but remained on his feet. There was no retaliating—the next swing came quick.

Flexed abs lessened the second strike with enough energy to sidestep the third swing. Catching air, his opponent skipped forward on his toes while hunched to try righting himself, but Lor hammered his gloved fists down onto the man's back.

Both men howled in pain. Gold snaked through the creases in Lor's hands and wrists.

The combatant swept his leg at Lor while unfurling to stand, but Lor leaped over it, feeling like a kid jumping rope.

Lor ducked and dodged and backed up with every swing. The crowed booed at him, shouting more insults and calling him a dirty cheat.

A glance to the calls of the crowd, and he swore he saw a bald man in his forties with thick rimmed glasses resting on his pink balding head. A second look and he suffered a solid blow to the jaw.

The jaw socket popped, rocketing pain up through his head, and he stumbled backward. As he stumbled, he took another hit to the nose.

Blood sprayed over his grain bag, and in reflex, he went to touch his face, only hitting himself again with the cold metal, falling to the ground.

He thought he heard, *Tap out, man!* but he couldn't be sure.

The crowd roared and laughed at Lor's broken nose. The attacker tried putting out a hand to help him, but he didn't see a hand—he saw a hazy red ring in his peripheral vision and his dead parents. Herbal greens filled his mouth, and the invigorating pull of pains knitting together... the child inside of him writhed in its death throes.

And then it was done.

Vacant eyes stared back at the Yeunish stranger attacking Lor. Dragging his nose across his short sleeve, he left a gory smear behind. The opponent withdrew his helping hand, putting fists up once again, but Lor struck, and he struck, metal on wrist bones that snapped with high-pitched wails.

Then a tooth arced into the grass. He didn't mean to hurt him that bad; it was Hammer's fault. Hammer's big block head, grinning his wicked red smile after murdering his mother... his father. Taking him away from his wife and babies for a stupid grudge. All for Paerli! The sour apple taste competed for his affection among the green life that wouldn't let him die.

The opponent was gone, standing by the wayside to watch as Lor pummeled the ground, feeling the earth collapse under his fists as Hammer's nose might. Each blow brought its sting, and he could almost taste the gold filling his mouth... but it was eneris. Pure green eneris.

It was in the silence of the crowd that he realized he was screaming.

"I'll kill you! I'll *kill* you!" His chant beat with every fist to the dirt. He carried on, throwing clods of fresh dirt and grass flying around him until he struck a hidden stone and his right glove burst open.

His shaking hand was a shock of swollen splits and black bruising under a veil of gold, and he stood to face the crowd.

With gasps and murmurs, their voices rose in chattering gossip. A woman from the back of the crowd shouted, "A golden fist!"

Gold Fist... Gold Fist... Gold Fist! Gold Fist!

They cheered for him, drowning out all other sound. Even his opponent cheered, pumping his broken fist with a toothy smile, showing off where Lor marred it.

Karl clapped him on the shoulder, dangling a cluster of small metal objects. "Got this for you." He slid one of the objects into a slot on the side of his other glove.

As he turned it, the glove snapped open, slapping the ground and revealing their dripping gold teeth.

The people cheered again at his freedom.

Freedom.

CHAPTER 40

Doing It The Right Way
Loren

SITTING BY THE FALLS, LOR took in the rushing sound of nature, squeezing his hand, where not just one standard hour ago, it had been littered with open cuts and bruises. No evidence of injury lingered after his dose of immortal green. Immortal Green. It had a ring to it.

People would start to ask questions. No cuts, no *brand*...each moment, his secret seemed more and more impossible to keep.

"Mind if I sit?"

Lor shook and whipped around to see Karl behind him. "Sure," he said.

"It's best if you don't have your back facing the open," Karl said as he sat down, slinging his bold-lettered pack-sack to the grass. There was no denying that he was right about that.

"Sorry I didn't tell you about the initiation. Things in the morass tend to be...unpredictable. We just thought it would be a good idea to toughen new people up when they get here."

"Nazagora wasn't enough?" Lor asked.

Karl laughed—a good belly laugh. "Ah, Nazagora. You'll learn after a while that nothing is what it seems."

Lor jerked his head toward the small town-sized group of people mulling about to see the teen Yeuni trying to touch Jack's swollen cheek as he rebuffed her angrily. "What about Zary?"

"In time," Karl said, then peered up at him under a bushy set of red-brown eyebrows. He had eyes the same color and a long, crooked nose. "You're immortal, aren't you?"

Lor hitched back with mouth parted. He reached up to feel his smooth forehead for the first time since freeing his hands. Not one wrinkle. The crescent scar on his arm still puckered under his touch. "Have many immortal friends, do you?" he said.

That belly laugh again. "It's not hard to see what you are with a trained eye."

"How many trained eyes are around here?"

"Just me."

"And who are *you*?"

"I'm just a man." Karl grinned. It was a charming grin, and crooked like his nose. He was bent on remaining cryptic, but Lor would learn his secrets eventually. Karl waved Jack and Zary to them, and they came from their place to the falls, Jack dragging his feet and Zary almost skipping.

"I need you to master your talent," he said, taking Zary's hand and pulling her toward Lor.

"What do you mean, *master it*? What more is there to know about being a Reaper?"

Karl tsk'ed and guided Zary in front of Lor. She went along with it, an eyebrow raised at Karl.

"Heal her brand."

They both gasped, then chuckled together. When Karl didn't laugh in return, their laughter died painfully awkward as they gaped at each other.

"I-I can't heal anyone, I can only pull eneris."

The wide grin that spread over his face felt like Lor had forgotten some shared secret and was going to re-learn it the hard way.

"You're Yeunish, right?" he asked.

"Yes."

"Heal her brand."

"I don't—"

"Here, you need to connect to her skin. This is how Adan did it." Karl yanked Lor's hand and hovered it over the raw bubbled "Y" on Zary's forehead. "He called it rhoe`tan."

Dancing his fingers in the air above her brand, Lor sighed. "What does that mean?"

"Dunno." Karl leaned back on the stone seat, waiting with that same grin.

Lor blew out a breath. Healing wasn't in his manual. He didn't actually have a manual, but if he did, it wasn't in there. Yeunish Reapers didn't exist... not to the cities.

They're just so good at them...

The sentence manifested in the forefront of his memory like a violent sneeze. Horace mentioned this in their quest for information, but Lor really only thought of Jack and his skill with formulation.

But what if I'm not Yeunish?

The heat of Zary's forehead radiated at his palm, and he was terrified.

What if I kill her?

Wide yellow eyes looked back at him, with her innocent smile plastered vacantly over her young face. It would be such a cruelty, to survive Nazagora together just to become a phial of silver and a wrinkled skin sack. He tried not to picture it as the electricity pulled his hand, pressing it against her skin as if the universe begged for it.

The hot sear in her flesh raked over the lines in his palm, and with a short, whispered prayer for relief from cirv`e's portal, he closed his eyes.

A blank space... with a wisp of blue smoke trailing in from the side. Zary's color. It curled around aimlessly until drawing an outline of Zary herself, being led into the roundsman cruiser.

"Ouch!" she cried, recoiling from Lor's touch.

When he snapped his eyes open, a dribble of silver clung to her brand, and she pulled away the drop with her finger, gawking at it.

"I'm so sorry, Zary!" Lor's hand shook when he saw her silver life resting in the cracks of his dry fingers.

"Just try again, but do it right this time," Karl said, picking at his fingernail.

"I don't know what I'm doing!" Lor shouted.

"You better learn fast out here, son. Do it again."

"She's just a kid, Karl!"

"All the more reason to do it right."

"You son of a—"

"It's alright, Lor, you can try again," Zary said, placing his hand back on her forehead. She closed her eyes with a pouted lip as if she might cry.

"See, she gets it," Karl said. "If you want to make it out here, you have to do the work to refine yourself. The cities baby you and make you soft... and when they feel like it, they'll cast you into the fire and you won't even see it coming. Did *you* see it coming? Did you see it coming when they snatched you from your family? When they arrested you for being something Audun hates for no reason? Do it again."

Lor pressed his teeth together, trying hard not to think about Hammer's fist beating his dad, or his mother's clothes soaking up the blood pouring from her body. Zary's blue smoke screamed under his lids.

She cried out again, more silver beading at the "Y." The skin at the right angle thinned, showing a peek of more silver underneath. Lor sucked his teeth, and he drew her into himself as she cried into his grain sack chest.

"I'm so sorry," he said as he held her.

The long stint he had at the city morgues had him in a routine. A routine of yaslecha... and he doubted himself. He doubted his ability to think past the life drain, his hold on himself, and even his heritage.

What if the tests were wrong? I can't be Yeunish...

Then the image of his daughter floated under his lids. Plump, pale cheeks and piercing yellow eyes that tested him. She came from him. She could be Zary someday. The poor girl was lost in the wasteland, and he had to protect her, just as he would his own daughter.

She pulled away from him with water glazing her eyes and blistered skin smoothing over, leaving a silver scar slashed at the angle where her skin had thinned. All that remained was the silver slash like Damaetra's "new tattoo."

"Your daughter is adorable," she whispered, wiping her eyes, then touching her forehead.

"You saw her?"

She nodded.

It seemed so simple after the fact. Rather than focus on their last moments, he had to feed them his—the good ones at least. Lor beckoned Jack with an outstretched hand.

Jack tittered. "I'm good."

CHAPTER 41

It Begins
GALE

TECHLIGHT FLICKERED IN THE WARM living room, where Gale had gathered the group.

"We've grown complacent," he said, standing in front of the white, ivy-carved fireplace. Flames crackled in the hearth. "And the Guilds are a lie."

Damaetra held a child in each arm as they slept through their grandpa's speech, a fresh bandage plastered over her forearm where he removed the golden bug. Eva sat next to her, a finger imprisoned by the Yeunish girl's little chubby hand and an identical bandage wrapped around her forearm.

"We've obeyed their every rule," he continued, taking a quick glance at Nico, who sat with his face in his hands next to Eva, "and we've worked hard for them."

Dill sat on the floor looking up—his visor glowing in attention as Emilia sat straight-backed next to him with her pearls reflecting the orange flames.

"They lied to us." His gaze moved to Eloria, wearing a Dill-branded tech halo encircling her head, then to Aedras and Thea sitting on the stools at the counter.

"And worst of all, we've grown careless..." Cae and Hare stood behind Nico, and Hare lowered his head.

"As much as I hate to say it, we're lucky we *only* lost Els'daegal. Lor and Jack are alive, I know they are."

A shining tear swelled at Damaetra's eye.

"They're hurt, I have no doubt. But they're alive. We need answers. We need help. I want to bring my son home to his children, and I want his people to be equal in the sight of Audun."

Gale pulled out a glossy black brochure that proclaimed: *The Maker's Magic,* on the front in glowing blue letters. "I found this in Loren's room."

"Dad, that's a cult," Eva said, bobbing her finger in the baby's fist.

"Yes. And what do they worship?" All eyes stared back, waiting for his answer. "Not the Maker," he continued, looking at Damaetra, "Not Maron." He glanced at Dill and Emilia. "Not even the breach itself." He turned to Nico.

Flipping to the center of the brochure, Gale opened to an image that he spun around to face everyone. "They worship *this*." He passed the image back and forth.

The image was meant to be an advertisement for the void brothers' calling. It was meant to look nice and welcoming, but nothing about it was that. Gale cleared his throat, growling out his next words. "They call it Cirv'e."

Damaetra gasped. "The beast," she whispered.

"The breach is this thing's home," Gale continued. "It plants corrupt ideas in the minds of good people. It grants corrupt powers to the powerless... it tells the cities lies about Lor's people."

He stuck the brochure in his back pocket and crossed his arms. The bright fire behind him made him nothing but a shadow as he scanned the room.

"And we need to send it back to hell."

Epilogue

The wind howled through the clearing, bringing with it gray clouds and a hint of rain. The most recent dry spell almost uncovered new earth under the marshes. Almost. Rain was near, and it was about time—dry times brought the Nazagora closer.

Lor jogged in place, squeezing the blood through his limbs with each move as Rik held back the oily Nazagora with the other beast tamer. Their howling pitch buzzed the ears, but he got used to hearing it. His hands, wrapped with old strips of grain sack and curled into fists, pumped at the ready near the sides of his face.

The usual shouts and jeers filled the circle... mostly harmless, but some renegades didn't actually like him too much. Not that it bothered him. He suspected their dislike came from fear, and he couldn't fault them for that. More banished were collected every standard month, but still no Reaper like him.

A chill curled over his bare torso, so he slapped it until red.

Across the way, his tall and vascular opponent stood stone still yet mirrored Lor's slaps for warmth into his bare chest. The stormy afternoon and all its aromas reflected the first day he had to face the Formulator formerly known as Cricket.

A fake right hook, duck, and leg sweep—all countered by the man who taught him those moves—and answered with two jutting knuckles to the nose bridge. Stumbling back and spurting, Lor shook his head and flung red drops in a cone around him. It was stupid to use Jack's own moves first... he should have started with Ivon's techniques. The crowd's soundtrack of cheering and boos swelled, and then he tasted it... the fresh wash of Immortal Green filling his mouth. Jack smirked as Lor's bloody nose slowed to a drip.

The moment blood stopped running from his nose, the first drops of rain landed on his cheekbones. The Nazagora's alien clicks and growls turned into hissing gulps as their neckless heads tilted toward the sky.

The minor irritation of drops plunking on his face became a blinding nuisance, but wet ground was where Zary's special moves excelled. No one turned away from a little water on the ground.

Every day for the past three standard years, he fought for her. Between whisperings of cirv'e and its constant presence under his eyelids, he dreamed about coming home to her every once in a while. He would stroll in to their home, find his children in her arms, and hold her for days. She radiated the fragrance of violet, and he almost tasted it when he woke. One day, that dream would become real.

The graying Princeps Renae sat on his blue and gold chair, poring over documents and holo forms when a short Danashi courier hurried silently along the cold marbled floor. A pair of roundsmen leaned in toward the princeps as the courier approached.

"Your eminence," the courier stated, clearing his throat, "I am Jedd from Celerity, and I come only with a report..." Eyeing the two stiff roundsmen, Jedd rolled his eyes at the unusually large one with round pink scars covering most of his arms and face. With a trembling hand, he presented a single transparent ticket scrawled with flash ink to Renae. "A-a report from the *South*... sir."

Renae's mustache twitched and he glared at Jedd from under wiry eyebrows. He plucked the ticket from him, and as his eyes darted across the news, each line of text disappeared until all he was left with was the glowing blue seal of Celerity City in the lower corner of a clear strip of plastic. With two fingers, he flicked the empty report across the glossy wood table. It skated half the length before floating off the edge to the floor.

"All you damn Readers are the same," Renae muttered, "formalities and ass-kissery." He leaned back and pulled a hand-rolled smoking cane from a dark box perched among the piles of documents and flickering holo forms. As he placed it on his lip, the smaller roundsman bent with an arc striker, but Renae waved him away, snatching the gadget and lighting the end himself.

Taking in a drag, he watched Jedd drop his jaw enough to show a thick pink tongue wriggling inside his mouth fighting the variety of words he wanted to spew. Renae smirked, blowing out a long wisp of orange smoke.

Jedd snapped his mouth shut, giving a slight bow. "I'm sorry, sir."

"Yes, yes, of course you are." Renae dismissed him with a hand wave and another stream of orange smoke. "So, my nephew is at it again, is he?"

"Sir?"

Renae folded a leg across the other, leaning deep into the blue cushion as the chair joints groaned. "The report. It's my nephew."

Jedd glanced around the room, unable to make eye contact. "I'm sorry,

I'm not sure. The report was written in flash ink, and I didn't want to risk losing the message—"

"Do I look stupid?" The black cane poked from under his curled mustache, almost threatening to spark the dry hairs.

"N-no, sir. No... I'm so sorry."

Renae leaned forward, teeth exposed with orange smoke leaking from his nostrils. "Come closer, please."

"I didn't mean to offend you, sir." Jedd glanced at the smaller roundsman, then to the larger, who snapped his knuckles one after the other.

"Just... come closer," his calm voice beckoned the shaking courier—a soothing hiss in the court garden.

"Please... my daughter—"

"Will be just fine with your estranged wife. Now, I'm going to need you to come just a little bit closer."

Both roundsmen draped fingers around their hollow riot clubs. Jedd's forehead greased up with sweat. In barely a whisper, he pleaded one last time.

When it was clear Renae wasn't going to stop asking, Jedd shuffled closer, wincing with each step as he studied the roundsmen, fingers curled about their weapons. When he was within reach, he stiffened as the princeps touched his hand. Firm, but gentle.

Holding on to Jedd with one hand, Renae stubbed out the cane with the other and turned to look back at him. "Why do you think I might be upset right now?" he asked.

The roundsmen tightened their grips on their clubs.

Jedd's eyes widened, and his mouth trembled. With a croak, he pushed out the tiniest utterance. "B-because he's family? Betraying you?"

"Ah, family," Renae said with a crooked grin. "Blood is thicker than water, and such and such..." He glared needles into Jedd's face, then sighed. "I'm tired, Jedd, my bumbling little Reader friend. I'm tired of our departure agents not doing enough to make sure our Yeunish refugees *die*.

"They crawl back onto shore, *bolder than ever*, and I'm tired of paying plat to every down-on-his-luck bastard that is better at catching them than our own agents are at seeing them dead!" He pumped Jedd's hand with each syllable as his voice crescendoed.

"I-I'm..."

"Sure, we could easily put a round in their thick, mutant skulls," he continued, squeezing Jedd's hand tighter as the roundsmen took small steps closer. "But I've always found the most diplomatic approach is to allow the people to see that it's just the harsh nature of the environment. We aren't truly killing them... we can't control the fact they're not equipped to handle basic survival skills. That's all, Jedd. Do you see? I'm a benevolent god."

Renae squeezed harder as the scarlet flush scrolled up Jedd's face.

"I'm... a *benevolent*... GOD."

Jedd howled as his fingers snapped. Threads of silver ribboned from his pores in wriggling arcs, splattering across documents and washing over marble. Jedd's dark skin faded to ash as his open mouth hollowed under thin cheeks. Thick silver jettisoned in rivers until he was nothing but a leather ball in Renae's fist. He tossed the Jedd ball onto the table with a thunk, and it wobbled over a petition for reform of harsh judgements of the Yeunish.

"Someone get the Foscans to clean this mess up," Renae said, pulling a swatch of cloth from his breast pocket. Flapping it out, he wrung it around each finger where Jedd's silver collected into the grooves. "And someone... *someone* find a way to stop feeding warm bodies to Karl's pathetic army!"

AUDUN RECOGNIZES THAT NOW, MORE THAN EVER, IT IS OF UTMOST IMPORTANCE TO STAY TRUE TO YOUR FAMILY.

In these times of uncertainty, having a support system in place can help alleviate any ill fate that may come, whether it be to yourself or a friend.

I, your Princeps, encourage you to absolve any grudge, right any wrong, and reconnect with those that matter most. With increased deaths attributed to rapid onset Weggevens malady, and further invasion by the Yeunish, we must stand together.

One thing I have found to help me in these trying times is my faith in the Maker's Magic. If you have never been shown the way, each of the Seven Cities will be hosting informational sessions to help guide you.

Head to your local branch today, and pick up a brochure. And as always...

Stay Vigilant!

Pick up a brochure today!

SIGN UP FOR THE NEWSLETTER!

www.reholdingauthor.com

WHAT YOU GET:

- Updates & Reviews
- Upcoming Works
- Early access to new projects
- Special discounts

Join the newsletter to receive CCB updates, special offers, reviews, giveaways, and more. Stay in touch!

Thanks for reading!

If you enjoyed this book, please consider posting a review! Reviews are critical for indie authors in an ever-evolving publishing space.

www.ingramcontent.com/pod-product-compliance
Lightning Source LLC
Chambersburg PA
CBHW031448160726
47994CB00005B/1935